Perilous Panacea

by

Ronald Klueh

Savant Books
Honolulu, HI, USA
2010

Published in the USA by Savant Books and Publications
2630 Kapiolani Blvd #1601
Honolulu, HI 96826
http://www.savantbooksandpublications.com

Printed in the USA

Edited by Jonathan Marcantoni
Cover images from U.S. Department of Energy photographs in the public domain
Front and back cover design by Helen Babalis

10-digit ISBN: 0-9845552-3-4
13-digit ISBN: 978-0-9845552-3-9

Dedication

To Helen:
For your constant encouragement and for always believing.

Acknowledgement

I am especially grateful to Jonathan Marcantoni, my editor, for taking my manuscript and finding the flaws, and then, despite my reluctance, having me see he was correct. This eventually led to an improved story, and in the end, it provided an education that should make me a better writer in the future.

Likewise, I owe a debt of gratitude to Dr. Daniel Janik, Publisher of Savant Books and Publications, for reading my submission, finding something there of merit, and giving me the opportunity to see the book I labored on for many years freed from its electronic file.

Perilous Panacea

$\mathcal{P}$rologue

Ian Deby arrived home from work, checked his e-mail, and found a message from his sister in England.

Dear Hassan,
Did you hear the rumors about Iran being invaded by the Israelis and Americans?
Can this be what we are praying for?
Love,
BahAmin

Deby checked his watch: almost 6:30. He grabbed the remote from the end of the couch, clicked on the TV, dropped onto the couch, and pondered BahAmin's words while he waited for the commercials to end.

"Good Evening on this Tuesday, January 4, 2011," the anchor woman for CBS Evening News said, continuing:

Today's top story is the surprise military attack carried out on nuclear installations in Iran, the objective presumably being the destruction of Iran's nuclear-processing capability to produce weapons-grade uranium that they have allegedly acquired over the past decade. Radio Tehran alerted the world to the raid late last night, when they reported an air attack on military and civilian installations. Iranian officials accused the U.S. and Israelis of making an unprovoked attack. Although Iranian officials have blocked all foreign news reporters from sending out pictures, Tehran has released video showing protesters in the streets with signs castigating The Great Satan and their Israeli lapdogs.

Earlier this afternoon, the Israeli Prime Minister's office released a statement confirming that they had carried out the raid, justifying the attack by citing the recent verbal threats by Iranian officials and stating that they could not stand idly by as Iran manufactured nuclear weapons. No U.S. involvement was indicated in the statement, in spite of reports of meetings between the President and the Secretaries of State and Defense that lasted well into the evening. Until an hour ago, there had been no official response to the Iranian accusations from the Gordono Administration. For details, we take you to Stuart Warner at the Pentagon.

Deby thought about his parents and his sisters and brother in Iran. What now? Would there be an uprising like after the elections last year? Would the U.S. attack Iran and help any revolt by the opposition? He turned his attention back to the TV.

The Gordono administration's response was delivered at the Pentagon by Press Secretary Jason Mayo who read a brief statement from Defense Secretary Romig denying U.S. involvement in the alleged attack. The statement said the United States understands Israeli concern about a nuclear presence in the area, but...

On the screen, the press secretary read his statement that added nothing new, after which the reporter came back on.

CBS has learned from various sources that at about 5 a.m. this morning in Iran, 8 p.m. last night Eastern Standard Time in the U.S., Israeli fighter planes attacked a secret installation thought to contain centrifuges to produce bomb-grade uranium. The raid destroyed the above-ground installation twenty-five miles southwest of the town of Turut on the northern edge of the Dasht-e-Kavir Desert. Israeli commandos invaded the site prior to the air raid and demolished strategic portions of the underground facilities with explosives, thus making them more vulnerable to the bomber attack. If, as reported, helicopters were used to transport the commandos, it would have been by sea, a capability the Israelis are not thought to possess.

2

Iran claims they are only interested in peaceful nuclear power and not in bombs. They are signatories of the Nuclear Nonproliferation Treaty and claim they are living up to the provisions of that agreement.

Russia and China condemned the attack, as did several European and South American countries. Russia's ambassador to the United Nations called for a Security Council meeting to condemn the actions of the United States and Israel. The Venezuelan ambassador called for...

Ian clicked off the reporter in mid-sentence, his thoughts turning to his father in an Iranian prison. Would this be his chance to get out? Would it be possible to get his family out of Iran to be with him and BahAmin? He dug his cell phone from his pocket and dialed BahAmin's number.

Perilous Panacea

Chapter One

Ian Deby switched the grocery bag to his left arm, unlocked the door, flicked the light switch, and bumped the door shut with his hip. The door rebounded, and the doorknob banged his hip.

A dark complected stranger stood in the doorway. "Hassan Mohammed Nagubi?" the stranger asked in slightly accented English.

"You've got the wrong person, my name is Ian Deby."

Of slight build and Deby's height—five-foot-ten—in a light-brown suit, white shirt, dark-brown tie, he pushed past Deby and glanced around the tiny living room. "Regardless of what you call yourself, you are Iranian, and your name is Hassan Mohammed Nagubi."

"Who are you?"

"I am Ahmed Sherbani, a representative of *your* Iranian government. We know who you really are."

He had short black hair, a gaunt, clean-shaven face and intense dark-brown eyes. A smile played on his lips, as if Deby's confusion amused him. "Your mother, brother, and two sisters are still in Iran, in Mashhad. They left Teheran to go back to her people after your father went away. You write to her every two months."

Deby studied Sherbani more closely. For a moment, he thought he was about to be scolded for not writing often enough. Sherbani was probably around his father's age, mid-fifties, his black hair flecked with gray.

"My father did not go away," Deby said as he wondered about the color of his father's hair. "The Iranian government put him in prison."

Recently, he hadn't thought about those days twenty-one years ago when he was seven, a distant time now that he was submerged in his new and busy life. His father planned to get the family out and sent him and his older sister BahAmin ahead with Uncle Behrouz. He was arrested a week

5

later.

"Your father was plotting against the government, plotting an assassination of the President."

"No way," Deby said, his voice breaking. He wondered about his father: was he a freedom fighter, or was he falsely accused by the Revolutionary Guards? "The Revolutionary Guards said…"

"They are the Army of the Guardians of the Islamic Revolution," Sherbani snapped. "They are protectors of the Iranian people. They are true Muslims."

"My father loves Allah as much as any man. He taught us the Koran and *Sharia*; the *Hajji* was in all his children's future."

"It has been a terrible time for Muslims for too long. It is even worse when Muslims fight Muslims, Iranians fight Iranians."

"You mean like what happened last year after the rigged election when the Revolutionary Guards shot protesters?"

"The election was fair. A few trouble makers decided to stir up the people by claiming the election was stolen. It wasn't. The majority of our people rejected them."

Deby knew it was useless to argue the point. He set the groceries on the floor next to the wall and turned to face the man. "What do you want with me?"

"I am told you are a brilliant nuclear engineer, and we need you," Sherbani said, stepping forward and stopping a couple feet from Deby, his gaze fixed on Deby's eyes. "We are going to build an atomic bomb. You've heard of the Islamic Bomb of Pakistan. We're going to build the *real* Islamic bomb."

"I am no longer a Muslim." It dawned on him that he had never said that before, or even thought it.

"A tiger cannot change his stripes, and you cannot change your birth. How can you live among these devils that invaded our country last month, invaded *your* country? Their women wear clothing that reveals their navel, their legs, their thighs. Would you want your sisters to dress like that? You are Muslim, and I am here to enlist you in the struggle of Islam."

"It's not my struggle," Deby said as his mind flashed to the young suicide bombers that kept blowing up themselves and others. What was the struggle? Were the Tehran protesters against the government his part of the struggle?

"Iran is a difficult land, thanks to our war with the Great Satan, and their Little Satan, their Israeli lapdogs. Iran is very difficult for a woman without a man. Your mother tries hard, but things could become difficult.

And then there is your uncle in England who raised you. Like your father, he is a traitor. I think you know why you will help."

Deby understood. His Uncle Behrouz was a lawyer in Iran; he now owned a restaurant in Birmingham, England, and lived in constant terror, expecting the "Ayatollah's men" to pounce at any moment, even though *his* Ayatollah, the Ayatollah Khomeini, died in 1989, the year they got out of Iran.

Yet, in every letter from Uncle Behrouz, he warned Deby to be wary of his father's jailers. To Deby, a dead Ayatollah had always been a dead threat, just as the present Ayatollah had never seemed a threat to him. He was wrong.

"I do not wish to threaten," Sherbani said. "I just explain how things are. Muslims are besieged everywhere, from Afghanistan to France, from Iraq to Indonesia to the United States. Look at the Palestinians in the refugee camps in Lebanon and Jordan and the oppression they live under on the West Bank and Gaza. The Israelis shoot women and children. Muslims are made fun of in books and the press. We Muslims are not vindictive, but the Koran says: 'And fight for the cause of God against those that fight against you; but commit not the injustice of attacking them first; verily God loveth not the unjust.'"

Deby remembered the passage: *Jihad*, The Holy War. "I'm not a Muslim. I am a British citizen."

"A *British* citizen? What a joke. You acquired a British passport and a British accent, but did your fellow students at the University of Birmingham accept you as British? No. Not even after you Anglicized your name. You were still a turban head. And things did not change at UCLA, did they? You worked for a Muslim professor for your PhD. Are things better here at the great Princeton University?"

Sherbani's mention of his British accent reminded him of torturous hours spent eliminating his Iranian accent and refining the speech patterns and mannerisms of his new British self. For years, he sought out Michael Cain movies and patterned his speech after him. He learned British slang and sayings so well Americans sometimes didn't understand him. All that work was about to pay off, for he would soon have a permanent academic position. His UCLA professor called last week about a faculty opening at the University of Wisconsin.

"To the Americans, you are a foreign lackey. To us, you are important. You can do much for your people. You can help them regain the respect Allah has deemed for us."

"I will not help a government that shoots its own people when they

7

protest in the street, a government that arrests someone for disagreeing with them, like they did to my father."

"We will see," Sherbani said and turned to leave. At the door, he stopped and looked back. "You want to see your father free, do you not?" Then he was gone.

- - - - -

Deby was in his bed above Uncle Behrouz's restaurant when the burglar alarm screamed, stopped, and then screamed again. He fought free of sleep, recognized he was dreaming, and the burglar alarm was the phone next to his bed in Princeton.

"Hassan? Is that you, Hassan?" a familiar voice asked in Farsi.

"Mother." He spoke in Farsi, his first use of the language in months. This was her first call ever. She didn't have his phone number, and she didn't have a phone or the money to make such a call.

After she gained control of her voice—they hadn't spoken in 15 years—they talked about family things. Then she mentioned a visit from a government man. "He said my job might be in danger, and we might have to move to a smaller apartment if you do not do what they want you to do. He said to tell you that, and now I did. Hassan, do what you need to do. That is what your father would want, and…"

The phone went dead.

- - - - -

That evening, Sherbani appeared carrying a thin black briefcase. He pushed past Deby, led him across the room, sat on the brown couch and motioned Deby to sit next to him. He spoke again about the difficulties of being Muslim. "But things are changing. Praised be Allah! Iran now has the leaders we need to win back respect."

"Israel just took away your bombs. They won't let you get another one."

"The U.S. devils took it away, but revenge is the father of glory."

"Do you have a scientific staff for the job? Do you have the nuclear material?"

Sherbani shook his head. "We have you, a brilliant nuclear engineer." He snapped open the briefcase and removed a book and a stack of papers—newspaper clippings. "Here is the answer to our bomb."

The book: *The Curve of Binding Energy* by John McPhee published in 1973. According to the dust jacket, the book explained the dangers of nuclear material being stolen from the United States nuclear program and

8

used to make an atom bomb. Deby shuffled through the copies of newspaper clippings, which dealt with the potential for diversion of nuclear material. Most of the clippings were from the last century—the seventies and early eighties. Headlines of two of them: *245 Pounds of Uranium Lost at Plant Since 1968* and *Could Steal Enough for Bomb without Detection*, the latter a quote from a U.S. General Accounting Office report. The *New York Times* article from 1978 began, "Enough plutonium for a nuclear bomb could be easily stolen from a federal reprocessing plant, and the government might not even detect it."

"This book and the newspaper stories are over thirty-years old," Deby said. "U.S. security has tightened since the 1970s. Do you have some of this nuclear material?"

"No. That is what we want you for."

"*Me*? *Steal* it? Then get it out of the country and make a bomb?"

"It could be difficult, but for Allah, nothing is impossible. We will give you all the assistance you need. Think about it. Read that material."

"I could never…"

"You will need to recruit scientific help. You have a friend who works for the U.S. government, a very bright and ambitious computer expert. Our scientists say computers are the reason we will succeed. Your friend is like most Americans, who will sell their mother for enough money."

"I could never ask him."

"We will pay several million dollars to you and any others that help. If you refuse, it could be difficult for your mother, brother, sisters, *and* your father."

"Could I get my father out of jail? Could I get my family out of Iran?"

Sherbani smiled. "It could be arranged. But remember, Hassan, you are one of us. Instead of your family leaving, you should come back to Iran. Come back to your Muslim roots. If you do this, you will be a hero."

Sherbani's offer to free his father stirred Deby's guilt. He dreamed of helping them. As the eldest son, his father expected it. Now he had a chance. Although there was no way he could do something like building a nuclear weapon, he said, "I'll think about it."

"There is nothing to think about. You *will* do it."

- - - - -

The day after Sherbani's visit, Deby picked up the phone to hear his

Aunt in England, her Farsi words jumbled by deep sobs. "Auntie Goli? What is wrong?"

Uncle Behrouz came on the line. "I didn't want her to call, but she insisted. Somebody set the restaurant on fire, but the damage was minor."

"Who did it?" Deby asked, but he knew the answer.

"We had a visitor last week who said something bad would happen if we didn't tell you to do what they wanted you to do. I told him to go to hell."

"You should have told me."

"Don't do anything you don't want to do. We are not in Iran anymore."

Early the next morning, his mother called to tell of another visit from the police. They spoke of catastrophes that could befall his sisters, like the young Iranian women who are kidnapped and taken to France to act as prostitutes; they said his brother could be arrested for plotting against the government, just as his father had been; they talked about bad things that happen to people in jail: "They often commit suicide by hanging themselves. It's the way it is."

That night Sherbani appeared and assumed his seat on the couch. He ignored Deby's pleas to leave his family alone and spoke of Dr. Austin, Deby's U. S. government friend. Sherbani said he learned about him when they investigated Deby. "We know your friend Austin is a computer expert at the Department of Energy in Washington. Presumably, he would have helpful information on the nuclear material we want to acquire."

"I'll do what you want. Just leave my family alone."

Sherbani smiled. "It is written in the Koran, 'War is prescribed to you; but to this ye have repugnance.' Hassan, my friend, you will be well rewarded by Allah."

Chapter Two

Ian Deby watched Steve Austin push the empty pizza pan aside and asked, "What brings you to Princeton this time?"

"The usual administrative bullshit. The DOE—your U.S. *Department of Energy*—is a micro-management disaster area. I'm here to make sure the Princeton fusion program stays on course."

Three months ago, Austin appeared in Deby's Princeton office. He said he saw Deby's name on the Princeton fusion staff list, and he knew Deby was a fellow UCLA alum because he remembered seeing him on campus. Deby did not remember Austin. Since that first meeting, Austin had shown up in his office twice. By coincidence, he called last night shortly after Sherbani left and invited Deby out for pizza.

Austin grabbed the pitcher of beer and filled their glasses. He was shorter than Deby, probably a little over five-foot-eight, and in contrast to Deby's dark-brown hair and eyes, Austin was blond with bright-blue eyes, and he wore the energetic good looks of many of the youthful UCLA undergrads that roamed the campus and populated the Westwood bars when Deby was there. Austin claimed not to have been like most UCLA students, saying he quickly got beyond surfing and sex, finished his PhD, and moved on.

"Why do you work for DOE?" Deby asked, remembering Sherbani's statement that Americans were only interested in money and sex. "Isn't money important to you?"

"You bet your ass it's important. It's freedom, escape from the bullshit. I went to DOE to learn how bureaucracies operate. Eventually, I intend to start my own software and consulting firm, so I can work on what *I* want to work on. The government makes a good customer—a *big* customer."

At a previous dinner, Austin talked about some of his life and achievements, beginning when he was nine and his father ran off with his twenty-three-year old secretary. His mother married a Stanford math professor, who tutored the young Austin. When he got to college, he was a math whiz and computer programming expert.

"Playing Grand Theft Auto soon became a bore," he said. By the time he was seventeen, he'd sold two computer games to a video-game company. Besides that, he'd developed an interest in electronics and built himself an advanced computer. He completed B.S. degrees in electrical engineering *and* computer science by the time he turned twenty; he had his PhD in computer science by twenty-three. He was now twenty-five.

With that background, taking a job at DOE made little sense to Deby. An expert in computer hardware design and software engineering could write his own ticket. Deby knew Austin would never take a chance on Sherbani's folly. There was no use asking.

A week ago, Deby was plagued with questions about his next job. Should he take an assistant professor's position at Wisconsin? Should he stay at Princeton after his post-graduate appointment ended? His UCLA professor e-mailed him about a job at MIT. Now, a job was the least of his worries. All he wanted was to convince Sherbani his idea for an atomic bomb was impossible. But with his father in jail and his mother and uncle at their mercy, he had no choice but to take the chance.

He fingered the cold mug. "How would you like to make a million dollars, Steve?"

"How many people do I have to kill?"

The question stunned Deby into momentary silence. It was something he'd thought about only in passing. The bombs would never be built. If they were, would they be used? Sherbani said they wouldn't. Not unless they were forced to by their infidel enemies.

"What I'm about to say could get me sent to jail."

"I promise not to turn you in."

"You do know I'm Iranian?"

"*Iranian*? *You* with that perfect British accent?"

Was that a compliment? He considered himself British. "I am a British citizen, but because of my background, I've been approached by the Iranian government to build a nuclear weapon," Deby said and then waited and wondered. Would Austin leave? Would he go to the FBI or Homeland Security? Was this the end of his dream of a professorship at Wisconsin? MIT? Would he be in jail tomorrow?

Austin stared, eyes wide. "It seems to me," he said, "Iran has tried a bunch of ways to get a bomb the last few years." He smiled, his blue eyes sparkling. "All attempts bombed, if you'll pardon the pun. It always appeared they weren't too bright. So what are they doing this time?"

"They want to steal nuclear material from the United States."

"From the DOE?" Austin laughed. "Never happen."

"It can be done." Deby described the literature Sherbani gave him.

"That's last century stuff. Things are different now. If it could be done, it won't be done by somebody who's screwed up every time they tried something."

Deby knew he was right. "It'll be different this time."

"If I agree to join you, what would I do? What are you going to do?"

Sherbani hadn't provided details, just what he expected, and what he expected was impossible. "If you join up, you and I would run the show, everything from figuring out how to steal the nuclear material to building the bombs."

"No shit? How did they pick you?"

That was the same question Deby asked Sherbani every time they met. "Like you said, up until now the Iranians buggered everything they tried. That was the old guard, so somebody figured they'd let the next generation have a go." One of Sherbani's convoluted explanations went something like that.

"What do you know about building a nuclear weapon?"

Another question he had asked Sherbani. "I'm a reasonably intelligent nuclear engineer. The theory of atomic bombs isn't difficult. Iran's nuclear scientists have studied it and have designs. All we need to do is get the nuclear material and build them."

Austin laughed. "That's all, huh?"

He told Austin about a report written by Iranian scientists that Sherbani gave him. It summarized bomb designs and information needed to build them. After reading it, Deby was as convinced as Sherbani that a computer expert would be needed—a bloody good computer expert—because computers would be needed in everything from bomb design to machining bomb parts. With an expert like Austin, they'd need only one or two other people once they got the nuclear material.

Austin drained half his beer, a smile spreading across his face. "A million dollars, right? I'd want to negotiate for more money, but first I'd like to see that literature."

- - - - -

With Sherbani's permission, Deby turned over the literature. Then he waited for the FBI, waited to be the latest Iranian caught with his trousers down. At least Sherbani would know he tried.

On the third day of waiting, he received a text message from Sherbani telling him to be in New York Saturday afternoon for a meeting at the Sheraton on Seventh Avenue near Madison Square Garden.

Sherbani answered Deby's knock at room 712. Deby stepped around Sherbani into the room and stopped dead in his tracks to stare across two double beds at Steve Austin sitting at a small round table behind a laptop computer.

"How you doing, Ian, old chap?" he asked, mimicking Deby's British accent.

Deby turned to Sherbani. "What is this?"

"We tested you, Hassan, to see if you were with us. Doctor Austin initiated this brilliant project and brought it to us. He needed a nuclear engineer. You were the logical choice."

Smiling, Austin waved Deby to a seat at the table.

- - - - -

Austin ran the meeting. "When we talked, Ian, I got the idea you didn't believe the plan would work. It'll work, because I'm not in the DOE Fusion Sciences Division, like I told you. I'm in NNSA, the National Nuclear Security Administration, *the* division responsible for security and for transporting and accounting for bomb-grade nuclear material in the U.S. That's where we're getting our nuclear material."

"You said you came to Princeton to meet with people on the fusion program."

He smiled. "I came to see you. We played it safe to make sure you wouldn't go to the police. We figured if you took a chance on recruiting me, you could be trusted."

"That's not all," Sherbani said his smile larger than Austin's, "he knows where all the bomb-grade material is that will fit the criteria for our bombs."

"That's right. Like you said, Ian, you need computers to do anything these days. I've got the skills, and I let the right people in DOE know about it. Now, whenever anybody has a computer problem, they call me."

Austin spent the next two hours laying out their plan. He concluded, "This job won't be easy and could take six months to a year. It's already taken me two years, but I've achieved our first objective by gaining access to DOE computers containing information on how bomb-grade material is stored and shipped. I run the computers that keep NNSA operating. *I* keep it operating."

"Access is one thing," Deby said, "but your plan will work only if you can manipulate the system."

"I agree. I've had experience hacking other people's computers. In that case, I first had to get passwords. Here, I've got passwords. By the time we are ready to go, I intend to control the computers that will be compromised."

Deby watched, amazed at Austin's confidence and wishing he was as cocksure of himself. He also wished he was anywhere but here. Two days ago he heard from Wisconsin. They set an interview date. With a little luck, he could reach his goal to be a British scientist teaching at an American university, maybe marry an American girl and raise a family.

Austin glanced at Deby, winked, and turned to Sherbani. "Before we go on, let's set Ian's mind straight. Tell him what you told me about what you intend to do with these bombs."

"Iran is a peaceful nation. All we want is to deal with the United States on equal footing, not from our knees. They have no right to tell us what we can do in our own country. We will get weapons they will not take from us. We will then negotiate as equals. We are no more anxious to use such powerful weapons than is the United States. But someone must show them they cannot dictate what the rest of the world can and cannot do."

Austin considered the reply, nodded, and glanced at Deby. "I understand, and I think Ian does too. Now that we've got the main part of our team assembled, the second thing we need to talk about is payment for services rendered if we are successful."

Sherbani now wore a constant smile. "Talking about money is difficult, Doctor Austin, but I say to you what I said before and what I told Hassan. You will be well rewarded."

Austin nodded, smile in place. "First, I want an immediate five-million dollars for bringing you this job. Then Ian, or Hassan, as you call him, and I want ten-million each to do the job. We want two million up front, as a show of good faith. We want further payments as the project proceeds, say two million when we steal the bomb material and two-million more when the first bomb is completed. Then we get the remainder when all bombs are delivered."

Sherbani's smile faded. "That is much money." His smile reignited, somewhat dimmed. "I need to talk to some people, but you will get your price."

"We also need access to cash, so we want you to arrange for us to get two-hundred-thousand in cash in the United States," Austin said. "I assume you can do that because you will have to get more cash for expenses for the project."

Sherbani indicated that would be possible.

Deby knew it was time to speak up. Act confident, he told himself. Be like Austin.

"You promised me something else," he said to Sherbani. "My family. I want my father out of prison, and then I want my family flown out of Iran *before* I agree to work for you."

"Do not be unreasonable, Hassan. It will take time, but we will work something out."

Deby stood, feeling Austin's gaze on him. "Either that, or I walk out right now."

"You know we can make it unpleasant for your father, *and* your mother. *And* you."

"That's my price."

- - - - -

Deby followed Austin through the revolving door of the hotel, onto the crowded New York sidewalk and around the corner into an almost-deserted bar. "We did it, Ian. We did it."

Deby felt as if he were in a daze. *"Why?* Why are you doing this?"

Austin laughed. "As you would say, my *British* friend, fifteen bloody-million reasons."

"But you're planning to give them a bloody atomic bomb. What will they do with it?"

Austin led him to a booth in the corner. "As our friend Sherbani says: they have as much right to one as anyone else. Where does the U.S. get the right to crash into their country and take their toys away?" Austin turned to the approaching waitress and told her to bring a bottle of Dom Pérignon. He turned back to Deby, laughing. "You talked me into this, remember? And now, I find out you don't think they should have a bomb."

"You better bloody well believe I don't."

"Maybe they should, maybe they shouldn't. But they *are* getting one. *We* are giving it to them and getting our ten-million. After that, who knows what might happen to the bombs?"

"What does that mean? You're going to double-cross them? They'll kill you."

Austin laughed. "You didn't hear me say anything about sabotaging the project. I intend to live up to our contract and give them the bomb. Enough of that, let's get down to the celebration of getting rich. I got the impression in our meetings over the last few months that you're still an up-tight Muslim and you've never gotten laid." He burst out laughing. "We're going to remedy that tonight."

Chapter Three

Ian now had a bank account in Switzerland with two-million dollars minus the two-hundred thousand in cash that Sherbani arranged for him and Austin in the United States. His cash rested in a safety deposit box in a branch of the PNC Bank in Princeton, New Jersey.

Despite Deby's insistence that his parents be out of Iran before he began work on the bomb, Sherbani insisted that would take time. In the meantime, he arranged for Deby to visit Iran. Deby considered taking BahAmin, his older sister who emigrated with him and now lived outside of London with her British husband, Malcolm Wilson, and their three children. Sherbani mentioned Uncle Behrouz, but not BahAmin. Why draw Sherbani's attention to her? Deby worried about not being trusted by Sherbani and therefore being watched or having his phone bugged, so he called her from a pay phone and told her what was happening. To keep from compromising her safety, he had her set up an anonymous e-mail account on Yahoo, and he did the same. They would use those accounts only to communicate with each other.

When he left for Iran, he told his Princeton colleagues he was going to England for a visit. Sherbani made arrangements under his Iranian name with an Iranian passport for an Iran Air flight from Amsterdam to Tehran.

The parents he found only vaguely resembled those pictured in his mind all these years, mental scenes enhanced by the few photographs Auntie Goli brought out of Iran. Streaks of gray pushed his forty-eight-year old mother's appearance to that of a sixty-plus grandmother, a change hastened by twelve-hour days spent cleaning government office buildings. On his first visit with his father, he discovered a completely gray prisoner with deep facial wrinkles that pushed his appearance well past his fifty-four years.

During his visit, Sherbani arranged for him to consult with the

Iranian scientists who had produced the report on atomic bombs that he had been given. These were older men, most of them older than Sherbani. Deby wondered if they would not rather be spending their time on other technical tasks.

When he returned to Amsterdam, he rented a car for a side trip to Zurich to check his new bank account and set up other accounts for later use. He spent a day looking for a place to settle his family when they arrived, but he then changed his mind about having them relocate there. Since they would come out of Iran on Iran Air, and since Iran Air had no flights to Switzerland, he decided to tell Sherbani to fly them to Amsterdam. Before his return to the U.S., he contacted an Amsterdam real-estate agent and used some of his new-found wealth for a six-month lease on a three-bedroom apartment in the Kinkerstraat district.

Back in the U.S., he e-mailed BahAmin with a tentative plan for when his parents were released. He included numbers for Swiss bank accounts for BahAmin and Uncle Behrouz, who was part of the plan.

He spent his last month at Princeton interviewing for jobs at Ohio State, MIT, Drexel, and Wisconsin. All but Ohio State offered jobs, which he turned down. When his postdoctoral appointment at Princeton ended, he announced he had a job with Conrad Engineering Consultants in Salt Lake City. Conrad Engineering's website described a virtual 90-person firm with e-mail addresses for the ninety phantom employees, thanks to Steve Austin. Ian Deby's new e-mail address, debyi@conradeng.com, would be used to communicate with friends and colleagues at Princeton and elsewhere. According to Austin, this would allow him to resume his former life once the bombs were built. At that time, he would return from a long-term consulting trip from somewhere on the other side of the world—Korea, China, or South Africa—and announce that he was looking for an academic position.

Three months after the New York meeting and a week after Deby left Princeton, they again met at the Sheraton. As before, Austin ran the meeting and with the aid of a PowerPoint presentation on his laptop computer, he laid out a bomb program that included preparation of facilities, bomb design, acquisition of nuclear material, and building and delivering the bombs. According to Austin, when the project was completed he and Deby would return to normal society. Deby had a difficult time believing it; he wondered if Austin felt the same way

After Austin laid out his ambitious program, Deby spoke up. "You sort of skipped over how you expect to steal the nuclear material. You said yourself that this isn't the 1970s when the *Curve of Binding Energy* was written, saying nuclear material could be stolen easily."

"Twenty-first century technology—cyberspace—makes it a piece of cake. I'll take care of it."

"You'll need other people to help with different parts of the project," Deby said. "It'll leak out. Nine-eleven changed everything in this country. Security has been upgraded considerably the last nine years."

"I agree. The more people that are involved, the greater the chance somebody will leak it. That's why we're minimizing the number of people involved, at least those involved voluntarily."

"What do you mean: *voluntarily*?"

"Don't worry about it. Only you, Mr. Sherbani, and I will know the whole plan. Everybody else will know only what they need to know. They won't know the other people involved. Those doing the hijacking won't know what's being hijacked. Only a few people besides us will know you're involved, and they won't know your real name. Everybody will be well paid to keep their mouth shut."

A week after that meeting, Ian Deby was reborn as Brian Applenu, and Steven Austin was reborn as Derek Hearn. The idea according to Austin was to keep their real names clean, so they could resume them when the job was completed. They had the required papers—birth certificates, social security numbers, credit cards, credit histories— everything a twenty-first century man needed to lead a respectable life in the USA in 2010, all thanks to Steve Austin—computer hacker extraordinaire—and a forgery expert Austin knew. Austin also gave Deby two other sets of identification papers should Applenu be compromised.

They would use their new names whenever working on the project, which for Ian, a.k.a Brian, was now a full time job. Since he was still a full-time NNSA employee, Steve didn't have the luxury, and would sometimes forget to respond when Ian called him Derek.

Austin had Deby buy two laptop computers, one for his communications as Ian Deby, the other for his communications as Brian Applenu. On this one, Austin installed an encryption program. When the job was complete, he could destroy the latter computer if necessary. He also bought a second cell phone, a Siemens S65, from which untraceable calls could be made by Brian Applenu.

Deby moved from Princeton to Washington, and as Applenu, he began designing a facility to safely turn nuclear material into atomic explosives. Actually, Austin had begun the process before Applenu arrived. After searching the country—the internet mainly—posing as Derek Hearn, he found and leased a new hot-cell facility down south that had been built but abandoned by a bankrupt nuclear fuel-element manufacturer before any nuclear material had been put into the facility. It was up to Applenu to modify the facility for their job and have it ready when they acquired the plutonium and uranium bomb material.

Applenu also helped Hearn design bombs. The ones in the Iranian report were not suitable for the nuclear material available for stealing. They would either have to be modified or new ones designed. As they struggled to estimate critical masses for uranium and plutonium, Applenu found it hard to believe they would ever build workable bombs. They lacked data to determine how explosive efficiency depended on mass and energy generation rates. They needed equations of state for bomb materials, which they finally obtained when Austin acquired the Rare Metals Handbook and Glasstone's *Sourcebook of Atomic Energy*.

The struggle eased considerably once Austin gained access to the DOE classified library and carted home copies of everything from designs for advanced weapons to critical mass summaries for fissionable materials. In reality, he didn't have to cart it home. He scanned the literature— actually, he had a librarian scan it—and carried it out of the library in his pocket on a tiny flash drive. In addition to information on designing atomic bombs, they assembled all the information they needed to process plutonium hexafluoride and uranium hexafluoride into plutonium metal and uranium metal, respectively.

While searching the DOE library files, Austin discovered that in the early 1950s before the hydrogen bomb—code named SUPER—became a reality, Atomic Energy Commission (AEC) scientists developed numerous atomic bomb designs with the objective of maximizing explosive yields while minimizing size. Bombs with names like Mike, Viper, and S.O.B.— Super Oralloy Bomb—were just three of the projects detailed in the classified reports he scanned.

With that information and computer-aided design programs, they developed new bomb designs. Hearn as Austin somehow acquired access to one of the world's fastest computers, a new CRAY supercomputer at Lawrence Livermore Laboratory, a computer used by DOE weapons scientists for their calculations. For good measure, he also acquired access to a second supercomputer at Oak Ridge National Laboratory in Tennessee. Tasks that took the Manhattan Project thousands of man hours to complete, took them but a fortnight. In some AEC reports, computational procedures had been worked out, and all they had to do was translate them into codes for the CRAY.

Hearn developed a computer code for simulated explosions he called

EXPLOVIEW. With it, they could change bomb parameters and determine explosive yields (kilotons). They designed bombs that approached a megaton, all of them vast improvements on the old AEC designs. To maximize the number of nuclear bombs they could build from material they intended to acquire, they decided on bombs averaging 40 kilotons, over three times the yield of the two dropped on Japan—and with much less weight.

The other part of the plan involved DOE, where six months earlier Austin submitted a massive report to redesign NNSA's nuclear transportation and security system. Everything was to be computerized, and the process coordinated on a classified website. This included hiring and assigning drivers and guards to trucks that transported nuclear material, organizing and approving the schedule for transporting nuclear material, automating inventory of nuclear material, etc. The report was immediately approved and funded. Austin was in charge of implementing the plan, and by now, the redesign of the system was nearing completion.

In conjunction with his work in Washington with Hearn, Applenu commuted from Washington to the bomb-making facility he was setting up down south. The plan was for Applenu to manage the factory where they would process the hijacked nuclear material that was liquid into powder and the powder into a solid that could be machined into a nuclear explosive for the bomb. Hijacked solid material would be machined directly.

To make it official, Hearn built a website for the factory, which they called Margine Nuclear Technology, a fuel-rod manufacturing facility, complete with e-mail accounts for dummy names that worked at marginenuclear.com. He said the site was for recruiting purposes.

Hearn recruited a young chemist, Eric Drafton, to work on processing the liquid and powder. Drafton visited Washington for three weeks to confer about the project. Hearn, who was vague on how he met him, turned over a large amount of classified literature to him and Applenu on procedures for processing the plutonium and uranium from liquid through powders to metal. Drafton spent most of his time at the factory getting it ready, thus allowing Applenu to spend most of his time in Washington.

Applenu figured Hearn worked fifteen-to-twenty hours a day—some as Austin on his DOE job, but most as Hearn on the project. Although Applenu's own twelve-hour days had him exhausted, Austin and/or Hearn never faltered. He even squeezed in time to party and spend some of his new-found wealth on a red Porsche Cayman. He knew how to party, and thanks to him, the former Ian Deby was no longer a virgin. That status changed in New York after their first meeting with Sherbani. After that, Austin introduced him to Patricia Hunter, a nice bit of stuff he had begun sleeping with on a semi-regular basis.

Simultaneously with designing the bombs, Hearn worked to acquire the bomb material. For that, Sherbani and Hearn brought in Bill Lormes, who Hearn described as a Russian ex-KGB officer who now "managed various enterprises," one of which was truck hijacking.

Applenu participated in the meetings to devise hijacking plans. The first part of the plan involved getting men hired as drivers and guards for NNSA's Transportation Division. Again, Hearn's computer skills greased the skids, as he was able to devise appropriate backgrounds for each man to ensure they got the jobs. As part of the redesign of the Transportation Division, Hearn made sure he was on the hiring committee. In essence, he was the committee—he and the Department of Human Resources computer.

Lormes—undoubtedly not his real name—was a burly, craggy-faced man in his late fifties, always in an expensive suit and tie. He spoke with a strong Russian accent. Meetings generally began with Lormes objecting to various aspects of Hearn's plans and then listening to Hearn convince him it was the best way to proceed.

Four months after Deby became Applenu, Hearn decided they should celebrate the successful completion of phase one of the project—bomb design, acquisition of manufacturing facilities, and planning for the hijacking. They sat across from each other at Morton's Steakhouse in Arlington, Hearn cutting a slice of "double-cut" filet mignon, Applenu chewing a mouthful of porterhouse. Between bites, Hearn quietly brought him up to date and then surprised him. "Lormes has everything in place for the heist of the century. You'll be manufacturing bombs in less than a month."

As they finished their meal, a young black man stopped at the table and spoke to Austin. "Steve, did you get hit yesterday? We were down all day."

"We weren't affected," Austin said. "We've worked hard on upgrading security."

"Maybe I'll come over to your place and get a rundown on your procedures."

"Sure," Austin said. "Call me next week."

After the man left, Austin turned to Applenu. "He's head of computer security—system administrator—for all mainframe computers on Capitol Hill. I keep in touch with him and other system administrators around town. Did you hear about the cyber attack, as the media termed it? Computers crashed all over Washington." He chuckled. "Ours didn't. I had a call this afternoon from the system administrator over at FBI headquarters. He thanked me for the help I gave him on security programs for his system. It didn't crash either. But then that was the plan."

"You were responsible for the cyber attack?"

He laughed. "I made the plan, and Sherbani provided funds to subcontract the job to some people I know, some very smart people. Between us we figured out how to shut systems down all over the world. Last week we confined ourselves to Washington."

"Hackers? What's this got to do with stealing the material?"

"Only everything." Another laugh. "It all goes down next week."

- - - - -

Five days after the celebration, Applenu was at the bomb factory when he got a text message from Hearn telling him to check CNN shortly after 7:00 pm. He turned on the TV a few minutes before seven. At seven, "The Blitzer Report" began with a gray-bearded chap interviewing a senator about an energy bill being debated in the Senate. Three minutes later, Blitzer was interrupted by a graphic announcing breaking news, and a blonde bit of fluff, eyes wide, appeared on screen, speaking in an excited tone.

"We've just been informed there's been a massive internet interruption that is affecting computers and communications over a wide area of the United States. The first indication something was wrong appeared about ten minutes ago." She paused, evidently listening to someone talking in her earphone. She resumed, "I've just been informed that some of CNN's computers in our Washington, New York, and Atlanta studios have been affected, and…"

Fascinated, Applenu watched for the next hour as Blitzer spoke with reporters in Washington, New York, and Atlanta about what was happening at their locations.

The Washington reporter: "We just learned that communications in Europe are also affected. As I said earlier, we are having difficulty communicating with our reporters, but we were able to get to our Pentagon correspondent by telephone, and she reports that many government computers were hit. Although not yet confirmed, a Pentagon employee, who wished to remain anonymous, said several of the government's super-security computers were hit." Blitzer came back on: "I have on the phone Professor Dudley Anderson, a computer-security expert from Georgetown University. Professor Anderson has been…"

It was clear to Applenu that this part of Hearn's elaborate plan worked to perfection. The objective was to disrupt communications between NNSA's Transportation Control Center in Albuquerque and the trucks carrying the nuclear materials. Everything needed to proceed in a precise fashion. Two minutes before communications were knocked out, the command car leading the truck convoy would receive a "Change in Route" notification originating from Hearn. A Change in Route notification requires the convoy commander to confirm the order, but before that could be done, communications would be interrupted. In addition to a loss of voice and computer communication, Albuquerque would also lose the GPS signals.

The original plan was to have the convoy commander be one of Lormes's recruits. However, since Austin was unable to make that happen, it would be necessary for Lormes's men to subdue the men not in on the hijacking. The commander's assistant riding in the truck with him was one of Lormes's men. Once they took over, the trucks would be taken off on a side road, where the nuclear material would be transferred to other trucks, eventually winding up at Applenu's factory. All GPS units on the trucks would be disabled, so Albuquerque would not be able to locate them when communications were restored.

It was after ten when Hearn called Applenu's cell phone. "We did it, Brian! I just talked to Lormes. Phase two, the acquisition, went as planned, like clockwork."

"It's over?"

"It's just beginning, old chap. Lormes and friends plan to have the product to you tomorrow. You got everything ready to begin manufacturing?"

Applenu hesitated; he had hoped it would never come to this, hoped that Austin would not be able to pull it off, thus getting him out of this quandary. "The facilities are ready," he said.

"For phase three," Hearn said, "you are the man, old chap. You're in charge of getting the stuff processed, machined, and shipped to the customer."

- - - - -

Three days after Lormes delivered the material to the factory, Applenu, on Hearn's orders, was at the Fontainebleau Hotel in Miami's South Beach for the American Society of Mechanical Engineers Meeting when Hearn called Applenu's cell phone. "Did you see our man?" Hearn asked.

"He gave an interesting talk on computerized machining, and he's giving another paper tomorrow morning entitled, 'Micro/Meso Mechanical Applications for Improved Precision Machining at the Microscale Level.'"

"Is he our man?"

"The chap's quite sharp, but he won't work for us when we tell him what we're doing. I can take care of the machining, and you can take care of the computer part of it, so we really don't need him."

"We need him and Surling for insurance. Maybe you can take care of the machining, but we've got to be sure. Reedan and Surling are experts. So it's up to you and Lormes to recruit him." He laughed. "Lormes can be persuasive."

"There are a bloody lot of things that could go wrong, and this is one of them."

"There were a *bloody* lot of things that could have gone wrong up to now, but they didn't. And they won't in the future. By the way, I sent our last product design off to our boss. It's the best design yet."

Hearn was referring to Sherbani, who showed all bomb designs to "his scientists at home," as he called them. Although Hearn referred to Sherbani as the boss, Applenu knew Hearn considered himself the boss. Applenu marveled at the pride Hearn expressed in his designs. Everything he did was done with excellence.

Hearn said, "I don't know if and when I'll be able to come down to the factory. I need to stay here to keep suspicion off me. Actually, I don't ever need to be down there, do I? You are the *man* at the factory. It's in your hands now. That's the way I planned it."

"What's happening with the investigation of the other guy?" Applenu asked Hearn, referring to Austin.

"DOE in-house security and DOD security is investigating. They somehow kept the FBI out of it up to now, but I know they are discussing when to bring them in."

"Have any investigators been to see the other guy?"

"They are concentrating the investigation in Tennessee and New Mexico, but two of them came to see him. They wanted to know how the computerized system works. One of them asked what happened to our super-secure system. I told them DOE computers were just one of many throughout the world that were hit. Although the computer that controls the transportation system in New Mexico failed, ours here at Washington didn't. I said we are looking into why the New Mexico computer failed. Of course, I didn't tell them I designed the entire system."

"So what happens if they zero in on you?"

"I've got plans for that. I've got explanations for everything. Eventually, when the time is right, I'll resign, saying I'm partly to blame because my computerized system failed. Oh, I've got plans. Don't worry about me."

"We succeeded with the hardest part of this project," Applenu said. "Maybe we should just end it here and walk away, just disappear."

"No way. Besides, you know you can't do that. You've got family involved. Buck up, old chap. Hey, I wish you were here, because I'm going out and celebrate. If you were here, you could call Patty and get laid." He laughed. "You miss getting laid regularly, now that you know what it's all about? We've got a lot to celebrate. And much *bigger* things are coming."

- - - - -

The morning after Hearn's celebration, Sherbani made one of his rare phone calls to Applenu in his hotel room in Miami. "Our colleague, Doctor Hearn is dead," he said solemnly.

"*Dead*? I talked to him last night."

"It was an automobile accident in his new Porsche. He was going too fast and lost control. The car exploded. His body was burned beyond recognition."

Applenu dropped into the chair behind the table he was standing at, his mind assessing the meaning of the news and it's effect on the project. Maybe this was the break he needed. He said, "We've got to cancel the project. We can't do it without him."

"We carry on just as before. Doctor Hearn served us well. He gave us some magnificent designs in phase one, engineered phase two, most ingeniously, and now phase three, the manufacture of the product, is up to you."

"He was our computer expert," Applenu protested. "We needed him to write programs for precision machining the product. He also made himself the chemistry expert on processing the fluoride solution to a solid."

"Why did Doctor Hearn send you and Lormes to Miami?" Sherbani asked and then answered his own question. "To recruit backup for the computerized machining, correct?"

"Yes, but…"

"And Doctor Hearn gave Mr. Lormes instructions on recruiting a backup chemist, correct? Doctor Hearn planned for all contingencies. He prepared documents on the chemistry and machining and gave them to you and Dr. Drafton. His plan all along was to have you run phase three without significant input from him. So we are right on schedule."

Applenu sighed with resignation as Sherbani continued in a soft voice. "When you make a long journey, your vehicle can break down. That does not mean you abandon your journey. There are other vehicles, some not as good as the one you started with and some better. Regardless, you continue the journey. You are now our vehicle, a better vehicle. I know you will not fail us."

Perilous Panacea

Chapter Four

Lori Reedan smiled as she threw open her front door, expecting to find Linda Bell. Instead, a squat, gray-haired man with a white walrus mustache squinted at her through purple-tinted glasses.

"Mrs. Reedan, I've got a message about your husband," he said in accented English, as he shoved his light-blue shirt into rumpled navy pants, his enormous stomach protruding over his belt.

"Curt isn't here. He's on a business trip." Nothing new there, she thought. Either away on business or isolated in his office, parked behind his computer. "I handle his business when he's gone." Curt's SOP to her: he made her vice-president of *their* company.

"I've got a message *about* him, not *for* him," he growled as he flipped off his glasses revealing watery blue eyes perched above purple pouches as wrinkled as his shirt. He scanned her bare legs.

Suddenly conscious of her brief shorts, she pushed the door forward and shuffled the lower half of her body behind it. "What do you mean, about him? Is something wrong?"

"Is Daddy home?" Beth suddenly squealed from behind Lori. In her pajamas, she danced merrily on tiptoes at the top of the steps that led down into the foyer.

"Beth, please get back to bed," Lori said, thinking again how good it would be to get her into kindergarten in the fall. Every day it got harder to get her to take a nap.

When Lori turned back to the man, he had the screen door open. She grabbed the door to slam it in his face, but she couldn't budge his massive bulk. "You can't come in here!"

He shoved her backward with the door, the soles of her leather sandals sliding on the slate floor.

"Mommy? What's the man doing?"

31

"Just take it easy, lady, and everything will be okay."

Head down, she leaned her weight against the door, her gaze falling on the chain lock Curt kept after her to use. She remembered the paper last week, where some guy on the other side of town came to this woman's door, forced his way into her house, and raped her. But that was three-thirty in the morning, not in the middle of the day.

"Mommy! Mommy!"

His steel-gray head now protruded into the house, his puffed cheeks and thick gray mustache less than a foot away from her face. Sweat beaded his forehead.

She strained against the door, but her feet glided backward. When she skipped forward to keep from falling, his momentum caught her mid-stride and shoved her farther back, the door now open wide enough for him to squeeze in. He grabbed her arms with damp hands, twisted her right hand from the doorknob and kicked the door shut. He jerked her toward him, his unbuttoned shirt flapping open to reveal a thick mat of gray chest hair, the air between them now filled with the odor of sweat—no deodorant. Up close, his body heat enveloped her as though she had just stepped outside; his breath reeked of liquor and onions.

Lori started to scream and remembered Beth, who stood at the top of the stairs, eyes wide open. Can't scare Beth, she thought, got to protect her from this madman. She flung herself backwards, but her arms were pinned as if in a strait jacket. She remembered the gun Dad wanted to give her ever since she left home.

Standing next to him, she realized he was short, about her height. His bulk dominated. She skipped forward and aimed a knee at his groin. "Get out of here, or I'll call the police."

With a twitch of his huge waist, he bowed slightly, causing her knee to barely graze his thigh. Reestablishing his grip, he held her at arm's length, a leering smile on his lips.

"No police, lady." He grabbed her shoulders and spun her around so she faced Beth at the top of the steps. Beth stared down, mouth open.

"Just get the hell up them steps, lady."

Lori twisted and squirmed in his grip, then threw her body to the floor, wrenching her shoulders free. She jumped up, but before she could turn and face him, he had both hands on her buttocks, his fingers probing as he boosted her toward the steps.

Lori screamed. She scampered up two steps toward Beth, whose eyes were mostly white.

"Mommy! Stop him, Mommy!"

Lori turned to face him.

"Lady, it's all up to you. You can calm down and not give me any trouble and you and the kid won't get hurt. And neither will your husband."

Chapter Five

When Bill Lormes said the job was his, Curt Reedan smiled and reached for his wine glass. He sipped merlot, savoring the flavor of his private toast to success, a toast to the completion of another stage of his career plan. "I'm looking forward to the job," he said as Brian Applenu refilled his wine glass, although it was still three-quarters full.

Sold at last, Curt thought. Now they could get down to the details of the job. Selling, there was always too much selling, although he felt himself getting better at it.

Curt shoved his chair back from the dining table, unfolded his long legs, and heard the familiar pop in the left knee. He glanced at the plush surroundings: a fourteenth floor Miami Beach hotel suite overlooking the Atlantic, the dining area set back in a corner away from the living-room area. He looked at Bill Lormes, who sat to his left, then glanced at Brian Applenu at the other end of the dining table from Lormes.

He spoke to Lormes, who had introduced himself as the president of Margine Nuclear Technology. "From what you've told me, I shouldn't have any trouble computerizing the machining operations. But we haven't really talked about what your company does. What's your product line?"

Lormes studied Curt's face. Curt had sensed Lormes's eyes on him throughout the meal, gray, penetrating eyes, watching him like a suspicious boss. "Our product line, as you put it, is atomic bombs," Lormes said, his voice, a heavily accented rumble suddenly stripped of its businessman-to-businessman joviality of their earlier conversation.

Words started to form, then froze on Curt's parted lips. He pumped out a too-loud laugh. "Oh, you're joking," he said, emitting more of his salesman's laughter.

Lormes's steel-gray eyes flashed above the white napkin he used to wipe at the wrinkles around his mouth. "It's no joke."

"What are you, government? I think my security clearance is still active."

"We're not government."

Curt sucked a deep breath to counter the alarm that pressured his chest and squeezed air from his lungs, leaving him partially winded. His head snapped from Lormes to Applenu, then back to Lormes. Who was this guy? Lormes's craggy face labeled him in his sixties, but his slick brown hair and the tailor-fitted gray pinstripe draped across his bulky shoulders probably knocked off ten years. Up 'till now, they hadn't discussed specifics of the job, but that wasn't unusual.

Margine Nuclear Technology was a legitimate firm. It had to be. When he received the e-mail inviting him to lunch, Curt looked at their website that described nuclear-related work they did at their plant in Blacksburg, Virginia. He figured they were located there to be near AREVA, the French nuclear company. Also, Lormes said they had talked to two of Curt's clients, and said he came highly recommended. They wouldn't do that if they were not for real. Both Lormes and Applenu called him last week to get him to visit their Blacksburg plant as soon as possible. When they found out he couldn't visit for two weeks and that he was giving a talk at the ASME meeting in Miami Beach, they made plans to meet him here.

"I don't understand," Curt said. "*Atomic bombs?*"

"It's simple enough," Applenu said, his words precise, delivered with a British accent that seemed more pronounced than when they talked on the phone. "We're going to build some atomic bombs, and we need you to help us computerize some remote-machining operations."

Lormes had introduced Brian Applenu as the brains of Margine Nuclear Technology. Slim, a dark complexion, about Lormes's height, five-ten or so, and Curt's age, around thirty, his face was mostly black hair. Thick black curls on his head tumbled from his forehead to his eyebrows. A black mustache dribbled down the sides of his mouth into a short black beard that covered his chin and jaw like chocolate pudding around a messy kid's mouth.

"We're going to be machining uranium and plutonium," Applenu said. "Since you worked at the Y-12 weapons plant in Oak Ridge for three years, you're used to machining those metals. We'll also be machining non-radioactive components to extremely close tolerances. We need the computer techniques you described in your talk today."

"I haven't worked with uranium or plutonium for over two years."

Applenu cocked his head like a curious animal, studying Curt as if he didn't believe what he heard. "According to what you just told us and what you said in your talk today, you've made metal fabrication a science. You can develop a computer program to machine anything. If that's so, you won't have any more trouble with plutonium and uranium than you would with carbon steel."

Curt remembered his salesman's motto: show the client confidence; talk a good game, even if clouds of doubt threaten peace of mind. Maybe it worked too well this time. Lormes's earlier announcement completed his career package for the next step: an MIT professorship coupled with long-term consulting jobs with companies like Y-12 at Oak Ridge and Margine Nuclear Technology put him right where he wanted to be. Success. Right?

A private company building atomic bombs? It was like the college junior designing an atom bomb for a class project that you read about. Just talk, anti-science talk. It had to be a joke. Curt had read articles about how easy it was to build an atomic bomb, but it had to be more complicated than that. "If you're not government, why are you building atomic bombs?"

"Let's not worry about *why* we're building bombs," Applenu said. "We told you up front, so you wouldn't be surprised later on. We need your expertise, and we will pay for it. Say two-hundred-fifty-thousand dollars for about a month's work."

"A quarter-of-a-million dollars?" That kind of money would accelerate his career plan by several years. "*Are* you kidding?" Are these guys al-Qaeda terrorists? Applenu, with the dark complexion: Is he Middle Eastern?

Applenu shook his head, smiling. "A quarter-of-a-million dollars, cash…tax free. Of course, we're also buying your silence. We know all about you. We found out that one of the reasons you're going to MIT is because you're into developing robots and you want to start a company. That money will go a long way toward getting you started. Patent lawyers are expensive."

Now he knew what was going on. It couldn't be. "What are these bombs going to be used for? What kind of organization are you running?"

"The less you know," Lormes growled, "the less you'll have to keep quiet about." Like rays from a bright light, the lines in Lormes's face emanated from his mouth.

With the quarter-of-a-million dollar figure still rattling around his brain, Curt decided he didn't want to know anything more about the job. He glanced around the room, trying to comprehend. A few minutes earlier the luxury of his surroundings had him thinking he had arrived at last, his reward for hard work at the ripe old age of thirty-one.

Even before this, Lori kept telling him everything was moving too fast. On the plane down, he tried to reflect on the future: the move to MIT, his consulting business, Lori's MBA degree and a possible job, and now, thrown in on top of it all, a new baby. Until he faced it on the plane, he hadn't taken time to consider the baby beyond the hope that Lori would still have her period, though the probability of that was about nil. The idea of a son had appealed to him, but not now.

Lori pestered him to sit down and talk about their life and make plans for *their* life. He knew where his career was headed, and they never got around to discussing plans. And he didn't waste any time on it on the plane. By the time the "Fasten Seat Belt" sign went off, his mind had wandered to the Vickers contract, and he reached into his briefcase for his laptop. Finish up Vickers and get back to the robot program. Vickers and Margine Nuclear Technology were tickets to the robot program, which was where he wanted to invest his attention, Now, Margine Technology needed to be deleted from that plan—immediately.

Lormes and Applenu stared at him as if expecting a momentous announcement.

Curt picked up his water glass, drained it, and stood. "Thanks for lunch, but I'm not your man. I've got to be in Cincinnati tomorrow, so…"

"You're not leaving," Lormes said, his accent heavier now and sounding Russian. In his haste to stand and throw his body in front of Curt, Lormes's wine glass toppled, sending a crimson shower to the gray carpet, the globules glistening like drops of blood.

Curt started to squeeze by, but Lormes shifted his mass, standing immovable like a bolder, his bulky shoulders balanced on a thick waist.

His path blocked on the right by the dining table and on the left by a wall of balcony windows looking out at the Atlantic Ocean, Curt started to turn just as Applenu eased in behind him.

Getting mugged in a hotel room because you wouldn't take a quarter-of-a-million dollars, Curt thought. Only one thing to do: go straight ahead, over or through Lormes, and drag Applenu with him if need be. "Listen, Mr. Lormes…"

Lormes yelled over his shoulder, "Beecher, Markum, get in here."

Across the room, the bedroom door crashed open, and a Mutt-and-Jeff pair in business suits hustled into the room.

Curt froze. Although he might bull his way past Lormes and Applenu, he could not get by all four of them.

The tall one cradled a laptop computer in his arm like a football. After he cleared dishes to the side, he set the computer down along with a wireless mouse. The short, stocky one took Lormes's place, staring up at Curt, smiling.

"We'd like to show you some slides of our operation," Lormes said, pulling his chair from the head of the table next to Curt's chair, sitting down and sliding the computer around in front of him. Behind him, Applenu pulled his chair to the other side of Curt's chair. Before Curt could move, the tall, broad-shouldered bull glided into the position vacated by Applenu.

Curt stared down at Lormes. "I'm not interested in the job. I've already got more business than I can handle."

Lormes reached for the mouse and clicked. A PowerPoint slide with a photo flashed onto the monitor, a green sign with white letters:

Welcome to the City of
OAK RIDGE
The Vision Lives On

"Margine Nuclear Technology's got a plant in Oak Ridge? I never heard…"

Lormes smiled up at Curt, and the lines around his mouth twisted into a whirlpool. The whirlpool sucked air. "*Sit down.*"

Halfway to his chair, Curt hesitated, a nerve touched by the tone of Lormes's voice. Get out now, he thought. No excuses just run. Trouble was, the big guy was anchored off his right shoulder, arms dangling like a gorilla. Curt figured the goon to be his own height, six-foot-four, but this guy was properly fleshed out, probably forty-five pounds of muscle beyond Curt's spindly one-seventy-five. Without his thick bush of dark-brown hair, it would have been impossible to tell where his neck ended and his head began. Instinct that urged him to run when Lormes blocked his way, now cautioned him to sit. Either sit or be sat down—and sat on.

Curt crumpled onto the chair as the monitor revealed another familiar green-and-white sign:

WILDEN LANE

"That's *my* street!" A chill coursed down his back as somewhere inside him a dam broke and panic flooded his guts.

The mouse clicked.

Curt jumped up. "That's my house! What's going on here?"

Two hands grabbed his shoulders and jammed him back into his seat; two large hands gripped his head like a vise and twisted it toward the monitor, where he saw the front of his brick house, the trees thick and green with summer foliage, a recent picture.

Click. The back of the house, taken from the woods.

Click. The back of the house, a woman on the patio.

"Lori," Curt shouted, turning to Lormes, who stared at the screen. She appeared anything but pregnant in the Kelly-green almost-string bikini that barely covered half of her bottom with the soft material he enjoyed rubbing his hand across—about the extent of his sex life lately. She never wore it in public; at least she wouldn't if he had anything to say about it.

Click. A close-up. She stared in the direction of the camera, a book in one hand, the other hand poking at coal-black hair that tumbled onto her tanned shoulders. She wore that faraway gaze he'd almost forgotten. Before he started dating her, that gaze turned him and his friends on back in Dref. Bedroom eyes, they called it, among other things.

Click. The lens zoomed in to catch her from waist up, hands behind her, breasts pushed forward and barely covered by the green halter.

Lori studied on the patio, while Beth played in her wading pool, both of them tanning for their Myrtle Beach vacation once Lori's classes ended. He kept telling her he didn't have time for a vacation.

Click.

Curt jumped up and shoved the chair backwards. It thumped onto the carpeted floor. Before Curt could move, the hulk glided in closer, his breath moist on Curt's neck.

"That is a nice set of tits," the short character said from behind Lormes, a voice with an accent similar to Lormes's. "Almost as brown as the rest of her." Another Russian accent?

Curt glanced at the screen. Just the opposite of him with her black hair and dark-brown eyes, she tanned easily. With his blue eyes and light-brown hair—Lori called it auburn—he quickly reddened as his hair bleached to a dirty-straw blond. He kept telling her sun tans were unhealthy, as if she didn't know. She recalled energetic summers during high school and college, driving a tractor on her dad's farm from dawn into dark, her tan deepening into a luscious dark brown. Back then, he enjoyed the glow that accompanied the color, but it's unhealthy now.

The tall one cackled. "She's got a hell-of-a nice ass and knows how to move it. Tall and sleek, too, like a model. Long, slim legs. What is she, five-nine?"

Another Russian accent, Curt thought. "Huh?" He mumbled, his body pressured by an expanding anger and a ballooning fear. He'd been had—an amateur hustled by pros.

"Her height?" the tall one behind him said, as he picked up the chair. "Five-nine?"

Curt turned to the big guy, who stared at the screen, a leering smile on his face. "Five-eight and three quarters." Her height bothered her when they first met. With him at six-four, he figured it helped him get her, although she denied it.

"*Sit down*," Lormes ordered. "Beecher there didn't go through all the trouble of getting those pictures of your wife's beautiful ass and tits so you could walk out of here."

Curt struggled to keep the alarm in his gut from exploding into panic. He clamped his arms tightly to his side, afraid his fear-charged body would propel them flailing in all directions. He glanced left, hesitated, and sat.

The photographer caught her from the waist up, just as she removed her bra. He knew she sun bathed without a bra, but in the *privacy* of their backyard.

Click. A blowup.

"She's a sharp-looking broad," Lormes said, his eyes on the screen. "And it's up to you to keep her that way."

"How did you get those pictures?"

"That's not important. What's important is that we need your help, and you're going to give it to us."

"I don't know anything about making atomic bombs."

"We don't need you for that," Applenu said with that deliberate British accent. He had been sitting back, taking it all in, seeming almost embarrassed, hesitant to join in. "You and I are scientists. We know where to go for technical information, it's all there if you do a little digging, and we've done all the work. We've got designs. Now all we need is some insurance on the manufacturing." He glanced at Lormes and back to Curt. "You're our insurance policy, mate."

Lormes fished a cell phone from his breast pocket and punched numbers.

Curt glanced around the room and decided this was no time for his usual approach to a problem, which included a detailed scientific analysis that considered everything from trajectory curves to velocity equations. Lately, as he got deeper into artificial intelligence, he had even taken to analyzing his own decision-making procedures.

He jumped up, spun around, his elbow bumping Lormes, the cell phone spinning from his hand onto the floor. Curt picked up the chair and shoved it into the tall one's midsection, causing him to stumble backward. In Curt's haste to turn and face the short character, his quick movement momentarily shifted weight onto his bum left leg and almost caused him to topple sideways. He regained his balance and shoulder-blocked the short redheaded guy backward against the wall. He headed for the door.

Behind him, the tall one called Beecher tossed the chair aside and moved around the table in the opposite direction to block Curt's way.

With his eyes, head, and body, Curt faked a quick move to his right.

Beecher reacted by doing the same.

A quick step and Curt headed left. But his left knee buckled. By the time he recovered, Beecher stood in front of him.

The stocky redhead moved in from behind, shoving something into Curt's ribs.

Curt turned, stepped back, and stared at a gun—a gun held by the sawed-off, freckled redhead—aimed right at his heart. Curt's head spun, and he wondered if he had drunk too much. No way. He had maintained his salesman's rule: one drink per hour maximum; one drink and hold.

Lormes retrieved the cell phone and ordered the short stocky one, Markum, to get Curt back to the table.

Curt limped slightly when Markum shoved him forward. Since he kissed his college basketball career goodbye, being quick on his feet wasn't a requirement for success. He still had the instinctive moves, he thought, just like in his basketball days. With a simple head and shoulder move, he'd faked the big guy right out of his jock strap. Then, after all these years, his bum knee bit him again. He had trained himself to walk without a limp, and the gimpy knee rarely crossed his mind. But remnants of the injury hid in the knee like a dormant disease and climbed all over him every time he tried a quick move.

Curt sat. On the computer monitor in front of him, Lori's breasts loomed in his face like two reproachful eyes.

"Hello, Max," Lormes said into the miniature phone. "Put her on. Mrs. Reedan? Yeah, he's okay... What? Hold on a minute."

Curt reached for the phone, ready to call their bluff. They couldn't have gotten somebody to Tennessee this soon. "Let me talk to her."

Lormes jerked the phone back and pressed his hand to the mouthpiece. "By now, you've got the picture. Okay? You tell her you're fine, but you'll be on a job for a few weeks. You tell her she will do what *we* tell her to do. It's for her own good. Okay?"

Curt hesitated, his breath rapid from the exertion. Was this for real? *"Okay?"*

Hand trembling as he reached for the phone, Curt nodded. "Hello, Lori?"

"Curt! What's happening? This man came to the door and forced his way in. He said you wanted to talk to me. Are you okay?"

"Did he hurt you?"

"No, I'm okay."

He fought to keep the trembling in his chest out of his voice. "I'm okay, too." He took a deep breath, and his mind flashed through their concerns of the past few weeks: whether they should move to Colorado or Boston, whether she would have her period, and if not, whether they wanted another child. Whether *he* wanted another child. Simple problems with easy solutions. Just sit down and talk them out. With the phone to his ear, he realized they did most of their talking on the phone, him talking to her from some city or other, in the middle of some business trip or other. And here they were again.

"Lori, I'm going to be on a consulting job for a few weeks."

"What? You can't..."

Lormes grabbed the phone out of Curt's hand. "Mrs. Reedan, we need your husband's expertise for a very important project. A very secret project. Now you might get worried if he doesn't show up for a few weeks. *Don't.*"

Lormes paused to glare at Curt; he tilted the phone away from his ear so Curt could hear when she replied. "Above all, Mrs. Reedan, *don't* go to the police. Because if you do, your husband will die."

"Die?"

"That's right. And we'll know if you go to the police, because Mr. Maxwell, the man who's with you now, or somebody else will be watching you at all times. Do you understand?"

Lormes waited, his lips pursed—an eroded volcano.

Curt sucked for air. He felt a giant hand squeezing his guts, trying to force out the nightmare scream trapped just below his throat. Vomit seeped into his mouth, a taste of rotten cheese and wine.

The eroded volcano of Lormes's mouth erupted. *"Is that clear,* Mrs. Reedan?"

"Yes. I'll do whatever you say."

"Good." Lormes reached for the mouse and looked at Curt, his steel-gray eyes blazing like synchronized laser drills. "It comes down to this, Reedan," he said clicking the mouse.

43

A half-naked Lori was replaced by a laughing little dark-haired girl in a yellow one-piece bathing suit splashing in a wading pool.

"Beth."

"The kid's five, right? You'd like to see her turn six, right?"

Curt stared at Lormes.

"I think you've got the picture, Reedan. You refused the money, so we're making you an offer you *cannot* refuse. We're offering you what's on the screen. You do the job we've got, or your wife and kid die. In fact, we will let you see them die just before we kill you."

Chapter Six

At first glance, Curt Reedan figured it could just as well be another of the forty-some business meetings he'd attended during the past year. Five men clustered around a circular stained-oak table in the center of a large room. Instead of arriving for this conference on another forgettable 757 flight, however, he felt as if he had materialized through a space warp: from Miami South Beach luxury to solitary confinement in one day. His cell was today's conference room, two folding cots along the back wall, facing the door. For two nights and now almost two days, he'd been locked away alone in the room.

Bill Lormes ran the meeting. "We're going to build the first atomic bombs ever built by private enterprise. This afternoon we'll get acquainted and tour the facilities. Then tomorrow we'll get down to the job."

Lormes beamed a smile to Applenu on his right. "Brian Applenu is the technical manager of the project. He's got a PhD in nuclear engineering from MIT." Lormes turned from the black-bearded Applenu to the thin, brown-bearded young man on his left. "Eric Drafton's got a PhD in chemical engineering, also from MIT. He'll be in charge of the chemical processing."

As best Curt could tell through the beards, both men were his age, but he didn't recognize either of them from his own days at MIT. Neither of them wore a Brass Rat on his finger like he did.

"We designed and built the chemical-processing facilities we'll use," Drafton said, a twitching smile poking through the scraggly beard, his youth hidden in the facial hair like a dark bird in a thick bush, only visible by a momentary sparkle in his sad brown eyes.

Lormes nodded across the table at the baldheaded man with rimless glasses at Curt's right. "Professor Robert Surling's got a PhD in chemistry from the University of Chicago. He's an expert in the chemistry of

45

plutonium and uranium. He'll be helping Dr. Drafton with the processing."

To Curt, Surling looked old, maybe seventy, about six-foot tall with a lean frame. Surling stared at Lormes with tranquil blue eyes, his tanned face with high cheek bones a blank, the only life an occasional flicker of light in his glasses.

"And what if I don't cooperate," Surling asked.

Lormes's steel-gray eyes flashed. "You'll cooperate. Or else your wife, daughters, and grandchildren will see some mighty interesting pictures and video of your latest *business* trip."

Curt realized he wasn't alone. Surling was the man for the other cot.

Lormes nodded at Curt. "Curt Reedan's an expert at metal fabrication with a PhD in metallurgy from MIT. It seems we only recruited from the best schools: three from MIT, and one from Chicago." Lormes coughed a laugh. "Everybody's a doctor but your old boss here, the *President* of Margine Nuclear Technology."

From instinct, Curt nodded, but caught himself before he automatically released his businessman's smile. How did this compare with being in Cincinnati, where he was supposed to be? Lormes made him call Carl Vickers from Miami and tell him he couldn't make his visit.

During the past two days, he'd had lots of time to think; he'd worked hard at shunting the fear generated in Miami to a remote corner of his mind, where it clung like a dull headache he tried to ignore. He decided the only way to hack it was to treat it like just another job.

"So how long will this job take?" Curt asked. He stretched his left leg to exercise his bum knee, still stiff from the exertion in Miami.

Applenu answered. "About six weeks. Then we'll pay you and turn you loose."

"Where did you get the fissionable material?" Surling asked, as he smoothed the few gray hairs that clung to his shiny bald head like isolated blades of grass on a rocky hillside. "What are you going to do with the bombs?"

"That's none of your business," Lormes said, his green eyes flashing and his accent heavier. "Don't worry. They won't be used in this country. We're not a bunch of cheap-ass terrorists."

"So you're going to sell them to some small country who'll wind up starting World War Three," Surling said. He spoke slowly, his voice flat, the kind of professorial tone Curt hoped to avoid when he began teaching.

Lormes ignored the statement. He pushed back his chair and stood. "We're ready for the tour." He stared down at Reedan and Surling. "You two know what's involved. We're not here to debate. You play along and promise to keep quiet, we'll turn you loose a quarter-of-a-million dollars richer." His eyes searched for Curt's, then turned to Surling. "If you don't cooperate...well...I don't think we need to discuss that."

- - - - -

Robert Surling watched the door slam. A key rattled in the lock outside. Their tour over, they wound up where they started. Surling stared at the two cots along the back wall and noted that someone brought his luggage while they were on tour. He glanced at Reedan, his cellmate in an asylum where the crazies held the key. Actually, up to now the only difference in the crazies here and the crazies running the university was that here they carried guns and locked you up. At least they didn't expect you to serve on committees and socialize with them.

He ignored Reedan and flopped on the scratched-and-frayed green-vinyl couch that stood along the wall to the right as you entered. Above it was a boarded up window, the only one. He rested his head on the back of the couch and stared at the three rows of fluorescent lights that ran three-quarters the length of the ceiling. Light reflected from the dirty aqua walls and ceiling and filled the room with the dull-green glow of a rainy day at the seashore.

Reedan, looking dazed, dragged a chair from under the oak table in the center of the room and sat facing Surling.

Keeping his face to the ceiling, Surling eyed his cellmate. Probably one of the contemporary replacements for the Whores of Babylon, he thought. They were everywhere. Today's whores arrived complete with a PhD in science or engineering and called themselves research scientists, professors, and consultants. Unlike the old days when he started his career, they no longer searched for nature's truths—science's ultimate goal. Instead, they gladly sold their ass to the bureaucrats of the university, government, and business for whatever they could get in the way of grants. For many, their highest objective was to be a manager, to become one of the bean-counting bureaucrats that squeezed the balls of those doing the work. Then they sat around and tried to figure out why the Chinese, Japanese, and Koreans, among others, were beating the shit out of us in technology.

On the tour of the facilities, Reedan played the role of the curious scientist, full of questions about the equipment, especially the computer. With his earnest face, he could pass for a first-year grad student, overwhelmed by the fantastic work ahead. Even if Reedan wasn't one of today's science whores, there were definitely two of them on the job, selling their services for all they could get. There was a difference, though. As opposed to most of the whores, who just talked and excreted paper, these assholes had assembled a hell of a factory and were out to make the world's most dangerous product.

Surling straightened up. "It's you and me against them, huh, son?" He flipped off his glasses, set them on the arm of the couch, and massaged his naked face. "I'd say they're Mafia. Russian Mafia, judging by the accent."

"*Mafia?*" Reedan asked.

Surling studied him: A typical drudge, never thinking beyond what's on his computer screen.

"That guy Lormes. Did you think he was one of your run-of-the-mill entrepreneurs? Did you think this was a government technology transfer of intellectual property project?"

Technology transfer and intellectual property: four of today's favorite buzzwords of the technology bureaucrats, a new way to siphon government money into their bureaucracies.

"Who else but Mafia could steal all that nuclear material? It's probably a new business venture for them. After drugs, what? Hire yourself a scientist with a British accent and go into the bomb-making business."

Surling dug a cigarette package out of his shirt pocket, probed inside, and crumpled it. He tossed it across the room at the beat-up green wastebasket between the white stove and matching refrigerator on the far wall. It landed far to the right, in front of the scratched white sink. We've got all the comforts of home, including a microwave, he thought. "Got a cigarette?"

"I don't smoke."

Surling sniffed a laugh. "I've wanted to quit."

"How about the facilities we saw?" Reedan asked. "That's a powerful computer."

"They were something, alright." Naturally, the kid would be impressed with the computer, although the tour encompassed five rooms, each containing the latest equipment needed to process any kind of nuclear material. And they had nuclear material, most of it still in the shipping containers. How the hell did they get it?

Their tour guides, Applenu and Drafton, led them first to a chemical-processing room filled with work benches and shelves lined with chemicals and reaction vessels. He should have such equipment in his university lab. Equipment included a brand-new dry box—an atmosphere chamber used to safely handle toxic materials. And plutonium *is* toxic. One whiff of plutonium oxide, and you're living on borrowed time. They visited four other rooms: a furnace room with another dry box, a hot cell, a computer room, and a machine room, all crammed with high-tech equipment that Applenu and Drafton explained to them.

"If we had equipment like that on the Manhattan Project, we'd have finished the bomb a year-or-two sooner," Surling said. The kid didn't respond, and Surling wondered if he knew what the Manhattan Project was. He laughed. "I'll make history twice: I was in on the first bomb in the forties of last century, and now I'll be on the team that makes the first free-enterprise bomb in this century." Surling shook his head. "Nuclear science, my life's work, it's a perilous panacea."

"We always knew that," Reedan said, "the bomb versus the reactor. But with nuclear reactors, we've got a chance to get free of Middle Eastern oil. With nuclear energy, we've got a chance to beat the greenhouse effect and global warming."

"Only if we can get people to believe in the panacea. The environmental crazies refuse to believe, and their propaganda and lies make it hard for everyone else to believe, so we scientists are not only to blame for the perils, but we don't get credit for the benefits."

"We're not to blame."

If he was like most scientists these days, Surling thought, he never considered it; he didn't think about anything beyond what his computer-generated thoughts registered. "You don't believe scientists are to blame, huh, son? Scientists go around opening up one Pandora's Box after another, looking for the panaceas, the magic cure-alls for the mess we've made of the world. As soon as a box is open, they're off trying to wedge open a new box to get the jump on their colleagues. And while they're off somewhere else, some asshole, who also calls himself a scientist, is turning their panaceas into the Love Canal. Or that town Bhopal in India, that got rained on by cyanide when Union Carbide's technological panacea went haywire. And in the fifties, before you were born, those poor bastards out in Utah got showered by atomic fallout. Later, the Ukrainians got a similar dose from Chernobyl. A whole lot of panaceas have morphed into deadly perils."

Without his glasses, he couldn't read the expression on young Reedan's face, although it probably didn't have much to say. "I'll grant you that most times those assholes are bureaucrats, but they are scientist-type bureaucrats. Now the panacea turned peril we've got here is the most dangerous of all: dime store nuclear weapons for two-bit dictators."

49

"I don't see how all scientists can be blamed."

He doesn't see, Surling thought. He shrugged. "So another country gets an atom bomb and starts World War Three. We knew it could happen."

Reedan appeared ready to protest, but instead said, "What about us, you and me? Like, where are we, for instance?"

Surling slipped on his wire-rimmed glasses and studied Reedan. The kid didn't seem to know how to take the grouchy professor. "Where are we? That's a good question for the world in general. Where are we mentally? Where are we historically? I'd say we're pretty fucked up." He faked a smile. "Where are you and I geographically? I'd say we're east of the Mississippi River."

Reedan told about his capture and the flight from Miami in an eight-passenger plane, all windows shuttered. They landed at a small airport with no traffic that he could hear, and they blindfolded him and drove here, a fifteen-to-twenty-minute drive.

Surling thought about his own "capture" in Philadelphia. An eighty-four-year-old professor should know better. Young blonde shows up at the hotel, says she's a lawyer who works for Margine Nuclear Technology, says she's there for Lormes, who couldn't make it for dinner and would see him at the plant in the morning. She pays for drinks and a great dinner at Bookbinders. Then more drinks at some dark bar she knew down the street. Next thing he knew, her hands were between his legs, his zipper open, hands inside his shorts massaging his cock. Then, at her apartment, her face was between his legs. An hour later, he was fucked in more ways than one. That's when he was introduced to Lormes and a tall monster with cameras and a gun. Screwed good by a Philadelphia lawyer.

No way would he give an account to this young twerp about how that whore did him in. He hadn't explained it to himself yet, especially after he turned over a new leaf when he met June. She was to be his one and only, *another* one and only. How many new leafs had to be turned over by a dirty-old man?

He told Reedan about Philadelphia, a gun, and a threat. He told how they made him call his wife and say he'd be on a consulting job for six-to-eight weeks. After that, the trip here, probably three hours on the same plane. "We're not in the northeast. It was hotter than Philadelphia when I got off the plane."

"We're probably not in the deep south, either. It wasn't as humid as Miami." Like a hiker lost in a forest on a cloudy night, Reedan, the scientist working without his computer, finally deduced that they were in one of the south-central states: Virginia, North Carolina, South Carolina,

Tennessee, or Kentucky.

Surling stood, went to the table, and grabbed a khaki shirt from the pile of work clothes left by the big goon. They'd be dressed for this job, he thought. No theoretical studies, unless you worked on computers like Reedan. "So we're south of New York and east of the Mississippi River. So what? The question is, how the hell do we get out of here?"

"There's no way. I tried that in Miami, and they stopped me cold. They've got guns, and one of them is outside the door day and night."

"Find a way, because we've *got* to escape. If we're still here when they finish their job, we're dead."

Surling watched Reedan's head snap back as if suddenly awakened. Obviously, he'd have to have his head extracted from his ass.

"They said they'd pay us and turn us loose if we cooperate," Reedan said.

"And you'll cooperate? You'll help those crazy bastards build an atomic bomb?"

"We don't have a choice. They'll kill us if we don't."

"You mean you'll help them build a bomb, take their money, and leave? You'll never worry about how those ten or fifteen bombs we make will be used, how many people they might kill? In other words, if they let you go, you wouldn't run straight to the police?"

"But they said..."

"They'll kill us," Surling said quietly. "They don't have a choice."

Perilous Panacea

Chapter Seven

Rick Saul listened to the vocal squirming of the outwardly calm men on the other side of the table as they went into cover-your-ass mode. According to agents who did this all the time, in Washington, somebody—Democrat or Republican—was always trying to save face. Saul knew what came next: whenever trouble surfaced for anyone with power, the immediate reaction was to try to tie the hands of the investigators.

"It's simple," George Spanner said from Saul's side of the table. "Lie-detector tests for anybody and everybody who could be involved. That's what, fifteen, maybe twenty people?"

Bart Kraft shook his graying, sand-colored head, but not a hair moved. "We can't," he said, his calm, blue-eyed gaze on Spanner. "Involve twenty people and the story will be in the *Post* and *Times* within twelve hours. Besides, it's not an internal problem." Although they were in Kraft's office, sitting at a small conference table across the room from his paper-free desk, the slim Kraft wore his light-blue sport coat buttoned.

Saul waited for the mundane details of a typical SGP—stolen government property—report. Because government agencies like DOE and DOD were into everything from food and office supplies to gold bullion, some employee was forever trying to get his share. In Washington, it was either stolen government property or some government-type using his influence one way or another to get a little something on the side, like some congressman forcing his affections on one of his female employees.

Since arriving in Washington eleven months ago, Saul had spent his eight-to-ten hours a day in the Bureau's Crime Records Division manipulating murder, rape, and robbery statistics on a computer. Everybody said getting called to Washington put you on the Bureau fast track, but for Saul, it was a boring track. At times, even Spokane looked good.

Saul didn't understand why Spanner brought him along on this case, especially considering the two men across the table. Kraft was Associate Administrator for Defense Nuclear Security for the National Nuclear Security Administration (NNSA) of DOE, and the man next to him, Doyle Logson, was Director of Security for DOD.

"So what do we do?" Spanner asked, his fleshy face reddening, a spark kindled in his pale-blue eyes. "You've lost—whatever *lost* means—some nuclear material and you don't want us to investigate too closely, at least not so anyone around here gets any dirt on him."

"You know what we mean, George," Logson said, smiling like he did every time he spoke, a smile that squeezed his eyelids into a caricature of a skinny, baldheaded Chinaman, although he was as white as most Civil Service employees at this level.

Saul figured Logson's emaciated look came from an addiction to jogging. Once he started to jog, his face shrank or his ears grew. Logson's bald head reminded him of his own mop of curly brown hair. Mary claimed he wasn't balding, but how do you measure recession? Every picture of his father Saul had ever seen showed him with an extremely high forehead.

"This is complicated," Logson said. "It involves a large amount of sensitive material."

"*Large amount? Sensitive material?*" Spanner's short gray hair and pink face labeled him the twenty-seven-year Bureau veteran he was. He jogged, but it didn't budge the extra thirty pounds he carted around on his five-nine frame.

Saul leaned forward, realizing he should have expected something big when a senior supervisory agent like Spanner abandoned his desk to trek out to Germantown, and they wind up faced with two high-ranking bureaucrats.

"First, we don't understand how three truckloads of SNM became involved. We usually ship only one at a time."

"S-N-M?"

"Special nuclear material."

"*Special?*" Saul said quietly, not sure if he should get involved in the questioning or let Senior Agent Spanner do all the talking. "Does special mean somebody could make bombs with it?"

Kraft nodded. "The shipments carried both plutonium and enriched uranium." He proceeded to lay out the scenario that somehow involved changes in the shipment contents made by unknown persons. All of the material was bomb grade, and it was considerably different from the original manifest.

"We haven't been able to determine who authorized changes in the shipment," Kraft said. "Then there was the convenient computer crash. This happened during the cyber-terrorist incident that hit the internet and all those other computers four weeks ago?"

Logson explained that the computer crash happened about thirty minutes after the shipment left the Oak Ridge Y-12 Plant in Tennessee headed for Savannah River National Laboratory in South Carolina. DOE's super computer in New Mexico crashed, just like thousands of computers around the world. Before the computers went down, Albuquerque had direct voice and computer communication with the convoy. They were tracking it by GPS. All contact was lost when the computer went down. When the computer came back online over two hours later, they were unable to reestablish contact. GPS contact was also lost. The three trucks had disappeared.

Spanner shook his head. "Unless there's been a change I haven't heard of, the FBI's got jurisdiction in all SGP cases, *including* nuclear material. Looks like that's what we've got here. Homeland should have been notified, too."

"We know, George," Logson said. "We didn't call you or Homeland sooner because of special circumstances."

"There are *always* special circumstances. But this was four weeks ago."

"We wanted to get you in right away, but the White House ordered us to look into it before you were called."

"The *White House*? You mean they couldn't come up with a quick plan on how to blame the previous administration?"

"I took a team of CID investigators to Tennessee," Logson said. "At DOD we've got excellent investigative capabilities, and we thought CID could handle it quickly."

Kraft broke in. "We knew the hijackers couldn't pull much of a terrorist act with the material in its present state. Some is liquid, and some is warhead material from dismantled nuclear missiles. They'd need considerable expertise to transform the stuff into bombs, and that takes time. We figured they'd contact us and try to ransom the SNM. The White House wanted that to happen without the public—the press—getting wind of it."

"You say some of it is liquid?" Spanner asked.

"There were over four-hundred gallons. It's stored and shipped as an aqueous solution. Before it's used, it's put into solid form by precipitation."

"So did the trucks ever show up?"

Logson nodded. "They were found in the woods early the next day, just outside of Loudon, Tennessee. Out of the ten people assigned to the convoy, only four bodies have been found, three dead and one critical. The dead included a driver, a guard, and the convoy commander. The critical was a driver. He's recovering."

"What do the others have to say about what happened?" Spanner asked.

"We haven't found them. They disappeared along with the nuclear material."

Saul remembered the nuclear disarmament rally Mary dragged him to shortly after they moved to Washington. One of her new interests, once she discovered it was one of the Senator's interests. Most speakers ranted about thousands of nuclear warheads the U.S. and Russia continued to hold—even in this time of supposedly cordial East-West relations. If only a few of them exploded, they would tear the old globe a new asshole. The speakers were mainly blaming the U.S. and wanted the U.S. to act unilaterally.

Somewhere between the repetitive tedium of young howlers and old squealers, a scrawny, middle-aged professor from Dartmouth got up and said the real danger lay in any number of petty dictators around the world that might somehow get a bomb, perhaps by stealing nuclear material. He mentioned Iran, North Korea, and Venezuela. Then he talked about the terrorists always on the lookout for ways to make a dirty bomb—use conventional explosives to spread nuclear material around a city. The nuclear material would not kill anyone immediately, but it would spread havoc and require a long time to clean up the mess to avoid people becoming ill in the long term.

Saul spoke up. "What if whoever stole the bomb material decided to get it out of the country, somebody like Iran. They weren't too happy about what the U.S. and Israel did to their nuclear program last year. This might be their way to get bomb-grade material without having to make it themselves."

"You mean like *your* people did," Logson said, the smile on his shiny face expanding, further slitting the eyes. "By the way, the U.S. was not involved in the raid on Iran. That was your people, too."

So Logson was that kind, Saul thought, his face growing warm. He knew what Logson meant, because the professor had mentioned it. He forced himself to smile and said, "*My* people?"

"The Israelis. They stole a boat load of uranium ore to make their first bomb."

"I don't think we're worried about the Israelis here," Spanner said. "Besides, if I read you right, the stuff these people got is a lot easier to turn into bombs than a boat load of uranium ore. How much stuff was stolen, all totaled?"

"Enough for fifteen, perhaps twenty atomic-type bombs," Kraft said. "Hiroshima- or Nagasaki-type bombs."

"*Twenty atomic bombs?*"

"It only takes fifteen pounds or so to make an atomic bomb," Kraft said. "That assumes they know how to use the material efficiently, which is highly unlikely. They also got some other radioactive material they'll have a hard time turning into bombs. In fact, if they're not careful with it, it'll burn them good."

"This is supposed to be 2011, not 1970," Spanner said. "Back in the seventies, the Bureau and the old Atomic Energy Commission worried about somebody stealing nuclear material. These days, DOE has a security system second to none, invulnerable. At least that's what you've been telling people."

Saul enjoyed watching Spanner cut through the bullshit. Although Saul hadn't seen much of Spanner, he'd heard Harry Bryson's story that Spanner, among others, had DOed— diversified out. According to Bryson, the diversity policy drove promotions at Spanner's level, so most mid-level, middle-aged white men hit a dead end. Morale for most agents suffered when they discovered they'd topped out because older white men at the very top had to justify their professed diversity policy. Many of the DOed quit or retired. For Spanner, however, being DOed gave him freedom to deal head-on with the bureaucratic chicken shit that came down the pike.

"Our security is excellent," Kraft said. "We knew we had a few problems given the funding restrictions we've operated under the last couple of years."

"We don't think they're terrorists," Logson said. "Or else we would have heard from them by now."

"They wouldn't have had to steal that much material to pull a terrorist act," Kraft said.

Watching Kraft operate made Saul pull himself upright. Kraft's upper body never moved. All business, hands resting on the table, he sat as if he had a steel rod shoved up his ass.

"So it's a foreign country, like *my* people," Saul said, remembering to smile. Mary insisted a Jekyll-and-Hyde character hid in the intensity of his dark-brown, deep-set eyes, and his charm only broke through in the carefree youthfulness of the smiling curly haired boy that first attracted her to him. Critical comments by her seemed to come more frequently lately, perhaps because his smiles didn't break through to her as often as they used to.

Logson's smile flickered. "I didn't mean *your* people to be taken personally. We agree. Either a foreign agency is behind it, or some enterprise hijacked it to sell to a foreign country."

"Who: Iran? North Korea? Venezuela?"

Logson shrugged. "We've got the CIA making discreet inquiries."

"You've *what*?" Spanner asked, almost coming out of his chair. "You called the CIA in before us, too?"

"Well, if a foreign country's involved…The White House suggested the CIA. Their man runs the agency."

After a brief silence, Kraft glanced at Saul, sighed, and spoke to Spanner. "George, you know it's always like this in Washington. You're asked to do a job, and then you don't get the money to do it. Cost cutting is the latest bureaucratic buzzword. My budget was cut twenty percent since I took over two years ago. Before this happened, the administration talked about more cuts. I don't have the people to do the job right. We protested, but nobody remembers that when something like this happens. If the media gets a hint of this, I'm through."

The bottom line, Saul thought. Kraft and Logson were stuck in the quagmire Uncle Nathan was trying to suck Saul into: a political career. Thanks to Uncle Nathan, Mary was already trapped. He should never have let her take the job on the Senator's staff. As if he could have talked her out of it after Nate dangled it in front of her like the keys to a BMW. Nate probably saw it as a way to guide Saul in what he considers the right direction—Nate's way of bestowing fatherly generosity.

Uncle Nathan called as soon as Saul got to Washington. He "gently" urged Saul to get in touch with the Senator if he ever got wind of something the Senator could use politically. Shortly after Nate talked to him, the Senator called to deliver the same message. Until now, Saul had spent his time behind a computer console massaging numbers, and there was nothing the Senator could use.

"So how do *we* fit into this case?" Spanner asked. "I'm sure somebody's concocted the rules we'll work under."

Logson nodded, smiled, and glanced at the ceiling. "It's been decided on high, *very* high. You got certain directions from the Director's office before you came over here, George, and you'll be getting more. The Administration isn't taking this lightly, no sir," Logson said, smiling at

Saul. "It's Operation SWISILREC, Swift Silent Recovery. Bart and I will report to the Assistant Secretaries of DOE and DOD, respectively. George, you'll report to your Associate Director Dowel. The Justice Department, Homeland Security, DOE, and DOD have formed a joint oversight committee for SWISILREC that includes the Attorney General, Director of Homeland Security, the FBI Director, and the Secretaries of Defense and Energy. Finally, there's a White House POC—planning and operations committee—with those same people, plus the President's National Security Advisor, the head of CIA, and the President's Chief of Staff. Of course, the President will be involved in SWISILREC on every level as he sees fit."

"The Washington way to a perfect solution," Spanner said. "Got a problem, form a committee. Two or three committees are even better."

Saul smiled at Spanner's comment, but neither Logson nor Kraft did. Now, if the Senator could get in on it, he could fire up the congressional committees.

Spanner nodded at Saul and asked, "So how do *we* fit in?"

"The FBI investigation will be low key in consultation with DOE and DOD. Bart Kraft will consult for DOE, and I'll represent the DOD hierarchy. You two will mount the investigation. *Just* you two."

"*What?*"

"You were picked because you can keep quiet," Logson said to Spanner. "Saul was picked because he's new to Washington and hasn't had time to build connections that could lead to disastrous leaks. It's just you and Saul in consultation with us. Use anybody else you want, just don't give them all the details. They can work on the hijackings and murders if you only tell them government property was stolen…say chemicals…or industrial silver…something like that."

Spanner chuckled. "With all the people involved that you just mentioned, along with the CIA and military security, it'll get out soon enough. This is Washington, not Beijing."

Color drained from Kraft's face. He unbuttoned his jacket.

Saul realized if he was to do most of the dog work on the case, he was looking at lots of traveling: Tennessee, New Mexico, and South Carolina, just for starters. He didn't want to be gone that long, but maybe this was the time to be gone. Maybe by being apart, he and Mary could think things out. Trouble was, she would still be around *them* at work, and he couldn't stop thinking about that, regardless of what she said.

Logson stood. "Let's just get the stuff back fast—the swift in SWISILREC. Nobody's going to build a bomb, but if whoever's got that material screws up and lets it get into the environment…that could be serious. Talk about a toxic-waste mess…I can't stress too much that the silent in SWISILREC is of utmost importance."

Kraft nodded. "Above all, keep it contained."

Chapter Eight

"They tried to blame it on us," Ray Woodward said to Saul in a strong southern accent as he fidgeted papers on his desk. Woodward was chief dispatcher for NNSA's Southeastern Office at Oak Ridge, Tennessee, the office that dispatched the lost shipments of nuclear material. He explained how CID and DOE investigators also wanted to know why three loaded trucks were sent out with only two escort vehicles, when their code four status required them to have four.

"Andy Jordan, my boss, said Washington instructed it to be a code two. Jordan figured it was an economy move. There's always a new economy move...on paper anyhow. That and reorganization."

Saul nodded. Everybody bitched about government work, but people like Woodward never quit. "You said they wanted to blame you for the hijacking."

"That's right. They claimed Washington never dropped it from a code four. There was no record of a change on the computer. Jordan told them the change was in an ED, electronic directive, but he couldn't find it on the web either, even though we both saw it. Goddamn computer. Used to be, we were covered up with paper and everybody said it would be better with computers. It isn't. We've got more web-based forms and directives than we ever had paper. It's a wonder we ever get a shipment out of here."

When Saul got to Andy Jordan, head of the NNSA's Southeastern Office, he got the same story about the computer and Washington, how the ED that changed the code was no longer on the web. Jordan said, "Someone must have removed it when they found out what happened."

"Do Washington people ever come down to look you over?" Saul asked.

"DOE and DOD people were all over the place when this happened."

"What about other times?"

"Fortunately, not too often. Washington types would rather visit California or New York than Tennessee. We get enough of them though, like the young pup we had here six-eight months ago, one of those computer whiz-bangs I was griping about, name of Austin. He wanted to know *exactly* how we operate. We wasted two days showing him the procedures for storage and transportation. We showed him the trucks and everything, although I don't know why he needed to see the trucks. He was studying how NNSA's communications network could be improved. A lack of communications didn't cause this screw-up. We weren't lacking security either, because this wasn't your run-of-the-mill hijacking. Security is what this job's all about. Our trucks cost over a million dollars apiece. They are more like an Abrams tank than a normal truck."

Saul nodded, knowing what Jordan was getting at. He and Spanner suspected the same, even before he left Washington, but he was happy to get out of there for awhile, although distance hadn't improved his relationship with Mary. When he finally got hold of her at the office today, they argued. She claimed she'd been working late last night, and then she went out to eat. It was *who* she went out with that interested him. That's when the argument started.

Jordan went on: "The trucks are called SSTs, Safe-Secure Transports. They're made of armored steel. If one is attacked, the driver can push a button and lock the axles." Saul had been briefed on the trucks, but let Jordan explain how they are tracked by GPS by the communications center at Kirtland Air Force Base outside Albuquerque. "And they're not being tracked by some two-bit rent-a-cop outfit with pins in a map and a walkie-talkie. There's a Cray supercomputer that knows what's going on at all times. It's a super-secure computer that nobody is going to get into from outside."

"I know what you're saying," Saul said.

"What I'm saying is that your problem isn't down here, it's back in Washington. Then again, a lot of us think most everybody's problems come out of Washington."

- - - - -

Saul's next stop was Tennessee State Police Headquarters, where he interviewed the investigating officers, who took him to the crime site. He learned nothing beyond what was in the DOD/DOE investigation report.

After a long phone conversation with Spanner, he got two FBI agents from the Knoxville office involved in the investigation. He told them everything but the contents of the shipment, which was classified, and which they did not need to know, at least not yet.

After Tennessee, Saul was off to Albuquerque. He wanted to go home, because the night before, he tried to call Mary seven times and never got her. Sometimes when he was out of town, she stayed with Joyce Able, but when he called Joyce's apartment, he got a busy signal.

In Albuquerque, he spent two days interviewing people involved with the fail-safe communications system that crashed. Just as in Tennessee, little new was learned beyond what was in the CID report. A system with dozens of fail-safe protocols failed, and the computer and communications experts at Kirtland Air Force Base could not say why. A couple people said the cyber attack and the hijacking had to be coordinated, but they expressed reservations that anybody could pull something like that, given the complicated nature of all the systems involved.

After Albuquerque, he flew to Augusta, Georgia, rented a car, and drove to Aiken, South Carolina, where the next day he interviewed people in the receiving office at the Savannah River National Laboratory (SRNL). As expected, they knew very little about the hijacked trucks that were scheduled to deliver their cargo to SRNL. Their only problem was that the manifest of the hijacked material did not agree with the one they received prior to the shipment, the one approved by NNSA headquarters in Washington. The hijacked shipment contained material they had not requested and would have no reason for receiving. Their conclusion: someone had used the computer to manipulate the shipment contents as a setup for the hijacking.

The next day he drove to Montmorenci, South Carolina to interview Luke Walker, the driver of one of the hijacked trucks. Walker, who had been shot in the head and left for dead was in his forties. He removed his red University of Georgia baseball cap to reveal a shaved head and a scar around the back where doctors had operated to remove the bullet. He spoke in a weak, southern-accented voice. "We were on this two-lane road…"

"Why were you off the interstate?"

"We wondered the same thing. We got this ED just after we took off that changed our route and took us off of Interstate 75 and put us on U. S. Highway 321 near Lenoir City." He told how they seemed to lose communications momentarily, then voice communications was reestablished, and they were told to take an even smaller road with almost no traffic.

"We figured it had to do with NUKE WATCH, you know, those

anti-nuclear peace protesters that sometimes follow us and harass us, take pictures and stuff.

"Anyway, we came round this bend, and there were four cars. It looked like they'd had one hell-of-a wreck. These two young women came running up to our truck with blood all over them. They waved their arms and screamed that they needed help back at the cars. Well, sir, we all got out to try and help."

"Did everybody get out," Saul said, "the two in each truck plus the four in the two escort vehicles?"

"Yes sir."

"Are drivers supposed to get out of the truck?"

"Only in an emergency, but we couldn't get by because the road was blocked by the wreck, or what we thought was a wreck. And there looked to be a bunch of people hurt besides those two women. This one woman had a bloody face, and the other one's arm was bleeding. Well, we thought it was blood. They had on these real-short shorts, and one of them looked like her clothes were about tore off her. These women led us to the cars screaming about somebody being dead. We barely got to the cars when a gun went off, and they told us to reach for the sky."

"Don't you carry weapons?"

"Yes, sir, the escort guards do. They probably pulled their guns, if they didn't leave them in the truck. Amos King pulled his gun; I know that for sure, because I saw them shoot him down. Just puff and he was dead."

"Did you get a look at these people?"

"No sir. Turns out some of them were drivers and guards. One of them was Ted Mitchell, the guy that rode with me. He was next to me when it started, and then somebody—one of the attackers—gave him a gun. He said to me, 'Sorry about that, Luke.' Then he shot me. They had to be in on the hijacking plan all along."

"Did any of them sound like foreigners?"

"Some of them in the cars did, yes sir." Walker hesitated. "Answer me a question, you being the FBI. How could all those guys get a security clearance to drive the trucks when they were really criminals? That ain't supposed to happen, is it?"

"I'd say that's a question that needs to be answered."

Chapter Nine

Lori Reedan yawned and reached out to Curt's side of the bed, the sheet cool and unwrinkled. Another restless night, but not because she slept alone, which she was used to. Her mind could not stop replaying the moment her attacker broke through the door and grabbed her legs...and the telephone call.

Rolling onto her back, she remembered how she had bounded down the steps, thinking she might shake herself up enough to start the flow. At least then she wouldn't have to put up with Curt's questions: "Are your breasts still sore? Are you still cramping?" If she felt miserable, there was a chance she would start and make him happy. Back before they got married, *he* talked about three or four kids, she didn't. That was when his mind still had room for something besides computers and robots.

She marveled at how she had gotten pregnant despite Curt's work habits. He woke early one Sunday morning and stayed in bed instead of heading for his computer. First his hands migrated to her side of the bed, and then he did, tangling his legs with hers. Not having seen him do anything that spontaneous and unpredictable in years, she didn't think about stopping him to get her diaphragm. If she had, he would have been up in his study when she got back to bed.

Timing of the pregnancy could not be worse: school and the move were enough to worry about. Two more courses, just six more weeks to her MBA; that's what she thought she wanted. Once Beth started kindergarten in the fall and they were settled in their new home, she would send out resumes. With her MBA in hand, she would welcome a move to Colorado—anyplace but Boston. Four years in Boston was enough. Curt mentioned Colorado on the phone from Miami, but she knew he still viewed MIT and Boston as his first and best choice. Knowing Curt, he had analyzed it thoroughly—probably programmed it on his computer—and found MIT the *only* choice.

She dragged herself out of bed, detecting a hint of the nausea that kept her from eating breakfast the last two mornings—the final determinant. Until that fateful day, her first stop every morning was the bathroom to check whether the red flow had broken through. Almost six weeks late, so forget it. Why couldn't Curt be happy with the prospect? Would this be a repeat of her pregnancy with Beth? That time, he was finishing his PhD: "It would have been better in a year or two...after we were settled."

Nothing had changed: "Things are unsettled. Maybe in a year or two...after our move..." It *would* be better this time. It *had* to be. If only that was all she had to worry about.

Like every other morning since that fateful day, she headed for the bedroom window and drew back the drapes far enough to search the street to see where *they* were—eyes on her bedroom window. Always the same: a deserted street or the familiar neighbor's car going to work. Next stop, across the hall in Beth's room to make sure she was safe.

All day she checked windows: the living room, the foyer, the bedroom. Nothing. Still, she felt their eyes on her body. The windows in back: maybe they were hiding in the woods with binoculars. She drew all the drapes and no longer studied on the patio.

Ten days since the fat man appeared and she talked to Curt on the phone. Did they really have Curt? Maybe he deserted her because of her pregnancy. No, never.

While driving the Oak Ridge streets, she eyed the rear-view mirror, hoping to spot a car following her. Nothing suspicious; everything suspicious. Cars bunched behind her and then disappeared. Another one behind her. The same one? One that was there before? One that was there yesterday?

On Mondays, Wednesdays, and Fridays, she left Beth with the sitter and spent the day in classes at the University of Tennessee in Knoxville. For thirty miles, her gaze never strayed from the mirror for more than a minute. Walking to class, she glanced back every quarter of a block, looking for someone. Nobody there, or just the typical male student, staring at her ass. Not the squat little man or anyone she'd seen before.

Studying came hard. She forced herself to work at the computer in her study, the spare bedroom next to Curt's office. Beth agitated to go outside, but Lori put her off. "You were outside at the sitter's house. Maybe tomorrow."

Today she forced herself to the computer to attack a term paper for

Finance III: *International Loans and the World Banking Crisis.* Who cares about a world banking crisis? Concentrate. After an hour of struggle, an outline took shape.

The doorbell rang.

"I'll get it, Mommy," Beth yelled from the family room downstairs.

"No," Lori screamed. "Just stay where you are."

Why did she yell? Nerves? Probably a neighbor. She could use a visitor and conversation, somebody besides Beth. Except for her classes, it had been just the two of them for ten days. A gun, she thought. For the past two nights, she debated whether to call Dad. Twice he offered her a forty-five. To Dad, anyone "in the city" and not on an Iowa farm like him and Mom was in constant danger. "With Curt traveling so much, you *need* a gun." He offered Curt the gun, but Curt reacted with indifference, his typical reaction to anything not issuing from a computer, or anything coming from her Dad. The two men in her life still treated each other from the distance that developed before they married. "Up to her," Curt said. She said no.

"Too many guns in the world, too many killings with guns," she said.

The doorbell rang again.

She hurried down the steps of the split foyer toward the door. Glancing down the steps to the family room, she saw Beth staring up at the door.

"Mrs. Reedan. I think you remember me."

It was him. "Yes…Mr. Maxwell." She remembered him as short, but the big man next to him squashed Maxwell into a short, fat, old man. She didn't remember him being that old, somewhere in his fifties, Dad's age. He wore the same mussed white shirt, black pants, same dark-rimmed, purple-tinted glasses that he again removed.

The tall man flipped off his aviator sun glasses and scanned her body, his gaze resting momentarily on her breasts. "I'm Larry Beecher," he said. Younger than Maxwell, probably in his thirties, he wore neatly pressed tan trousers and a dark-blue knit shirt, but with the same foreign accent as the fat one. "We are checking to make sure you are doing what we asked."

She wondered if she could still shoot. You didn't forget, not after all those Sunday afternoons down by the creek shooting cans. At fourteen she could outshoot her three brothers with the twenty-two pistol, picking off three cans at twenty-to-thirty feet with six shots or less. She always won the game, and after a year, it took only three. Only Dad did it better.

"Yes, I did what you told me to do," she said to the tall one. This one was Curt's height, but more massive, with a large round face, small light-brown eyes, and a rather thin pointy nose. She longed to hide her body behind the door, away from his stare and exaggerated smile, his gaze dropping slowly from the front of her sleeveless blouse to her bare legs, but she didn't move. She would call Dad tonight and have a forty-five in a week. Although good with the twenty-two, she was even better with the forty-five.

"Good to hear it," Beecher said. "You might get the idea that because we're not staying at your house, you can call the police. Don't try it, because we will know. And that would be too bad for you and your husband." He smiled and motioned his head to indicate Beth at the bottom of the steps. "*And* your little girl."

She nodded, her hand on the door knob trembling. If she had a gun, could she shoot them? She couldn't watch when Dad and her brothers shot rats out by the corn crib, always squeezing her eyes shut at the sound of the first shot, hating the sight of the little bodies ripped open, blood splattered in the dust. The bloody bodies of the rabbits and pheasants they dragged home from hunting trips twisted her insides; the dead deer and antelope were horrible.

Beecher waited for her to speak.

"I...I won't go to the police."

"That's good, because I don't think you would like somebody with you all the time, would you?"

Her mind raced, trying to understand. Somebody with her, he said. He said they'd know if she called. Were they listening to her phone calls? She would write Dad. But what if Dad called to ask why she changed her mind about a gun? "You won't have to keep anybody with us."

"Just go about your business like you do when your husband is on a trip."

She nodded. Karl Eberhard, her neighbor, was a hunter and gun owner. Maybe he had a forty-five she could borrow.

"We'll be watching you, even if you don't see us," Beecher said, smiling as he moved his gaze back to her breasts. "You've got a nice tan, lady."

She refused to get behind the door. "Is Curt okay?"

"He is fine. And he'll stay that way if you do what you are told."

"I will." Behind her, she heard Beth creeping up the steps toward her.

Beecher glanced at the shorter man. "It might be a good idea to move in with her, eh, Max." They both laughed.

"I'll do what you told me."

68

As soon as she closed the door, Beth scrambled up the steps to her, sobbing. Lori's heart pounded and her legs trembled. She resisted the urge to sink to her knees, hold on to Beth, and cry with her. Instead, she grabbed Beth's hand and hurried her up the steps and into the bedroom, where she eased back the drapes far enough to see their shiny big black car.

She needed a gun and a plan.

Chapter Ten

Ten minutes after Saul dragged himself into his office, Uncle Nathan called. "Hey, *boychik*, I heard they finally let you out from behind your desk and right onto a big case."

No way could there be leaks already, Saul thought. But if only some of the stories he'd heard from Bureau veterans were true, in this town, you never knew.

"Did your lovely bride tell you she and I had dinner together last week?"

"No. I got in late, and we didn't get a chance to talk." But plenty of time to argue. Everything was fine until he asked where she'd been on three of the nights he called. That question exploded ten minutes after he got home, even though he lectured himself for a week not to ask. He also asked who she'd been having lunch with and who she was working with, all the things he'd been hammering at for the past few months, ever since he visited her office and saw all those young guys and everybody joking and having a ball "running the government." She wanted him to believe she was just "one of the boys" in the office.

Why did he shout those things? Why did he feel that way? Enthusiasm for her job threw him, even though she insisted she just loved her job, especially after not being able to get anything but secretarial work in Spokane. "I've told you a hundred times I'm not interested in anyone else," she said. But the idea invaded his brain like a malignant growth.

In the heat of the argument, she yelled "separation," Harry Bryson's magic word. According to Bryson, "Once they mention a trial separation, it's the beginning of the end. After that, you'll soon be hitting the bars again, looking for pussy just like the old days."

"Mary said you were gone for nine days," Uncle Nate said. "It must be a mighty important case."

"Just routine."

"The reason I called was to tell you that Mary's worried about you. She's one great *shikse*."

"That's not what you called her when I told you I was getting married."

"I didn't have great expectations considering you were marrying a *shikse* from some small burg in Indiana. I probably said, better you should marry a nice Jewish girl, and knowing me, I probably said a JAP. So I was wrong."

"You called her a typical empty-headed blonde *shikse* with a great tush and boobs. You didn't want Mama to wind up a *bubbe* to a bunch of *mishling* brats. Your advice was to slip her that old kosher *schlong* until I got her out of my system."

"Tactful, I'm not. Now, I'm telling you, this *dreck* you're giving her about her looking for somebody at work, who needs it?"

"She told you that?" If she ever slept with somebody else, Nate would know before he did. Would he tell him?

"Who else can she talk to? Better you should worry once in awhile to make sure you don't take her for granted. I should be so lucky."

Listening to Uncle Nathan one-on-one, you'd never know that in public he looked and sounded like a handsome Ivy League English professor. And when there were women around, he turned on the charm to accompany the elegant words.

"Anyway, this big job that takes you away from your computer and out of town so long, could the Senator capitalize the information?"

"No, it is nothing like that."

"Hey *boychik*, the only way I'll ever be governor is with his help. His name's been mentioned as a future vice-presidential candidate. Any help you give him is help for me...and for you and Mary. Once I'm governor, I'll be able to help the both of you."

- - - - -

Dressed in a tan jacket, crisp white shirt and tan tie, Bart Kraft reigned from behind his desk, empty except for two pictures and a pad of paper. Everything in the paneled room had its place, from books on their shelves to the computer on the table behind his desk.

Only Saul didn't fit, sweaty in a wrinkled brown suit and out of breath from the sprint-walk from the parking lot—out of breath despite membership in Arlington Health and Fitness Club which Mary had talked him into "investing" in. Now she wanted him to invest in a wardrobe.

"I'm not sure why you came out here," Kraft said. "I told you everything I knew last time. Besides that, Doyle Logson can't make it."

"I wanted to talk to you since DOE was responsible for the lost shipments, even though it was DOD material being transported."

Kraft's broad smile only lightly wrinkled his tanned face. "Our security failed, but with the budget cuts...Have you made any progress?"

"I've been to Tennessee, New Mexico, and South Carolina. The answer isn't at any of those places."

"Then where is it?"

The bastard knew as well as anybody, Saul thought. "Its here in Washington, at DOE."

Kraft reached to the right side of the desk top and touched the frame of a blonde woman's picture set at an angle to a picture of Kraft standing with two young men about college age. That's what he and Mary needed: kids. Fortunately, he hadn't brought that up last night.

Kraft looked directly at him. "If you're saying this was an inside job, you're wrong. Everyone involved with security here at DOE has been thoroughly checked and cleared."

After eleven months in Washington, Saul had encountered enough guys like Kraft, and they were starting to grate. Smooth in everything they did, they filled most upper levels of government he'd come in contact with; the Bureau had more than their share. Saul remembered last Election Day when Mary gave him hell for not voting, as did the holier-than-thou TV commentators. Since being in Washington, he'd found a reason for him and the other fifty percent of eligible voters that didn't vote: you don't vote for the Krafts and the Logsons; you don't vote for congressional staffers like Mary, who stand at their great man's side and whisper wisdom into his ear. *They* run the government. Well, maybe not Mary—not yet, at least.

"Whoever did this had detailed information they could only get in your division."

Kraft squared the pad of paper with the edge of the desk. "If I allowed you to snoop around here, in no time at all every big-dick reporter would be as well."

Evasion, political expediency, it was everywhere, even where nuclear weapons were involved. But in this town, why would they be different? From his limited observations, Saul had concluded all anyone cared about was their career *development*. For many, that meant blending a proper government career into a better out-of-government career. Mary kept saying he wasn't serious enough about his career *development*.

Earlier at headquarters, he found out Spanner was running into the same stone walls. Maybe that was sufficient reason for going to the Senator. Once the story hit the press, there would be action, at least public relations action to give the story the proper spin.

"I'm not interested in snooping around. To start, explain your operation to me."

Kraft glanced around the office, obviously trying to figure out how to get rid of Saul. "Well…a shipment is arranged between the two contracting installations, as we call them, the shipper and the receiver. Then we schedule transportation. Everything is done by computer on a secure website." He pointed to the darkened computer monitor on the table behind his desk and explained how they had recently updated the sophisticated program they used to arrange shipments.

Kraft explained how all the information was logged in, including dates, destinations of all past shipments and all shipments planned for the next month. All security arrangements, travel routes, everything was there at the click of a mouse. "Every shipment is tracked using a Cray supercomputer at Kirtland Air Force Base. They have access to the same information we do."

"I visited Kirtland, and they know everything except what's in a shipment. Tell me about Savannah River, the destination of the shipments. The people there say they did not request most of what was hijacked."

"The computer tells a different story. Their request and agreement to receive the shipment were logged in and the SAVE was approved." Kraft explained SAVE, the Shipment Agreement and Verification Evaluation process package. "The first step is an agreement between shipper and receiver on shipment contents. Then the shipper puts together a shipping plan that includes the manifest and the DSP—Detailed Security Plan—and these and other documents make up the SAVE package that is submitted for approval by SPAC, the Strategic Planning and Authorization Committee. The entire process is on our secure website."

"Who is on SPAC?"

"Mr. Logson and I make up the committee."

"And you approved this SAVE package?"

"Well, I really could not recall the exact SAVE, but then I read and approve many SAVE plans and other documents, and I can't be expected to remember the details of all of them."

"What about Logson?"

"He didn't remember this specific SAVE either."

"Would you or Logson normally approve a three-truck convoy as a code two?"

"Well...regulations state...no, probably not."

"But the computer said you approved it, right?"

"Well, according to the computer, an ED was sent to people who needed to know. The *secure* website was checked during our investigation, and all approvals were in order. Neither Mr. Logson nor I remembered it."

"So it comes down to this, Dr. Kraft. Someone in your division did this. The computer makes your job easier, but it also made it easier to set up the hijacking."

Kraft stared at Saul, his face pale. "I can't believe anyone here did it."

"How many people in Washington can access the website information on shipments?"

"Access is tightly controlled. Probably only ten people."

"I'll need their names."

Kraft took a deep breath. "I've got to protest."

"We won't talk to anyone without getting approval from on high."

"I hope not. Because if the newspapers or TV get wind of this..."

- - - - -

Saul tapped the keyboard and another personnel record splashed onto the screen.

KRAFT, BARTHOLOMEW ARTHUR
DOE EMPLOYEE NO: 013967
BORN: March 13, 1971
EDUCATION: PhD...

Saul glanced quickly through the record: PhD in Nuclear Engineering from Michigan University. Worked at GE and then went back to Michigan as a Professor in the Nuclear Engineering Department before being nominated to his present position at NNSA two-years ago. He listed reading and chess as hobbies.

He leaned back in his chair and glanced around his cubicle: paper-cluttered desk, file cabinet, and another chair, fenced off from three other cubicles by portable gray fabric-covered partitions. By now he had combed the files of thirteen probables from Oak Ridge, New Mexico and Savannah River, the ten names from NNSA Kraft had given him, plus seven more he'd picked because of their management roles and top-secret clearances.

He wondered why he saved Kraft's file for last. Did he expect Kraft to be most interesting or least interesting? In all, he examined files of twenty-two men and six women with degrees from places like Yale, Michigan, Northwestern, Cal Berkeley, all the good schools. Not an interesting hobby among them.

He considered taking a break to straighten up the desk. Twice in the last month he was told by Bureau veterans that such an office would not have been tolerated in the good old days. He picked up an e-mail memo from the travel office: "Minimization of Rental Car Expense." He tossed it back on the pile and returned his attention to the computer.

What now? Run a PPI on the people Kraft gave him and on Kraft? Comb their lives to try and turn up inconsistencies, like spending too much or having an excessively large bank account somewhere? In the end, it always came down to money.

Saul tapped at the keyboard to access the National Crime Information Center computer. He entered the twenty-eight names to check for a criminal record. Nowadays, with drugs everywhere, unexpected names popped up in those files all the time. Drugs meant money—a lot or not enough. None of the names turned up in the NCIC computer.

He typed a request to the NNSA computer for all people who worked in the Security and Safeguards Division during the last year. Then he asked for names of personnel who no longer worked in the division and when they terminated.

```
JOHNSON, GREGORY LEE      15326    AUG 22, 2010
BROWN, RANDOLF GEORGE      17265    MAR 30, 2011
AUSTIN, STEVEN ALLEN       19223    JUN 15, 2011
```

Interesting: Austin quit only a month ago.

Saul focused on Austin. Jordan said a computer expert named Austin visited them at Oak Ridge. He typed:

DOE PERS FILE: AUSTIN, STEVEN ALLEN, 19223

The computer replied:

FILE INACTIVATED, 06/24/2011

Inactivated? Why? Files were rarely inactivated that soon after termination. To check that, he punched the keyboard for the files of Johnson and Brown, who were terminated over three months ago. Both files flashed on the screen with their new positions: Johnson retired and Brown moved to the Labor Department—still hadn't found his high-paying out-of-government career position.

He checked Austin's security-clearance file. No unusual notations, just a regular guy, PhD and all. So why did he leave just a few weeks after the robbery?

Saul grabbed the phone, and in the next hour, he spoke to people at Kirtland in Albuquerque and at Savannah River National Laboratory. It turned out Austin had visited both facilities, in addition to his visit to Oak Ridge. At Kirtland, Austin helped them revise their computer programs to improve the NNSA communications and security system.

Saul had one more call to make. After a lot of stalling by the secretary and insistence by Saul that it was urgent, Kraft came on the line. Saul asked if Austin was involved with scheduling nuclear-material shipments.

"Steve? No. He was a computer expert. He put together the new secure system for handling the shipments. He developed the SAVE process."

Saul's pulse quickened. Austin was their man. "Why did he leave the division? Where did he go?"

A long pause: "He was killed in an auto accident while driving his Porsche. You know how young people are with fast cars. It was a terrible loss."

- - - - -

Contrary to Saul's expectations, Spanner didn't protest when he requested permission and manpower help to do a PPI on everyone with access to the NNSA's Security and Safeguards Division computer files in Washington, Oak Ridge, Savannah River, and Albuquerque.

A PPI—Preliminary Personal Investigation—was a low profile secret investigation into a person's financial standing to determine where their money came from, where it went, whether there was a lack of it, and whether there had been any large deposits other than the paycheck. PPIs on the thirty-one individuals were completed in four days. Unreal: not a suspicious character among them—at least the live ones.

Saul ran a check on Steven Allen Austin, deceased. Accessing Austin's security-clearance records, he found that Austin obtained the clearance when he worked for Congressman John Tilton, Democrat from

California. With his top-secret clearance in place and Tilton as reference, getting a job with DOE was a snap.

Austin was cleared by Agent David Zachary of the Security Investigation Division of the Office of Personnel Management. Because Zachary's name was not in the SID OPM Directory, Saul called a SID agent he knew to get Zachary's present station.

"Dave Zachary? He retired five or six years ago."

"Are you sure? He hasn't cleared anyone in the last three years?"

"Positive. I spoke at his retirement party."

Chapter Eleven

Hunched behind the computer monitor, Curt Reedan typed:

X, Y, Z: 12, 120, 72

The computer responded:

NOT ADMISSIBLE: UNDEFINED COORDINATES.

Curt typed a new set of coordinates for a program to machine a precision part on one of Applenu's many CAD/CAM drawings.

For over two weeks now, they isolated him in the sparsely furnished twelve-foot-square computer room studying numbers and diagrams on the monitor. When in touch with a computer, Curt escaped to a state of oblivion as far as the world around him was concerned. Alone, his mind attuned to the computer, he temporarily escaped the doom generated by Surling's warnings.

The silence of the room was shattered when Surling and Drafton entered to announce lunch. Drafton strolled around Curt and stood behind him, studying the monitor, his right hand resting lightly on Curt's shoulder. Curt sat facing the door, where Surling watched them.

Of their captors, Drafton was the friendly one; he treated them as scientific colleagues. At times, Curt felt Applenu also tried to treat him as a scientific colleague. Drafton and Surling spent most of their work time together. To Curt, Surling seemed overly friendly with Drafton.

Drafton began extolling the virtues of the high-powered computer that consisted of a High-Performance Cluster system that took up half of the room, while Surling drifted to the table next to the monitor, opened a binder and studied the top drawing of bomb parts Curt was working on. He turned to Drafton. "How are you getting these bombs out of the country, Eric?"

"That's Applenu's department now that Derek is no longer with us. He's connected to the client country, although about the only thing left to ship is the nuclear material. Everything else was built earlier and shipped. Derek handled that through a contract in upstate New York."

"Are you saying Applenu designed and built those devices, and then they went out and stole the nuclear material they needed?"

"Applenu didn't, Derek did."

Surling shook his head in disbelief. "What about the trigger mechanism?"

"Triggers are electronics, and Derek was an electronics genius."

Surling turned to Curt. "The principle behind an atom bomb is simple enough," he said, assuming his dry professorial tone. "You just squeeze a sphere of enriched uranium or plutonium into a critical mass—a supercritical mass, really—or else you force two hemispheres of plutonium or enriched uranium into a supercritical mass. Once that supercritical mass is assembled, an uncontrolled chain reaction starts, causing a rapid buildup of energy that's released in a gigantic explosion. On the Manhattan Project, we had a hell of a time compressing the metallic sphere into a perfect spherical configuration. Any shape aberration lowers the yield or gives you a dud. We put conventional explosives around the outside of the sphere. On detonation, the conventional explosives compressed the sphere to a supercritical mass. To get a perfect spherical shape, we built a complicated system of lenses that properly concentrated the shock waves from the explosives."

"That's the implosion technique," Drafton said, stroking his brown beard. "Derek's designs use that in some of the bombs. He even tested instrumented charges to verify the trigger design. Worked like a charm. You've got to remember that back in the forties you didn't have computers."

"I know. These days, you can model everything and anything with a computer. Guys like Curt are putting old experimentalists like me out of business."

Drafton nodded and smiled at Curt. "Derek modeled the lens system as well as the initiator. He designed and modeled bombs using the gun-barrel method, where you explosively propel part of a critical mass down a tube and mate it with material at the other end to get a supercritical configuration. Derek used the computer to check out all designs," Drafton said, walking around to the back of Curt and resting his hand on the chair so it touched Curt's shoulder.

Curt twisted around so he could get Drafton's hand off his shoulder. "If you people could do all that, why did you need Bob and me?"

Drafton looked down at Curt and quickly jerked his hand back, as if Curt's shoulder were red hot. "You two have the expertise we needed on processing and machining nuclear material. I know Derek could have handled it, but he wanted a sure thing. He didn't leave anything to chance."

"So where is this genius Derek?" Curt asked.

Drafton's eyes clouded. "He got killed in a car wreck."

"But why would bright young guys like you and him get involved in something like this?" Surling asked.

"Derek and I...hell, the work's challenging, and the money's good. With the money we were getting for the job, Derek and I figured to be set for life. We had plans."

"It's not worth it," Curt said. "With a PhD, you'd have found a good job."

"Terrorists have wanted nuclear weapons for the last twenty years," Surling said, "and now you guys are giving them one."

"They aren't going to terrorists. Derek cleared that up with the customer before he started."

In their discussions, Curt and Surling agreed these guys might do some real damage, but they could never successfully build a working atom bomb. Now, it was like seeing your basketball team, a twenty-point favorite, lead the whole game only to lose that lead with a second left.

Curt saw Surling glance his way, and he knew what Surling was thinking: they had to be stopped, and it was up to them to do it.

Chapter Twelve

Brian Applenu watched smoking metal chips spiral from the steel rod in the spinning lathe and plunge into the oil bath, like downed jetfighter planes into a black sea. He glanced sideways at Reedan, who sat behind a computer monitor and keyboard and gazed around the large machine room: two lathes, a milling machine, a grinder, and a drill press, all new. The lathe they worked at stood in the far right corner as you came into the room from the hall.

Cued by the computer in the next room, the lathe ground to a halt. On the lathe, calipers automatically moved across the work piece, a dummy part being machined to check Reedan's computer program. Tomorrow they machined the real thing, a complicated part from non-radioactive material required to complete the firing mechanism for the plutonium bombs. Measurements complete, the lathe began to turn.

Applenu watched their machinist adjust his goggles and approach the lathe for a closer look. A graying, dark-complected man in his early fifties, Perk Simmons arrived four days ago. In addition to being an excellent machinist, he would help Drafton with the chemical processing. In his e-mail saying Simmons was coming, Sherbani wrote, "Simmons is one of us." Based on his appearance and his relatively good English skills, Applenu fingered him as an Iranian who had been in the U.S. for some time. He wondered if Simmons was there under circumstances similar to his own.

That e-mail was the first communication Applenu had with Sherbani since he got the phone call telling him Austin/Hearn was dead. What a hard kick to the gut. Although Applenu had no particular love for Austin since he had been as responsible as Sherbani for getting him involved in this process, Austin had hinted in their New York conversation that they might be able to affect the effectiveness of the bombs if and when they were made. To Applenu, it appeared that Austin was as worried as he was concerning how they might be used. In addition to that, he would have been useful as an intermediary if and when he had to challenge Sherbani on getting his family out of Iran. To that end, Applenu replied to Sherbani's e-mail asking when his family would be brought out of Iran. Sherbani had not replied.

Applenu turned to Reedan and wondered how he could connect with him, since they were in the same fix, neither wanting to be here. "It is a bloody nice program, Doctor Reedan. All the machinist has to do is apply lubricant and change the tool."

"It was a difficult program to write," Reedan said, appearing uninterested in the process. He glanced back at the door.

Applenu looked back, and through the window in the door, he saw Beecher patrolling the hall. Whenever Reedan and Surling were in the hall guarded by one of Lormes's men, you could read their eyes, always glancing furtively at the exits. If he had his own way, Applenu thought, he'd go out the door with them. They were obstinate blokes, he thought, remembering their first meeting where Surling pressured Lormes into defending himself as not being a terrorist.

Applenu glanced at Beecher again, noting the video camera strapped around his neck. He had been in earlier to photograph the machining setup. Sherbani wanted pictures and videos of all operations that showed how the bombs were manufactured. He wouldn't say why. Was there to be a written report on the project? Politics back home?

Regardless of his dilemma, Applenu knew that technically everything was working better than they had any right to expect, especially considering where they came from and all they had been through in the last six months. With that sinking feeling in his gut that a bomb was now inevitable and he knew of no way to stop it, he turned to Reedan. "I believe we are going to pull it off." From the startled look in Reedan's eyes, it appeared he was becoming a believer, too.

Across the room at the lathe, Simmons changed the tool while Applenu strolled up behind Reedan to study the dimensions on the monitor. It can't be, he thought. He moved quickly across the room and grabbed the machine drawing on the bench next to the lathe. Those numbers had to be wrong. Out of the corner of his eye he caught sight of Reedan, his tall frame hunched over his monitor. The bloke knew what was happening. He was about to speak to Reedan as Beecher ambled into the room.

Beecher surveyed the scene and seemed to understand. "What did Reedan do?"

Applenu hesitated, not sure what Beecher might do to Reedan. "Reedan seems to have screwed up the machining program."

"Is that right, Reedan?" Beecher asked, setting the video camera on the table next to the monitor. "I would have thought you knew better than to pull shit like that."

- - - - -

Curt was ready for the challenge, "What are you talking about," he asked, first looking at Applenu, then staring up at Beecher, the tall bull from South Beach. Curt turned to the monitor to study the numbers that summarized the damage.

"Something *wrong*, Reedan?" Beecher asked.

Slow and easy, Curt told himself. Playing games with management came with the territory of being a self-employed consultant. "I was just going to check the drawing," he said. He stood and started toward the workbench, but Beecher stepped in front of him, his face inches from Curt's face.

Applenu ordered Simmons to measure the work piece.

"I just did. It's out of tolerance, ruined," Simmons said, his dark-brown eyes wide open and filled with fear, as if he might be blamed for the error.

"Surprised, *Doctor* Reedan?" Beecher asked. "I suppose you *accidentally* put the wrong numbers into the computer. Or was it a *computer* error?"

Curt realized it wasn't playing out as planned, a delaying action to slow them down until he and Surling could escape. "Well...uh...most new computer programs got bugs. I'll fix it, but..."

"You're damned right you'll fix it," Beecher said. Before Curt could think up a reply, Beecher's sledge-hammer fist smashed into his stomach. He doubled up, fighting to pull enough air into his lungs to eject the pain exploding up into his chest. Slowly, as if sinking into quicksand, he settled to his knees, tears blurring his vision, a cough erupting from his gut as he attempted to exhale the fire igniting in his lungs.

Beecher reached down and grabbed a handful of the front of Curt's khaki shirt and jerked upward. Curt stared up into Beecher's tanned face, his lightbrown eyes glowing with pleasure. Beecher cocked his right fist.

Curt raised his arms to cover his face.

"That's enough," Applenu said, touching Beecher's raised arm.

Beecher tossed Curt aside like a crumpled piece of paper.

Applenu stepped over to Curt and yelled down at him. "That's a lot of balls about bugs in the program. A bloody college freshman knows any machining program worth a crap is going to have limits so something like this doesn't happen."

Sitting on the cold concrete, Curt poked gently at his aching stomach and chest, wondering about broken ribs. He tried a deep breath, but stopped short when pain ripped at the inside of his chest. "I was going to..."

"Shut up," Beecher yelled.

"That's right," Applenu said, glancing at Beecher. "We'll be machining dummies on everything so you don't muck up valuable nuclear material."

"Any more obvious screw-ups like this," Beecher said, "and what you just got will seem mild. Next time, I won't just stomp *your* ass." He laughed. "What I'll be doing is handling your old lady's ass. I might even be gentle with her."

Chapter Thirteen

Rick Saul fled Bart Kraft's office without anything new on Steve Austin. All Kraft wanted to talk about was Sheena Mosely. That was all Spanner talked about before Saul left the Bureau, because that was all his superiors wanted to talk about. Mosely appeared, and instantly everyone forgot somebody stole enough nuclear material to level Washington, half of Chicago, and a minor city or two in between, like Cleveland and Pittsburgh.

Maybe Uncle Herbert was right: A scientific career was the only option available for anyone who wished to live by logic. Logic gave way to chaotic chance when you dealt with people—especially government people and politics. In science, even chance operated by precise mathematical rules.

Somehow, Sheena Mosely, an AP reporter from Atlanta, appeared to have stumbled on a "rumor" that a truckload of bomb-grade nuclear material had been hijacked. No one knew how or where she got the information, but in her mad dash to confirm it, she was ringing phones all over Washington and asking for comments on or off the record. At present, she pursued the story alone, probably hoping for an exclusive that would earn her a Pulitzer.

Now, some manpower assigned to SWISILREC would be pulled off to find the leak and shut him or her down. He recalled Logson implying that if a leak occurred, it would be from Spanner or him.

Saul realized that Mosely provided a plausible reason to tell Mary and Senator Hughson, since once Mosely published, the Senator, Uncle Nathan, and Mary would come down on him, wanting to know why the Senator was not informed immediately. Politics: a team game where team members played only for themselves. Chaos within chaos, an exciting game, but one Saul was not ready to play.

His present game involved the elusive Steve Austin. First, nobody in Congressman Tilton's office knew the name or recognized him from his DOE badge picture. Second, Austin's remains still lay unclaimed at the morgue. A problem surfaced when they went to examine the body. There was no body, just a box full of charred bones and ashes, because Austin's Porsche with him inside left the road in rural Virginia, turned over, and burst into flames, leaving no fingerprints to be run through the Bureau computer.

Since Saul had finally been authorized to talk to someone at DOE besides Kraft, his next stop was the office of Ralph Ebert, Deputy Associate Administrator for NNSA's Defense Nuclear Security.

"Austin was Bart Kraft's boy all the way," Ebert said from behind a cluttered desk that looked more like Saul's than Kraft's. "He hired Austin, and within a year, he was heading the Computer Operations Section. Kraft never consulted anyone about his hiring."

"Does Kraft hire all personnel for the department?"

"Yes, but usually the top people in the division interview a candidate and give Bart their evaluation. In the case of Austin, Kraft came in one day and introduced him as our new computer specialist. He touted Austin as a computer genius the department couldn't pass up. From my contacts with Austin, I'd say Bart was right on that score."

Ebert, a thin, gray, bespectacled man, had spent twenty-nine years at DOE. His engineering career began with a mediocre position at Westinghouse, which he shucked early on for DOE, where he aged into a moderately high position. He verified Saul's assumption that Austin had access to all classified files as soon as he was hired because he already had a top-secret Q clearance. He was quickly promoted to section head, a logical choice, according to Ebert. Once promoted, he revamped everything, from a more efficient computer-controlled security and transportation system, beginning with the Cray supercomputer in New Mexico and then extending it to the entire NNSA computer system. He also completely revamped, automated, and integrated the special nuclear materials storage, inventory, and transportation format for NNSA complete with a new and improved security format.

Ebert explained how, when setting up the system, Austin visited field offices and even went along in an escort vehicle for a plutonium shipment from Los Alamos to Pantex near Amarillo.

"You can't get anymore direct knowledge than that, but I never saw anything to make me suspicious that he was doing something illegal."

"Did Kraft consult you on his promotion?"

"Sort of, but he did it after the fact. Austin was Bart's man all the way. They worked together, probably because ever since Kraft became division head, he pushed to upgrade computer operations. Kraft and Austin usually ate lunch together, long lunches." Ebert coughed a dry laugh. "I might have thought they had something queer going on if I hadn't seen Austin at a bar in Gaithersburg with Marge Alsop from the DOE library. She must be twenty-five years older than Austin."

"Are you saying Kraft is homosexual?"

Ebert's eyes widened; then he laughed. "That was a joke." More forced laughter. "Kraft's married with two boys. I just meant he and Austin spent a lot of time together. From what I saw of Austin and Marge Alsop, they had more than a mother-son thing."

Back in his car, Saul consulted his laptop to determine that Marge Alsop was the Chief Librarian of the DOE Technical Library. She was a forty-nine-year-old divorcee, mother of two with three grandchildren, and she had a Q clearance.

In person, Saul found a tall honey blonde with an aging face and a figure rounding into middle age. Facing her across her desk, he knew Austin was after something besides companionship. "How long did you know Steve Austin?"

"About nine months. What a loss. I kept telling him not to drive so fast. He was always in a hurry."

Saul hesitated, but knew he could ask. "Were you two lovers?"

She blushed and nodded hesitantly. When he asked why they broke up, she described an argument after Austin introduced her to a young man he said was his roommate. She got the feeling there was more between them, and she asked Austin about it. "Steve got mad and stormed out of the house." Tears welled in her eyes.

"Do you think Steve was homosexual?"

She smiled through the tears. "He never gave me any reason to think so before that. I wonder if he staged the scene just to break us up." She reached into a drawer for a tissue. "I was a little older than him."

"What was the other guy's name?"

"Eric. I don't remember his last name."

"Did Austin use the library?"

She blew her nose and recounted how they met when he asked for help in researching a book on the history of the atom bomb. His interest was in old reports on building one.

"Classified reports?" Saul asked

"Yes, but they were from the forties and fifties. Nothing was relevant for today."

"Since he had a Q clearance, why did he need your help to get classified material?"

"Well…you know, he didn't have a need-to-know."

"So he slept with you in return for the reports."

Her eyes flashed. "You make it sound dirty."

"Did you let him make copies?"

She nodded rapidly, her face reddening. "I had one of my girls scan the reports for him. But it was old stuff, and he was a history buff."

- - - - -

Once his feet hit the sidewalk outside the Hoover Building, Saul shrugged off his coat and loosened his tie. At nine-thirty, even the tourists had deserted Pennsylvania Avenue. For Saul, it was another long day of slogging through endless fields of paperwork, of frantically trying to cover all possibilities that would bring SWISILREC to its swift and silent conclusion. Every day the amount of e-mail from the field doubled, as more agents reported their progress. Today, there was little progress to report.

A task force was examining records of past non-nuclear hijackings to determine if anyone implicated in those cases could have been involved in this nuclear caper. That effort involved agents manning computers in Washington, while others tracked down convicted and suspected hijackers and got the word out to snitches that the FBI was interested in such information. Today an e-mail report arrived from the Boston office about an informant who heard about two men implicated in two past hijacking cases being out of town for several weeks at the end of May and early June. Agents had not yet tracked them down.

Saul headed up Tenth Street toward the Ford Theater and his car. A click-click of high heels on the pavement behind him sliced through his thoughts a moment before he heard his name called by a female voice with a British accent. He turned.

"Mr. Saul, I am Sheena Mosely from the Associated Press. I'd like to buy you a drink and give you a chance to verify some extraordinary information I've come across."

Chapter Fourteen

From where Curt sat at the table, the insistent slap-tap of Surling's footsteps hammered his brain like a dripping faucet. Every evening the same thing: Surling jogged in place for one-thousand steps, slap-tap-tap... then ten times around the table. In the morning, there were pushups, sit-ups, and more jogging, slowly driving Curt insane.

Curt considered exercise, although jogging was out because of his knee. Three years ago he started rowing and abruptly gave it up—too much to do to waste over an hour a day.

One last time around the table, and Surling collapsed in the chair across from Curt. He peeled off his glasses and wiped his face with a towel. For a moment, the two men dropped into their thoughts. Surling sucked air.

Curt's mind wandered a path now worn bare. "We've got to get out of here," he said.

Surling's breath pumped in and out in short explosive bursts. "You ready to admit these assholes have got to be stopped?"

"That, and I want to save my skin. But how do we do it?"

"I figure we've got two choices. The first one is straight forward. We make a break for it." Surling toweled his bald head as he studied Curt. "The second one is trickier. Drafton's queer, and Derek was his lover. Derek's all he talks about."

Curt stared at Surling. Was that why Surling and Drafton seemed so close? It was more than just working together all day, every day. Was Surling bisexual? When did they find the time? Did they do it in the furnace room?

"So how will that help us escape?"

"He's all torn up about Derek's death. He told me you remind him of Derek."

"*Me*." That hollow feeling from Miami exploded in his gut, the feeling of being conned.

Surling positioned his glasses on his face and brought it back to life. "I figure you could play up to him, play on his sentiments about Derek, and maybe take Derek's place. If he gets to like you he will help you—help us escape."

"No way," Curt said.

"Just play up to him. That's *all*."

"*No way in hell*." Curt bounced up, strode over to the couch, turned and looked down at Surling. "Let's go with the first choice. How do we do it?"

"If they show up tonight, we'll wait for an opening and go."

"There's no way both of us can escape."

"That's right. One of us runs, while the other tries to delay them." Surling pulled a quarter from his pocket. "I'll flip you to see who makes the break."

- - - - -

Applenu sipped scotch and glanced around the Howard Johnson lounge, now filling with women, a few his age, many older, much older. Like Marge Alsop, he thought. Steve Austin joked about Marge and her search for youth: a grandmother hanging out in singles bars with other grandmothers.

Applenu studied a long-legged bit of skirt that strolled past his table. God, this country had a lot of blondes. Or maybe he noticed them more now. This one displayed physical similarities to Patricia Hunter, the bint on Congressman Morgan's staff Steve fixed him up with. "Her legs reach all the way to her ass," Austin said. And they did. God, how he would like to see her again—see *all* of her again.

He recalled his trip to Iran, the streets filled with women in black *chadors*. What would it be like making it with one of them, pushing up under the long black skirt and getting past the veil to her face? He remembered his mother, who had to go back to it following the Revolution. Her mother had made her wear it when she was a child, but she abandoned it when she got married, because his father did not like it. His sisters hated the costume.

One of the few passages he remembered from when his father read them the Koran: "You are allowed on the night of the fast to approach your wives; they are your garment and ye are their garment. Now, therefore, go in unto them with full desire for that which God hath ordained for you."

With full desire, he thought, as he watched the blonde join two older women at the next table. His mind wandered back to Patricia Hunter. While he went to her with full desire, Steve Austin took care of the Thornton woman. Not your nice bit of crumpet that one, but you'd never have known by the way he treated her. Steve would do anything to complete the job. While getting into her knickers—not too difficult for him—he somehow sweet-talked her into allowing him to use her computer password for access to government-classified information sources other than those he had access to with the DOE computer. With that access, he simply hacked his way to security clearances for the men subsequently hired to transport the nuclear material they hijacked.

If Austin or Hearn was here today, they would have women. He worked hard and played hard: twelve hours of work, six hours of play. Then get up and do it again. Seven days a week. He had to admit that they accomplished a lot while Hearn was around and had fun in the bargain, even though he would like to be any place else but in the situation he found himself.

With Hearn gone, there was nobody even to have a drink with, much less to party with. Lormes and his men dealt with him on a business only basis. That pouffe Drafton pursued other interests. Old Mustafa Mohammad, alias Perk Simmons, was out of the question. He was Sherbani's man all the way, not someone to have a drink with without Sherbani hearing about it—assuming Simmons drank, which wasn't likely, given the fact that he dragged his prayer rug around with him and used it at the appropriate five times a day for *Salat*. Sherbani used Simmons as his messenger to let Applenu know there would be a call.

Across the room, the band was getting ready with someone on a guitar running up and down the scales. The blonde glanced his way, and he momentarily caught her eye. He glanced at his Rolex: 8:58. The couple-thousand dollars he spent on the watch was essentially the only thing he'd spent any of his millions on. He had seventy thousand cash with papers for two other identities in a knapsack in his apartment ready for an emergency escape, the rest in a safe-deposit box in a Princeton bank. He didn't need any of that money because Sherbani, through Lormes, provided expense money—five-thousand dollars a month, some of which wound up in the knapsack. The only other outlay was the money he wired his sister and uncle for their plan when the rest of the family got out of Iran. Family: he needed to bring that up to Sherbani again.

At 8:59:30, he strolled into the hall off the hotel lobby, moving toward the bank of pay phones. *Was all this necessary*, he thought. Hearn had set up a sequence of public phones for Sherbani to call, so he never had to call the same phone twice. Even though the U.S. government said they were not monitoring phone calls, Sherbani did not trust the security of cell phones. Thank God for that. Without having to go out to a phone booth, he might never get a drink or meet any women.

The phone on the end of the row rang. He picked it up. "Brian here."

"Yes, Brian." Sherbani's accent seemed stronger on the phone, his voice choppier. "How is the enterprise going?"

"First we need to talk about my family. I want them flown to Amsterdam as we agreed."

"It is being taken care of. I will know something definite next week. Tell me about the enterprise."

"Everything is on schedule to deliver a competitive product by September."

"The reason I called was to tell you we decided to go ahead with the diversion."

"Why? Nothing has been made public about the product."

"The lack of publicity is politics. One faction of our competitors is keeping knowledge of the problem from other factions in their organization, because those others will want to know why the problem occurred, what is being done to fix it, and who is responsible for the problem. If you have watched the organization on other problems, you know that those left in the dark always like to fix blame."

"So you are going to give it to the media."

"We have a saying, Hassan, 'Don't get between two fighting dogs, you might get bit.' We also know that fighting dogs bite each other."

Chapter Fifteen

A nasal voice shoved country music from a CD player on the table next to the green-vinyl couch. For Curt, the songs conjured up a bitter taste of home.

Back roads, I've traveled them all,
In summer's heat, spring, winter, and fall.
You're never where you were.
I can't replace you with her.

Tonight's the night, Curt thought, as he studied his hole card. He called tails and "won" the right to try to escape.

For the last three nights their guards, Beecher, Markum, and Maxwell, the older fat one they called Max, showed up for poker. At other times, one of them was camped on the portable cot or chair they kept outside the door to their quarters.

Sitting at Curt's left, Markum said, "Bet a dollar."

Max: the name nagged at Curt's brain.

Sitting next to Markum, Surling called. Maxwell called and reached for a cigarette. At Curt's right, Beecher flipped his cards, stood, and headed for the refrigerator. "Anybody want a beer?"

Curt called the bet and glanced at Beecher, who bent to reach into the refrigerator, his tan shoulder holster popping from under his left armpit like a misplaced erect penis. Although Curt knew he was drinking too fast, he called for another beer.

Markum raked the pot and blew cigarette smoke onto the table as he collected the cards and shuffled. Beer, cigarette smoke, and country music, just like Friday nights at home eleven years ago in Dref, Iowa, after the accident.

We had a home, our home.
Then you started to roam,
Back roads that took you from me,
Back roads from what used to be.

Curt remembered. "*Max. Maxwell*, you're the one."

"Huh?" Maxwell blinked; his flabby face wore a hound-dog sleepiness enhanced by his gray walrus mustache. Behind the gold-rimmed, purple-tinted glasses, everything appeared a faded blue-gray.

"You were with my wife when I talked to her from Miami."

"So?" Maxwell straightened his thick body and swiped a hand across his puffed face that was as rumpled as his gray jacket.

"So why aren't you watching her now?"

"Just let it go, Reedan," Beecher said quietly as he set a Sam Adams in front of Curt and lowered his large frame into his chair. Beecher's face displayed no emotion, the same expression as when he pounded Curt's stomach in the machine room.

Curt turned back to Maxwell and wondered what kind of pounding he would get if he didn't escape. "If you're here, that means she's so scared you know she won't go to the police."

"Goddamn you, Reedan," Beecher growled, his gaze straight ahead. "I thought that shot in the stomach showed we mean business."

"My family *is* my business."

"We can tell him, Beech," Markum said, his accent thicker than that of the other two.

"Huh?" Beecher's head snapped left as he looked past Curt at Markum.

Short and stocky with a coarse, freckled face with blue eyes, Markum, like Beecher, appeared to be in his mid-thirties. His long red hair seemed to have slipped from the top of his head onto his collar, leaving an elongated forehead. "What's to tell?" he asked, glancing at Curt and Beecher. "We got somebody else watching her."

"That's not it," Beecher said. "He's a goddamned wise ass, and he's going to fuck around until we have to knock the shit out of him."

Curt felt Surling watching him and sensed his irritation. If they picked up and left, there would be no escape attempt. "Bet a dollar on the pair of fives," he said, letting his mind wander back to the escape attempt. What would happen to Surling if he escaped?

Conversation dried up, leaving cards, beer, smoke, and country music. The music died unattended.

Curt peeked at his hole cards, ace-three, then sipped at his second beer, his limit, a lesson from watching Dad embarrass himself. He slipped up once in high school and puked his guts out. He didn't try alcohol again until grad school. Tonight he needed an extra beer to get through the next hour.

"This is a goddamned wake," Beecher said, flipping his cards over. He went to his jacket on the couch and rummaged through the pockets, rattling keys. When he returned, he dropped a gray pipe and a clear plastic bag of green leaves on the table. "Since we don't have any women, maybe a little weed will liven up this party."

Curt called the bet and glanced at Surling. This was something new.

"*Professor* Surling, do you play cards as well as you *fuck*?" Beecher asked as he filled the pipe with crumpled green leaves. "Or is *fucking* your academic specialty?"

"What?" Surling asked, glancing at Beecher, then grabbing Markum's package of cigarettes.

Beecher turned to Markum. "Let's look at them pictures I took up in Philly."

Markum roared into a laugh, tossed in his hand, and stood.

"Maybe we could get Lormes to bring Marti and Carol down here for you two," Beecher said. "Even you scientists have got to get fucked once in awhile. Maybe it is more often for you, *Professor*." More laughter

Maxwell dealt another round up, and then he and Curt called Surling. Beecher lit the pipe and filled the table with smoke that smelled like burning rope. Maxwell dealt another round.

Curt glanced at Beecher. Was this the time? Was there a right time to challenge three men with guns?

Maxwell and Curt called Surling, and Maxwell dealt the last card face down.

Beecher handed Curt the pipe. "Take a puff."

Curt hesitated. Got to stay alert, he thought. No way would he challenge those guns with his head messed up with booze *and* drugs.

"Go ahead, try it."

Curt took the pipe. Dope surrounded him in college, and although he took flack, he never smoked. In high school, Dad convinced him he'd only be great at basketball if he kept his body free of drugs and alcohol. People didn't believe him when he said he'd never smoked marijuana. Lori tried it in college and tried to talk him into trying it. They argued about it, and after that she never used it again. At least not that he knew.

He inhaled, and the smoke clawed its way down his windpipe like an angry tomcat. He roared into a cough; tears flooded his eyes.

Beecher howled and grabbed the pipe: "Smaller puffs, hold it in." He demonstrated, hissing and popping noises issuing from his mouth. He handed the pipe to Curt and watched to see that he followed his instructions.

Can't get high, Curt thought, but he played along. He choked back the cough that tickled his throat trying to escape.

Surling raked the pot. He realized he was smoking and stubbed out the cigarette, three-quarters unsmoked, obviously remembering his pledge to quit.

Markum returned and tossed a packet of color pictures on the table.

Beecher, holding the pipe, grabbed the top picture and handed it to Curt. "Here's how we got the professor: giving oral exams." Markum broke into a loud cackle.

Surling lay on his back, glasses off, a naked blonde's face between his legs.

Beecher handed Curt a close-up photo of the blonde's face and Surling's penis. "For you *scientists*, the technical term for that is fellatio."

Markum giggled, his face blooming as red as his thinning hair. "You got some great pictures, Beech." He dug through the stack and laid four of them in front of Curt, pictures of Surling under or over the blonde, but always inside one of her openings. "She really handled you, eh, *Professor*."

"Too bad we don't have the laptop here to show the video you got," Markum said.

Beecher pointed with the pipe at the picture of Surling being sucked by the blonde and looked at Curt. "Does that sharp wife of yours give good head, Reedan?" He turned to Surling, "If you had a wife like Reedan's, *Professor*, you wouldn't have to screw everything around. I just hope that when I'm eighty-four like you are, I'll still be able to fuck like a mongrel dog. You're my hero, *Professor*."

Loud laughter from the three goons filled the room.

Maxwell turned to Curt. "I'd go down on your wife in a minute, Reedan. I'd gladly let her wrap those long legs around my neck while I wallowed in it." Beecher and Markum roared. "Or maybe I'd have her wrap her luscious lips around my cock, while that long black hair of hers tickled my balls. If my wife would have been anything like her, I'd still be married."

Curt restrained himself from rushing around the table and grabbing the slob.

Beecher loudly exhaled smoke. "So you see, Reedan, we're

definitely keeping our eyes on your wife. We've got our eyes on everything from that sweet ass of hers up to those perky tits."

Curt's face burned; his breathing accelerated. He figured he could get one swing at Maxwell before they grabbed him. Just hold on for now, he told himself, stick to the plan. He grabbed the gray pipe from Beecher and studied the stem, shiny like a minnow, wet with saliva. Feeling Beecher's eyes, he inhaled. No more, he thought. It was time to move while everyone else's mood was mellow.

When Surling got the pipe, his eyes darted to Beecher and Markum; Maxwell kept his head down. Surling went through the motions of inhaling deeply.

"Quite a high, huh, Reedan?" Beecher said.

Curt nodded and smiled; he felt nothing.

Beecher looked at Surling. "You smoked before, Professor?"

"A few times."

Like dog and master, the pipe followed the cards around the table, clockwise. When his turn came, Curt put a dollar in the pot and took the pipe. One more puff wouldn't hurt. He inhaled, held it, and passed the pipe.

It hit. Like a TV set with the contrast suddenly properly adjusted, everything in the room flipped into sharp focus: Markum's red hair blended into a pink scalp that merged into his pink forehead. Beecher's liquid eyes were pools of scotch with small drops of cola in the center. All light in the room reflected from Surling's head and flashed off his glasses. A smile rippled Maxwell's puffed face when he peeked at his hole cards; he quickly smoothed his gray mustache.

Curt shook his head. This wasn't supposed to happen. Not after five or six puffs. Lori claimed that the first two times she smoked, nothing happened. His body tingled; his arms and legs felt as if they were packed with vibrating springs, his face cold, freezing. Should he call it off? Beecher held the pipe, now empty. A chance to come down.

To Curt's left, Markum rubbed his arms and babbled on about Surling in Philadelphia and the video. "You should see him doing her doggy style," Markum said amid a roar of laughter. "Beecher's mongrel dog couldn't do it better."

On Curt's right, Beecher, a perpetual motion machine, jiggled up and down as if in the cab of a bouncing truck. Suddenly, Curt climbed in the truck, legs jiggling, shoulders and head bobbing.

"Feelin' no pain, boy," Dad would say when he and Uncle Artie staggered in from the Country Lane Bar, each with a six pack. After Dad put on some records, he and Artie popped a beer and sang along with a scratchy Hank Williams record: "Your cheatin' heart…" Dad never drank before Curt's accident.

Maybe feeling no pain would pull him through the next few minutes: no pain from a bullet in the back, a fist in the stomach, or a kick in the balls.

Dad drank and Mom prayed: prayed for Dad to stop drinking, prayed for Curt to make it at Iowa State, then at MIT. I hope you're still praying for me, Mom, he thought. It was now or never. He tossed in his cards and stood. "Anybody want a beer?" he asked, heading for the refrigerator, his step light and his body ready to float, a giddiness jiggling his brain. *Trip the light fantastic to wherever the next few minutes might lead*, he thought. *May I have this dance?*

Beecher and Maxwell called for a beer.

Act natural, he told himself, make them think you're high, but don't get lost in the high. Be ready: ready to feel no pain, see no pain, and hear no pain.

He uncapped two Sam Adams and grabbed one for himself, unopened. As he set Maxwell's beer in front of him, Surling glanced up, his eyes stretched vertically into robin's eggs by the angle of his glasses. Questioning eyes: *You going to do it or not?*

He set Beecher's beer down, saw the gun under Beecher's arm, and quickly looked at the pictures. Surling and sex. Sex: Surling's alternative to escape.

"Reedan," Beecher yelled, "start that CD player."

"You've got it." Curt said. Was his speech slurred? "Nothing beats country music and beer."

"And weed," Beecher said. "Don't forget weed."

"And weed." Curt laughed, a laugh that threatened to transform itself into a giggle. He tried to remember what day it was. Friday? Uncle Artie was dead, and according to Mom, Dad only went to the Country Lane the last Friday of the month, and he usually came home early and sober.

As he punched the button on the CD player, he remembered the jingling keys in Beecher's coat. He turned up the volume and quickly probed the coat pockets and found the keys.

A minute or two of your time,
That's not too much to ask.
Once everything you had was mine.
Now it's behind a mask.

"Don't deal me in this hand," he called. "Got to go to the john." He stumbled. An act, he told himself, as he staggered toward the door, carrying his unopened beer, his weapon of choice. "Feelin' no pain," he said.

Time to put their plan into operation. A simple plan: one man would accompany him to the bathroom. Once inside the large room that served as shower room, change room, and bathroom, he'd maneuver to get behind the guard and smash him with one of the metal chairs lined up against the wall. He hefted the Sam Adams club. A slight change in plan. After he clobbered him with the beer bottle, he would run like hell.

The music played on:

It's all behind a mask,
Hidden behind a mask.
If only I could know,
Your love will once more grow.
From seed behind that mask,
Hidden behind that mask.

Between the alcohol, the drug, and the fear, he realized part of the put-on stagger was real, making it difficult to walk a straight line. He needed to go to the bathroom, bad.

He opened the door and looked back. Nobody moved. Answered prayers? He stepped into the ten-foot wide hall, the door to the change room directly across the hall. Fifteen feet to the right, past the guard's cot along the wall, the hallway intersected a similar-size hallway that ran the length of the building. All the work rooms were on that corridor. His objective was twenty feet to the left, a large dark-green sliding door with a smaller dark-green man-sized door next to it.

Closing the door to their prison, he accelerated into an easy jog, careful of his knee, which felt good, although the drug had him feeling good all over. He examined Beecher's keys and identified the car keys and the unlock button on the digital key pad as he stepped from air-conditioned cool into a wall of heat and humidity. He bounded down five concrete steps next to a loading dock on his left and jogged toward a big car at the end of the long warehouse-like structure. *Home free*, he thought, a giggle about to break through the giddy feeling that suffused his body.

Behind him, the door banged open. "Stay right where you are, Reedan," Beecher yelled as he pounded down the steps.

Curt tossed the Sam Adams toward the building and grabbed the door handle. Locked. He quickly punched buttons on the key pad; the car lights blinked. He opened the door and slipped into a plush leather seat of what he now recognized to be a Lincoln Town Car. He slammed the door. The lock, where is it? Forget it. The ignition, where's the ignition? He felt along the steering column and located it. He jammed the key into the ignition just as Beecher jerked open the door.

"Just hold it right there, asshole," Beecher said through shortened breaths. He shoved a gun into the lighted interior and pressed the hard steel muzzle against Curt's temple.

Markum, his gun drawn, pounded up next to Beecher. "Thank God, you got the bastard."

Curt stared through the windshield, sweat dribbling into his eyes. Surling would be ready with his alternate plan, and Curt was chosen—without a coin toss.

Chapter Sixteen

This time Rick Saul inhabited his home turf, a Bureau interrogation room, sitting behind a long metal table with Doyle Logson on his side. Bart Kraft sat at attention on the other side, alone, no wife's picture to touch, no sons smiling up at him. It was time for Kraft to come up with answers about Steve Austin.

Kraft glanced around the room, the only decoration a picture of the President on the white wall behind Saul and Logson. "What did you call me down here for?" Kraft asked, unbuttoning his tan jacket and then buttoning it. "I've got a lot of work waiting for me at the office. Besides that, I've got Sheena Mosely hounding me. Somebody better figure out what to do about her, or SWISILREC will be smeared all over the media."

Sheena Mosely was every Washington bureaucrat's worst nightmare come true. Fortunately, she was a Washington outsider, and although she had been nosing around DOE and DOD for a week, as far as they knew, she made little progress. She hadn't hit Capitol Hill yet—at least Mary and the Senator didn't know about her.

"We called you down here to talk about Austin," Logson said.

"I told Saul everything I know."

Saul worried that Kraft might be telling the truth.

Austin, for want of his real name, they still called him that. Although Saul and twenty-one other agents now on the case in and around Washington had turned over many rocks, they had few clues to Austin's true identity.

Austin's social security card was obtained with a birth certificate for a long-dead baby in Detroit. Unburned remains of his wallet at the morgue held a Maryland driver's license with a fake address and little else, such as credit cards or anything that would connect him with anybody but who he was trying to be. Although his job application at DOE stated that he worked for California Congressman Terrance Tilton, Tilton's office never heard of him. From the congressional payroll office, they found out he worked for Congressman Clarence Morgan of Florida. They had agents questioning people in Morgan's office, but they were hampered because Morgan and four of his top assistants were on a "fact-finding" trip to Southeast Asia.

His resume listed a PhD in electrical engineering from Carnegie Mellon University in Pittsburgh and a B.S. and M.S. from Columbia University in New York City, both phonies. If he earned degrees from those schools, they weren't obtained under the name of Steve Austin.

Regardless of his degrees, he was a computer whiz-bang, as testified to by Kraft and others at DOE and as attested to by his success in hacking the SID computer to award himself a security clearance. Then he played his hacking games in NNSA's computer at DOE and NNSA's supercomputer at Kirtland Air Force Base in Albuquerque, and now somebody had enough nuclear material for fifteen-to-twenty atomic bombs.

After many agent days spent turning D.C. upside down, they found only two people who had really touched Austin: Kraft and Marge Alsop. Marge knew Austin, but knew nothing about him. Kraft claimed to have known Austin only as a co-worker, so there was no way he could know anything about him. Rick Saul now knew better.

"Bart, we know that you know more about Austin than you've been telling us," Logson said, his Chinaman's smile flickering on his bald face.

Before Kraft could deny it, Saul said, "You and Austin were lovers."

Kraft's head jerked from looking at Logson to Saul. His right hand reached out, dropped onto the white plastic table top, and then slid back into his lap, his shoulders straight. "What are you talking about?" He turned to Logson, eyes pleading. "You know me, Doyle. You've met my wife and family."

Logson's smile drained away.

Saul tried to put himself in Kraft's position, but couldn't. What was he looking for? He tried to picture them together naked. Why? Kraft didn't look like someone bored with his job, someone who needed extra kicks. With guys yet. Women, Saul could understand, the wife not measuring up to the picture on the desk. But *guys*?

"Where did you go for lunch yesterday?" Saul asked.

Kraft's shoulders drooped slightly; he undid the button on his jacket and rubbed his hand across his brow.

"You went to Georgetown and had lunch at Mister May, right?"

At the mention of Mister May, a light-red shadow crept from below Kraft's collar up into his face. "You've been following me."

"It's a gay bar, and you didn't go back to work yesterday afternoon. You went with…"

"You've got no right to follow me. I turned in leave time for yesterday afternoon. You can check the record."

"Okay, Bart," Logson said, his voice husky, his face almost as red as Kraft's. "Let's talk about Austin. You spent time with him, right?"

"Jesus, Doyle, it's not what you think." He held up his hands. "Martha and the kids don't know anything about that part of my life. I don't know *why* I do it."

Saul wondered how many Washington bean counters spent lunchtime yesterday at a gay bar or in bed with someone other than their spouse. Only Kraft got caught. "*Austin.* What about *Austin*?" Saul said, wishing this part of the process was over.

Kraft shrugged, his head dropping onto his chest. "About two years ago, Austin came up to me at a bar. He knew who I was. I don't know how he found out, because I was always discreet. I always made sure nobody knew where I worked. I always used a false name."

"So you met Austin in a bar, and you had sex with him. So why did you give him a job?"

Kraft rubbed his hand across his mouth. "A few days after we met, I got a letter with his resume indicating he was a computer expert with a Q clearance. There was no direct threat of blackmail in the letter, but I could read between the lines. So I had him in for an interview."

"There wasn't any reason for a threat, because you gave him a job. Right?"

Kraft held out his hands, palms up. "Why shouldn't I give him the job? He was a straight-A student, and he had good references and a Q clearance. Our security people verified it."

"It was a fake," Saul said. "Austin accessed OPM's SID computer and gave himself a Q clearance. Did you check his references?"

"No," Kraft said, his voice barely audible. His body sank slightly in the chair. He reached up and loosened his tie and undid the shirt button. "He said he was working for Congressman Tilton, but he wanted to get back to technical work because the job with Tilton was too political. Why should I check? As far as I knew, he had a Q clearance, and he knew all about computers. These days, my department's nothing but computers, and we needed an expert. I didn't think there was any way he could hurt our department…or the government."

Logson shook his head and looked at Saul. "He didn't think. So you gave him carte blanche with your computer."

"Yes. He redid the transportation security, uranium and plutonium management, and storage programs and greatly improved them."

"You let him visit field offices, right?"

Kraft looked around the room as if hoping for a way to disappear. He nodded and ran his hand through his hair. "When he began the revamping, he said he needed to tour some field offices to see how they operate."

"And you continued to have homosexual relations with him," Saul said. "I assume you found out something about his personal life."

It turned out Kraft found out absolutely nothing that would lead to Austin's identity or, more importantly, lead to the people Austin worked with. This, despite the fact that they had spent many lunch hours at Austin's apartment in Rockville. He never met any of Austin's friends and knew nothing about Austin and Marge Alsop.

"Nothing that I can remember," Kraft said for about the sixth time.

"Our only hope is that we can turn something up in his apartment," Logson said, "assuming Kraft can find it."

He now had his handkerchief out and wiped his brow. "I'll take you right to it."

Kraft stood, his hair mussed, tie undone, and started toward the door. Halfway there, he stopped and turned to Logson. "Doyle, what about me? The job...Martha and the boys?"

Logson looked as if he could barely stand the sight of Kraft. "The first thing you should do when you get back to your office is prepare your resignation. Somebody will let you know when it's wanted."

"You can't fire me because of my sexual preference."

"Nobody's going to fire you, Bart. You're going to resign."

- - - - -

Kraft led Saul to an old, red brick duplex in Rockville. After dropping him at a Metrobus stop, Saul went to see the landlady, who lived in the adjoining apartment. In her late sixties, she was only too happy to talk about "that nice young man. Such a tragedy."

"Who told you about the accident?"

"The men who took his belongings away. They showed up two days after Mr. Austin was killed. They had a letter from a lawyer that said they could take his personal belongings and return them to his folks."

"Did they tell you where his folks lived?"

She shook her head. "If they did, I don't remember."

"Did Mr. Austin have a roommate?"

"No, sir. He had friends who visited him a lot. Quite a few times they stayed overnight."

"Men or women?"

"Both."

"Can I see the apartment? Maybe he left something behind."

"There's nothing of Mr. Austin's in there. A nice young couple moved in three weeks after they moved Mr. Austin's things out."

Chapter Seventeen

"You're crazy, Bob," Reedan said. "*Me* and *Drafton*? No way!"

Surling wanted to scream at the futility of Reedan's argument. Over and over they examined all possibilities; there was no other way. That, or wait for the end. Getting another escape chance like the one Reedan fucked up last night was increasingly unlikely.

"Goddammit, Curt, we're not talking about turning you into a queer. We're talking life and death, namely, *ours*."

Although they sat at the oak table eating dinner, Surling thought Reedan looked sick—sick of the idea and the argument, and also sick of him. "We've *got* to do something. They've got your wife scared shitless, and they made me call my wife again yesterday to tell her everything's okay. Drafton is our only chance."

Surling shook his head. He began agitating for the alternate plan after Reedan's screw up: he hadn't even gotten a look at a license plate to see what state they were in. He saw a sign on the building that said they were working for General Nuclear American Company. So it wasn't Margine Nuclear Technology, like he was told when they were "recruiting" him and like the website they gave him to look at. Big goddamn deal, Surling thought. He spends his time before the escape attempt drinking beer and smoking pot, and then has the gall to say that if he had been five seconds faster getting the key into the ignition, he'd have been out of here in a Lincoln Town Car. And now he fights their only other plan.

Reedan pushed his half-eaten meal aside. "Why can't we just play on Drafton's sympathies?"

"We don't mean anything to him. He's young and naive, too, and he still believes they'll pay us and let us go. If you mean something to him, we'll be able to convince him they intend to kill us." Surling sipped coffee. "If you two, you know, get it on, he'll have a stake in you...and me."

"What about AIDS? We'll get out of here, and I'll die of AIDS."

Here we go again, Surling thought. The guy was great at thinking of all possibilities for why something shouldn't be done. "How many times do I have to tell you, it won't come to sex. Besides, he and I talked about AIDS. He said he hadn't been with anyone since Derek, and they had safe sex."

"Safe sex doesn't mean anything."

"It's a chance we'll have to take."

"*We'll* have to take?"

"Okay, if it ever comes to sex, *you'll* have to take the chance. Safe sex or not, we're dead for sure if you don't take it." Safe sex, Surling thought. As he was coming in the blonde in Philadelphia, the thought had flicked across his mind: You're supposed to use a rubber, not that this was the first time he didn't use one or that he thought about it after the fact.

"What am I supposed to do, seduce him?"

"Why go over it again, Curt? Seduce him, or let him seduce you, what's the difference? For now, just be friendly, play it as it comes. I've been telling him about you, and he's interested."

"Yeah. He's been in the computer room a few times. He never says much, just stands behind me and watches the monitor while I work. He talks about how good Derek was on the computer. Once or twice he touched my shoulder, rubbed it."

"There's your chance. I told him you and your wife are having trouble and might split."

"*What?*"

"You said you argued about your job change and moving to Boston. I figured if Drafton knows that, he won't think we're trying to pull something."

"My wife and I are doing fine."

"*Goddammit*, Curt, you're not going to Boston *or* Colorado, but to an early grave unless we do something. *Now.*"

"It's just that I don't think I could ever… What would I actually do?"

Reedan's question took Surling by surprise, since it was the first time they'd spoken about the act. What did he want to hear? "I guess you blow him and he blows you. That and anal sex. You have had a blow job, haven't you?"

Reedan hesitated and then shook his head. "I've been rather… conventional…I've been busy."

"You've never had a woman go down on you? You've never gone down on your wife? I guess you never had another woman besides your

110

wife either."

Reedan stared at him.

Surling smiled. "I'll let you get in a few licks on me." He began to laugh.

Reedan didn't laugh.

"That was crude," Surling said quietly. "I can see there are some pleasures you haven't experienced, my young friend. And a whole lot of pain." He smiled. "But why are we talking about sex? It won't get that far. What's he going to do, tell Applenu he wants to take you back to his apartment so you two can sleep together? Or will they move me out of here, so you two can be alone? At worst, you might have to hug him a few times."

Reedan nodded. "I know. It's just that…Hey, I told you we're going to have a baby. I'd like a son, but another daughter would be fine."

Surling marveled at Reedan's naiveté as he remembered his own son, who was about Reedan's age when it happened. "I'm sorry it has to be this way, Curt. You'll see your son." He smiled. "I had a son once, too."

- - - - -

Lori picked up the phone after the fifth ring.

"Hello, Lori. I'm checking to see how you are doing all by yourself."

She recognized the leering voice of the tall one. This was the second time he called.

"If you are lonesome, Lori, I'll come and keep you company." He cackled.

She cringed at the way her name sounded with his foreign accent. "I'm fine." She had to get a gun.

"Just don't get any ideas about going to the police, because we're watching and listening."

What good was a gun? Could she have him come over and then shoot him? What would she tell the police?

"I won't tell anyone." She said.

"You better not, or else it's the end for your old man and little girl. It will be the end of you, too."

- - - - -

Curt was behind the keyboard in the computer room when Drafton walked in and sat on the chair at the other end of the long table. After a few awkward moments, Drafton began talking about the work Curt had been doing. Although he would rather break his leg again, another compound fracture of the tibia and fibula, his foot pointing ninety degrees in the wrong direction, Curt knew Surling was right. Reluctantly, he changed the subject to Derek.

Drafton's face lit up, and he began to describe Derek Hearn the computer genius, how Derek put the project together, how he had known Derek in college and Derek contacted him to work on it.

"God, I miss him," Drafton said.

"So why didn't you get out after he died?"

Drafton tugged at his bushy brown beard, his eyes glistening. "They convinced me to help finish what Derek started. Besides, I didn't have anywhere else to go."

Ever since high school, homosexuals were queers, fags, and fairies to Curt, the butts of locker-room jokes. Face-to-face with a real one, all he wanted was to get away from the sad sack, get back to his quarters. But like the escape attempt, it was again now-or-never, life-or-death time if he were to believe Surling.

"You know what it means to lose somebody you love? Yes, love." Tears surged but did not flow. "I loved him. You might not understand. Most people don't. I'm not sure Derek did." Tears flowed.

Curt remembered a joke. Drafton didn't talk like that, his voice about the same pitch and tone as Curt's. He had to get out of there, but in his mind, he heard Surling: "Make a move. Now."

Drafton rubbed his right eye with his index finger and talked about how there was nobody he could talk to about Derek, certainly not his parents, since he had fought with them about his lifestyle ever since they found out. Large wet drops rolled into his beard and disappeared. "Why can't people understand?"

Parents, Curt thought. What would Mom think of this? Dad would shoot him. "Screwed up his basketball career out on that farm, and now he turns queer." Where were Mom's prayers? He sat, unable to move, Surling's voice rattling in his brain: "*You* make the move."

Thoughts were Curt's domain, everything in the mind. Ever since the summer after his sophomore year in college, physical action held little appeal. After his recovery he quickly connected with the computer and the metallurgy department at school. He sometimes wondered if he lived too much inside his head or in the wrong part of his head to understand sex. During his junior and senior years in college, a portion of his brain was occupied by sex, at least when he was with Lori, although they never went all the way until they were married. Surling got a laugh out of that and the fact that Lori was the only one. Maybe he *was* queer.

He wanted to believe Surling was right: nothing sexual would happen. He knew he should go to Drafton. Can't do it, he thought. Why didn't Surling do it? Surling needed sex. Surling started him thinking about his own sex life, which was as limited as his thoughts on the subject. Like Surling asking him if he'd ever had a blow job. Lori wanted to experiment; she bought a book and wanted him to read it. She teased him in bed a few times, kissing his penis and playfully licking at it, asking if he wasn't up for something a little different. They never got there, because he quickly steered her back to the tried and true. He wasn't ready for this.

By the time he and Lori married, he was entrenched in the mental life. MIT wouldn't have it any other way. At first, five times a week, with no time wasted. He liked everything about it. After two years at MIT, he was always busy, and they were down to twice a week: Saturday night or Sunday morning; Wednesday or Thursday after dinner. Quickly over and back to the lab or the computer, where he immersed himself in mathematical modeling of alloys during deformation and sought computer solutions of three-dimensional stress equations. Same thing now, but the average had deteriorated to below twice a week. Well below. Sex still occupied a corner of his mind, especially at night in a hotel room his mind often turned to Lori. When he was home, he was always too busy getting ready for the next trip. When he finally got to bed, Lori had been asleep for several hours, and he didn't feel he should wake her.

Drafton said, "Since Derek got killed, I've been lonely, and there's nobody I can talk to."

Curt nodded, still glued to the chair. Since the first year of their marriage, only once did he have an irresistible urge that could be satisfied only by sex. That came with Lori nine months pregnant, waiting for her day, and...What an ass! Maybe he was queer.

Time to get out of here, he thought. *Now*. He stood and forced his legs forward, mentally swatting away thoughts that would trigger the nausea primed just below his Adam's apple ready to explode like coke from a shaken bottle. Think of robotics equations. He held out his arms. "I understand, Eric."

Drafton stood and rubbed at his flooded eyes, the tears tumbling down his cheeks and soaking into his beard. He lurched forward, arms encircling Curt. He buried his face in Curt's shoulder, his body shuddering. Warm tears soaked through Curt's khaki shirt.

Curt held him. "I'm sorry, Eric. I understand." He understood nothing, least of all himself. Only doing a job, he thought, a life-and-death job.

After an eternity, Drafton's body quieted. He pulled back, their faces inches apart. Tears glistened on his beard like dew drops on grass. "I knew you'd understand, Curt."

He forced himself to look into Drafton's flooded blue eyes. Lori's eyes were brown, dark brown, and he wondered when he last looked into them.

Then it happened. They kissed, mouth to mouth. No way should that happen. He didn't know who made the first move—Surling would say Curt should have. He tried to remember the first time he kissed Lori or the first girl he'd kissed. He couldn't remember.

He thought of Maxwell in the hall beyond the door. At least the window in this door was translucent, and he could not see in.

They kissed again, quick, almost natural. Drafton's wet mouth covered Curt's lips, both their mouths open. Before Curt could react to his emotions, Drafton hugged him and pulled back, a pathetic smile smeared onto his tears.

Still in each other's arms, Drafton's eyes probed the depths of Curt's. "You *do* understand, Curt, you *really* do. We'll get together soon." He turned and hurried out of the room.

Curt scrubbed at his mouth, erasing the taste of the salt from Drafton's kisses, now indelibly etched onto the surface of his brain. It all happened so fast, too fast to get sick.

Only after his numbed mind recovered from the shock did he realize he had a partial erection. "Oh my God! No! No!"

Chapter Eighteen

Rick Saul eased his head from the pillow, checking the heft. Not too bad, considering all the Glenfiddich and the wine with dinner.

The phone beeped in the other room. Spanner? Emergency?

Mary answered. He hadn't heard her get up and wished he could roll over on top of her and continue the celebration.

Besides Saul and Spanner, SWISILREC now had about thirty other agents pursuing leads around D.C. and helping keep track of the e-mails and telephone calls deluging headquarters from about eighty agents around the country investigating various aspects of the case. Twenty-to-thirty new agents were being added each week as different areas for investigation became evident. None of the agents knew the exact nature of the case, just enough to allow them to operate.

Although Spanner coordinated SWISILREC, he spent most of his time explaining to "people in high places" why they hadn't found the bomb material and the people who stole it. That meant Saul spent most of his time coordinating the investigation and assimilating information for Spanner's daily reports to upper management.

SWISILREC boiled down to Steven Austin. Saul's big investigation, his ultimate opportunity for Bureau recognition and advancement by way of the Washington fast track, quickly degenerated into a series of dead ends and petering-out leads. Steven Austin had all the trappings of a twenty-first century citizen, from birth certificate to social security number to PhD degree. His reality was a virtual one that had no correspondence with official electronic memories around the country. No Steven A. Austin appeared in the electronic memories of computers at Columbia and Carnegie Mellon Universities, which according to his job applications were the universities he had graduated from.

The Steven Andrew Austin on the birth certificate died in Detroit in

1984 at the age of eleven months. The 2011 Austin with properly validated death certificate was just as dead, his tracks since the 1990s as ephemeral as the electronic signals that conferred his self-generated existence. Although Steven Austin crossed the lives of Marge Alsop and Bart Kraft, he left no traces of the intersection, only memories of his youthful charms.

Instead of chasing Austin through his mind, Saul turned his memories to last night: Italian food and dancing afterward, their private celebration of Mary's promotion to become the Senator's press secretary.

In the other room, Mary chatted away, her words indecipherable through the door. Across the room, his pants and shirt lay on the floor, inside out. Mary's pink dress hung across the chair. They got in about two and started making love in the living room: her panty hose off, his pants and shorts down around his ankles, groping and poking their way into the bed. Maybe after she got off the phone, he could coax her back.

When Saul got to the kitchen, Mary was perched on a stool at the breakfast bar, hunched over a story in the *Post*, her stocking-clad feet propped on the stool, knees poking out from under her skirt. She grunted a greeting without looking up.

Ambling up behind her, he slipped his arms around her waist, pulled up alongside her satin-smooth cheek, and buried his face in her long, thick blonde hair. As he inhaled the fragrance, his cock did an expectant jig under his robe.

"Don't mess my hair," she said, unloosening his grip from her waist. She swiveled the chair to face him, her dark-blue eyes searching his face before she pecked him on the mouth.

His expectations sank when he realized she was dressed for work: tight navy dress with white polka dots. A perfect outfit to go with the long blonde hair and blue eyes, just like all of her clothes these days. Nothing like the washed-out Levis and shapeless sweat shirts she lived in at Notre Dame and Spokane. Her dress, which she would say was appropriate for the press secretary of the *Honorable* Stanley M. Hughson, accented the fact that in the past five years she blossomed from a skinny blonde giggler to a beautiful full-bodied woman, the woman he had always desired. That's what worried him.

Saul bent forward for a real kiss, but she pecked at his lips and pulled back. When he reached for her, she grabbed his hands. He jerked back to free his hands and get at her body. "Come back to bed for awhile. We'll finish what we started last night, finish the celebration."

She laughed and tightened her grip on his hands. "I'd say you finished pretty well. Besides, I've got to get to work." She sucked at her lips, like she always did when she debated what to say or how to say it. "That was the Senator on the phone."

"What did that pompous ass want this early in the morning?" He regretted the words as soon as they were out, knowing that the probability of getting her to bed had just hit zero.

She swiveled the chair back to face the counter and slid the newspaper to her left "He told me that you made the *Post*." she said as she pointed at a story on the front page:

NUCLEAR BOMB MATERIAL STOLEN IN TENNESSEE
Sheena Mosely, Associated Press
Washington—Associated Press has learned that a truck or trucks loaded with nuclear bomb-grade uranium and plutonium were hijacked in Tennessee on June 6, shortly after they left the Y-12 nuclear facility in Oak Ridge, TN. The trucks were en route to the Savannah River National Laboratory outside Aiken, South Carolina. An unspecified number of men—drivers and guards—were killed. The hijacking occurred on a lonely county road near Lenoir City, Tennessee.

Julia Vargas, the spokesperson at DOE's Washington Headquarters, stated there was "no information to report on stolen material," and that "for over 25 years the department has transported weapons-grade nuclear material in convoys of special tractor-trailer sets called Safe Secure Trailers (SSTs) over four-million miles without ever losing any material...

"How the hell did Mosely get all this?" he asked as he read about how the cargo had enough nuclear material for 10 bombs like those dropped on Japan that killed 100,000 people, how Kraft did not return her calls, and about what Kraft's predecessor had to say about it.

According to AP sources, who wish to remain anonymous, the FBI has launched Operation Swift Silent Recovery (SWISILREC) to recover the nuclear material. Special Agents George Spanner and Richard Saul from FBI headquarters in Washington are heading the investigation. Three weeks ago, Saul spent several days in Tennessee, South Carolina, and New Mexico investigating the case. When reached in Washington, Saul declined to comment on the investigation...

After quickly scanning the rest of the article, he headed across the room for coffee. Sheena Mosely had struck, and he'd wound up a target. How the hell did she learn about his trips? Thank God he didn't have to go to the office until after his visit to Germantown.

"Did somebody really steal nuclear material?" Mary asked.

"What you see is what you get." He poured coffee and brought the mug back to the bar so he could study the article.

Mosely had covered much ground—the bitch. She found out Amos King of Aiken, South Carolina was killed, and she interviewed his daughter and the undertaker. She didn't get much there.

"Come on, Rick, the Senator needs you," Mary said. "If he can get on top of this, we can generate media space and time. It'll help with name recognition when he makes his move."

"What move?"

She chewed at her lips. "It's still hush-hush, but he's going to run for president."

"That *asshole* is running for president?"

"*Rick*, he's as capable as the other people being talked about. In the past few years, he's generated good media capital out of the nuclear proliferation issue and the thing with Iran before the Israeli raid. This is right up his alley."

Media capital, media space, he thought. Media: How many times a day did she use that almighty Washington buzzword? When she went for coffee, his eyes were assaulted by the amount of long legs revealed by the short dress.

"Jesus, that dress is short."

"Not that again, Rick. It's the style."

"A skirt up to the crack of your ass is style? It looks like advertising to me. You know what guys at the Bureau call those dresses? C-skimmers, and C doesn't stand for cute."

She ignored his comment, brought her coffee to the counter, and sat down next to him. "You can help us, Rick."

He didn't answer. Her dress reminded him of Julia Thornton. Florida Congressman Clarence Morgan finally got back from his fact-finding trip to Southeast Asia, and they got a chance to talk to Morgan and his top assistants. Austin worked for Morgan for seven months, just as the IRS and congressional payroll records indicated. It turned out Austin got the job by seducing Morgan's office manager, Julia Thornton, thirty-three-years-old and not as attractive as Marge Alsop. Thornton's skirts swooped toward her ankles, but Austin didn't mind lifting them. He got into the government classified computer files by first getting into her pants.

"It's to your benefit to help the Senator," Mary said. "He can help Uncle Nathan—and you."

"Help him with a media opportunity? I could write my own ticket, huh?"

"You could. He likes Uncle Nathan. He'd like you, too, if he got to know you."

To get to know his staff, Hughson had invited them and their families to his Pennsylvania farm one weekend earlier in the summer. Saul refused to go. He'd met the guy a couple of times at Nate's house. Did Nate really like the guy? The only thing Saul could see that the Senator and Nate had in common was their political need for each other. Their friendship began at Penn State, where they became Republicans to piss off their fathers. Uncle Nathan worked his way from a powerful Philadelphia city councilman to mayor. While doing that, he helped Hughson, a former mayor of Pittsburgh, become a senator. Now Nate needed the Pittsburgher's help to become governor.

"Hughson's a phony," Saul said, "always playing to the press."

"He's not," Mary said. "He does what's necessary. In this town, communication is key to everything. Communicate to legislate, communicate or vegetate."

She spoke like a new press secretary with a degree in communications, Saul thought. "This town is bullshit or forget it," he said.

She slid off her stool and sidled up to him, leaning her body against his back. "Come on, Rick. That *Post* story means it'll all come out soon. Let us be on top of it from the start." She wrapped her arms around his chest, rubbing her breasts against his shoulders. Her hand slid under his robe.

Seduction? Would she go back to bed for his secret? Was that their *modus operandi* now? Julia Thornton and Marge Alsop with Steven Austin? Mary Jane with…?

Although tempted, he slipped off the stool and out of her arms. "I've got to get to work." He slapped his hand on the newspaper story. "An interesting start to what should be an interesting day."

- - - - -

Saul straightened in his chair, wishing for a cup of coffee to help keep his eyelids pried open and his head upright while he concentrated on what Doctor Tomomuro—"you can carr me Tom"—Sukiomo was rambling on about from the head of the table, occasionally switching his pronunciation of "Ls" and "Rs", as the Japanese are wont to do. Sukiomo was a nuclear weapons specialist from Los Alamos, who Logson brought in to brief them on nuclear science.

Across the table, Ralph Ebert and Doyle Logson fought their own battles against sleep. Ebert suffered occasional setbacks, eyes glazing, head sinking forward slowly and then bouncing quickly off his chest to an upright position, eyes wide open. Next to Saul sat a squat young man who Ebert introduced as Kyle Orman, the new System Administrator for the NNSA computers—Steve Austin's replacement. Orman appeared wide awake, his full attention focused on Sukiomo's slides. Spanner cancelled out of the meeting because of two other ones where he would battle the raging Mosely fire.

They sat around the conference table in Bart Kraft's old office, which was now Ebert's due to his new role as Associate Administrator of NNSA's Security and Safeguards Division (acting). Although there had been no public announcement, Kraft had been "reassigned" to a non-position. Later, if the shit hit the fan and it looked like some important people would get splattered, Kraft would be dealt with publicly. According to Spanner, this was one of many aspects of crisis management strategy being diagrammed by the White House Planning and Operations Committee for SWISILREC.

White haired, in his late fifties, the short and skinny Sukiomo addressed the intricacies of nuclear chemistry and the manufacture of reliable nuclear weapons. PowerPoint slides flashed onto a screen at the front of the room: graphs of kilograms of nuclear material required for bombs that deliver kilotons and megatons of TNT, tables and diagrams of damage parameters and zones of destruction, and charts describing how many kilograms of uranium or plutonium were needed to take out New York City or just the Empire State Building. After several more bounces of Ebert's head, Sukiomo finished and sat down next to Logson.

Saul waited for someone to speak and realized they were waiting for him, hoping he had new leads. "That's interesting," he said, "but how's it going to help us find these guys?"

Logson nodded, his Charlie Chan smile in place, looking more oriental than Sukiomo. "We thought you needed a background briefing on nuclear weaponry of the type these people are probably planning to build."

"So now you think they're going to make a bomb?"

Logson turned up his smile. "Face facts: the information you turned up on what Austin got from the classified library can only lead to that conclusion."

In Washington, people believed in facts, especially if their bosses believed them. "They might still be smuggling the material out of the country."

"No way," Sukiomo said. "The materials they store are too bulky. Only way they smuggle liquid material is after they transform it to sorids. They can then machine the sorids for bomb parts to make them compact enough to ship."

"So you think they're making bombs right here in the U.S.," Saul said.

When there was no reply, Ebert told Orman to brief them on what he had learned about how Austin had used DOE computers to pull off the hijacking.

Orman plugged the projector cord into his laptop, and soon more PowerPoint slides appeared on the screen. One showed the Shipment Agreement and Verification Evaluation form followed by one of the Detailed Security Platform for the shipment followed by a slide of the approval by Strategic Planning and Authorization Committee. Finally, slides of EDs approving the SAVE and DSP sent to Oak Ridge, Savannah River, and Kirtland Air Force Base flashed on the screen.

"In other words," Orman said, "the paperwork was in place approving the doomed shipment. Trouble is, they were all fakes put together by Dr. Austin."

"How do you know they were fakes?" Saul asked.

"As you recall," Logson said, "you found that nobody at Oak Ridge, Savannah River, or Kirtland remembered seeing these documents on a three-truck shipment, and Kraft and I didn't remember approving the SPAC."

With a laser-pointer red dot bobbing about the screen, Orman explained how Austin let the original request by Savannah River for three shipments go through the approval process, after which he forged the SAVE, DSP and ED documents that changed shipping plans for three individual shipments in SSTs with individual guard vans into a convoy of three SSTs and two guard vehicles. Then Orman turned to the hijacking itself.

Orman paced and flashed slides of e-mails that Austin had sent human resources personnel that hired the SST drivers and escort guards. "It appears Austin was able to affect the hiring of six men by forging more documents. All six were hired after Austin came to NNSA, and they all supposedly had security clearances when they applied for the job. Furthermore, all six were on the ill-fated convoy, and all six disappeared with the nuclear material. The three dead men and the one wounded driver, who obviously was also supposed to be dead, were not part of the Austin hiring intervention. It's unclear how Austin managed to forge documents for the six. Our best guess is that he got into the SID computer as Agent Saul previously surmised and gave them new identities and forged security clearances. That makes sense, since Agent Saul verified that he did just that to get his own clearance."

"He not only got those men resumes with security clearances so they could get the truck-driving and guard jobs," Orman said, "he went in later and erased all information on those men, including their badge pictures."

"That's why you couldn't find anything on those people when you asked for their files," Logson said to Saul.

"Did Austin do all that and engineer the cyber attack?" Saul asked.

"He recruited help," Orman said as he flashed a slide of a world map and blinked his laser pointer on Russia, Poland, Italy, and Canada. "The outage was engineered by simultaneous attacks from those four countries starting at 18:57 hours on June 6. We assume that when the outage caused Kirtland to lose contact with the convoy, Austin contacted the convoy via computer messaging and posing as Kirtland, he ordered them onto the deserted road where the hijacking occurred. He could do that from our NNSA computer here at headquarters, since he made sure it was not shut down by the cyber attack."

"Why was Kirtland shut down? Their security should be as good as or better than yours."

"We always thought they were better...at least that's what Austin told us," Orman said. "Kirtland is still trying to determine what happened."

Saul shook his head. "It looks like Austin was one of the few bureaucrats in Washington who knew how to use the computer for something besides generating useless paper." When Sukiomo was the only one who laughed, Saul turned to him and said, "With Austin dead, the bomb makers are without their computer expert. What do they need a computer expert for at this point?"

"Many things," Sukiomo said, "They need to use computerized machining methods on sorid uranium and the prutonium after they convert the prutonium hexafruoride solutions to metal."

"Chemistry of plutonium," Ebert said. "You found out that was another subject Austin got classified documents on. That and A-bomb design."

"Which means they might be out an expert on nuclear chemistry, assuming Austin was going to handle that task," Logson said.

"Ergo, no chance at a bomb," Ebert said.

"Unless they recruit some new experts," Saul said.

"You don't just put an ad in the newspaper or a professional journal for experts to make atomic bombs," Ebert said.

"But they might recruit them directly," Saul said. "Find out who the expert is and buy him, like they bought Austin. We found out he paid about eighty-thousand cash for the Porsche he was driving. If they can't buy the experts, they can go out and kidnap them."

Saul rested his elbows on the table, leaned his head into his hands, and rubbed his eyes. Last night's relaxed feeling had evaporated as the frustrations of the past days and weeks reestablished their grip on his brain. "You know how many computer experts there are in this country? How many chemists there are? Where the hell do you start to look?"

"Wherever it is, you better get there fast," Logson said, smiling. "Because your little Miz Mosely has us all standing around naked waiting to get our balls sliced off."

- - - - -

Back in his cubby-hole office, Saul found a stack of phone messages and a ringing phone, all welcoming him to media land. Myron Shorahm of CBS News wanted to verify the AP story. "Let's meet for lunch and talk about it."

Saul told him to call the Bureau's Public Information Office. For certain, PIO had a story, but not one Shorahm wanted. Saul figured PR flacks in the Bureau PIO and PIOs in government offices all over Washington must be brainstorming like crazy. Since the director constantly solicited "publicity to adequately and fairly portray our organization," maybe he could make this a PR windfall—unless they did not immediately recover the bomb material. Shorahm persisted, but Saul ducked all his questions until the newsman gave up.

He barely dropped the phone before it rang again. "Rick, Senator Hughson here. Tell me about this lost uranium."

"I'll tell you what I told Mosely and what I told Mary: there's nothing to tell."

"You're not talking to some bitch reporter, Rick. You and I are a team. Meet me for lunch in the Senate Dining Room about one."

Who said there was no free lunch? Saul thought as he looked up to see George Spanner materialize in front of his desk. "I can't make it, Senator."

"Listen, Rick, I've made my share of points coming down on

123

government ineptitude. I smell another chance here. One o'clock."

Is this arrogant bastard who we need for president? "Senator, I don't have anything."

"I hope you remember who got you out of Spokane as a favor to your Uncle."

Saul wondered how Hughson pulled that off. Did he know somebody in the personnel department? Or was it somebody higher up in Bureau management?

Hughson went on. "Nate and I have talked big things for you. You're like a son to him. If I have anything to do with it, Nate will be governor soon and, say six-to-eight years from now, you can be in congress. After that, who knows? And Mary's got a great future, a most intelligent young woman."

He remembered Hughson's "bitch reporter" remark and wondered how the great man really saw Mary: his bitch press secretary? The senator's supposed reputation with women was another reason he wanted Mary out of that office. Fortunately, he had not yet mentioned that to her, although the temptation to do so nipped at him every time they argued. Last month he saw the Senator on TV in a press conference with Mary standing behind him, smiling, once leaning over to whisper in his ear.

Saul glanced up at Spanner, who had backed away from the desk and was watching Saul. Thank God Spanner could not hear what Hughson was saying. "I know what you're saying, Senator, but I don't have anything."

"It's your future, Rick. I know you want a lot for yourself and Mary, and so do I."

Saul wondered if he ever did get into politics if the Senator's getting him out of Spokane could be construed as using undue influence. Before that, Uncle Nathan greased the skids to get him into Yale Law School. Then to show that he didn't need his help, Saul rejected Yale and got a scholarship to Notre Dame to be one of their representative Jews. Why? "He wants to be a *smarkasth*. Why else?" Maybe so.

A long silence on Hughson's end, then, "Get back to me when you've got something. It's for your own good."

"Who was that?" Spanner asked when Saul put down the phone.

"Senator Stanley Hughson of Pennsylvania."

"You've hit the big time. You're new to Washington, Rick, so let me warn you. You'll soon discover that every time your name is associated with a case, you'll hear from all kinds of politicians and media people. My advice is to keep your ass clear of politics and the media. Especially politics."

"I didn't…"

The phone interrupted, and before he could answer it, Spanner motioned Saul to follow him to his private office. When they were on their sides of the new desk, Saul reported on his DOE meeting and how they could go about looking for missing chemists and computer experts.

"Let's get to the subject everybody wanted to talk to me about," Spanner said. "Did you tell that Mosely broad anything she's holding back?"

"I didn't say anything beyond telling her I had nothing to say. I asked her how she got my name. She said she got an anonymous phone call."

Spanner fished a sheet of paper from his cluttered desk and waved it at Saul. "MEDIASCAN didn't even have her in the files when her name surfaced, but they remedied that. Our Miz Sheena Mosely is fifty-one years old, your basic left winger, probably with reason. She was born Bernadette Sheena Feeney, March 22, 1959, in Belfast, Ireland, to an IRA radical. Her mother was a Scot, and when her husband died—killed in a shootout with the British army—she moved back to Glasgow with her two youngest children. Our girl was ten at the time. Two years later, her mother married a chief petty officer in our navy who was based at the Holy Loch submarine base. A year later they moved to Norfolk."

As Saul listened, he shuffled through the phone messages he brought along. He was popular with TV correspondents and newspaper reporters: NBC, *New York Times, Newsweek,* and *U. S. News and World Report* were among those represented there. Where was *Time*?

Spanner continued to read from the MEDIASCAN report. "While in high school and then in college at William and Mary, she wrote anti-war articles for the school newspapers, and she got arrested for drug possession with some of her friends. She got probation, but her stepfather cut off her education funds. Two years later she was busted for dealing coke, and she spent eleven months at the Virginia State Prison for Women. Our investigators haven't found out what she did immediately after she got out, but eventually she wound up working for a newspaper in Petersburg, Virginia. From there she worked up to bigger papers in Virginia, eventually working her way into this job with AP. Sometime in there she married George Mosely and divorced him two years later. Mosely owned the Petersburg newspaper.

"MEDIASCAN's run down a couple of anti-U.S. diatribes she published in some small magazines in 2005 to 2008 during the Iraq war, along with a couple on the imperialist U.S. policy in the Middle East and Latin America. She normally works out of AP's Atlanta office, but since she turned up this story, they turned her loose on it."

Saul waved his stack of messages. "AP is not the only organization that's got people on it. You said she was born in Northern Ireland. You think the IRA is involved?"

"The IRA," Spanner said shaking his head. "It seems like I've heard about one hundred other organizations mentioned the last few days." He went on to complain about the daily meetings he'd been attending, where he came in contact with representatives from DOD, DOE, CIA, and the White House. "Do you realize how many damn guys in this town are advisors of some sort or other to someone or other? Everywhere you turn you find college professors, industrial executives, retired generals, and private consultants of one kind or another. At the White House alone, you got guys acting as your congressional advisor, science advisor, national security advisor, advisors for domestic affairs, foreign affairs, military affairs…you name it they've got one or more advisors. Anyway, it seems like one of each type from the White House, Pentagon, CIA, and DOE show up at these meetings. They've all got a theory on what happened and who did it. Once congress finds out, we'll have three times as many people involved and six times as many theories. That will come soon enough.

"Our *experts'* favorite scenario is that Al-Qaeda is behind it to pull the ultimate terrorist act, but then it could be Hamas, Hezbollah, Egyptian Islamic Jihad, and on and on. Instead of taking out an embassy or two, they figure somebody's ripe to take out a city or two. They'll blow it away and then notify some TV or newspaper guy—say Mosely—in some other city, of course, who did it and give some perverted reason why they did it."

Saul nodded. "First, bomb a few embassies, the USS Cole in Yemen, the airliners in Scotland and Toronto, and the big one, the twin towers of the World Trade Center and the Pentagon. Now nuclear bombs in New York and Washington: the inevitable progression."

"That's the favorite theory. I've heard theories on the North Koreans, Chinese, Iranians, disgruntled Russians, Libyans, Pakistanis, Iraqis, Albanians, Venezuelans, Japanese…"

"Japanese?"

"A state department type figures Japan has everything *but* nuclear weapons. Maybe one of the heads of their large industrial concerns wants to regain some of the military glory they had before World War Two. According to her, they might not have much military glory these days, but they got excess dollars. So this Japanese patriot takes some of his company's surplus funds and buys them some atomic bombs. Hell, I don't know what the dumb shit was going on about. I also found out that the

Russians know we lost the material."

"How could they know?"

"We've got CIA agents everywhere making *discreet* inquiries, trying to figure out if maybe somebody actually got the stuff out of the country. You've got to figure what the CIA knows, the Russians soon find out. Then again, you know how open the Russians are supposed to be with us these days. So then we're open with them. For all I know, the Administration might have gone right out and consulted with them, as well as the European Community, the Japanese, the Chinese…"

Spanner spun his chair to the side and stared at the seashore picture on the wall. He sighed. "It's an eye-opener when you rub elbows with this country's movers and shakers. I enlisted in the army right out of high school. From what I saw there, most of the low-level officers and noncoms were some of your everyday Joes, your ordinary and extra-ordinary fuck-ups, bumbling along, barely keeping things running. I figured they were there because that's the only people they could get to stay in the army. I figured those same people would have been at the bottom of the heap outside the military, and most of the high-ranking officers, your colonels and generals, the ones your ordinary nineteen-year-old private didn't come in contact with, they must be the sharp ones who ran the show. I also figured people in high places in government and industry, those that ran the country, were sharp, and that's why things stayed on an even keel."

Spanner spun his chair back around to look at Saul. "I found out a long time ago it isn't that way. The same bumbling assholes and fuck-ups that were sergeants and second lieutenants are now the colonels and generals. They're also the big shots running this country and, I assume, running the world."

He sighed, his face a tired red mask. "Sometimes I think the higher up you get in the government, the worse it gets. These guys get themselves elected to the senate—or to the presidency, for that matter—and they come in here knowing everything there is to know about running the government. They don't want any mere government workers like us messing up their heads with facts. A bunch of them 'high government officials,' as the media call them, just have a meeting and decide what's best for everybody. Most times that's fine, because they're just playing with themselves. But at times like this, the system scares the shit out of me."

- - - - -

Things were looking up at last, Saul thought, as he hustled back into

127

his office late in the afternoon, hoping to catch Spanner before he left for his five o'clock meeting. They had their best live lead yet, thanks to Patricia Hunter, a secretary in Congressman Morgan's office. It turned out Austin fixed her up with a friend of his, a Brian Applenu. In his late twenties or early thirties, Applenu told Hunter he worked as a scientific attaché at the British Embassy. They went out four or five times, and then Applenu went back to Britain. She was waiting for him to return.

The phone rang. It was Mary. "Rick, we need your help. We've got sources at the Pentagon and at DOE, but we need facts."

"A lack of facts never stops anybody in this town, much less your senator."

"The Senator is going to be interviewed by Sheena Mosely, and he will hold a news conference. Our sources gave us information that wasn't in Mosley's piece. We now know there were three trucks in the hijacked convoy. We want you to verify the numbers."

"Talk him out of the interview, Mary. This is not your everyday political bullshit. It's serious. Throw in the typical public reaction whenever they hear the word nuclear, along with the press, and there's no way to gauge what the people who've got the bomb material might do."

"What do you know about the people with the bomb material?"

"Nothing. But you never know how a media story might spook them. Then what?"

"So you're not going to help. Well then, we'll see you in the newspapers."

Chapter Nineteen

"You've got to admit it worked better than we planned," Surling said, pouring coffee for them both. They were on a coffee break in their quarters. "He's making plans for the two of you when the job's finished."

Curt wanted to smack the smug expression off Surling's face. "You said it wouldn't come to sex." What a two weeks, he thought. Kissing Drafton was one thing, but now Drafton showed up in the computer room every night, a blanket stuffed into a large briefcase. First, he convinced Applenu he needed Curt to make some calculations for plutonium-conversion reactions and that they could do it after normal working hours. Then he told whoever was on guard duty they weren't to be disturbed in their "work."

"I can't keep doing it," Curt said. "What do you call it? Whoring?"

When Drafton first told him they were going to meet, he let Surling convince him of the necessity of it, a life-or-death situation. Mentally, he pumped himself up and did it. It's a job, just like becoming a consultant when you really wanted to build robots: you go out and do what's required. Anything the client wanted, you delivered. You whored. In consulting, it was either whore or go back to working for someone else and have still less time for robot design. Necessity, the mother of invention: just like the prostitutes promenading most city streets seeking to feed their kids or their drug habit.

"Whatever it is, the alternative's a lot worse," Surling said.

"But you don't have to do what I'm doing. What's so pathetic is the guy needs me. He was shattered by Derek's death, and I'm his savior. He talks about us being partners for life."

"It'll get us out of here. That's what matters. Hey, have you ever needed anybody?"

Curt considered the question, another of the innumerable personal questions that invaded his mind the past weeks. Before this, he'd wasted little time pondering non-technical questions. He left feelings to Lori.

"I probably haven't needed anyone until now. Ever since my leg was demolished, I've been busy making my own breaks and trying to take care of myself."

One lousy farm accident ruined his basketball career and propelled him toward Miami Beach and Drafton. Of course, the accident gave him his successful career and Lori, when she strolled into his hospital room one afternoon, looked at his leg hoisted up by the rope hanging from the ceiling, and said, "Scott can be such an asshole." Her brother Scott's reckless driving flipped him off the hay truck and shattered his leg and knee.

Now, for the first time, he needed her. He wanted her to be pregnant. This time he would not miss the experience. But would his head hold together until the baby came? Would he be there when the baby came?

Surling stared at his coffee. "That was me once. I had everything and didn't need anybody to get in the way of what I was doing. Then Al died. I lost one of my most important possessions, and up until then I didn't even know it was important."

"Al?"

"My son. After he was killed, everything I was busy with seemed pointless. My life's work was just a big mindfuck boiling down to so much egotistical, self-serving bullshit. I was like Drafton, I needed something… somebody, and there wasn't anybody there. They all left while I was writing my books and papers, studying nuclear chemistry. My daughters were married, and my wife was torn up about Al. She and I had gone our separate ways years before. She had friends to help her get through it. I didn't have anyone, not even her."

Curt stared at Surling, wondering if he should go to him like he went to Drafton. Surling's words echoed Lori's complaints about his too many trips and too many late hours. God, he wanted just one of those nights back that he passed up for a session on the computer.

Surling tried to look Curt in the eye. "Drafton needs you, but *we* need Drafton more."

Curt wondered why he wanted to please Surling. Did he remind him of Dad? When Curt turned five, Dad began molding him into a basketball star. From grade school through college, up to the time of his accident, Dad was his wise coach and cheerleader. The accident devastated Dad, and then transformed him. Would Curt's death have affected him more?

The day after doctors told him Curt's basketball career was over, he showed up at the hospital drunk, ready to sue Lori's father. Two days later, sober, he told Curt they'd prove the doctors wrong. By the time Dad got around to a lawyer, Curt would not go along with the suit, because he and Lori were in love. Ironically, Lori's father didn't want her to have anything to do with Curt either. His reason, according to Lori: "He comes from a family of losers."

Curt wanted to prove to Surling he would do anything to save their lives, but for the first time in ten years of proving he wasn't a loser, his mind was a hopper full of uncertainties and fears that he wanted to empty and forget. "I'm trying, Bob. My wife: what about her? Drafton keeps saying I'm bisexual, like Derek. He keeps saying he loves me."

"It's survival. Your wife will understand."

"Will she? I sure don't."

Surling tried to laugh. "What if it was Erica Drafton, a good-looking blonde? You'd make a token protest and then fuck her. You'd understand that, but your wife would have a harder time."

"You don't understand. How would you get yourself up for a homosexual act? For awhile last night, I thought I wouldn't be able to, you know, get it up." He pictured the scene, recalling Markum's comment about Surling doing it "doggy" style. "I finally decided to let myself go. I just let Drafton take over. But this is what slays me: I think I enjoyed some of it. Will Lori understand that?"

"Maybe that's the best way. Enjoy it. Fantasize about an Erica."

"Don't you have a conscience? A person can't mess with his head and come out okay."

Surling reached out and patted Curt's hand. Curt jerked away.

"It'll be okay. What's more obscene: you giving Drafton a blow job or these guys building atom bombs that blow away a few hundred thousand people? Think about that."

Bob Surling turned professor and explained how he and Drafton had precipitated plutonium oxalate from nitrate solutions, separated the precipitate with a centrifuge, put it in a furnace, and fired it to get plutonium oxide. They put the oxide in a reaction vessel with calcium metal and reduced oxide to plutonium metal.

"Drafton is up there right now taking more oxide out of the furnace. Then we'll make more metal, from which we will make a plutonium casting that you will help them machine. After that, an atom bomb is a slam dunk."

Surling stood to go for more coffee. "Everything worked so well in the process that Applenu had Beecher come in and take before-and-after photos and videos as if they were going to publish the…"

Surling was interrupted by a muffled pop from outside the room. An alarm growled to life in the hall.

"Was that an explosion?" Surling asked, setting down the coffee pot and heading for the door. "It's got to be a radiation alarm in the chemical-processing room. Drafton's up there."

He banged on the door. After a short wait, Markum appeared, but blocked the doorway.

Curt went to stand beside Surling. He sniffed for smoke, hoping. Nothing in the air but the normal mustiness.

Maxwell shouted from somewhere in the other hall, his words indecipherable over the roaring alarm. Applenu and Simmons hustled up the other hall toward the chemical-processing room. Applenu yelled for someone to shut off the alarm. Markum shoved Surling and Curt back into the room and slammed the door in their face.

Like an angry, wounded giant that finally gives up his ghost, the alarm sputtered and died. The door opened, and Markum, his face pale, ordered them out into the ten-foot-wide hall and shoved them toward the intersecting hall that ran the length of the building. To the right, the hall was bounded by the machine room on the left and the wall of their quarters on the right, and it ended at a door with an attached warning:

EMERGENCY EXIT
ALARM SOUNDS WHEN DOOR OPENS

Markum forced them the other way, past the computer room (next to the machine room) and the hot cell on their right, and on the left was the shower room, then a solid metal door marked SUPPLIES, and one with a frosted-glass window marked OFFICE.

Applenu waited in front of the dark-green door at the end of the corridor, the entrance to the chemical-processing and furnace rooms. "It's Drafton," he said, his black eyes like beacons energized by panic, the wild-eyed gaze of a man plunging from a forty story building. "There was a bloody explosion in the furnace room."

Relief flooded Curt's body. With Drafton dead, his nightmare ended. Only the nightmare of Surling's prediction of sure death for the both of them remained.

"How the hell did that happen?" Surling asked.

"Who knows, but what do we do now?"

Simmons and Maxwell stood next to Applenu and kept glancing

down the hall toward the exit.

Surling yanked open the door. "Let's go."

Applenu's head jerked back as if hit by an invisible fist. "No bloody way, mate. All our radioactive materials are in those two rooms. That bloody shit can kill you."

Surling glared at him, started to enter, and then turned to Curt. "Come on." When Curt didn't move, Surling grabbed his arm and jerked him through the door.

To get to the furnace room and Drafton, they had to go through the chemical-processing room. Before that, they had to pass through an airlock, a device that prevented the transfer of radioactive contamination from the chemical-processing room to the corridor.

This airlock was an eight-foot-square room under negative pressure with two air-tight doors, one to the corridor and the other to the chemical-processing room. One wall contained bins with protective suits to wear inside the chemical-processing and furnace rooms whenever a danger of contamination existed. After working in a contaminated area, the suits were disposed of in airtight bins in a roped off area on the other wall.

Surling and Reedan slipped into bright yellow coveralls that fit like a baby's pajamas and covered them from their feet to their necks. Sleeves tied off tight at the wrists. They tied a yellow "cape" around their necks and snugged a yellow hood to their heads. After pulling on long yellow gloves, they donned black breathing masks with a canister filter that protruded from their right cheek like a bulbous growth, giving them the appearance of moon men.

Surling grabbed a gray, lunch-box size instrument with a dial on top and a microphone-shaped probe attached to the box by a three-foot cord and led Curt into the chemical-processing room. Halting just inside the door, Surling reached as far forward as possible with the probe and checked the dial. After another step and another check of the dial, he motioned Curt into the room.

Glass and metal chemical-reaction vessels stood undisturbed on shelves and work benches. Also undisturbed was the atmosphere chamber, its glass windows dark in the center of the room. The long black rubber gloves used to manipulate toxic material inside the chamber hung limp from entry ports, like the hands of strangled occupants unable to escape from within.

In the far corner, unopened shipping containers with their yellow-and-red triangular radioactivity warning labels triggered chills in Curt's spine. Across the room, another air-lock door beckoned, the only barrier between them and Drafton in the furnace room.

When he worked at the Oak Ridge Y-12 plant, Curt rarely strayed from his computer, staying as far as possible from radioactivity. His secret: he was scared of the stuff, and that terror now threatened to paralyze him. He watched Surling, hoping he would turn back. What if the radiation counter didn't work and the room was full of radioactive particles? What if the filters in their masks were not the right ones? Nausea knotted his gut, crowding in beside the fear and uncertainty that seared his insides the past weeks. Applenu wouldn't come in. What did he know?

Surling inched his way toward the bank of instruments on the wall with the airlock door, his probe arm sweeping the air in front of him, scanning for an invisible hazard. After checking the instruments on the wall, he peeled off his mask and motioned for Curt to do the same.

Curt hesitated and then stripped off the mask, allowing the air-conditioned room to cool his sweat-soaked face.

"Nothing got into this room yet," Surling said. He waved at the dials on the wall. "But the activity in the furnace room is ten-thousand times higher than it was this morning. It's the alpha radiation from the plutonium."

Surling studied the gauges, his nose practically scraping the wall as he tried to see without the glasses he couldn't wear under the mask. He flipped a switch on the wall, cleared his throat, and called into the intercom speaker, his voice calm. "Are you there, Eric?"

Like bodies down the escape chute of a crashed plane, Drafton's words hurtled through the wall. "The vacuum furnace exploded open, and the powder just rushed out at me."

"Did you get a critical mass together?" Surling turned to Curt. "A critical mass could set off a miniature atomic explosion."

"No way," Drafton said. "We checked those calculations too many times. The glass viewing port failed. The glass didn't cut me, but plutonium oxide powder flew out at me, all over me and into my face. Bob, I breathed in a lot of fine powder." Drafton paused, his next words squeezed through the wall like tooth paste from an almost empty tube. "I'll...I'll die...from lung cancer."

"You'll be okay, Eric."

Surling turned to Curt. Without glasses, his blue eyes stared. He motioned Curt to the speaker. "Eric, Curt is here."

"Curt. Hey, thanks for coming, buddy."

Curt struggled to erase thoughts that wished Drafton dead. Back to his job, he thought. "We're here to help, Eric."

"Is Brian there?"

Surling winked at Curt and shouldered him away from the speaker. "Applenu's not here. Curt and I will get you out without spreading radioactivity beyond that room."

"Thanks. I'm in the airlock. I put my clothing in the contaminated containers and showered. How long before I...before I die, Bob? I'm only twenty-eight. I've...we've got plans."

Drafton's talk of plans only half registered on Curt's brain, his attention hijacked by radiation-warning signs all around. Got to get out of here, he thought.

"Have you checked yourself with the radiation counters?" Surling asked.

"My body's okay, but when I breathe into the counter, it goes off scale."

"That'll die down." Surling's voice was firm, his unseeing blue eyes staring at Curt. "They can use calcium compounds to remove plutonium from your body."

As Surling droned on about possible treatments, fear liquefied in Curt's spine, its chill coursing into his legs and igniting the shakes. Although he had not spent much time around radioactive materials, he knew the dangers of breathing plutonium-oxide particles. A controversy raged about how large a particle inside the lungs was necessary to cause cancer. The amount argued about was the difference between a microgram and a tenth of a microgram, the difference between a gnat and a gnat's head.

Curt shuffled toward the door to the outside, steadied himself against it, and held his breath, not trusting the counters. For the last several days, his mind had been locked in a battle with itself, trying desperately to eliminate terror that gripped his gut like flesh-eating bacteria: Miami Beach, Beecher's fist in the stomach, Surling's predictions of doom, and lover's trysts with Drafton. Now all that fear focused itself in the yellow-and-red radiation signs that stared from all directions like waiting vultures.

"Bob, let's get out of here."

Ignoring Curt, Surling instructed Drafton to put on clean clothing and come out.

Curt swallowed to force back the nausea and gain control of his voice. "Bob, I've got to get out of here."

"Easy, Curt. We'll get out now."

For Curt, stepping into the hall was like coming down from the thin air of the Himalayas. Although weak from the trip, he could breathe again.

Applenu paced just outside the door. Halfway down the hall, Simmons, Maxwell, and Markum huddled against the wall next to the door marked OFFICE, throwing panicky stares at Reedan and Surling, then down the corridor toward safety.

"Is it bad?" Applenu asked. "Is the project shot?"

Surling's face reddened. "The first thing you've *got* to do is get that young man to a doctor, a specialist that treats radiation poisoning. His lungs need to be flushed—irrigated. Calcium compounds can eliminate radioactive material from his system through the kidneys and bowels. Then he'll..."

"*Okay,*" Applenu said. "I'll take care of it."

Surling called Perk Simmons from down the hall and handed him the radiation counter with instructions to check Drafton and see that he got an emetic and his beard and head shaved. Like a cornered dog about to take a beating, Simmons's eyes, mostly white, darted to Applenu, who nodded his approval to Surling's instructions.

A flustered Drafton staggered from the chemical-processing room. Without any clothes under his floppy white coveralls, his body seemed to have shriveled. His gaze shuttled between Curt, Applenu, and Surling, searching for something. Then he fixed on Simmons, who shuffled toward him with the detector.

Simmons halted at well over arm's length from Drafton, stretched forward, and ran the detector the length of his body. He breathed into the counter, and Simmons's head snapped back like the end of a bullwhip.

"Curt, come here," Drafton called over Simmons's shoulder, his sad brown eyes filled with the longing Curt saw when they were together. Love, maybe?

Curt hesitated. Why wasn't he dead? He sucked a breath to gear his mind back to his job, and he started toward Drafton.

Applenu stepped in front of him. "Stay here." He turned and walked slowly toward Drafton.

"Brian, I want to talk to Curt."

"Later, mate."

Drafton looked at Applenu, his eyes pleading. "Where were you, Brian? Why didn't you come in and get me?"

"We'll talk about that later."

"I'm going to die, aren't I?" Drafton's voice quivered like a faraway radio station. "I'll get lung cancer."

"Take it easy, mate. First, we'll empty your stomach and get rid of any plutonium oxide you might have swallowed. We'll flush your nose. It's a good filter. You'll be okay."

"I want to talk to Curt."

"Later."

Applenu signaled down the hall to Markum to take Curt and Surling to their quarters.

Inside their room, Surling flopped on one end of the couch. "He doesn't have a snowball's chance."

"Lung cancer?"

"He won't live long enough to get lung cancer."

Curt slumped onto the other end of the couch. Now he believed. Deep down, he always knew Surling was right, but he wanted to believe otherwise. Just as they had to sacrifice Drafton for the success of the project, they *had* to kill him and Surling. "I think I'm going to be sick."

Surling ignored him. "He won't live long enough to help us escape. He was our *only* ticket out of here."

Chapter Twenty

When Saul crawled out of bed at 6:30, Mary was already gone, and he remembered she had mentioned a breakfast meeting. On the kitchen counter, he found the *Washington Post* on which Mary had circled a front-page story with a broad black marker, and using the same pen, she wrote, "I'll call you."

ENOUGH WEAPONS-GRADE NUCLEAR MATERIAL STOLEN FOR 6-TO-20 BOMBS—Hijacking of Nuclear Material was Inside Job
Sheena Mosely
Washington (AP)—The AP has learned...

"*Holy Shit,*" he mumbled. "How the hell did she get Austin's name?" And they had a picture of him to boot, the same NNSI badge picture the FBI had.

As if that was not bad enough, Hughson had injected himself onto the scene:

In an interview yesterday in his Capitol Hill office, Pennsylvania Senator Stanley Hughson, the ranking Republican on the Senate Armed Services Committee, discussed the consequences to be expected from this incident. Hughson has been a critic of the Gordono Administration's stance on nuclear weapons, and he pointed out the irony in this "regrettable incident" in that when the cold war ended, the U.S. spent many millions to ensure the former Soviet Union's weapons would not fall into the wrong hands. "While that was going on," he said, "we evidently ignored our own vulnerabilities.

Hughson then turned on the bullshit, talking about North Korea, Iran, Osama Bin Laden and Al Qaeda and how they were all after the bomb. The final paragraph should scare the shit out of a lot of people, Saul thought.

Finally, Hughson recalled a suggestion by Richard L. Garwin, IBM Fellow Emeritus and a former weapons scientist who helped develop the hydrogen bomb. Garwin believes the best way to deliver nuclear weapons is to smuggle them into the enemy's country and place them in the enemy's major cities. Then, in time of war, safe delivery is assured, and it could not be thwarted by a missile defense system. Garwin suggested this scenario during the height of the cold war, suggesting at the time that the U.S. and Russia may have already deployed such weapons. Since the cold war has long passed, Hughson suggested North Korean, Iranian, or Al Qaeda agents may have hijacked the nuclear material as part of a Garwin-type scenario.

- - - - -

Applenu waited in his rental car parked next to an empty phone booth outside The Pantry, a convenience store near the center of town. Whenever he tried to contact Sherbani, he wound up waiting. According to Austin when they set up the system of numbered phone booths, Sherbani could not use cell phones to talk to them—too easily monitored. Once more he glanced down at the passenger seat, where Sheena Mosley's story naming Austin stared back. He wondered what Austin would do in this situation.

He called Sherbani two hours after Drafton dragged his bumbling arse out of the furnace room, but Sherbani wasn't there. Applenu had no idea who he reached at the number with a New York area code. He assumed it was someone from Iran's United Nations delegation. Whoever it was gave him the number for the next phone booth and said Sherbani would call in three hours.

Afterwards, he went back to the factory, and he and Simmons dressed out in protective clothing and surveyed the furnace room. It was bollocked up alright. Fortunately, before he and Hearn started the project, they prepared for every eventuality, including this one, and he knew what to do. To accomplish the decontamination, he got Lormes to assign Markum and Maxwell to him; with their help, he estimated the room could be decontaminated in a couple of days.

The phone rang, and Applenu hustled out of his auto and into the booth. He debated whether to tell Sherbani the accident would make it necessary to call off the project, but he knew Sherbani wouldn't accept that decision. Also, if it was discontinued, he would not get his family out of Iran.

"You wished to talk to me," Sherbani said.

Applenu described the Drafton situation in cryptic words and told how he had Simmons, Markum, and Maxwell working on decontamination. "We need Drafton, because he's the only one besides Surling who knows the techniques for processing the material, but the bloke insists he needs medical treatment to speed removal of ingested material. Bloody Surling fed Drafton a lot of balls that experts can do that."

"So take him to a doctor."

"We can't. It wouldn't be anytime before the Bobbies were involved."

"Let Mr. Lormes find him a doctor. That is why we hired him. He has many resources. Find out what kind of doctor Mr. Drafton expects to see and what such a doctor would do. Then let Mr. Lormes have one of the doctors he has at his disposal carry out the procedure."

"Drafton will know the difference."

"A man weighted down by uncertainty sees only the extended helping hand. By the way, did you see the newspaper stories? Do they not spread havoc in the councils of our adversaries like I said they would? One senator fights another, and the White House is doing everything possible to hush it up. We have a saying: You cannot see your enemy if your friends stand in front of you."

"You should have waited until they got closer to us."

"You produce the product. We will keep them from ever getting close. Are you still getting pictures and videos of everything you do?"

The pictures again, Applenu thought. The last three times they talked, Sherbani asked about the pictures and videos. Why? "Beecher is taking pictures and making videos of everything."

"Good. Those pictures will help agitate our adversaries. The chaos we have sowed up to now is minor compared to what we have in mind."

Applenu took a deep breath. "One more thing," he said. "I want my family out of the country and in Amsterdam by the end of next week, or I walk away from the project."

"I told you that…"

Applenu hung up before Sherbani could finish his reply.

- - - - -

Saul picked up the phone and hoped it wasn't Mary again, or Uncle Nathan, both of whom called earlier to get him to give Senator Hughson something he could use to get into the papers and on TV. Most of the rest of the morning he and Spanner wasted time meeting with Associate Director Herbert Dowel trying to figure out the Mosely leak and how she got Austin's name and picture. They also had to convince Dowel they were not the leak source.

It was Kyle Orman, NNSA's computer expert, who had just returned from Albuquerque. "We found out that the Kirtland computer crash during the hijacking wasn't due to the cyber attack. It was caused by a Trojan horse and a trap door."

Although Saul was familiar with the term, Orman explained that the "Trojan horse" was a program surreptitiously installed on the Kirtland computer sometime before the hijacking. The program was set to cause a computer crash at 18:57 hours on June 6, the same time the world-wide cyber attack began. "The program took control of the computer and kept it off line for two hours, after which the program shut down, and the computer could again be brought back on line."

"Are you saying the computer was programmed by the Trojan horse program to go down at the exact time of the cyber attack and come back on when the attack ended to make it look connected?" Saul asked. "Austin did this? When?"

"Who else could have done it?" Orman asked. He explained how Austin spent a week at Kirtland six weeks before the hijacking. "Ostensibly, he was there to help the Kirtland computer department bring their computer in compliance with his revisions of the overall NNSA security and transportation system. While he was there to help them improve security, he had complete access, and it was simple for him to load the Trojan horse program to subvert security."

"How could he know that far ahead of time that he would want it to shut down on a given date and time?"

"That's where the trap door came in." Orman explained that the trap door allowed unauthorized access to the computer to someone with another computer outside of Kirtland "Once he knew the time and date of the cyber attack, he used the trap door to get into the computer and entered the date and time information into the Trojan horse program."

"The bastard."

"Based on what Austin did at Kirtland, we went through NNSA's computer programs," Orman said, "and we also found a Trojan horse and a trap door program. This Trojan horse was different. It allowed an unauthorized person with another computer outside of NNSA to enter the computer and act as system manager, which would allow him to access passwords and other people's files."

"Why would Austin do that?" Saul asked.

"You tell me. You're the FBI."

Chapter Twenty-One

Immediately after Drafton's accident, Surling and Reedan were confined to their quarters. They waited and talked, ate lunch, and waited some more. Finally, Surling declared cocktail time. After two beers, Surling stretched out on his cot and smoked a cigarette, watching as Reedan went to the refrigerator for his third beer. There was always plenty of beer when they were off work. Beer and magazines of all kinds constituted their recreation, and the evening meal usually included wine. Part of their captor's plan seemed to be "Keep 'em stoned" when not working. More and more, he and Reedan accommodated their plan.

Surling studied his cigarette and wondered why he had begun to smoke again. Then again, why not? He glanced at Reedan, who sat at the table nursing his beer. Maybe the beer would get his mind off Drafton, he thought. That's all he talked about. Surling remembered the punch line from an old joke that summed up Reedan's attitude toward himself: "I built all those bridges, but nobody called me a bridge builder. I sucked one cock, and I'm forever a cocksucker."

To get Reedan thinking about other things, Surling turned the conversation to Reedan's desire to be an MIT professor. "Once, a university like MIT was a good place to be, like when I first started teaching," Surling said. "But the whores fucked it up." He put the dig into Reedan about the bureaucracy now entrenched in academe, as impenetrable as any bureaucracy Reedan had escaped when he left the weapons plant.

It was comprised of technological whores who weren't interested in teaching or research. They obtained science or engineering degrees because those degrees held the promise of good-paying management and government jobs, and they spent their time deluging the scientific staff with paper to "assure that the institution lives up to its commitments."

Most young professors arriving on the scene joined right in.

Reedan protested Surling's gloomy picture, and a lively discussion ensued. Turned out Reedan liked teaching, but for him a MIT professorship was a ticket to launch his career as an entrepreneur. He and another MIT professor had plans for a robot for nano-metallurgical applications. They figured to follow in the footsteps of many others who used MIT as a stepping stone to their own company.

"So you'll build your robots and become rich."

"I'm not sure what I want anymore. Before Drafton, I had time to think, and it dawned on me that one of my goals in everything I've done for the past ten years was to prove to my father I can make a success of something besides basketball and to prove to my father-in-law that I'm not a loser. I figured money was the only thing they'd understand."

Perhaps Reedan was a little more complicated than the whores, Surling thought. The whores eschewed deep thinking, having no thoughts beyond their next promotion. Reedan reminded him more and more of his own son.

"You've probably noticed my limp," Reedan said. "It's the result of an accident on my father-in-law's farm between my sophomore and junior years in college. Before that, my dad and I had our minds set on a pro basketball career. Lori came to see me in the hospital, and against both our dads' wishes, we wound up married. Her dad never thought I was good enough for her. Mine figured I'd never amount to anything other than a basketball player."

"So you're going to become a millionaire to prove both of them wrong?"

"Stupid, isn't it? I can see now what I've been doing wrong, especially with my family. Until Drafton, I was starting to look forward to the new baby—instead of seeing it as an intrusion on my career. I realize now that's how I looked at Beth. Then along came Drafton...and now I can't even sleep anymore."

Surling saw himself forty years earlier, but when it came to his family, he never took the time to think things out. "You'll forget Drafton," he said, "and you'll succeed with your robots. Your dream won't give you time to think about other things. And if you don't fuck it up, you'll have your family to help you."

"Like you've got your family, getting caught in bed with a non-technological whore. You don't seem to enjoy your career, always knocking the university, knocking your fellow scientists."

"Things change when you get older. They shouldn't, but you don't

Ronald Klueh

plan on your son dying before you do either."

He told Reedan about that day he remembered as vividly as he remembered Drafton's pained voice from the furnace room this morning. The call from the detective came to his office at ten-thirty at night; his son's roommate had found his body hanging from a tree in the back yard of their rented house. Before that call, the most anxiety he'd known was when he realized he was going bald. Perhaps a stronger man would have pushed on as before. He couldn't concentrate anymore. After that, he just went through the motions.

"What about your wife?" Reedan asked. "Why go to prostitutes, at eighty-four years old, yet?"

"I'd been too busy for her before that. She raised the kids, although I thought Al and I were getting along better just before he died. After his death, she had her church and her friends. They helped her, but I wasn't into the religion thing. It wasn't prostitutes then, just other women to help me forget."

How many times had he asked himself why he did it? He remembered the first one, Ellie Hendrix, his wife's good friend. Three days after the funeral, she found him at home alone. She burst into tears and grabbed him, pulling her soft and warm body into his. After holding on to him for a minute or more, her lips found his, and the next thing he knew, they were sprawled on the couch, half undressed. It happened several more times before guilt consumed Ellie. By then, he'd discovered that Joan Bracher also wanted to help him forget. Trouble was, he couldn't.

"Why don't you go to a marriage counselor?" Reedan asked. "Or just get a divorce?"

Surling stood and went for a beer. How easy the solution sounded to someone who knew he could do anything, except forget his homosexual acts. He now felt a twinge of remorse over the fact that he suggested to Drafton how he and Reedan could get together: "Just tell Applenu you need Reedan to make some calculations," he had told him, and Applenu bought it. Remorse or not, Drafton would never have helped them if he and Reedan hadn't been intimate. Now Drafton would not be able to help.

"Maybe I should have tried to save you from the Drafton thing. All he probably needed was sex. I could have seduced him, as torn up as he was. God knows, I've developed more lines of bullshit than a Chicago politician. When you're like me, what's the difference between fucking a man or a woman?"

Surling was glad to see Applenu and Lormes arrive with dinner, this one catered by Markum and featuring a New York strip. Just as there was

147

always plenty of beer after work, they always ate well, too.

"We invited ourselves to dinner to discuss the accident," Lormes said as he poured dark-red wine into plastic glasses. He looked at Surling. "Drafton told Brian you think he needs a doctor."

What were these guys after now? Surling wondered.

"He doesn't need just *any* doctor. He needs one that specializes in radiation medicine. Plutonium can be eliminated from the body with the right treatment. The sooner it's eliminated the better chance he's got."

"The longer cancer can be delayed," Applenu said, his mood as dark as his beard. Lormes chewed and listened, the wrinkles around his mouth rolling like constantly shifting sand dunes. "Do we really know if he inhaled that much plutonium oxide?"

"That's why he needs medical help. They can determine how much he ingested." Surling explained urine and feces analyses and chemical treatments to speed elimination through those routes.

"I think we've got someone who can do that," Lormes said to Applenu.

Surling understood: they were picking his brain so they could get a doctor to convince Drafton he was okay. "You'll need a specialist on treating radiation sickness."

Applenu perked up and turned to Lormes. "We'll acquire the expertise." He waved his hand as though his fork were a magic wand. "How do you think we did all this, the whole operation, the hot cell, atmosphere chambers, the ventilation system that kept the radioactivity confined to one room? Government labs don't have better facilities. I took Simmons, Markum, and Maxwell into the furnace room this afternoon to start decontamination. We will have it decontaminated by tomorrow night. If we can do that, we can bloody well acquire the medical knowledge we need for Eric."

Lormes smiled. "That's what I've been telling you, Brian. It's just a minor setback."

Surling sipped wine. "You don't have time to acquire that expertise. Granted, maybe we're talking about the difference between ten and twenty years before cancer strikes. But if he ingested enough plutonium oxide particles, he might not last more than a few weeks."

"Cancer doesn't strike that fast," Applenu said.

"The greatest danger is his immune system. Irradiation knocks the hell out of the white blood cell count. After that, a minor infection could kill him." Surling chewed his steak and watched Applenu and Lormes digest the new information. "Since Drafton has the expertise on the

148

processing equipment, you're going to need him."

The light areas of Applenu's face darkened, as if a shadow had passed over it. He put down his fork.

Lormes wiped his wrinkled mouth with his napkin and turned to Applenu. "I'll make sure Drafton gets out here tomorrow morning. You and Simmons can learn his job. Meantime, I'll find a doctor for him."

Perilous Panacea

Chapter Twenty-Two

Rick Saul sighed, looked around his office, and decided to call it a day. Another long day of digging through mushrooming e-mails from field offices, trying to ferret out information on their quarry. Every day more agents came into SWISILREC and had to be let in on details. Every day he and Spanner prepared reports for Bureau management to pass on to Administration officials at the endless meetings held to "contain" the crisis.

The phone rang.

"Mr. Saul, Sheena Mosely here. *Finally*, I got through to you. How do you like my stories thus far?"

"Like I told you when we met on the street, I've got nothing to say," he said, fingering the report on his desk from the hijacking task force: no progress. They tracked down the two Boston men rumored to have been away for a couple of months in May and June. Both claimed to be in Texas looking for jobs in the booming oil industry.

"I won't need your help for the next story that goes into more detail on the hijacking and who else besides Austin was involved."

To Saul, her British accent seemed stronger on the phone. Was it Scottish or Irish? He wondered as his mind clicked over people who knew details of the thefts. Kraft, bitter with a ruined career, was a possibility, because the picture of Austin was his NNSA badge picture, to which Kraft had access. The only trouble with that was that Mosely was on the story well before they knew about Kraft and Austin. Then again, Saul probably knew only a small percentage of the people who knew the details and could pass on the information as well as the picture.

"Where do you get this information?" he asked. "How did you find out about Austin and get his picture?" He remembered the Trojan horse and trap door in the NNSA's computer. Could that have been used to get information? Who but the late Steve Austin could use the trap door? "Do you have a government source?"

"That's why I called. My source is some guy on the phone who also e-mailed the Austin photo. I know the official government word is that what I wrote is a rumor and no nuclear material was stolen. You and I know better. So I'll make you an offer. If you are willing to admit the investigation is going on, just send somebody to my office and tap my phone for when they call again. That's what you guys do, right? Meantime, I'll forward the e-mail I received with Austin's picture. Maybe you can trace its source"

His computer dinged, notifying him of new e-mail—the forwarded message with picture attached. The originating e-mail address was: info4u@yahoo.com. Saul wondered how Mosely got his e-mail address. Would Spanner, Dowel, and the POC agree to tap her phones, thus admitting there was an ongoing investigation?

"Now that you got what you want, Mr. Saul, tell me about the investigation."

"What investigation?"

"Why play games, Mr. Saul?"

"If there was an investigation, I am sure it would be going great."

Really going great, he thought. After his meeting with Logson, Ebert, and Sukiomo, he and Spanner decided that when the hijackers lost the genius of Austin, they would need to recruit a new computer expert. Because the sign-out record of Austin's foray into DOE's classified library indicated his interest in chemistry of plutonium and uranium, they also needed a chemist. Saul spent time in the NCI computer missing-persons files. He found no missing scientists, although it usually took weeks before missing persons turned up in NCI files.

Once Saul and Spanner agreed on an approach, Spanner had to sell it to the Bureau hierarchy, who had to sell it to the Planning and Operations Committee for SWISILREC at the White House. Approval by POC or not, Spanner figured the course they proposed would be "like trying to find a Winston-Churchill-type statesman in Washington." When POC approved, Saul ordered field offices to determine if any scientists or engineers were missing in their area.

"If the investigation's going so great," Mosely said, "how soon before you make arrests?"

Arrests? How about a suspect, he thought.

"Are you saving your insights for Senator Hughson?" She continued. "Since his press secretary happens to be your wife, it must be easy to get information to him."

152

"I keep my information confidential."

"I guess that's right, since Hughson didn't have anything but your standard senatorial bullshit. What do guys like you see in young blondes? You are older than your wife, aren't you?"

When he didn't answer, she said, "She's like most sweet young things these days, the thick golden hair, dyed of course. She likes to toss it back and run her hand through it whenever she can't think of the right thing to say. They really go for that type on Capitol Hill. She was ever so attentive to the great man during our interview, laughing at all his jokes, like a college sophomore. Is she that way with you?"

What's with this bitch? "She graduated from college."

"I'm sure her college degree and other *credentials* got her that job. But that college-girl act must get old to someone as sophisticated as you, a man with a law degree. What you need is an older woman with sophistication, one with experience."

Saul recalled Spanner saying Mosely was fifty-one. When he met her on Tenth Street, it was too dark to get a good look at her. He'd seen her interviewed on TV, and she looked pretty good there. "What are you proposing?" Was she using her cunt to get the stories she'd been writing?

She laughed. "Me, with an FBI man?" She laughed again. "I'm sure you've seen my record with the law. Lawmen aren't my type, although I'm sure I could show you some things a cute little sophomore never heard of. Then again, she might be getting lessons from some mighty experienced persons. I understand her Senator is quite the cocksman."

Enough of this shit. "I appreciate your call, Miss Mosely, and your offer to have us set up surveillance on your phone."

"I thought maybe we could make a trade."

Saul had an idea. Perhaps they could get her to turn up the identity of Brian Applenu and Eric. Their only leads were Austin's DOE badge picture and the sketches of his two friends that they had not yet released to the public. Applenu was not the science attaché he claimed to be. Nobody at the British Embassy ever heard of him or recognized the sketch, and he was probably not a native of Britain based on Patricia Hunter's description.

Trouble was, the accuracy of the sketches was questionable. Marge Alsop had little recollection of Eric, since she'd only met him once. Although Patricia Hunter wouldn't admit it, she slept with Applenu. Presumably, the sketch made from her description was better. Unfortunately, both men wore beards, and sketches of men with dark beards had a tendency to all look alike.

How to distribute the sketches while maintaining government

secrecy was a problem. Saul and Spanner wanted to release them to the press along with the story of the lost nuclear material. "Not just yet," was the POC's first reaction. Then yesterday, POC decreed that the sketches could be released, but under a cover story that the men were wanted for a brutal double murder. In that form, the best they could expect was for the story to show up on back pages of a few newspapers scattered around the country. How about a leak to Mosely?

"What kind of trade did you have in mind?" Saul asked, glancing up and seeing Jeremy Slaughter in the doorway.

"The way I figure it, in the next few days, you fine upstanding law enforcement officers are going to leak information whenever it benefits you. I'd like to be the person you leak to. I'll show you mine, if you show me yours." She began to laugh.

He decided to check it out with Spanner.

When Saul didn't reply, she said, "I'll take your silence to mean you're thinking about it. I'll keep in touch, okay?"

"Suit yourself," Saul said and hung up. He looked up at Jeremy Slaughter and motioned him to the chair in front of the desk.

"I see where you're a regular item in the newspapers these days," Slaughter said, laughing and plopping his lanky body into the chair. Slaughter was System Administrator for FBI Headquarters computers. He and Saul hit it off because of Saul's electrical engineering and computer background, and they often discussed computer hardware and software.

"I came by to tell you I knew Steve Austin and considered him a friend. He was sharp. He helped me upgrade our computer security. From what I know from friends in the same business Steve and I are in, he was known by a lot of government computer people. Fact is, I met him through a friend who runs the computer complex on Capitol Hill."

"Are you saying Austin had access to our computers here at Headquarters?"

When Slaughter nodded, Saul explained the Trojan horses and trap doors on the Kirtland and NNSA computers. "Could he have done the same thing to our computer?"

Slaughter shrugged. "Maybe. He helped me write code for the security upgrade, so he had access to our machines. But what could he do with it?"

"That's the question I've been asking myself about the trap door on the NNSA computer," Saul said, looking to Slaughter for an answer but getting none. "How about this: he was intending to quit NNSA, maybe just leave when things got hot after the hijacking, and the trap door would allow him to get back into the computer so he could keep track what was happening on the case?"

"Sounds plausible," Slaughter said, standing. "He could get even more information from our computer. I better get back and see if there's a Trojan horse and trap door on ours."

"Do that. However, even if they are there, they aren't important anymore, since the *late* Steve Austin is no longer in the picture."

- - - - -

Despite Applenu's plan, Drafton didn't show up the day after the accident or the next day. According to Applenu, they sent Drafton to a specialist in New York.

Applenu sent Curt to the computer room, while he, Surling, Simmons, Markum, and Maxwell spent the next two days cleaning up the radioactive mess in the furnace room caused by the explosion. On the third day, Applenu and Simmons spent their time with Surling to familiarize themselves with Drafton's job on processing plutonium. According to Surling, Applenu spent his evenings studying Hearn's and Drafton's notes on processing. If Drafton didn't make it back, they would carry on without him.

Left alone in the computer room with Beecher patrolling the hall outside the door, Curt wrote machining programs for plutonium, happy to have the computer to help him forget Drafton. Even with Drafton gone, his mind would not shut down the memory. Trying to forget was like throwing away a boomerang. Regardless of what subject it pursued, it always circled back to Drafton.

Curt was also happy to get away from Surling. Embittered by the loss of their escape ticket, Surling turned to drinking, and it had the same effect liquor had on Dad after Curt's accident. He went from being a decent guy to being your sarcastic buddy.

Sitting behind the computer, Curt combed his brain for escape ideas, searching a mind stuffed with metallurgical facts, computer programming techniques, ideas about artificial intelligence, and robotics. Escape plans defied scientific analysis and led to thoughts of prayer. Maybe Mom's prayers would spring him. At least salvation no longer hinged on homosexual intercourse.

That's what he thought, but five days after the accident, a thin-faced stranger appeared at the door to their quarters. "Are you guys ready to get to work?" He asked.

Curt and Surling stared up from their breakfast, simultaneously recognizing a clean-shaven Drafton, his brown hair shaved down to his white skull, giving him the appearance of a concentration-camp survivor.

Drafton's eyes locked onto Curt.

Chapter Twenty-Three

Brian Applenu jumped when the "Applenu" cell phone chirped, since neither it nor the "Deby" phone rang often. Was it Sherbani or Lormes, the only people with the number? Good news or bad? He pushed back from the desk and fished the phone from his pocket. "Hello."

"How goes it old chap? Long time no talk."

"Ste...Derek? You're...you're...what happened? How can..."

"It is *I*, mate, alive and well. You didn't really believe I could stay in that job after the incident? I had our Mr. Lormes arrange a transition, all part of the detailed plan. Now I am the strategist for our program."

"I thought the original plan had you down here to help manufacture the product."

"We set you up to run that part of the project. We even recruited employees to help, and you're doing a great job. I understand you had some problems recently, but you are handling it. How is our friend doing?"

"He needs specialized medical treatment. He'll be happy to hear you're okay. Maybe you can get him the medical treatment he needs."

"Don't tell him anything about me."

"Why..."

"Just *don't*," he said, his friendly tone of voice transforming to gruff. "The reason I called was that I understand you've made some demands on our boss and given him an ultimatum. He's not too happy about that. We lived up to our bargain on the payments: two two-million payments, and as soon as the first product is machined, there will be a third payment of two-million. When will that occur?"

"In a few weeks, say four-to-six, if my demands are met."

"Great! After that payment, the other four-million will come when you finish the job. You are a rich bloke, mate, and when you finish the project, we'll also deliver your personnel. If we gave you that part now, you might just walk away."

"You and I know that wouldn't be possible, because our bosses would be watching me and my personnel. I know what our bosses can do. I want my personnel transported to Amsterdam within five days, or else I *will* walk. I don't trust them to deliver after the job is finished."

"Your walking won't help your personnel. Besides, we know you cleaned up the mess our friend made, even though you said you wouldn't."

Applenu realized Simmons had reported. "Give me what was promised or else."

"I'll get back to you. Keep up the good work, old chap."

- - - - -

Curt stared at the computer screen: the last program for machining radioactive uranium was finished. When would he and Surling be finished? Once again, everything depended on Drafton—their savior and Curt's demon.

Since Drafton's return a week earlier, everyone threw themselves into their work. Surling complained about Applenu's determination to get all he could from Drafton, for if Drafton went down, Applenu would step in and carry on.

Drafton and Surling produced the first plutonium metal in quantity that was ready to be machined with one of Curt's programs. In addition to plutonium, they transferred several pieces of uranium into the hot cell for machining into a bomb-ready nuclear explosive. They would soon have nuclear explosives for their first bombs.

Atomic bombs were the least of Curt's worries. Immediately after Drafton returned and he and Surling were again alone drinking coffee, the first thing Surling said was: "He's a goner."

"He said he's fine." Drafton told them earlier that the nausea and vomiting he experienced the first few days after the accident had gone away. Two doctors in New York had treated him and couldn't detect any radioactivity.

"They probably had him examined by some doctors they've got on their payroll," Surling said. "The quacks could go to the literature and see what procedures are used. But that's a long shot for your ordinary doctor to carry out effectively."

"In other words they're sacrificing him."

"What else can they do? They can't go to a real specialist and say, 'Look, we've got this guy who inhaled plutonium oxide.'"

Curt tried to ignore the mix of feelings that stirred inside, tried not to think about what he wanted for Drafton.

"He's our only hope," Surling said. "Now we've got to hope he lasts long enough to help us. Another long shot."

Curt sipped his coffee, waiting.

"Did you see how he looked at you? We don't have a choice. You don't have a choice."

- - - - -

Despite hearing Austin's voice last night, Applenu found it difficult to believe he was alive, but he knew he needed to take advantage of this unexpected turn of events. He had made a threat, and now he needed to carry it out.

He got out his laptop and went to his Yahoo e-mail account and composed an e-mail to bigboom20@yahoo.com, the address Austin set up for himself for them to communicate anonymously. In the e-mail, he laid out the terms of his threat. He promised to keep working as usual for the next five days. However, if his parents, sisters, and brother were not in Amsterdam by the end of that time, he would disappear from the project.

After a brief hesitation, he clicked the send button.

- - - - -

"I wish we could go somewhere and really relax," a rail-thin Drafton told Curt as he pulled up his pants. They were in the computer room again, alone, the blankets spread on the floor in front of the computer. When he pulled his shirt over his head, his ribs rumpled his chest like the slats in Beth's doll bed. "It won't be long now, Curt. We'll be finished, and we can really be together."

Curt stepped into his khaki work pants. Together, he thought. He wanted to be together with his daughter, sitting on the edge of her bed reading a bedtime story, a task he resisted in the past. Lori read the stories and took Beth for walks, while he slaved away at his computer. When he tried to conjure up thoughts of him and Lori in bed, he saw only Drafton. Right now he just wanted to return to the safety of his prison. Trouble is, there was another selling job, and he always did his jobs. Always selling, always doing favors.

"You'll make sure Bob and I are set free, won't you, Eric?"

Before Drafton could answer, he coughed, drawn out explosions that erupted from deep inside his chest. He dragged the chair from under the

159

table with the bomb drawings and sat facing Curt. "Why do you keep worrying about that, Curt? You'll be paid and set free. I talked to Brian about it, and he says that's the deal."

"That assumes Applenu is in charge. Lormes and his men with the guns might not go along with him. Will they trust us with what we know?"

Curt's mind reverberated with the turmoil that shattered all possibility of mental peace. Did he want to be free? Forget that and sell, he told himself. Press now or Surling won't forgive him. He tried his businessman's smile. His lover's smile?

"They're going to kill us, Eric. Applenu's a scientist, and he probably wants us to go free. Lormes and his people don't care about Bob and me... or about you, for that matter."

"They will let you go. There will be conditions but..." He clamped his handkerchief to his mouth and roared into it. His face blossomed a bright red as he fought to regain his breath. "When it's over," he wheezed, fighting to stifle a cough, "we'll be together...companions forever."

Forever: Eric's constant refrain. "We'll be together only if you help us escape."

Drafton stood, waited for Curt to stand, and threw his arms around him, hugging Curt, his smooth cheek nuzzling Curt's, reminding him of Lori. They kissed.

Kisses: Curt kissed naturally now, trying not to think. Mind over matter? Don't think, just do the job. Drafton's kisses seemed different since he got back, a different wetness to his mouth.

"Please help us escape, Eric."

"Everything will turn out okay."

All for nothing, he thought; it wouldn't work. The clammy hand that threatened to rip out his guts in Miami Beach again had a firm grip. They held each other until Drafton jerked loose to cough.

- - - - -

After long weeks of waiting and having accepted her pregnancy, Lori Reedan finally discovered blood. Before Beth, there had been a miscarriage, preceded by the same reddish-brown spots on the tissue she now found when she wiped. Not heavy, just enough for another worry. When pregnant with Beth, the spotting became heavy, and the doctor put her on extensive bed rest during her second and third months. Spotting came along with the morning sickness.

More bad news appeared in the *Oak Ridger* and *Knoxville News*

Sentinel, for now she knew what they were mixed up in. Now she could tell the police why Curt was missing. Trouble is, she had no information to help them find Curt, only enough to get them all killed.

On TV, a senator spoke heatedly about a foreign country stealing nuclear material to get an atom bomb. The tall one and the older fat man that threatened her were foreigners; the man on the phone from Miami sounded foreign, too. Maybe that would help the police.

There was *no way* she could go to the police.

- - - - -

Surling studied Drafton out of the corner of his eye, watching him suck the flattened cigarette. No use lying to myself, he thought. The skinny queer looks like shit. Each day his eyes receded further into the hollow sockets of his naked face, like a wild animal backing into a dark hole. And that cough: a death chant.

For the past four evenings, Drafton appeared for dinner, although he hardly ate anything. Afterwards, the three of them sat around the oak table and drank Drafton's wine and smoked his weed. Evidently, Drafton was too tired to go to the computer room with Reedan anymore, which cheered Reedan up, as if anything could cheer him.

Reedan's worries had expanded to include AIDS, even though they wouldn't be around long enough to catch another cold. Now Reedan sat across the table, silently waiting for a chance to inhale all the smoke he possibly could. And he claimed he'd never smoked the shit before.

"I've thought about what you two are worrying about," Drafton said, reaching out to Surling for the cigarette. "Maybe you're right. Maybe Lormes can't turn you loose."

Why did it take young people so long to see the truth? Surling wondered. If only his son Al hadn't acted so rashly. "They'll never be able to trust us," Surling said.

Drafton glanced at Reedan. "There's no way I'm going to be involved with murder. I think Applenu's like me, a scientist who wouldn't even think about such a thing. He's in charge of getting the bombs made, but I'm not sure this is where he wants to be. I think they've got something on him, and he has to be here. I'm also having second thoughts about helping them—whoever them really is. I had the same feeling when Derek first brought it up, but he insisted. He wanted to get rich."

Drafton paused and contemplated the cigarette between the thumb and index finger of his right hand, then quickly brought the balled up handkerchief in his left hand to the front of his face, anticipating another cough. Choking it back, he smiled, his water-filled red eyes threatening to overflow. "A couple of times Derek fantasized about collecting our money and then delivering inactivated bombs. You know, making them turn out to be duds. He might have found a way to do it, too, although sometimes I thought it might be an act to make me feel good about what I was doing."

Drafton sucked on the cigarette. Smoke barely hit his lungs before he twisted sideways and coughed into the handkerchief. Once, twice, and then it caught in a continuous rasping convulsion that shook his entire body. Eyes brimming with tears, he sucked a deep breath to stifle another cough, and then smiled at Reedan and handed him the cigarette. He turned to Surling. "You two helped me when I got into trouble, so now I'll help you."

Surling caught Reedan's victorious glance, as if to say they did it. Maybe now Reedan would be convinced he was justified in his actions. Surling smiled at Drafton and wondered how much time the spindly fairy had before plutonium got him. Could he possibly last long enough?

"We'll need a plan, perhaps…" Drafton's words drowned in the cough that seemed to erupt from a greater depth each night, as if gradually engulfing his skinny body.

"Have you seen a doctor about that cough?" Surling asked.

Before Drafton could answer, another one erupted, his small head of close-cropped hair atop his thin neck waving wildly over the table. Between coughs, he unfolded his handkerchief, and on the next one, a crimson splash shot onto the cloth.

"When did you start spitting blood, for God's sake?" Surling demanded, realizing now it was only a matter of time before their reissued escape ticket would be completely invalidated.

"Yesterday morning," Drafton wheezed. "The doctor said it was a lung infection. I'm taking antibiotics." Drafton's voice ignited another cough, rattling his entire body.

Surling tried to remember what he'd learned years ago about radiation sickness: loss of weight, bleeding from mucous membranes. It was all there. He glanced at Reedan, who held the cigarette poised in front of his face while he watched Drafton spit blood into his handkerchief. Reedan studied the soaked end of the cigarette Drafton had just handed him. After a couple seconds of mental debate, he stuck it into his mouth. Eyes closed, he sucked the smoke into his lungs.

- - - - -

Only after five chirps could Applenu extract himself from his deep sleep to recognize that it was the cell phone and not the alarm clock. Eleven and twelve hour days were exacting a toll. Almost four o'clock, according to the glowing dial, two hours until the alarm.

He blinked himself fully awake before he turned on the light. Although each morning he ached to turn over and go back to sleep, more and more he looked forward to work. It excited him that they were about to complete a job that everyone thought was impossible. Besides that, once finished he could get away from Sherbani, and now Austin again. More importantly, he could help his family if Sherbani lived up to his promise.

Not too long now. They had already machined enough uranium for two bombs. Like an automobile body without a motor is not an automobile, a bomb body and firing mechanism without a nuclear explosive is not an atomic bomb. You mate the body and engine and you've got an auto; once they mated the machined material to the bomb mechanism—only a matter of mechanics—they had a bomb.

At the sound of Hearn's voice, he suspected trouble. "I've got some good news and bad news, old chap. The bad news is in the latest newspaper story. They have your picture and have you connected with the missing material. They also have our sick friend's picture."

Applenu sat up, now wide awake. "How did they get that?"

"They are not really pictures, but sketches, and not very good ones. With the beards, it would be difficult to identify you, even for someone that knew you."

"How did they connect us to this?"

"They have you connected with our late friend, whose picture they've had for some time. They found someone who connected the two of you to our late friend, and the story says you two are 'persons of interest' that the FBI wants to talk to. I think you know who fingered you." Hearn chuckled. "You probably fingered her some."

Patricia Hunter! They obviously traced Austin back to the Congressman's office. Applenu had looked forward to seeing more of her, a lot more, but now he could forget it. Worse than not seeing her, where would he go once it was over? His picture was just the start of what they would discover. Where *could* he go? Iran? No bloody way. And what about his family? How could he help them if he had to go into hiding?

"They have your first and last name, but they only know our sick friend's first name."

"Well, they won't find us, that's for sure."

"Maybe you should shave your beard. Do not give your name unless you have to. And then use another one."

These days he didn't see anyone, except when he went out to eat. He'd been out twice with the bit of stuff he met at the Howard Johnson Lounge, but not in the last few weeks. Too busy. Told her his name was Nigel Williams. American birds liked British names like Colin, Ian, Nigel, Trevor. When they started the project, Austin set him up with other alternate identifications, which he could use as required. The papers were in the knapsack with the cash.

"Keep our sick friend under cover, and get the product finished as fast as possible." Hearn said. "In the meantime, we will give the pursuers something more to think about than looking for two people they only have some rough sketches of."

"You also said you had some good news."

"Check your e-mail for flight information on the arrival of your personnel into Amsterdam. Make arrangements to have someone meet them."

"They are really getting out."

"They will be in Amsterdam on Monday."

As soon as he was off the phone, Applenu went to his laptop and accessed his e-mail. They were to arrive at Amsterdam's Schiphol Airport on Iran Air 659 at 17:20 hours on Monday. He e-mailed the information to BahAmin and told her to put their plan into operation.

- - - - -

Curt was in the computer room with Applenu when Surling burst in. Surling started to speak to Applenu, hesitated in mid sentence when he saw him without his black beard and mustache. He looked ten years younger. "You've got to get Drafton to a doctor," he said, talking faster than usual. "He can barely stand up, and he's spitting blood. Plutonium irradiation affects the immune mechanism, and…"

"It's not plutonium," Applenu said. "It's a lung infection. He saw a local doctor, but we're sending him to New York this afternoon."

Although Curt and Surling had watched Drafton's daily deterioration over the past week, at the words immune mechanism, Curt panicked. "It *is* the plutonium oxide he inhaled, isn't it?"

"Nothing like that," Applenu said. He rubbed a hand over his smooth chin. "It's a respiratory infection. According to the doctor, it could become pneumonia. I'll go send him back to his apartment."

When Applenu left, Surling exploded. "*Goddammit!* Plutonium just got its first victim and ripped up our ticket to freedom. Couple a lung infection with an immune system shot to shit, and he doesn't have a snowball's chance. His white blood count is probably zilch."

"Immune system means AIDS, right?" Curt said. "It's AIDS, isn't it?"

"*What?*" Surling asked, walking over to Curt.

"AIDS. With AIDS they lose their immunity to disease. I'll get it, too. I did all those things for nothing. We're not going to escape...I can't sleep...I can't live with myself, and now I'm going to wind up with AIDS. Even if I get out of here, I'm dead."

"It's the *plutonium*. His immune system is shot, okay, but from *plutonium*. Forget AIDS. Concentrate on finding a new way to save our asses. I was thinking maybe we could get some plutonium oxide and threaten to turn it loose on them. But how do we do that without doing ourselves in?"

"I *know* it's AIDS. We didn't use condoms because Eric said he'd tested safe."

Surling ignored him. "I've thought of rigging the ventilation system—some kind of timed device. We could rig it up so it would push contaminated air at them, but they'd just evacuate the building and wait us out."

It was Surling's fault, Curt thought. "I can't blame Eric. You shouldn't have made me do it. Maybe I deserve AIDS for what I did."

"*Goddammit*, Curt, snap out of it. It was either them or us. And that skinny faggot was one of *them*. Forget AIDS."

Curt stared at the monitor. No answers there.

They were jerked from their thoughts by yelling in the hall. The door banged open, and Markum ordered them out.

At the end of the hall outside the chemical-processing room, Applenu and Simmons were crouched down and bent over something on the floor. A coughing Drafton lay sprawled on his back, a bunched-up white lab coat under his head.

As Curt and Surling approached, Applenu looked up. "He just keeled over. Either of you know what to do?"

"Get him to a hospital," Surling said.

Applenu and Simmons stood up. "He keeps asking for Reedan," Applenu said, rubbing his bare face.

Drafton saw Curt and mumbled something that degenerated into an indecipherable wheeze. Curt inched toward Drafton as Simmons backed away rapidly, obviously glad to escape out of coughing range.

Curt squatted down and saw his future self reflected on Drafton's face, blood-laced saliva seeping from the corner of his mouth, a trickle of blood oozing from one nostril. His red, watery eyes beckoned Curt forward. Mouth quivering, his first word triggered a cough that rattled through his body in spasms, stiffening it until it seemed about to levitate above the gray-tiled floor. When the cough eased, his eyes brimmed with tears. With a blood-soaked handkerchief he swiped weakly at drool dribbling from his mouth, but he succeeded only in smearing the pink saliva across his chin.

Curt started to grab the handkerchief, but held back. He wasn't about to touch that AIDS-contaminated rag. He wanted to run, his body shaking worse than the day Drafton got his radiation shower.

"Curt," Drafton gasped, "I'm sorry I let you down." He paused to force in a breath, his eyes rolling back to locate Applenu, who had stepped back to talk to Surling.

Curt leaned in closer, his ear six inches from Drafton's mouth, Drafton's damp breath warm on the side of his face.

Drafton squeezed back a cough. "You and Bob may be right. They might not turn you loose…I…I'm sorry I can't help." He began to cough.

Curt stared at Drafton and remembered the purple-blue face of the drowned man he saw on the banks of the Mississippi River when he was eleven, his only other direct encounter with death. Tentatively, he touched the back of Drafton's hand. "You'll be back, Eric."

Drafton's head rolled side-to-side on the lab coat as he fought back a cough and tried to breathe. "I always worried about that bomb. The prototypes they built…that they've still got in this country." He stifled another cough, and when he saw Applenu move in behind Curt, he tried to talk fast. "Thanks for everything, Curt. I…I love you."

Curt rubbed Drafton's hand and stared at the empty husk that fought to remain on the floor when he coughed. When would this end? How do you respond to those words? AIDS or not, he and Surling used him, and *he* apologized for not helping *them*.

Out of the corner of his eye, Curt saw Markum and Maxwell down the hall, watching, leering smiles on their lips. No way to think straight. He asked for AIDS when he decided to do what Surling asked.

Curt started to stand, but instead reached inside himself and pulled out words that he never seemed able to use the way they should be used. Lori accused him of it once during an argument, and although he denied it and said he could use them at the right time, she was right. He couldn't use them with his parents and hardly ever used them with Lori, even though he sometimes felt it. No, not now. This was not the time. He squeezed Drafton's sweaty hand. "I love you, Eric," he whispered.

Drafton's smile barely lit his face before a new spasm rumbled through his body and shook it away.

Curt stood and looked at Applenu. "You've got to get him to a hospital."

Applenu motioned to Maxwell and Simmons. "Take him to the car."

Each man grabbed an end of the limp body, and when the middle sagged between them like a hammock, Markum grabbed the waist. Surling hustled to the other side to help. As they trudged down the hall, Surling glanced over his shoulder at Applenu. He sidled right toward the door marked OFFICE.

Markum motioned with his head for Applenu to grab Drafton. With his hands free, Markum reached into his jacket and came out with a gun. "Hold it right there, Surling."

Surling stopped.

"Now, get back here."

Like members of a funeral procession, Curt, Surling, and Markum trailed the three men and their burden toward the door marked OFFICE: another blocked escape route.

Chapter Twenty-Four

Surling stopped pacing and stared through the thick lead-glass window of the hot cell, trying to ignore the ache in his head from too many beers the previous night. The headache reminded him why he didn't turn to alcohol after Al died.

Surling, Simmons, and Reedan waited in the hot-cell room for Applenu. Simmons perched on a high stool next to Surling, silently staring into the cell. To their right, Reedan sat hunched over the computer keyboard, diddling with the machine while he studied the monitor.

Since they carted Drafton away the previous day, nothing had been said about him. Surling knew why but asked anyway. "Did you get Drafton to that New York doctor?"

Simmons glanced at Surling, and then stared back into the hot cell. "He died at the apartment two hours after he left here."

"*Died*," Reedan said.

Surling watched Reedan attack the keyboard with violent keystrokes, as if trying to enter his thoughts into the computer in the next room and merge his brain with it. Whenever one of the keyboards was around, Reedan slipped behind it. Evidently, the computer did his thinking, and he'd probably let the computer do his grieving, although grieving was not what Surling called it. How do you grieve for a queer who sold his ass to help a bunch of assholes build an atomic bomb? Then again, they would be grieving for themselves soon enough.

After they carted Drafton off, Reedan crumbled like a dead cactus in the Arizona desert, just because Drafton told him he loved him. Surling couldn't figure out whether Reedan was more torn up because of what Drafton said or because he reciprocated. Said he felt obligated. Probably wonders if he meant the words, probably wonders if he might be queer. Reedan actually expressed sorrow for how they—he and Surling—used

169

Drafton. *Used* him? Misused him, according to Reedan. That, and AIDS: Reedan was convinced he would get AIDS.

Dumb fuck, Surling thought, as he watched Reedan type. What about their own deaths, which now loomed as inevitable as this bomb? What did his computer say about that?

Reedan stared at the output on the monitor, probably using the data to scare away new visions of death before they got their claws into his brain. Death's sting, Surling thought. For an eighty-four-year-old man, death should probably always loom in the mind, but until he wound up in this hell hole, it had not dogged him. Over the last few days though, it had clung to his entire being like a constant ache. At eighty-four, maybe he should be thankful for being around this long, still able to get it up without the Viagra crap. But he was still not ready to accept the end of it all.

Surling turned to Simmons, who continued to stare into the cell, his crinkled steel-gray head shaking ever so slightly, like a leaf in a negligible breeze. "Why didn't you take Drafton to a hospital?"

"We couldn't."

"So you killed him," Reedan said, then loudly smashed three keys and watched the screen fill with columns of numbers and letters.

Reedan and computers, Surling thought. According to Reedan, computers could do anything and everything; you just had to figure out how to use them. Earlier in his rambling on about Drafton and AIDS, he said that the computer would get them out of this mess.

"How?" Surling had asked.

"I'm working on a plan."

Maybe he could blow it like he blew Drafton, Surling thought, because it was obviously a sexual object for him. Given his obsession with the computer, he had to be completely fucked up sexually even before he ran into Drafton.

Simmons tried to get Reedan's attention, speaking down at him. "He *died*. It was an accident. I liked the boy. We all did."

When Reedan didn't look up, Simmons turned to Surling. "They were going to take him back to New York. Nobody thought he would go that fast. He choked to death. You saw how he was coughing. He just turned blue and stopped breathing."

Surling ignored Simmons. "Where the hell's Applenu?" He growled as he studied the lathe, milling machine, and grinder inside the hot cell. Hooked to the computer next door, the machines in the cell were operated through the computer, just like the ones in the machine room where the non-radioactive material was processed. By machining plutonium and uranium in the isolation of the hot cell, all the excess radioactive "hot" material removed from the bomb parts would remain isolated in the cell and would not contaminate the rest of the building.

Surling grabbed two hot-cell controls on the ends of the metal arms that dangled from the ceiling like jointed metal grapevines. The feel of the cold steel manipulators in his hands revived memories of how he once maneuvered such controls like a pro, memories of long hours struggling to bring forth a bomb to save the world from Hitler. Memories of youth. Build a bigger and better bomb and save the world. They succeeded, at least in building a bigger and better bomb that blew the hell out of a Japanese city.

He glanced around the inside of the hot cell, so different from those jury-rigged boxes at Los Alamos in 1944, and so much safer. This cell consisted of a ten-by-twenty-foot room with lead-lined, concrete-and-steel walls several-feet thick that protected operators from high-energy radiation that can penetrate normal thicknesses of concrete and steel.

Surling, Reedan, and Simmons—the operators—were in a six-foot-wide room that ran the twenty-foot length of the cell. Through the three-foot-thick lead-glass window, Surling spotted the dummy steel specimen that simulated the plutonium that would eventually be transferred from the furnace room next door into the cell. It would then be put into the lathe, and the computer would take over. Today, the dummy specimen would be machined exactly like the plutonium would be machined later. Applenu insisted on a trial run for everything.

Surling turned his attention to a crescent wrench that lay on the work bench in the front part of the cell. He pulled and shoved on the control in his right hand, and a three-fingered metal hand on the end of a metal arm inside the cell dropped from the ceiling and grabbed the wrench. Another flick of the wrist, and the hand behind the window quickly traversed half the distance of the chamber to the lathe, where it fit the wrench to a nut.

While he worked the controls, he mulled over the possibility of using Simmons to escape. "Now that you've gotten rid of Drafton, how do you feel about killing us?" he asked as he shoved his metal-extended left arm toward the floor. On the other side of the window, a second arm descended from the ceiling toward the wrench. Surling twisted his hand, and motors in the controls whirred. Inside, the second metal hand adjusted the wrench. With a flick of his right hand and more whirring motors, the first hand fit the wrench to the nut. A twist of the wrist outside resulted in a twist of the wrench inside.

Simmons chuckled. "Nobody's going to kill you."

171

"You believe that? Drafton didn't."

"Sure, I believe it. If you guys are smart and don't go to the cops... you will be...let go."

Surling twisted the metal hands and released the wrench from the nut and lifted it into the air. He turned to Simmons, his hands gripping the controls. "Maybe they won't need you either when they get their bomb. Maybe you'll know too much, too."

Simmons's eyes registered momentary panic before he could force a loud laugh.

With a wide grin, Surling's hands dropped from the controls to his sides. Behind the massive window, the wrench tumbled silently to the workbench, like a TV picture without sound.

"We all fall down," he said. "Just like Drafton."

- - - - -

Although his mind was distracted by the latest Mosely article, Rick Saul scanned the numerous e-mails with field-office reports on SWISILREC, waiting for George Spanner to return from his meeting in the Director's office.

Spanner arrived and flopped into the chair next to Rick's desk, happy to escape his office phone. "I just came from the Director's office, and he and Dowel are highly pissed because the White House is highly pissed about Hughson and Mosely. They figure either you or I leaked Austin's picture and the sketches of Applenu and Drafton."

After talking to Mosely previously, Saul suggested leaking the photos to Spanner, who liked the idea. He presented it to the oversight committee, who rejected it. "Did you tell them we didn't know anything about it?" Saul asked.

"I told them we didn't give hard copies *or* digital copies to anyone, which sealed his case that the leak had to come from you or me. So how did she get them?"

"Did you check your e-mail recently?" Saul asked as he tapped keys on his keyboard and pointed Spanner to the screen. "Mosely forwarded this e-mail with the sketches attached. It's from the same address as the previous one she sent with Austin's picture. This one has a message explaining the sketches and is signed An Inquisitive Friend."

Jeremy Slaughter appeared in the doorway and excused the interruption. "I've got some news on the Trojan Horse and trap door we talked about," he said. "We found the programs on our computer. I checked with Orman at NNSA, and ours are identical to those they attributed to Austin. He obviously put it on ours when he helped us with security, and he probably used the program to monitor e-mails on SWISLREC before he cashed out. What is ironic is that the Trojan horse program is Carnivore."

"The sniffing program the Bureau uses to monitor e-mails on ISPs?" Spanner asked.

"That's right. But instead of installing a removable disk on the computer like the Bureau does when they get a court order to monitor someone's e-mails, he stored e-mails in a file on our computer. Then he used the trap door to download the file and learn what is going on in the case."

"So now we know where the leak is," Saul said. "Our inquisitive friend knows how to get into our computer."

"But who is it?" Spanner asked, motioning Slaughter to the other chair in the cubicle. "We agreed Austin put the Trojan horse on the NNSA computer and planned to use the trap door to follow what was going on at NNSA after he left. But if he's dead, he can't use the trap door."

"That leaves three possibilities," Saul said. "He either gave the information to somebody else, or the trap door is not the source of the leak. The only other possibility is that Austin isn't dead."

"That's it," Spanner said. "It was part of his elaborate plan, which included him faking his death with a pile of burned bones. That smart, sleazy son of a bitch is still alive and working the rest of his plan, which is to keep us jumping through hoops."

"So he did us a favor, since we wanted to release the photos of Brian Applenu and Eric," Saul said.

"But he accomplished his goal of stirring things up here, at DOD, DOE, and the White House, and he didn't lose anything because he knew we would eventually release the pictures. He did give us one other thing: we now know he's alive."

"There are still the other two possibilities, and we've got a pile of Austin's bones in the D.C. morgue," Saul said, turning to Slaughter. "Did you trash the file of e-mails the Trojan horse program uses?"

"Not yet. We wanted to investigate the details of how it was used. We checked when it was last accessed, and that was at 05:35 this morning. So it probably won't be accessed again today."

"Good. I suggest we keep the program in place for now, and we monitor the file to make sure there isn't anything in there we don't want to get out. In addition, I will send an e-mail to George containing false information and see if it shows up in a Mosely article. That will confirm how the information is getting out."

Spanner agreed, and they composed a message from Saul to Spanner describing how the FBI arrested two men in New York City that were alleged to be involved in the hijacking. After they finished, Spanner instructed Slaughter to send Saul all the messages in the file that had not been seen by the intruder. Slaughter agreed to set up a file to receive all field-office reports without them being sniffed by the Trojan horse program. From now on, the Trojan horse file would only contain innocuous field-office e-mails prepared to deceive the intruder.

"Can you set a trap for whoever enters through the trap door and trace them back to the computer they are using?" Spanner asked Slaughter.

"We can try, but they probably go through some other computers to make tracing them impossible."

"We also need to send somebody to tap Mosely's phones and try to trace the source of the e-mails, although that's probably a lost cause. When are our people going to admit the whole story and quit hiding behind national security?" Saul asked.

Spanner laughed. "The Director says they want to keep politics out of SWISILREC, and that's impossible if the press and congress is involved. Even so, he's having Dowel form a committee with me and the PIO to plot ways the Bureau can enhance its image when the Administration does go public. Or when we capture the people who stole the material, whichever comes first."

After Slaughter left, Saul turned to the computer and pointed to an e-mail that had come in just before Spanner arrived. "We might be making some progress. This e-mail is from Phoenix in response to our search for missing chemists and computer experts. The Tempe police have an unofficial report from Arizona State University of a possible missing chemistry professor."

"Unofficial? Possibly missing?"

"Seems this Professor Surling had a consulting assignment in Philadelphia over a month ago, and the university hasn't heard from him since. He was supposed to be gone a week. His wife says he's not missing, because he called three times from Philadelphia to say the consulting job was extended indefinitely and not to worry. She didn't know exactly where in Philadelphia he was. He told her it was a secret project."

"So why are the university people worried?"

"Surling's got five graduate students, and he's never gone off for more than a week without leaving instructions for them. Even when he left instructions, he'd check back frequently to keep updated. This time, he hasn't called them once."

"Did they try to call him on his cell phone?"

"They tried, but his cell must be turned off."

"Think he's our man? Or is it another false alarm, like that missing computer expert we turned up last week? Must be as many kooks in colleges as there are working for the government," Spanner said, referring to the Northwestern University professor who'd been reported missing. After checking up on him, it turned out he'd been reported missing twice before. Seems he had a habit of taking off for parts unknown without telling anyone, like the time he took a three-week train trip across Canada to Hudson Bay.

"I'll have the Philadelphia office check on what happened to him up there," Saul said. "If he's missing, he's been kidnapped. If he was in on it, he'd have made sure nobody reported him to the police."

"Now all we need is a missing computer expert, although maybe they don't need one if Austin's alive."

"Sukiomo thought the most likely place they'd need a computer expert at this stage was for machining the nuclear material. Although Austin was a computer expert, we should still assume he was not an expert in computer-controlled machining." Saul outlined how they were tracking down experts on computer-controlled machining. They started with government facilities that machined radioactive material to find out who their experts were and determine their present status. Once those government possibilities were exhausted, they would expand the search to other industries.

Spanner stood. "This Surling thing might mean we've lucked out. If they had to kidnap somebody, they couldn't go right out and make a bomb. The longer it takes to make a bomb, the better chance we've got to catch them before they can do whatever they intend to do with it."

- - - - -

Applenu hunched himself into the small phone compartment, his back to the cramped lobby of the hotel as he listened to Sherbani congratulate himself on getting Applenu's family out of Iran as promised. "They are on a plane to Amsterdam at this very moment. Just remember, there will be a place for all of you in your homeland when this is over. You will be a hero, my friend. A man with friends always has a refuge."

Not my homeland, Applenu thought.

"One other thing," Sherbani said, "we deposited the two-million in your account, since you reached the third goal, completing the first unit of our product. We always live up to our promises. Is there more progress to report?"

"Five units are complete," Applenu said. He explained the progress as he contemplated his money, now six-million dollars. He could disappear, and then reappear with another new name, in Paris say, or Berlin, Munich, Tokyo or Seoul, or South America—a big world to disappear into, but he still hoped to stay in the U.S. as Dr. Ian Deby. He told Sherbani they would ship the eight units in two days. He knew he had no other choice.

Sherbani changed the subject and talked obscurely about how they would soon give the government some false leads, referring obliquely to Hearn's strategy. "We have a saying in our country: Set your enemy on the path of the wind, and you will be safe in your home. So, my friend, everything will work out."

Everything worked out for Drafton, too, Applenu thought. At least Drafton didn't have to worry about his picture in the paper or worry about what to do when they finished the project. Although he and Drafton had nothing else in common, he liked him, and sure didn't want to see him peg out the way he did, even if his head was cocked a little off center. That business with Reedan and Surling toward the end could have caused trouble. Drafton asked twice what the plans were for the two of them. Applenu told him they'd be turned loose when it was over. That's what he'd do, if it was his decision. He would talk to Lormes about it.

Other problems to worry about now, he thought, waiting for Sherbani to conclude his discussion on diversionary tactics to keep the FBI off balance. Sherbani finished, saying, "We will persevere. As the Koran says, 'But they who believe, and who fly their country, and fight in the cause of Allah, may hope for Allah's mercy: and Allah is gracious, merciful.' Always remember, that is our strength."

Applenu waited. His gut burned with the annoying feeling of being in a desperate race, but the finish line had been moved and he had no idea to where. How could he ever hope to win?

"We need to make a video to go along with the photos you've been collecting," Sherbani said. "We will use them in the diversionary scheme to keep our pursuers chasing the wind while you finish the rest of the product."

"Why do we need that now?"

"Our strategist will be in contact with you to talk about it. One more thing, my friend. Do not try to take the money and run out on your commitment now that your family is out of Iran. We would track you down and deal with you…and with your family."

Chapter Twenty-Five

Applenu said goodbye to his mother and father, shoved the cloned cell phone into his pocket, and sat back and smiled. They talked for over an hour, and his father could not stop thanking him for what he had done for the family. His father had been overwhelmed to find his brother Behrouz waiting for them at the airport.

In Applenu's plan, Uncle Behrouz could be there because Sherbani and his people knew about him. By design, BahAmin was not at the airport to meet them, although she and her husband, Malcolm Wilson, were waiting for them at the Kinkerstraat apartment. They filled his parents in on the elaborate disappearance plan that Applenu, BahAmin, and Uncle Behrouz had put together. The plan was not mentioned in the phone conversation.

Suffused with the happiness and satisfaction for having been able to play the good son, Applenu detected a sadness lurking in this happy ending. How, he wondered, would he ever be able to go to Europe and see them? Would that require him to also disappear?

- - - - -

"Ricky, *boychick*, my nephew the FBI agent, what can I say?" Uncle Nathan crooned on the other end of the phone. "Your father, may he rest in peace, he would be proud of you for what you have accomplished, and for your great future. Now, haven't I treated you like the son I never had? And after all I've done for you, the time has come for me to ask for your help. This thing is getting hotter, and our Senator is completely frozen out. He needs the information you're sitting on."

Saul knew he owed much to Uncle Nate, but not this. Spanner's news about the Administration being upset about Hughson's statements to the press and TV made it imperative that Saul didn't give them anything. If they were looking into how Hughson got his information, they would soon enough find out that Mary worked for the Senator. He needed to be extra clean.

Saul sipped his beer and batted down Nate's requests as soon as he set them up. He had beaten Mary home and was waiting for her so they could go out to eat. He heard Bob Dylan singing from the living room:

There must be some way out of here,
Said the joker to the thief.
There's too much confusion,
I can't get no relief.

He began playing the CDs of Dylan's old songs two weeks ago when his disjointed memories of some of the bizarre lyrics began to make more sense than the real life craziness crashing around him.

"I can't give it to him, Uncle Nathan," Saul said again. "Eventually, somebody would figure out where it came from. If I wasn't directly involved, then…"

"So now he's directly involved? A few days ago, he didn't know from nothing about the case. Hey, the government's got more leaks than there are urinals in the Pentagon. So why should they blame you? Better you should take a chance and give the Senator something he can use. Go talk to him. That way the rest of us can relax a little bit."

Directly involved, Saul thought. And for sure, he had information the Senator could use. They now had an Austin pseudonym, and they also knew Austin was a pseudonym; they were also more convinced than ever that Austin was still alive. Since they left the trap door open for the present and filled it with bogus information, someone had used it twice. They were trying to track down the computer using the trap door, but that did not appear possible. One time they traced the origin of the computer accessing the file to Italy, and another time the computer was in Russia. They concluded that Austin or whoever was at the other end was going through several computers to keep from being traced. They were now waiting to see if the false information of the arrests in New York would be published by Mosely, assuming Austin was feeding her the information she published.

Did he have information the Senator could use? Earlier today, he and an expert on ethnicity and craniofacial identification had interviewed Patricia Hunter in Congressman Morgan's office to try to narrow down the nationality of the British-accented dark-complected Brian Applenu she met through Austin. Based on her viewing of about 200 facial sketches and photographs, the origin of Mr. Applenu's ethnicity was narrowed down to the countries of Azerbaijan, Turkmenistan, Uzbekistan, and Iran, which in Saul and Spanner's opinion meant Iran was behind it all.

Mary walked in, decked out in a silky white dress covered with a red floral design and red shoes to match the flowers. At least the dress was long and full. Saul smiled and waved at her, expecting her to come over and kiss him, since she had not seen him for two days. She ignored him and headed toward the bedroom. Oh, shit, he thought. Now what?

"Relaxation I could use," Saul said to Uncle Nathan.

"Like you think I want to make like an *utz*. It's politics."

"And you want me to get into politics."

"Mainly, it's okay. Hey, a *mentch* Hughson's not. But we're on the same side...at least most of the time."

When he finally got Uncle Nathan off the phone, he turned up the stereo and headed for the bedroom. Dylan sang about Frankie Lee and Judas Priest.

Mary lay across the bottom of the bed, staring at the ceiling, the end of the spread doubled over her, and her dress draped across a chair.

He crossed the room and bent down to kiss her. She turned away.

"Was that Uncle Nathan? Are you going to talk to the Senator?"

"Let's forget work."

"That's fine for you to say, you bastard! You know how much shit I had to take the last few days because of your Sheena Mosely's latest story, the one *you* gave her?"

In the other room, one Dylan song ended and a new one began. Dylan sang:

When your mother sends back all your invitations...

"Who says we gave it to her?"

"Just forget it, Rick." She pointed toward the living room. "I see you're regressing to your drug music again. Did you go back to smoking dope, too?"

His face burned, but he choked back his anger. It still pissed him off that somehow she had associated Dylan with drugs well before he ever mentioned discovering Dylan during a summer of smoking dope and listening to his records. She didn't know anything about Dylan, and she knew less back then. Nevertheless, she called it drug music on one of their first dates when he played a B.D. tape on his car stereo. She said it jokingly that time. Thank God, he never mentioned Diane Fosbury, who had introduced him to Dylan. "Where do you want to go for dinner?" he asked.

"Leave me alone."

"You have a nice lunch with one of the boys from the office, so you don't need to eat with your husband? Your husband's okay, as long as he supplies information for the office, is that it? If you don't get any information from me, maybe the boys will shun you, is that what's the matter with you? Will it cause a short circuit in the old career trajectory?"

"Fuck you!"

"I like it when you use government talk."

The phone rang in the other room.

She stared directly at him, her blue eyes dark with anger. "Rick...Oh, the hell with it! Answer the goddamn phone."

He didn't bother to turn the music down this time, he just sang along:

Sweet Melinda,
The peasants call her the goddess of gloom.
She speaks good English,
And she invites you up to her room.
And you're so kind and careful,
Not to go to her too soon,
And she takes your voice
And leaves you howling at the moon.

"Hello, Mr. Saul," Sheena Mosely said, her British accent in full bloom. She paused a moment, then said, "Hey, did the big FBI man find Robert Zimmerman of Hibbing, Minnesota, who was missing and presumed renamed?"

"You a Dylan fan?"

"Sonny, I was around when he first sang about a rolling stone, about the times they are a-changin', back when you were still in diapers—or more likely not even born. Back then, we sat around and drank wine, blew smoke, and listened to Baez and Dylan and thought we'd change the world by singing songs and talking about peace and justice. Now we know the world isn't changed by long hair, love-ins, and peace signs."

"You don't think so?" Over the years he hadn't met many fans besides Diane Fosbury. Although Dylan was still around, most people Saul's age and younger never heard of him.

"That world Dylan sang about back then hasn't changed for the better for many people in places like Central America, Northern Ireland, and the Middle East, but him and the other people from back then don't give a shit anymore. They turned into the over-thirty people they didn't trust."

"And you haven't changed? You're still out to reform the world?"

"No, not really. Maybe I'm just bitter because I sold out cheap. Remember I told you the last time you need to be exposed to a *mature* woman. Maybe we could get together and listen to Mr. Zimmerman. Then, if you could momentarily forget that you're the big FBI man, we could do some smoke."

Saul's thoughts wandered back to that summer job in Silicon Valley after his junior year; his memories were mainly on the after-work activities: Dylan, dope, and Diane Fosbury's hands and mouth all over his body, and his hands and mouth all over hers. Did Sheena Mosely have good hands and mouth? He wondered what happened to Diane, a *mature* woman way back then, five years older than him.

The music clicked off in the living room, and Mary appeared in the doorway in black bikini panties and bra. Saul clamped his hand over the receiver, waiting for her to say something. She just stood there.

"You didn't have to turn it off on my account, love," Mosely said. "I called to see if we could maybe exchange information. I received more from my source."

"What did he say?"

"You know, if the government admitted they lost the material, you could have tapped my phones, and you would already have the information. Can we make a trade?"

Saul looked at Mary, posing, her bare legs at just the right angle.

"What did he say?"

"He said they have a prototype bomb they'd like the government's bomb experts to see. They figure if the government sees what they've got, then the government will know they're serious when they get around to making their demands."

"You mean he isn't a government informant? You've been in touch with the people who've got the material? Where and when are they going to give us this demonstration?"

"He mentioned Saint Louis or Indianapolis, or a city like that. You can read all of this in your morning paper."

After they discussed Saint Louis and Indianapolis some more, he remembered Mary and glanced back at her. She stared back at him, a slight smile on her face.

"Now, what do you have for me?" Mosely asked.

He rummaged his brain for something Mosely would find out soon enough anyway, assuming the White House went ahead as planned. "We found out Dr. Steve Austin also goes by the name of Derek Hearn."

Mary's smile disappeared, and her face reddened.

They had a call from a Philip Jarome who ran a computer refurbishing shop in Newark, New Jersey, and Saul had just returned from spending almost two days there. Jarome recognized Austin's picture in Mosely's first story as someone who came to his shop six months ago looking for servers and data processors. Austin called himself Derek Hearn, and he told Jarome he was setting up a computer cluster at the Center for Molecular and Behavioral Neuroscience on the Rutgers-Newark campus so they could do modeling studies on Parkinson's disease and memory disorders. Unfortunately, that was all the information Jarome could provide. Hearn paid in cash and did not give an address. He picked up the CPUs himself, rather than have them delivered.

Saul spent this morning on the Rutgers-Newark campus, but nobody in the Center for Molecular and Behavioral Neuroscience could identify Hearn-Austin's picture.

"I know about Hearn being Austin," Mosely said. "You got the information from a guy that reconditions computers in Newark. That's already part of tomorrow's story. It was..."

"*What*? How did you get that?" That information was not in the Trojan file, so how could they have gotten it? He e-mailed the information Jarome gave him to Spanner yesterday. Did whoever used the trap door previously have other ways of finding information in the FBI computer? Or was there really a government source? Spanner?

"That information was in the e-mail from our inquisitive friend that I got a few minutes ago. I forwarded a copy to you." Mosely said. "How will knowing Austin used the name Hearn help you? Austin...Hearn...whoever, is dead."

"That is a problem. It looks like I don't have anything to trade."

"I guess you'll have to owe me."

"One more thing," he said. "Could you please keep Indianapolis and Saint Louis out of the story? Something like that could panic a whole lot of people real fast."

"I could probably do that, at least for the time being."

"Also, if you want to keep up with this story, you'd better be in Washington tomorrow."

"You mean the government's finally going to come clean?"

"They might. I'd check at the White House about a news conference. After that, you'll hear from us about the phone taps."

When he put the phone down, Mary blasted away. "What kind of shit is this, Rick? You can't give me anything, but then you turn right around and broadcast information on the phone," she said, her arms flapping as if trying to fly away. "Who were you talking to? It was Mosely, wasn't it? You *are* giving her information. You *bastard*."

Seeing her in panties and bra, her legs bare, he wondered if she had come in here to seduce information from him after he got off the phone. Jumbled thoughts as chaotic as Dylan's lyrics tumbled through his head.

"Mosely gave us information, so I had to give her something in return, but she already had it. I'll tell you exactly what I told her and what she told me."

"Who are they? Who's behind it all?"

He repeated the information he gave Mosely, all the information she'd overheard on Austin.

"What was that about Indianapolis and Saint Louis? Is that where they're making bombs?"

"No, nothing like that." He was not about to give her that information.

"It had something to do with a demonstration they're giving in one of those cities. What kind of demonstration? That's where they're building the bombs, isn't it?"

"Not really. Anyway, all this is going to be out in the open tomorrow."

"*Bullshit*," she said and huffed out of the room.

Saul got his laptop from his briefcase, and accessed the e-mail forwarded by Mosely. He forwarded it to Spanner and then dialed his number on his cell phone. Indianapolis or Saint Louis, he thought. They couldn't have a bomb. Could they? They wouldn't use it in this country. Would they?

- - - - -

Applenu rushed to get back to his flat for the 10 p.m. news. Last night Hearn called to say the government had identified him—Hearn—as Austin, and that the White House had called a news conference to confirm the theft of the nuclear material, although Sheena Mosely didn't leave the White House much to disclose, since her story in this morning's paper disclosed all the latest, including the Austin-is-Hearn information. Applenu wondered how Hearn found out these things that he then turned over to her.

So they knew the Austin/Hearn connection. Would they be able to make the Applenu/Deby connection?

Applenu surveyed the CNN weather girl, who appeared every night just before the news presenters. Newscasters, he thought to himself, the Yanks called them newscasters. This tall reddish-blonde bit of fluff in a tight, bright-orange outfit that displayed her excellent shape strutted in front of the map and chatted about the weather in Boise and Denver and Chicago. Her appearance stimulated memories of his nights with Patricia Hunter.

He'd much rather be thinking of weather girls or Patricia Hunter—being in her snappy apartment in Alexandria would be even better—than being terrified every time he picked up a newspaper or turned on TV, afraid of what happened today, what the news would disclose. Was the FBI getting closer? Then tomorrow he'd have go through it all over again.

Patricia Hunter: a nice bit of work that was, but in the end she bloody well buggered him. If Austin hadn't fixed him up with her, they'd never have found him out. They should have seen that. Austin probably did see it, but he figured to give them Applenu with no connection to Ian Deby, thus protecting his Deby identification.

Although bone tired from the long day spent processing plutonium, he knew he'd have trouble sleeping. Same as last night and the night before: too much to do during the day, too much to think about when he closed his eyes at night. He leaned back on the couch and sipped whiskey, hoping to take the edge off. Just a drink or two to calm down—Chivas Regal on ice, the first bottle of liquor he ever bought. With almost six-million dollars tucked away in Zurich, he decided he might as well spend some—while he still could.

After the weather girl, two newscasters appeared with the "CNN Evening News." A perky black-haired piece of skirt named Donna Kelly began: "Today's top story is the presidential press conference that confirmed reports circulating in Washington for the last several weeks concerning stolen nuclear material capable of being made into atomic bombs. When asked why the government took so long to verify the reports, the President said they needed time to study and analyze the situation and its grave national security implications. For the latest on the story, we take you to our White House correspondent Frank Sesno."

Applenu drained his whiskey as they showed the President making a brief statement: "I want to make two important points: First, our best scientists believe it highly unlikely the hijackers can ever build a working nuclear weapon. Secondly, I want to assure the American people that the perpetrators will be quickly apprehended and brought to justice. I think the American people know that this Administration will see to it that this is done with no American citizen's life being placed in danger."

After the President's statement, the FBI Director took over and described the hijackings and discussed the investigation. In great detail, he described how they determined that the heist was masterminded by the late Steve Austin, an employee at the Department of Energy, who had also used the alias Derek Hearn.

Finishing his discussion of Austin, the FBI Director said, "We also identified two other suspects, who go by the name of Brian Applenu and Eric, last name unknown. Both names are probably aliases." Sketches of the two of them with beards flashed on the screen.

Applenu rubbed his beardless face and decided it was time to drop the accent and talk like an American. As long as Deby was isolated from Applenu, he might just walk away from this and start over—somewhere. Trouble was, he needed to ensure his family's survival. BahAmin's latest e-mail said that the next step in their family-relocation plan was set to go next week. How would Sherbani react to that?

- - - - -

Curt stared at Surling's calendar and diary, a series of tick marks on the wall next to the couch, one for each day of captivity. Surling started it shortly after they got there, but back dated it to June eleventh—the day Curt arrived. It ended today, August fourteenth. Surling occasionally lengthened marks and scribbled memorable events, like Drafton's death.

What a week, Curt thought. Ever since Drafton left, Curt's mind cooked a stew of thoughts and dreams with Drafton haunting every one: Drafton as corpse, Drafton as lover, Drafton as friend willing to sacrifice his life for him and Surling, Drafton and AIDS, and always, Drafton and Lori. Drafton understood Lori. Deep down, Curt knew Lori would understand Drafton. He could not understand either of them, much less himself.

The turmoil hammering his brain drove him to the computer. In its electronic thoughts, he created the order his brain lacked. As long as he established contact with an island of calm and logic in the deranged sea that raged all about, there was hope, at least the hope for peaceful isolation. He knew if he could just concentrate long enough, the computer would spring them out of there. They didn't need Drafton. They never needed Drafton.

While Curt wrestled with his demons, he became aware of Surling plummeting into his own sea of mental discord. His confidence in the future oscillated, but mainly deteriorated. Every evening, he sat at the table and stared across his beer, like a lost sailor searching for land he knew he would never see. Dark half moons glowed beneath his eyes, and his glasses now rimmed the eyes of the eighty-four-year-old man he was. Below the table, his right leg jiggled away the hours. Momentarily in touch with his inherent need to compute, Curt estimated a rate of 200 leg jiggles a minute, 12,000 in an hour.

Tonight, Curt sat for a while with his own beer and listened to Surling, who more and more fit into the mold of his embittered Dad after the accident. When he could no longer stand the jiggling leg, Curt stood and paced.

Surling's conversations inevitably involved death: Drafton's death, their impending deaths, and the death of his son Al. At least once every night, he said, "We can't just sit around here and wait for the fucking United States Cavalry." Tonight, he added: "They've machined all of the uranium, and it's been shipped out of here. We've also got about half the plutonium processed. Today, Applenu casually dropped the bomb that they won't need me much longer. We both know what that means." Surling slashed his hand across his throat.

"Applenu wants to finish with me at the same time. He's been learning the programs and says he intends to take over the computer operation when the plutonium is machined," Curt said.

"That means we're both fucked."

"Maybe, maybe not. I think I've come up with an insurance policy."

"What? How?"

"The computer, I've…"

"You and that fucking computer. You make a big deal about what your wife will say about you and Drafton. She's used to you having a lover that takes up most of your time and energy. How long have you been in love with that fucking machine? I bet you'd rather diddle a computer any day than fuck your wife."

Surling's words stung because of the truth they held. He would change after this was over…if he could forget Drafton.

"I've even been thinking that maybe we should be praying," Surling said without a smile to indicate he might be joking. "My wife's forever after me to go to church with her, to be born again. According to her, that would get me back on track. I used to go to church back when my kids were younger. I don't know if I ever believed. You got religion? You believe?"

"I was raised Lutheran, but I quit going back in college. My

188

insurance policy isn't prayer. It's a little sub-routine I wrote for the plutonium-machining programs. None of the programs will execute properly unless the subroutine is run first, and a password is needed to get to the subroutine. And I'm the only one who knows the subroutine and password."

"What if the password isn't used?"

"The computer will butcher anything in the machine."

"How do we use it? At most it will keep you alive a while longer. Then you're back where I am now."

"Maybe. Maybe not."

Chapter Twenty-Six

"So it's a goddamned hoax," Martin Dowel said from the head of the mahogany conference table, "another fucking wild-goose chase."

A corner office with windows and carpet, Saul thought, everything his own office lacked. In this three-man meeting, Saul sat to the Associate Director's right, Spanner to his left. It was Saul's fourth meeting of the day in somebody else's office, three of them in Indianapolis, his plane arriving from there less than an hour earlier. This followed meetings yesterday in Saint Louis. All he wanted now was to go home, have a couple of beers, something to eat, and then get some sleep.

Tall and thin with intense blue eyes and thick white hair, Dowel was an easy-going Texan in his sixties. Although his words indicated anger and his normally pink-white face reddened, his words oozed in a soft drawl. "That Mosely bitch holds back on publishing the names of the cities, just like she promises, and then about the time we decide there is nothing in Saint Louis or Indianapolis and we wouldn't have to say anything about those cities, that fucking Hughson announces there are atomic bombs in Saint Louis and Indianapolis."

Here it comes, Saul thought. Spanner said Dowel was upset at Saul "about the Hughson thing."

Dowel glared directly at Saul. "And Hughson's announcement sends people into a panic," he growled.

Although he could have retired several years ago, Dowel served as the Director's drinking buddy and stayed on as Associate Director because the Director liked the way Dowel handled the details he couldn't stomach—like dealing with Saul and Spanner. Dowel collected details, and then later over drinks, he pumped them into the Director for use tomorrow morning or whenever he was called on by important members of the government.

"So, Mr. Saul, what's in Saint Louis and Indianapolis? An atomic bomb?"

Saul, tense and waiting for the explosion on Hughson, ran a hand through his hair while his mind changed gears. "As you know, DOD immediately got NEST to both cities, and NEST concluded there are no bombs out there."

Dowel jotted something on a pad of paper and then looked up. "Tell me again what NEST stands for."

"Nuclear Emergency Search Team. They're based out of Andrews Air Force Base. They were established in the 1970s specifically to locate terrorist nuclear weapons should any ever be planted inside a city or anyplace else in the country."

"At least we were prepared for something. How are they supposed to find them?"

"They admit it's like looking for a diamond in a gravel pile. They've got the latest nuclear detection technology mounted on helicopters and in trucks. If they get a fix on nuclear material, they've got panel trucks loaded with detectors to zero in on it. They've even got detectors in briefcases."

"And they didn't find anything?"

"We didn't figure they would," Spanner said. "Those people wouldn't tip us off where the bombs are so we could go out there and find them. They're playing head games with us."

"Mosely didn't say they told her they were going to show us a bomb in those cities," Saul said. "She said those cities were mentioned."

"So they used Mosely to throw us off," Dowel said.

"That's my bet," Spanner said. "Trouble is, we've got to respond to every tip, and they know that."

Saul reported details on Saint Louis and Indianapolis, from the search by NEST to the panic of the citizens, who were driving the FBI and local police crazy with calls of suspicious characters carrying suspicious packages, to the pickets around the federal buildings in both cities. All the panic hit after Hughson's announcement.

That report finished, Spanner moved them on to other business. "We now feel certain that Professor Surling was kidnapped, although his wife disagrees. She says he called her four times since he went to Philadelphia. One call came last week."

"So why don't you believe her?" Dowel asked.

"We believe he called her, but the fact that he hasn't told his people at the university anything is highly unusual based on his past actions. Besides that, we've learned that he worked on the Manhattan Project. He's an expert on the chemistry of plutonium and uranium, just the type of expert we thought they might need."

"Anything on what might have happened to Surling?"

Spanner reported how Surling checked into the Hershey Hotel in Philadelphia on June twelfth and checked out on June thirteenth. According to his secretary, he was going to consult with Margine Nuclear Technology, a company with a website that says they are located in Blacksburg, Virginia, but the address is an empty lot.

Saul reported on the search for a missing computer-controlled machining expert by checking the whereabouts of each expert from DOE weapons plants. Until now, everything was negative, although they were still trying to verify the present location of two men in Boston, one at Argonne, and two at Oak Ridge. If those also proved negative, the simple portion of their search—government facilities—would be exhausted.

"What was the reaction on high when you passed on the information Saul got about Applenu being an Iranian?" Spanner asked.

"According to the Director, the White House and the State Department are consulting on how to handle that," Dowel growled. "There's a rumor of ongoing private diplomatic talks with the Iranian government exploring better relations. It sounds like they're doing the Neville Chamberlain waltz with the bastards that run that country and kill their own people—women and kids for God's sake—when they want a little freedom."

He shook his head in frustration. "It's over two months since the hijackings. We figured to have SWISILREC wrapped up long before we had to go public."

"We've still got time," Spanner said. "Our nuclear weapons experts figure it'll take months, maybe even years, to build a bomb. Besides that, if they had to kidnap at least one expert to help, that'll slow them down. That crap about showing us a bomb was a confusion factor to keep us off guard and keep the media stirred up."

"We've got to get those bastards and quick," Dowel said, his face darkening. "There are all kinds of pickets across from the White House. Then there's the newspapers and TV. Did you see the *Today* show? *Good Morning America?* Fucking so-called experts are coming out of the woodwork to tell us what's wrong with our government, saying they told us so. And, of course, our old buddy Senator Hughson's been anywhere and everywhere he can squeeze his ugly mug onto the tube."

At last, the Hughson scene, Saul thought, knowing the script Dowel was playing. He and the Director were on a search-and-destroy mission for scapegoats below them to take the heat off. They played the Kraft scene during the government's announcement, stating that they had accepted his resignation. Eventually, they'd need somebody else. Spanner might be a possible stopgap sacrifice, although he was not big enough to take all the blame. Dowel would get to Saul soon enough.

"That's to be expected," Spanner said. "It's just politics as usual."

"But it's going to get worse, unless the Administration can show they've stopped these people. The President's scheduled for a speech in Chicago in two days, and there are at least five groups organizing demonstrations at the airport and outside the Hilton where he's speaking."

"We've now got over three-hundred agents on it," Spanner said.

"Do you think organized crime is involved?" Dowel asked. "Was this a for-profit caper, like drugs?"

"If they are, we haven't been able to verify it. We've alerted all our undercovers, and we've drawn blanks."

After a short pause, Dowel looked at Saul and said, "That leaves just one more thing: leaks. As I understand it, the information Mosely published on Austin using the alias Derek Hearn was not released by the Bureau, yet she somehow got hold of it."

Spanner was ready. He again explained the calls to Saul from Mosely and how she had all the information the FBI had by way of the e-mails that she sent to Rick. He reviewed the information on the trap door and Trojan horse programs on the FBI and DOE computers and how computer experts at each agency had observed the computers being accessed by an outside source. "That's got to be the leak source, and it means Austin must still be alive. He accesses our computer and then forwards the information to Mosely. Once he knows what we've got, it doesn't matter to him if it gets out to the public, because he knows that when it gets out there it will get everybody in government who isn't in the know all stirred up, which makes it harder for us to do our job of catching him."

"Three days ago you told me you had him blocked from getting anything important from our computer, but you were allowing him to get false information that you arrested two people in New York. That wasn't in Mosely's story, but the information you uncovered day-before yesterday on the Austin-Hearn connection was."

"We have that remedied now," Spanner said.

Saul explained how they found Austin's Trojan horse sniffer program and how they allowed only fake e-mails into the file. "However, although Austin or somebody else accessed the file with the fake information after they discovered it, for some reason they decided not to pass it on to

Mosely. When Mosely got the Jarome leak about Austin's pseudonym, Slaughter put a watch on the trap door and found that Austin, or whoever came in the trap door, went to another file that was now being used by the sniffer program. Slaughter found the original program was written so that if the first file was discovered, the sniffer program would send e-mails and other pertinent information to another file. Unfortunately, that was only discovered after they got the Hearn information. The trap door has now been blocked and the Trojan horse program removed."

"Okay, but it's the Saint Louis and Indianapolis thing that's got the White House on the Director's ass," Dowel said. He glared at Saul. "They want to know if, you, Mr. Saul, gave Hughson that information. You told us Mosely agreed not to put those cities in her story, and then Hughson goes public with it. Some people in the Administration want you off the case. The Director's fighting that, insisting the Bureau is nonpolitical. Are *you* nonpolitical, Mr. Saul? What is your relationship with Hughson?"

"I have no relationship with Hughson."

Dowel turned to Spanner. "We really fucked this one up, George. We took Saul away from diddling statistics because we wanted a Washington-scene virgin, one without local contacts that would lead to leaks. So we have Dickson in personnel run it through his computer, and he comes up with Saul, who has been in D.C. less than six months and mostly riding a desk. Now, after a little investigating, we find out his wife is Hughson's press secretary."

So some of the three-to-four- hundred agents on the case were snooping on Hughson and Mary, Saul thought. "I didn't tell my wife anything that wasn't in the press. She overheard me talking to Mosely and mention Indianapolis and Saint Louis. She assumed that was where they were building the bombs, but she said she didn't tell Hughson. The next day after the Mosely story appeared without mentioning those cities, she said Hughson's office received an anonymous e-mail with the information on those cities. She said she then corroborated it."

"Hughson's a rabble-rouser," Dowel said, the pink in his face drowning in red. "Rumor has it he intends to run for president. That's all this fucking country needs."

"Sir, it seems to me this is beyond politics. If somebody made a bomb, and..."

"You mean somebody might try to blow up Washington...like your friend Hughson suggested. Never happen. Right, George?"

"We'll get them, sir. *Before* anything happens."

Dowel cleared his throat and looked at Saul. "Even if somebody else gave Hughson that information, there's still pressure to get you off the case."

Spanner broke in. "Rick's done a hell of a job coordinating this case for me. Perhaps if he keeps a low profile..." He glanced quickly at Saul, his eyebrows raised in exasperation.

"I can do that, sir. Except for Mosely, I've avoided the press."

"Okay. But if your name winds up in the news again, or if Hughson winds up with any new information, you'll be wiped off this case quicker than birdshit off the President's limo. And that won't be a political move. It'll be a Bureau necessity, for the protection of the Bureau's good name."

- - - - -

Curt cashed his insurance policy the next morning. They were back in the hot-cell room preparing to machine the first plutonium, when Applenu announced one more dry run.

"And this time," Applenu said, "Simmons and I will handle everything." He motioned Curt to get up from behind the keyboard, and he sat down. "The sooner we know the complete operation, the sooner we'll be able to send you two home."

A live demonstration, Curt thought, glancing quickly at Surling. This was much better than their planned announcement. Once Applenu saw the consequences of the program adjustment, he would have no choice but to deal with him and Surling on their terms.

Curt and Surling moved to the back of the room to make way for the other two men.

Simmons reached over his head for a pair of the remote manipulators. He shoved and twisted with both hands. On the other side of the window inside the hot cell, two three-fingered hands on the end of their long metal arms moved to open the door to the transfer chamber—a small airlock in the wall between the furnace room and the hot cell. Two metal hands grabbed the dummy sample from the chamber and carried it to the lathe at the front of the cell.

Applenu typed commands for the computer, his black head bobbing over the yellow keyboard like a bumblebee over a daffodil. After typing several statements, he stood and watched the lathe on the other side of the window go silently into motion. As if operated by an invisible hand, adjusting wheels spun, and the cutting tool advanced to contact the dummy plutonium sample.

Curt and Surling stared into the cell, waiting.

196

To Curt, everything in the room flared into sharp clarity, like the effects of the crazy cigarettes, but in an atmosphere charged with energy different from the relaxation that percolated through his body on the smoke molecules. His brain clicked into a ready state; he concentrated on the sequence of events about to unfold, analyzing alternate possibilities and responses he and Surling might have to make to Applenu's response. He searched his imagination for a reaction by Applenu that they may not have anticipated.

Applenu typed his command to the computer, and a screen appeared asking for a password. Applenu turned to Curt. "Where did this come from? There wasn't anything about a password before."

"Hit enter," Curt said.

When Applenu hit the key, READY appeared on the screen. Applenu typed: PROCEED MACH 492. He stood to watch the lathe, his right hand rubbing his clean-shaven chin.

Inside the cell, the motor started and the lathe turned. Chips curled rapidly from the dummy specimen. Blue smoke rolled from the whirling machine and began to envelop the cell like a morning fog filling a mountain valley.

Applenu dropped into the chair behind the keyboard. "What the bloody hell's going on?" he yelled, his face reddening. Like a pianist at the height of a Brahms concerto, he hammered at the keys:

END MACH 492

Large letters appeared on the monitor:

ILLEGAL COMMAND: PROGRAM IN PROGRESS

"Illegal command? The bugger's gone bonkers! It won't accept the command to shut down."

Curt stepped up to the keyboard, leaned around Applenu and typed.

Inside the cell, the lathe ground to a halt.

Applenu glared at the word: REBUFF. When he spun around to look up at Curt, his curly black hair streamed down his forehead, his dark eyes burning through. "You did this, Reedan, you son of a bitch." He swiped at his hair. "You made the computer ruin that sample."

"That's right, but it's a dummy. I did it to prove you need us on this project. You need us alive." He pointed to the cell now clearing of smoke. "That's how all your machining efforts will end up unless you make a deal

197

with us."

Applenu jumped up. Standing on his tiptoes, he stuck his crimson face next to Curt's chin. "What the hell are you talking about, a *deal*?"

Curt didn't move. At last he would show Surling how the computer would get them out of there. "The computer's been programmed to carry out all of the machining operations you'll need to finish the project. Surling and Simmons are about finished reducing all the plutonium oxide to plutonium metal. You and Simmons can finish the rest. So you don't need the two of us anymore."

Applenu stepped back, nostrils flared, fuming like a rocket on the launch pad at ignition. "Sod you! You can't ruin the project, nobody can."

Things were going their way, Curt thought, marveling at his coolness. Occasionally, when making a presentation to clients or a technical audience, his heart raced and his knees turned to rubber. Now, under the greatest pressure ever, he had contacted that confidence to gain control, like that brief moment in Miami Beach when he decided to make a run for it.

"We don't want to ruin your project. We just want to save ourselves. The programs are there to machine the plutonium. All you need is a password to run the program correctly, and I've got the password."

Applenu pushed past Curt to get to Surling, who stood behind him, taking it all in. "Was this your idea, Professor?"

"Does it matter?"

"That's right," Curt said. He dropped into the chair vacated by Applenu. "All the two of us want is to be free. You free us, and then I'll give you the password and how to operate the programs."

Applenu glanced at Simmons, who stood in front of the hot-cell window, his hands still on the controls. Simmons's eyes filled with panic. He stepped back, looking as if he were about to be dragged into quicksand. Applenu looked back at Surling. "We couldn't trust you to give us the right password after we let you go."

"We'll play straight with you if you play straight with us," Surling said. His eyes glowed from behind his glasses. With the scent of freedom, youth seeped back into his face. "We can work it out so you can verify that the programs operate before we're completely free."

"I don't trust you."

"We don't trust you either," Surling said, a faint smile threatening to break through to his lips. He cocked his head and his blue eyes ducked behind the glare of his glasses. "Look at it this way. We know you've got material machined for eight uranium bombs. So what's the difference to us if you make ten more plutonium bombs?"

"You'll bring the police down on us."

Surling's eyes fixed on Applenu's. "How're we going to do that? You've eluded the police so far, haven't you?"

"You could give them our names and descriptions."

"But we won't. We know you could turn your people loose on us with their guns. There'd be no benefit for us to go to the police."

Applenu turned and stared at Curt, then turned back to Surling. "I think you two chaps have a deal... Maybe...if we pay you, too... Anyway, there are some details we'll have to work out, things like how we'll verify that you've given us the programs."

Curt and Surling nodded eagerly.

"I'll have to consult my colleagues, but I think we might make a deal."

Chapter Twenty-Seven

As Applenu followed the massive Beecher into the living room of Lormes's apartment; his thoughts were on Surling and Reedan and what he told them: "I need to consult my colleagues." Bloody "colleagues" had only non-technical solutions to problems. Why did the buggers have to pick today? This morning in Amsterdam, BahAmin and her husband were putting their plan for the family into operation, and he wanted to get to his e-mail to see if it succeeded.

After the family got out of Iran and settled in Amsterdam, Uncle Behrouz hired a private investigator to determine if the family was being watched. They were, night and day. Uncle Behrouz's and BahAmin's next task was to recruit help from the pool of Iranian dissidents they knew and trusted in Britain, who got them in touch with trusted dissidents in Amsterdam.

Every Wednesday morning since the family arrived from Iran, Applenu's parents, his two younger sisters and his younger brother took a taxi to the Kinkerstratt Tenkatemarkt at about 09:30 hours. They returned to the apartment around noon with their needs for the coming week. They would do the same this Wednesday—today. There was one difference about this Wednesday. At 08:30, a panel truck pulled up to the back entrance of the apartment building, and six painters dressed in white coveralls and caps emerged carrying ladders and buckets of paint and entered the building. Shortly after the family returned from shopping, six painters dressed in white coveralls and caps would emerge from the building and go to lunch. Only one of the painters—the driver—would be the same as the painters that entered the building earlier. The other five "painters" had left earlier by the front door, and they would return with the driver after "lunch" and remain until 17:00 hours, after which they would leave with their ladders and buckets.

Beecher led Applenu into the living room. Lormes greeted them from the end of a white couch, where he lounged next to a blonde much less than half his age. He shared the rented apartment with her, although he periodically flew back to New York to visit his wife and kids. Applenu tried not to stare at her, clad as she was in short shorts and a red halter.

"So you've got a problem, Dr. Applenu," Lormes said, his eroded mouth smoothed by his smile. He turned to the blonde and told her to go outside and take a long walk. When she protested it was too hot, he stared at her, but said nothing. She stood and hurried from the room on long tanned legs, followed by the sound of the outside door opening and closing.

Lormes motioned Applenu to the other end of the couch. Beecher dropped into the chair across from the couch. Applenu explained the problem posed by Reedan and Surling and the proposal they had for remedying the situation.

Lormes listened, nodded occasionally, his penetrating eyes fixed on Applenu. When Applenu finished, Lormes broke into a loud laugh. "I see you not only lost your beard, you also lost the British accent," he said, his Russian accent subdued today. Another loud chuckle, his laughter amplified by Beecher's high-pitched cackle. "I think we can take care of the problem. Do you agree, Mr. Beecher?"

"I think I can solve the problem by tomorrow morning," Beecher said. "I know just the way to solve it."

"I'm not sure violence will work on these guys," Applenu said, looking directly at Lormes. "They're worried they will be killed when their job is done. I hope that is not their fate, because I don't want to be mixed up in murder. They promised not to go to the police if we let them go."

Lormes turned to Beecher. "He doesn't want to be mixed up in murder."

Applenu looked at Beecher then back to Lormes. "Why not just pay them to be quiet and put them on your plane and drop them off somewhere in the middle of the country. There's no way they would know where they've been and where we are."

"And then they'll go to the police and identify you, me, Beecher, and everybody else. They've seen you with and without your beard. According to this morning's paper, the FBI knows Surling is missing, and they have him connected to the missing nuclear material." Lormes shook his head. "We can't leave loose ends when this thing is over."

"What's a loose end?" Applenu asked. "Will I be a loose end?"

Lormes laughed. "I hope not, but that will be up to your bosses."

- - - - -

Lori had just finished frying chicken when the doorbell rang. She planned an early dinner, so she could get back to her studies. It rang again, and she hurriedly wiped her hands and rushed toward the door, hoping to keep Beth downstairs with the TV. Maybe whoever was at the door would give her a chance at some adult conversation for a change.

Finals week: one more night of study for one last final exam in the morning, and then a week until graduation. At times, she felt guilty about carrying on while Curt remained a prisoner. She considered quitting school when this thing started, but realized she'd go crazy with nothing to keep her busy while fate ran its course.

Outside of her classes, she had hardly talked to anyone but Beth. She needed to talk to an adult about anything, but she hesitated to call friends, afraid she would break down and blurt it all out. Several times, just lying in bed at night, she couldn't hold back the tears. Next morning, it was business as usual. What else could she do?

Although in a hurry to answer the door, she resisted the urge to race barefoot down the steps, even though there hadn't been any spotting the last four days. Same thing happened with the last two pregnancies: it came and went. One pregnancy ended early, and the other went all the way. Easy does it, she thought, as she ran her hand across her abdomen: barely a bulge.

As soon as she turned the knob, the door banged back at her, shoved open by Beecher, who rushed past her into the foyer. Maxwell tagged along behind him carrying a briefcase.

"Long time, no see," Beecher said.

They hadn't been back for over a month, the only contact being the frequent phone calls.

"What do you want?"

Next to Beecher, Maxwell, who reminded Lori of a giant slug, leered at her through his colored glasses.

"Just get your sweet little ass up there," Beecher said, grabbing her arm and jerking her toward the steps. "You cooperate, and we'll be out of here in no time. We wouldn't be here if your pansy husband would do what he is told to do."

"Mommy! What's happening?" Beth screamed, running up the steps to Lori and grasping for her hand.

"Just keep the kid quiet," Beecher growled, yanking Lori's arm to force her up the steps and propel her into the living room that was separated from the steps by a wrought-iron railing. He shoved her toward the couch. As on his other visit, Beecher strutted, his huge muscles inflated, shoulders jacked up, this time dressed in cream-colored pants and a dark-blue knit shirt.

Lori sat and Beth scrambled into her lap. When Lori saw Beecher scanning her bare legs, she wished she had left her slacks on when she got back from today's final. After they came the last time, she quit wearing shorts. Then they quit coming. Why now?

Maxwell straggled into the room, the giant slug in wrinkled black pants and a red knit shirt with broad white horizontal stripes stretched outward by his huge protruding stomach. "Smells good in here," he said, breathing heavily from climbing the steps. "Fried chicken? She looks good and cooks, too." He set the briefcase on the coffee table in front of the couch, snapped it open, and extracted a camcorder and a digital camera. He handed the camcorder to Beecher, and then stepped back from the couch and pointed the camera at Lori and Beth.

"We are going to get some pictures of you and the kid," Beecher said, his fake smile countered by his brutal Russian-accented growl.

"Smile," Maxwell said from behind the camera.

Lori forced a smile and pushed Beth to the front of her lap to hide her legs behind Beth's. Thank God, she left the ruffled blouse on. At least it wasn't a T-shirt.

A flash erupted, and Maxwell checked the display on the back of the camera. Meanwhile, Beecher used the video camera.

"Why are they taking pictures, Mommy?"

"To show your daddy," Beecher said, "to remind him why he should cooperate with us."

After studying the digital picture, Maxwell pointed the camera at them. It flashed twice while Beecher continued with the video camera. Maxwell took two shots of Beth alone, followed by three of Lori alone. Before each shot, Maxwell checked her, his wide-eyed stare all over her. If rape was a visual act, she thought, she'd be ravaged.

Beecher shut off the video camera and handed it to Maxwell, who set the digital camera on the coffee table.

"Now let the kid go watch TV so the three of us can talk," Beecher said."

"I'll take you downstairs to watch cartoons, honey," Lori said, leading Beth out of the room.

"I want to stay with you, Mommy."

"Do what Mommy says," Beecher snapped.

On the way through the foyer, Lori had the urge to open the front door and run for it. They'd never catch them before they got to the Eberhard's. But then what would they do to Curt?

Back in the living room, she found Maxwell and Beecher on the couch laughing as they examined the video on the camcorder viewing screen.

Dad used to tell her: "You're a farm girl, you can do anything." This too would end, she told herself. Just stay with it; show them you can be firm.

Beecher and Maxwell stood. Maxwell pointed the camcorder at her and began recording.

Beecher motioned her to the couch and loomed above, looking down at her. "We don't want to hurt you, Lori, or your husband." He spoke as if talking to a child. "All you have to do is cooperate."

"I am cooperating. I haven't told the police or anyone."

"Good. Trouble is, your husband isn't."

Maxwell moved closer, the camcorder pointed at her face.

"He will. Just...just give him a chance."

Beecher moved closer and towered above her, making her lean back to look up at him. "That's why we're here. To make you convince him to do our job."

Without warning, his right hand smashed into her left cheek and jolted her head around to the right, pain blazing across her face and into her jaw. She screamed and grabbed the side of her face. For a moment she thought the flash of light was from the digital camera, but Maxwell still lurked to her left with the camcorder, the digital camera still on the coffee table.

Beecher dropped onto the couch beside her.

"What do you want?" she asked.

Beecher lunged at her and grabbed her wrists. He shoved her backwards and pinned her against the couch, her scream muffled by his massive chest that smothered her face in the odor of cigarette smoke from his shirt. Immobile, every muscle straining to escape, she felt his lips brush her cheek, his breath sour. She twisted her head sideways, but could not detach his damp lips now plastered on her left cheek.

Maxwell crouched at the front of the couch with the camcorder pressed to his face. "Give it to her, Beech."

"Quit! Please quit." She wriggled her shoulders and tried to move her arms to push his hand off the inside of her thigh and moving toward her crotch. Her face burned.

With her body pinned to the couch by his massive body, he grabbed her face with both hands and twisted it around to him. He kissed her on her open mouth, his slippery wet tongue thrusting inside. "We're going to give the pansy a demonstration of what's going to happen to you if he doesn't cooperate."

She fought to free her arms. "Goddammit," she mumbled, her anger damming the tears that threatened. "He'll cooperate."

Beecher released her and sat back.

Maxwell stood, the camcorder still pointed at her.

Lori straightened up and wiped at her mouth, trying to slow her breathing.

Beecher reached out with both hands, grabbed two handfuls of the blouse material, and ripped it to shreds.

She screamed and shoved at his arms, protesting and promising.

"You scream again and bring your kid up here, you'll regret it."

Maxwell chuckled from behind the camcorder. "I think it's fun time, Beech."

"Let me go, please. I've done what you asked me to do. Curt will do the job, I know he will."

- - - - -

As soon as the two men were on the steps down to the front door, she grabbed her underpants and shorts. Beth, she thought, can't let Beth see me like this. She dropped the slimy underpants and pulled on the blue shorts, remembering how Maxwell used the underpants to wipe himself.

The front door slammed, and they were gone.

She collapsed onto the couch, the mess on the coffee table catching her eye: the greasy plate with chicken bones and four empty Budweiser cans. Sometime while Beecher was…Maxwell went to the kitchen and brought back the chicken and beer, which must have been in the refrigerator for six months, she thought, trying to distract herself, trying to relax long enough to think—and to forget. An ashtray filled with cigarette butts stunk up the room. Got to get them out of here, she thought. She shook her head to forget and noticed the ache. No way could she forget the taste in her mouth. She bolted for the bathroom, her hands plastered across her mouth.

Afterward, she lay on the bathroom floor, her head next to the cool toilet bowl. She wiped at her mouth and eyes with a wet cloth, hoping the nausea had passed and the headache subsided. She struggled to her feet and stumbled into the bedroom, where she wrapped herself in her yellow robe. In the mirror, she examined her left cheek, red and swollen from where Beecher hit her. A shower, she thought, long and hot.

"Beth!" Momentarily, she'd forgotten Beth. She called her, and while waiting for her to respond, she went to the window and pulled the drape aside.

There they were, leaning against their car. Maxwell ate chicken and licked his fingers. Beecher smoked while he scanned the video on the camcorder screen. He reached down to his crotch and tugged. She couldn't hear what he said, only the derisive laughter.

"Mommy! Mommy! Are those bad men gone?"

Lori fought the tears as she stooped to hug Beth. "They're gone. Everything's okay."

She stepped back to the window and watched them eating and smoking, taking in the evening.

She hurried across the room to the phone and dialed Sarah Eberhard and asked her to take care of Beth for a couple of hours. On her way to the closet, she instructed Beth to go next door by way of the back door. She felt a cramp start; the pain nucleated deep in the abdomen and halted her in her tracks. When it eased, she pulled on a white blouse. Back at the window, she saw them getting into their car.

By the time she got her car out of the driveway, the big black car with out-of-state license plates was at the end of Wilden Lane, turning left onto Outer Drive.

"Where to, bastards," she asked, her loud voice suddenly making her aware of her cursing, remnants of summers working with Dad in the fields, his infrequent outbursts inducing her to quiet laughter and infrequent imitations, unlike Curt, embarrassed by his father's obscene language. A hell of a time to wonder about all that, she thought. They escaped from Iowa, but for what? This?

The big black car, headlights now on in the dusk, followed West Outer to Newridge, then to Nebraska and onto the Turnpike. She had no plans beyond finding out where they went: to a hotel or the airport. Maybe they just flew in for their mission, their sport. She would follow them to hell if she could deal with them.

When they turned right on Vanderbilt Drive, she figured they made a wrong turn, wanting to turn at the next right onto Illinois Avenue to take them to a hotel or the Knoxville Airport.

Up ahead, they turned left into a parking lot for one of the many

Garden Apartment buildings along Vanderbilt. She and Curt lived in an apartment farther down Vanderbilt when they first got to Oak Ridge. The appearance of the apartments hadn't improved in the past five years—a series of long, sand-colored brick boxes on both sides of the street.

She followed and parked in front of a fire hydrant just inside the road leading to the parking area for two of the buildings set in an L-shape. From there she watched the two men go up the outside stairs to a second floor apartment of the building that paralleled the far side of the parking area.

Why were they in Oak Ridge? Were they really watching her? For the first few weeks, she had searched for them and never saw any indication that anyone followed her. She had driven both directions on Outer just to see, but nothing. So why did they have an apartment in Oak Ridge?

A pain jolted her abdomen, and she gripped the steering wheel. It began like a hard menstrual cramp and built from there until she felt she had to scream. Then it broke.

She sighed and tried to relax back onto the seat and let the numbing pain drain slowly away. What now? Wait? Wait for what? What could she do? She needed a gun. She started the car. "I'll be back, *bastards!* You can count on it."

- - - - -

Lori rubbed her burning cheek and wondered where she could buy a gun. She remembered the sign for guns on the front of a pawn shop and sports equipment store on the Turnpike. Before she could get out of the car at the shop, the most powerful cramp yet seized her midsection and doubled her up against the steering wheel. She held on and waited for it to run its course. Sweat beaded her forehead as the pain built to a peak and drained away, slowly, the pain as excruciating as when she had Beth. Got to lie down, check for spotting. With the pain came an awareness of wetness between her legs, forgotten during the last half hour. She glanced down at her shorts, soaked through. *"Bastards!"*

In the mirror she saw the mess of her face and hair. She brushed her hand through her hair and debated whether to forget about the gun and go home to Beth. Her head ached.

Just inside the dimly lit store, another cramp hit, momentarily inducing dizziness, the lights flickering as she gasped for air. Confused, slightly nauseated, a cool wetness tickling her thigh, she stood next to piles of half-off orange University of Tennessee T-shirts on a display counter. Where are the guns?

When Lori saw the young woman behind the counter eying her, she glanced down at the wetness and remembered that she had forgotten to put on underpants. What would she do if she ran into someone she knew?

She glanced back at the clerk and decided she didn't know her. Her mind wouldn't stop: Haven't you ever seen anybody that's just been raped, lady? If you lived in the world I do, you'd know it happens all the time.

Her thoughts were interrupted by another pain starting to build. Or was it a remnant from the last one that never quite faded away? Get out of here and go home, she told herself.

Across the room to the left, she saw a display case filled with bows and arrows. Hunting equipment. Guns.

With her eyes staring straight ahead, her mind trying to ignore the pain and the nausea, she shuffled forward. She wove her way through racks of hunting jackets, baseball caps, and equipment bags, everything exuding a sickening odor of newness, of plastic, rubber, and fabric. Behind it all, she found a display case filled with all kinds of pistols.

"May I help you, ma'am," the young woman asked as she stepped from behind the counter to follow Lori to the front of the case, her eyes wide as he looked Lori over.

Lori swallowed, trying to beat back the revolution in her stomach. What must she think of her? Had she seen her before? "I need a gun, a pis…" The cramp threatened to pound her to her knees, and she grabbed the glass display case to steady herself. She needed to vomit. She saw a trickle of blood inching down the inside of her thigh.

The clerk saw it, too. "You okay, ma'am?"

Lori sucked a deep breath. "May I…may I use your restroom?"

Inside the cramped quarters, she dropped to her knees and hung over the commode. After much gagging, she threw up, a cloudy, viscous liquid that clung to her throat and ran down her chin when she tried to spit it out. She gagged again, but nothing emerged.

She stood, pulled down her blue shorts, and found dark-red liquid covering the crotch of the shorts and streaming down the inside of her thigh. A powerful cramp, then another smashed into her midsection, doubling her up. Somewhere down inside, a dam broke. She collapsed onto the toilet and watched as blood gushed into the bowl, clots splashing like pebbles into a pond. Another prolonged cramp, and a couple of large chunks splashed into the bright-red pool.

Exhausted, eyes blurred with tears generated by the pounding pain, she leaned back, closed her eyes, and listened to the stream of liquid subside to an occasional drip.

Chapter Twenty-Eight

"Ring, bloody phone, ring," Applenu mumbled to himself. He rubbed a hand across his scraggly beard and wondered what he was doing in broad daylight next to another phone booth in another car park of another of the numerous combination petrol stations and grocery stores in the city. Car park, petrol, bloody, he thought; got to change that. Think and talk American. He changed his speech patterns once, he could do it again. No more playing Michael Cain. He had not shaved for two days, uncertain what to do about his beard, since there was now an artist's sketch of an unshaven Applenu, although he didn't think it resembled him any more than the bearded one.

After his visit with Lormes, Simmons gave him the message that Sherbani would call at seven. How did he get his messages to Simmons? Applenu had not spoken to Sherbani recently, as Hearn was now working through the problems that Sherbani had once handled.

As he waited, he wondered if Sherbani had found out about his family's relocation. At least part of his day was looking up. BahAmin's e-mail said their family relocation project went as planned. When would Sherbani find out about that? Was that the reason for this call?

Applenu glanced at the sports page of the newspaper he'd been reading, full of stories of the local college football team and the Yanks' bloody baseball scores. He avoided the front page, where the sketch of his bearded and shaved face now appeared regularly. Similar sketches of Drafton were there next to his. Up to now, all they had were the sketches, and the stories indicated they were digging up more on them. One thing they would never dig up was Drafton. At least they better not. Lormes was supposed to be jolly good at making sure of something like that.

When the phone rang, Applenu looked around before he got out and answered it. "You've got to call the apartment or my cell phone from now on," Applenu said after the usual greetings. "Somebody's going to recognize me. With all this news media stuff, maybe we should stop work and cut away."

"I say again, do not worry, my friend. We will finish what we started and walk away, and they will never find us. Mr. Lormes called to say he was taking care of your personnel problem. Mr. Lormes said it would be solved by tomorrow morning. He also said you were worried about the fate of our employees when the project is completed. It is not your job to worry about such things."

Applenu thought of Reedan and Surling in their quarters back at the factory celebrating their success. What was Beecher doing? How was he going to fix the problem? Would he be making a call on them this evening? "I was worried that..."

"I repeat, that is *not* your job," Sherbani said, obvious anger in his voice. He cleared his throat. "The reason I called concerns the photos and videos you sent our colleague. He said this is the third time you sent it, and although it is close to what we need for the next phase, it is still not right. He wonders if you are dragging your feet and whether we should have Mr. Lormes talk to you. I assured him you were probably busy with other things and did not consider the pictures that important. They *are* important, and we need them quickly, because arrangements are being made for the presentation."

"I thought I sent what he wanted." The colleague he referred to was Hearn, a name they no longer spoke since it was revealed in the news media. Austin/Hearn had a new name, but he had not told Applenu what it was. He told Applenu to just call him Al.

After clarifying what was needed, Sherbani said, "At this moment, we are making arrangements for the first international shipments of the product you manufactured. We are applying for the export license," When Applenu did not speak, he said, "That is a joke, my serious friend."

"What is the video for?"

"It will be a commercial to confuse our competitor. When your enemies are searching two-thousand hills, you will be safe in one-thousand valleys."

- - - - -

Though round, the oak table separated them like a fence, Applenu and Beecher on the side nearest the door, Surling and Reedan on the opposite side. Beecher tossed a brown envelope onto the table and set a laptop computer with a large screen in the center.

Curt held his gaze as steady as Applenu's. Inwardly, he smiled. Once he and Surling had made their play to Applenu, he felt his confident self re-emerge from the shadows of his mind. Though bombs would be built, he and Surling would live. And just maybe, they could help the FBI stop them.

Curt flashed his businessman's smile, ready to begin some more selling. "Bob and I figured a way we can all get what we want. You can have your men take us to an airport, say Saint Louis or Chicago, a city in the middle of the country and…"

Beecher roared into a loud, mocking laugh. He turned to Applenu, who sat to his left and stared across the table. "You hear that, Doc, they figure we can *all* get what we want."

Applenu continued to stare across the table at them, his mind seeming to be elsewhere.

Next to Curt, Surling's leg began a nervous 200 jiggles per minute.

Smiling directly at Curt, Beecher snapped on the laptop and grabbed the brown envelope, from which he pulled out a packet of photos and tossed two of them into the center of the table: pictures of Lori and Beth; a third picture followed, a picture of them together. God, he thought, I just want to get back to them.

Beecher typed at the keys of the laptop, and then he turned the screen toward Curt and Surling. "I want you to take a look at this video we made on our visit to your home."

- - - - -

Lori heard Beth's voice a long way off.

"Get up, Mommy, you'll be late. You've got to take your test today."

Lori's body jerked twice; she shrugged her arms, as if trying to get loose from something that pinned her down. She sat up, dazed, out of breath, trying to get her bearings. Then she remembered.

"Mommy, your face is red. One side's bigger than the other."

She probed the swollen left side of her face and eye where he hit her. Along with her face and head, every fiber in her body ached.

"When's Daddy coming home, Mommy? I want to see Daddy."

Lori reached for Beth and pulled her up on the bed. She kissed her and hugged her to her body and wondered if the three of them would ever be together again.

"Today's your test, Mommy."

Nine fifteen on the clock. "What test?" A night in bed, she thought, but still as exhausted as if she hadn't slept.

"Your test at U-T."

"Oh, that test. Not today." More important things to do, she thought, although just then she didn't know what. Who needs an MBA anyhow?

Her first item of the day remained the same as every other day for the past two months: check herself for blood. When it all began, she checked in the hope her period would start. Once she accepted the pregnancy, she hoped no blood would show. Today, she didn't know what to hope for. She found the pad only moderately soaked and the blood mostly dark brown and dry. She would decide later whether to call the doctor.

Rest, she needed rest. Anytime she managed to fall asleep, images of yesterday's waking nightmare cascaded through her mind.

Relax, clear your mind, she told herself. The method got her to sleep after a night of studying, but not last night. Chaos flooded back, her mind reliving every touch, every word: the creeps crawling over her body, squirming their way in and then pounding relentlessly. Beth calling from downstairs. Beecher strutting in front of her, standing there like a rock and ordering her to kneel in front of him. Three-thirty came and went without sleep. Somewhere between then and now, she dropped off, only to thrash around trying to run from the terror.

How would Curt react? Surely, they wouldn't show him the last pictures and video they took. Regardless, he would see the shorts she wore. Would he think she was asking for it? He knew better. Didn't he?

By noon, she felt like moving again, and after dropping Beth at the sitter, she headed for the Garden Apartments. By constantly checking the mirror and following the common TV-police-show procedure of making several turns that took her away from the direct route, she convinced herself no one was following. In the mirror, her dark glasses worn to hide the swollen eye and swollen cheek reminded her that she had to do something. What?

As she drove into the Garden Apartments parking lot, she glanced down at the large black-leather shoulder bag that held her revenge.

- - - - -

When she emerged from the bathroom at the pawn shop last night, she asked the clerk for a moderate-size pistol easily concealed.

"What a lot of women are buying and what I personally own, is a thirty-eight caliber," the clerk said. "Mine is a Rossi Model 88 with a stainless steel handle that won't rust. If you shoot somebody with a

214

thirty-eight, they'll stay down. Not like your twenty-two."

Her face burned and her stomach stirred with a faint nausea. "I'll take it."

"Well, we don't have a Rossi on hand right now, but it's like this Taurus thirty-eight here in the display."

"Is that a forty-five?" Lori said pointing at a black pistol in the display case. She remembered shooting targets on the farm with a forty-five and the hole it put into a beer can.

The clerk nodded. "It's a Taurus 1911B, but it costs $719.95. Maybe you ought to wait for the Rossi, ma'am. It only costs about three-hundred, and…"

"I'll take the forty-five now. And I'll need bullets."

- - - - -

This morning she had to figure out how to carry it. She tried a backpack but then settled on the large shoulder bag that she bought several years ago and rarely used. Next, she spent ten minutes in front of the bathroom mirror practicing how she would grab it from the shoulder bag, aim, and fire. It was heavy—three pounds with a loaded magazine. She decided to wear the handbag on her left shoulder, so she could draw with her right hand. She wanted to take it out in the country and practice, but there wasn't time. Her stance and aim felt familiar. Maybe you never forgot, like riding a bike.

Parking as far as possible from where Beecher and Maxwell had parked last night, she searched the half-empty lot for the big black car. Not there. She debated whether to wait for them, decided against it, and picked up Beth at the sitter.

They heard the phone from the garage. She didn't hurry to answer it, because there was nobody she wanted to talk to. Nobody she *could* talk to. It kept ringing until she got into the kitchen.

"Where've you been, Lori?" Beecher asked. "We've been trying to reach you for the last hour. You didn't go to the police, did you?"

His voice ignited a shiver that rattled her body. "No, I didn't."

"That's good Lori. Just don't get any ideas, or I'll come out there and live with you every minute of the day…and night." He laughed.

She didn't answer, just toyed with the zipper on her leather shoulder bag. What if she invited them out and then used the gun to force them to tell her where Curt was? Impossible.

"Are you still there, Lori?"

215

She remembered the taste in her mouth and felt ill. "I'm here."

"What do you say, Lori, should I move in with you? Just you and me?" He began to laugh. "We can have some lovely times. Just like we had yesterday." His laugh accelerated into a high-pitched cackle.

She hung up.

Chapter Twenty-Nine

Saul had just settled into his office for another day of slogging through e-mails and phone calls when Agent Jerry Fortner of the Knoxville, Tennessee, office contacted him. "We located Barry Everly," Fortner said. "He's on a job in Idaho."

Everly was one of two unaccounted-for computer-controlled machining experts who had left the Y-12 weapons plant in Oak Ridge within the past three years to become private consultants. Everly moved to California, and they had been unable to contact him immediately.

One down, three to go Saul thought. One more at Oak Ridge, one in Boston, and one in Albuquerque. "What about the other Oak Ridge possibility?" Saul asked as he rifled the reports on his desk for the name. "Curtis Alfred Reedan."

"People at Y-12 say he's a metallurgist who's an expert in computer applications to metal fabrication. I didn't check on him because the Y-12 people know what he's up to: technical consulting out of his home in Oak Ridge. He talks to Y-12 regularly, because he consults for them."

"Check him out like you were told. Find out what he's been up to the last month or so."

"Hey, okay," Fortner said, anger creeping into his voice. "I just got on this job yesterday when Abbot came down sick. I barely got any information on what the hell you guys want."

"So now you know. And we want it yesterday."

"What is this anyway, another drug case? Money laundering? If so, it doesn't sound like Reedan's our man."

Jesus, where has this guy been? Even if he just got on the job yesterday, he was an FBI agent and should have put it all together. "All you need to know is we're looking for a missing scientist." Saul hung up.

The telephone rang, and the secretary who was answering his phone to keep away reporters said, "I've got a Miz Mosely on the phone. I tried to get her to talk to a PIO, but she insisted on talking to you. She says it's a matter of life or death."

Mosely came on, her British accent suppressed by her anger. "I thought you and I were working together. So why don't you tell that bloody bitch to get me through when I call? I don't want to talk to any goddamned Public *Information* Officer and get a lot of P-R bullshit."

"Well, she..."

"I don't have time for that crap now. I just had a phone call from our guy, who told me he was sending an e-mail with some important information. Remember back when he told me they were going to demonstrate that they know what they are doing when it came to making bombs?"

"I remember. I wasted two days in Saint Louis and Indianapolis."

"Yeah, yeah. I didn't say those were the cities just that they were possibilities. Anyway, they're ready to give you that demonstration."

"Where? When?"

"Today, in Chicago."

"The President is in Chicago."

- - - - -

When Lori got to the Garden Apartment complex parking lot at four-forty-five, over half the parking spaces were empty, and there was no big black car with out-of-state plates. She parked in the sun as far as possible from where Beecher had parked, determined to wait until six. She reasoned that if they kept regular working hours, they would return shortly after five.

With her Taurus 1911 .45-caliber pistol snuggled in the shoulder bag on the seat beside her, she hunkered down, locked in her thoughts, a suffocating heat building in her burgundy Honda Accord. Sweat beaded her forehead, and she started the engine to run the air conditioner. Three barefoot kids playing in the yard in front of the building nearest her stopped to watch. Kids reminded her of Beth and her lost child, who would never run barefoot in the grass.

She fought drowsiness, the aftermath of another sleepless night. Each night her mind replayed words and actions, her still stiff and sore body a constant reminder of that frightful day.

By five-fifteen, home-from-work cars began filling parking spaces. People in arriving cars studied her. At five-twenty-five, a man and a woman got into the car parked next to her and drove away. What if Beecher came back and parked there?

She remembered Beecher standing in front of her, grabbing her chin in his huge hand and twisting her head so she had to look up at him. What was she doing here? What about Beth if they caught her? If they didn't see her, they would go into the apartment and leave her sitting there sweating. Then what? She touched her shoulder bag on the seat next to her. Would she go in and shoot them? Even if she could pull the trigger, how would that help Curt?

She started the motor and went to pick up Beth.

Five minutes after they got home, the phone rang. Just like the last time. Were they actually watching? Did they really know when she came home?

"Hello?"

"Hello. Mrs. Reedan? This is Special Agent Jerry Fortner of the FBI. I'd like to speak to your husband."

She paused. "He's not here. He's away on business."

"Where is he? When will he be back?"

Should she tell the truth? "He's...he's in Pennsylvania." She told that lie several times before to Curt's clients and to MIT and the Colorado School of Mines when they wanted Curt's decision on their job offers. It's what they told her to say. "I'm not sure when he'll be back, probably in a couple of days. What do you want with him?"

"Just some routine security clearance questions for his consulting job at Y-12. Can you be more specific about where he is and when he'll be back?"

She rubbed her hand lightly across her swollen cheek, now taking on a blue tinge below and around the eye. She could tell the FBI. If anybody could help, they could. What about Beecher? What would they do to Curt? What if they were listening to this phone call?

"The last time he called, he wasn't sure when he would be back. He goes to Pittsburgh quite often. Call back the day-after tomorrow. Maybe he'll be back, or if he calls, I'll tell him you want to talk to him."

"Please give me his cell phone number or his hotel so I can call him."

How to answer? "When we talked, he mentioned his cell phone wasn't working. I'm not exactly sure where he is in Pennsylvania."

"Well...Okay, I'll call back."

Lori collapsed onto a kitchen chair. Day after tomorrow, she thought. What will she say then?

219

- - - - -

As soon as Saul got off the phone with Mosely, he called Spanner, which spawned another meeting in Dowel's office, this time with the Director present. The Director had notified the chairman of the White House Planning and Operations Committee for SWISILREC of the message, and the POC was to meet in an hour. After some discussion, Spanner and Dowel recommended that the Director tell the POC that the President should go through with his Chicago talk, since the bomb makers would not tell Saul and some nuclear experts to be in Chicago for a demonstration at the same time the President was speaking if they were planning to detonate an atomic bomb.

At 7:25 pm, Saul, Spanner, and Chicago Special Agent Mel Hubbard entered the Monroe Street entrance of the Palmer House as instructed by the latest e-mail Mosely forwarded forty-minutes ago. Hustling up a long stone stairway, they entered the cavernous two-story hotel lobby with its ornate columns and cornices and murals on the curved ceiling. A piano and violin duet superimposed "Old Man River" onto a rumble of voices emanating from the suit-and-tie and evening-dress crowd clustered around the glistening lobby bar.

Hubbard, a tall, well-built black man, walked with Spanner, fifteen feet ahead of Saul. Once in the lobby, Spanner and Hubbard separated, and Saul strolled toward the registration desk, a long marble counter straight ahead as he came up the steps. Following instructions in the e-mail, he asked the girl behind the counter if there was a message for him.

Saul read the note she handed him, wadded it, and casually dropped it to the floor for Spanner to retrieve. As instructed by the note, Saul headed for the phone with the out of order sign at the end of a bank of four phones in a narrow corridor next to the counter.

Spanner and Hubbard strolled around the lobby, checking to see if anyone watched Saul. Three other Chicago agents had entered another door and were watching the lobby from the balcony.

At seven-thirty sharp, the phone on the end rang.

"Saul speaking."

"This will not take long, Mr. Saul. What was your wife's maiden name, her home town, and what was her major in college?"

"What is this, twenty questions?"

"Just answer the question, or I will hang up."

Saul didn't recognize the accent, maybe Russian—Iranian?—which meant he wasn't talking to Applenu or Austin.

When he didn't say anything, the voice said, "Answer the question or else I hang up."

"Her name was Jahn, from Jasper, Indiana, and she majored in communications."

"Good. We just wanted to make sure the FBI was following our commands. I'll also assume you brought nuclear experts, as we requested. The item you came to see is in Chicago's convention and exhibition center, McCormick Place, only about a mile from where your president is supposed to be giving a speech tonight. Am I to assume his speech is still on?"

"Yes it is. Where exactly in McCormick is this exhibition, or do we have to search all of the building?"

"We set up an exhibit for you in the Lawless Room. It's set up like a museum display. You will not be disappointed. By the way, Chicago has some excellent museums, as you will soon find out."

He hung up.

- - - - -

Hubbard maneuvered their dark-blue Ford Taurus through light evening traffic, heading south on Michigan Avenue. Saul and Spanner sat in the back, Trent Marshall, the head of the Chicago office, sat in the front. The car behind them contained two more agents from the Chicago office and two nuclear weapons experts, Tom Sukiomo from Los Alamos and Ted Lassiter from Lawrence Livermore National Laboratory in California. When Spanner heard about them being flown in, he said, "It verifies my suspicions: there's nobody in Washington anymore who knows how anything works."

They swept past the Chicago Art Institute with its two dirty stone lions guarding the entrance. A few blocks later, they passed the Hilton, where policemen formed a barrier to keep a crowd of demonstrators back, their signs castigating the president for not protecting them from nuclear weapons in the hands of terrorists. A knot of sign-waving demonstrators also patrolled the sidewalk across the street.

After wasting nearly half an hour being directed and misdirected by various guards and managers of the seemingly endless complex, they were met in the parking garage for McCormick Place East by Janos Lubanski, night security manager for all of McCormick Place, and his two black assistants, both of whom were on cell phones. Lubanski led the entourage into the deserted building and down a long dimly lit corridor past meeting rooms 20W 1-14, the Olive-Harvey and Jane Adams rooms to the Theo

Lawless Room.

Although eight enormous chandeliers blazed from the ceiling, most of the light seemed to be sucked away by the dark-brown acoustical tiles on the ceiling, the reddish-brown carpet, and the dark-stained wainscoting on the walls. In the front half of the room, straight-back, brown leather-covered metal chairs were set up for a meeting.

"Are you here to review the slides?" Lubanski asked.

"What slides?" Spanner asked.

"We just helped two guys set this room up for a meeting of the Bootstrap Bombers tomorrow morning," Lubanski said, leading them to the raised stage at the front of the room. A lectern on the left end held a laptop computer. "They said Mr. Saul would be here later tonight to review the slides on that laptop."

"I'm Saul."

"They said they left instructions on that crate," Lubanski said, motioning to a large wooden box the size of a refrigerator on the other side of the screen.

Saul found an envelope on top of the box. "It's addressed to Mr. Saul and interested people." Although he knew it was a futile gesture, he took a pair of surgical gloves from his pocket, pulled them on and opened the envelope.

"So what the hell does it say?" Spanner asked.

"It says they've got a slide show set up for us." Saul went around the wooden box and simply lifted off the side, reached in with both gloved hands and brought out a small digital recorder. He set it on the wooden box, then reached back into the box and came out with a long roll of blueprints and a three-ring binder filled with graphs and tables. "That's it."

"That's all that's in that big box?" Spanner asked, looking back at the two weapons experts at the back of the room and motioning them forward. "Have a seat, and we'll play the thing."

"You want to dust for prints first?"

"Later. You know there aren't any. For now, we'll play it and look at the slides," Spanner said. He turned to Marshall and told him to get everyone but the scientists out of the room, including Hubbard and himself.

Saul brought the tiny recorder over to the scientists in the front row of chairs and pressed PLAY.

"Gentlemen: what we are about to demonstrate should convince you that we have constructed several atomic bombs," a deep voice said with a slight unidentifiable accent.

"It's not Austin," Spanner said.

"Or Applenu," Saul said. "Not a British accent."

"First, the wooden box you see is the size we would use to transport one of our bombs. Had we chosen to, we could have easily placed a bomb in this room or anywhere in Chicago, as close to the president as we wanted to. Even in the Hilton, although for the type of bombs we have constructed, such proximity is not important. Of course, we could place our bombs any place, say the Empire State Building in New York, the Capital Building in Washington, or the Arch in Saint Louis.

"We considered showing you a real bomb, minus the nuclear material. But why should we give up something we worked so hard to produce? Instead, we conceived another method to convince you we mean business. Now, please turn off this recorder and have someone dim the lights and touch a key on the computer. Then double click the icon on the desktop. Everything we have to show and tell you is in the slides and video you are about to view."

Saul took care of the lights and then touched the space bar on the computer, which brought the monitor and screen in front of the room to life with the desktop and a PowerPoint icon, which, after several more clicks was in slideshow mode, and a PowerPoint title slide appeared:

Advanced Bomb Designs
by Bootstrap Bombers

The slide show was really a narrated video, and when the next slide flashed on the screen showing a complicated mechanism it was accompanied by the voice on the digital recorder who described the mechanism as a finished bomb without the nuclear material. As new slides flashed on the screen, the narrator kept up a detailed technical description of what was being displayed.

The first series of slides showed how this bomb mechanism was built, including the addition of conventional explosives used to detonate the nuclear explosion. Complicated calculations used to verify the placement of the conventional explosives were described, and a slide showing the calculation setup was displayed along with graphs and a table of results.

Videos followed, the first one showing containers of nuclear material, supposedly taken from the hijacked trucks. They could easily check that, Saul thought, as he pulled out his notebook. The video led the viewers through nuclear handling facilities that the narrator claimed were used to handle the radioactive material safely. The video panned around a computer room filled with an eight-node computer cluster used for the computerized machining of nuclear material.

The video of the facilities completed, slides of nuclear material in various stages of processing followed, from the liquid solution right through the machining of solids to the point where the material stood ready for insertion into the bomb. Finally, there were slides showing diagrams of atom-bomb designs, for which the narrator rattled off results of modeling studies on a supercomputer to produce calculations of explosive yields for the different designs. Tables and graphs were used to demonstrate the bomb specifications and characteristics. The narrator indicated that more detail on the various designs described could be seen on the accompanying blueprints and the contents of the three-ring binder.

Throughout the video presentation, Sukiomo and Lassiter carried on a rapid-fire conversation, using terms Saul didn't understand.

The demonstration ended like it started, with a slide of the assembled bomb mechanism. This time, however, the slide showed it next to the wooden box that stood in front of them with machined uranium set on top of the box.

The voice said, "Now all that remains is for the uranium to be inserted into the bomb mechanism. Once the uranium is installed, we can deliver a bomb anywhere in the country...or the world. This ends our demonstration."

Before anyone could move or say anything, the slide with the bomb mechanism changed to one that read:

A FINAL DEMONSTRATION OF OUR SINCERITY WILL BE AVAILABLE IN A SHORT TIME AT THE CHICAGO ART INSTITUTE

They seemed to have a fascination with Chicago museums, Saul thought, remembering his phone conversation.

As soon as the screen went blank, Sukiomo and Lassiter began jabbering. Saul groped his way back to the light switches, wondering where the bomb makers were leading them. Some BD lyrics floated into his head:

When you're lost in Juarez,
And it's Easter time too.
And your gravity fails you,

And your negativity won't pull you through...

Spanner paced around the box, looking at the blueprints and binder the taped voice said would provide further proof for the validity of their design. Spanner turned to the two scientists. "So what do you think?"

"It could be, very well could be," Sukiomo said.

Lassiter nodded. "We wondered about the triggers, figured they wouldn't be able to get any. In 1990 after Iraq tried to buy some, the government made them impossible to get. These guys built their own. They've got them. I believe they can do it."

"What's next?" Spanner asked.

Lassiter answered. "We've got orders to get all this information back to Washington as soon as possible. A committee of experts has been convened for tomorrow morning to evaluate the data."

The door in the back of the room crashed open, and Marshall rushed in. "George, we just got a call on the radio that there's been an explosion down on Michigan Avenue in front of the Art Institute. A car blew up. Evidently blew the hell out of the front of the building as well as some buildings across the street."

Spanner looked at the two scientists, then at Saul. "A car bomb. They exploded a goddamned car bomb right in the middle of Chicago."

Chapter Thirty

BOMB MAKERS CLAIM RESPONSIBILITY FOR CHICAGO
MUSEUM EXPLOSION
Sheena Mosely
Chicago (AP) An anonymous informant to AP claimed a
connection exists between persons who stole enough nuclear
material for fifteen to twenty atomic bombs and the car-bomb
explosion that rocked downtown Chicago last night. The
explosion, which injured eleven people, caused extensive
damage to the Chicago Art Institute and shattered windows in
buildings as far as three blocks away.

When the explosion occurred, President Gordono was
delivering a speech at the Hilton Hotel, less than four blocks
from the explosion. The President was rushed by helicopter to
O'Hare Field, from where he flew back to Washington on Air
Force One. As yet, the White House has not commented on
these developments beyond a press release saying that
government experts were analyzing this new turn of events.

Senator Stanley Hughson, a member of the Senate Armed
Services Committee, did have a comment after he arrived at
the damaged Art Institute last night shortly after the explosion.
He said that this incident invalidates his previous speculation
that an enemy of the United States might be building a bomb
that could then be kept inside the United States until hostilities
broke out between the two countries. He now believes that
whoever has the bomb intends to make terrorist demands on
the U.S. Government. According to Hughson, the Chicago
demonstration was meant to insure that when those demands
are presented, the government will know that there is a bomb

somewhere in the country. Hughson called on the President to join Congress to explore ways to head off a possible catastrophe.

The explosion, which demolished the two stone lions in front of the Art Institute as well as doing extensive damage inside the museum, was estimated by Chicago Police Chief Ben Westman to have contained...

- - - - -

Applenu set down the phone and leaned back in his chair. He tried to concentrate on the CAD/CAM drawing on the monitor that went with Reedan's latest program, but his mind remained on the phone conversation. It was that pesky local newspaper reporter again wanting to know when they would begin operation and how many people they would employee. He talked to her several months ago, when she called wanting information on the new business in town. Even after he gave her answers she liked and allowed her to write an article, she wanted to come out and interview him, tour the plant, and take pictures. He suggested she call at the end of next month. By then he hoped to be well away from this place.

A key rattled in the outside door, and Lormes strolled in carrying a newspaper. What did *he* want? Applenu wondered, since he rarely showed up at the plant. He assumed it wasn't a social call at this time of the morning, because he usually hung around his apartment or was off on some trip, never saying where he was going. Applenu didn't ask or care, as long as his people were available when needed.

"What in hell are Sherbani and Hearn up to?" Lormes asked, waving the newspaper. He unfolded it and pointed to the front-page story by Sheena Mosely.

Applenu had seen it. "Hearn and Sherbani say it's a smoke screen to keep the FBI busy and distracted. That way we can finish our work and cut away." That's what they said, Applenu thought, but could you believe them? Applenu argued against making that video or having Beecher take pictures of their operation.

Lormes pulled a chair next to the desk and sat. "I'm all for keeping them off our ass," he said, "but I know something about bombs, and that one in Chicago was a warning. He's saying, 'We can do the same thing with the atom bombs we're building.'"

Applenu nodded. They didn't need Lormes upset. "That's the message, but it's just to keep the FBI chasing their bloody tails."

"You think so? Hey, I've killed some people who needed killing, and I'll probably do it again. Along the way, some innocent people got whacked, like the ones that died when we hijacked this nuclear stuff. That's regrettable. But there was always a reason. You know, ends justify the means. But I don't want anything to do with exploding an atomic bomb in this country, killing a lot of people like those bastards did on nine eleven. Hey, I love this country. It's done a lot for me."

Applenu pointed to the newspaper. "You've got to admit he's got the FBI so they don't know bugger all about what's happening. One day they're in Saint Louis, the next day it's Chicago. If they're in Chicago, they're not banging *our* door down."

Lormes nodded. "They've used the Mosely broad to our advantage, but one thing doesn't sit right. I was told that the material we stole would be smuggled out of the country after it was machined. Once they had it in your country, they would safeguard it from the U. S. and Israel, and after that they wouldn't be pushed around by those countries."

Lormes wasn't supposed to ask such questions. He was hired to do the job and collect his large fee, not to analyze foreign policy.

"Sherbani talks about negotiating from strength," Lormes said. "Once they get the material out of the country, it'll be up to the diplomats to calm things down and get Sherbani's country the respect he thinks they deserve. But this shit with the car bomb makes you wonder what they plan to do with the atomic bombs."

"I'll speak to Sherbani and Hearn about your concerns."

Lormes stood and started for the door. "You do that. Tell them I'm not going to let them explode any atomic bombs in this country. That wasn't in the deal."

The deal, Applenu thought. What about his own deal? All he really wanted was a professorship at Ohio State, or even one back in England, say at the University of Birmingham where he started. He never thought dirty old Birmingham would look so good.

Lormes paused at the door and looked back. "You are doing good on getting rid of the British accent. Only problem is, you still say 'bloody' a lot."

- - - - -

Surling stared across the table at Applenu and wondered what brought the bastard here this time. He just invited himself to lunch for the first time, saying there were things to discuss. Then again, maybe it wasn't bad news, since none of his goons came with him.

Surling glanced at Reedan, who'd been quiet throughout the meal. He'd been quiet ever since the last time they sat across the table from Applenu. Reedan had been through it alright: first Drafton, then his wife. Slapped the shit out of her, felt her up good, and let him see and hear it. Based on how Beecher acted and talked when he stopped the video, they did a lot more than just feel her up, and Reedan knew it.

During lunch, Applenu did most of the talking, directing his conversation at Surling, talking about processing the nuclear material and the imminent success of the project. He was working hard at losing the British accent, although on occasion he slipped up by interjecting a "bloody" or some British slang into the conversation. He was growing his black beard again, after being clean shaven for a week or so.

With lunch over, they sipped coffee. Then Applenu dropped the bomb. He looked at Surling, smiled, and said, "It looks like we're through with your part of the project, Professor. You did a good job, and we quite appreciate it. You can pack this evening, and later tonight we'll get you on your way back to Philadelphia."

It couldn't be. Not yet. They hadn't made alternate escape plans. Surling tried to plan, but Reedan was too preoccupied about his wife and AIDS.

Surling tried a smile and happy act at the news. "You're really going to let me go?"

"We're sending you home to your…" Applenu laughed. "I was going to say wife." He turned to Reedan. "Did he tell you he's grinding two women? Three, if you count his wife, although from what I hear, he hasn't shagged her for awhile."

"How did you know about them?" Surling asked while forcing a man-to-man chuckle. These bastards had done their homework, okay. But then he made their job simple: Bill Surling, the original dirty old man. Just hire a whore to smile at him, pull his dick out of his pants, suck it, and he'll follow her anywhere. Jesus, when would he learn? Why did he keep on doing it? They probably found out all about him by asking around the campus. How many people back there knew?

"We investigated you, Professor." Applenu turned back to Reedan. "On most days for lunch he goes home with a secretary from the Civil Engineering Department. They tell me the bird's young enough to be his granddaughter. Then he's got a widow, forty-something. Sees her every Wednesday night and Sunday morning when his wife's at church. She thinks he's interested in marrying her. They say he's been chatting up one of his graduate students, a bit of fluff by the name of Nancy Gleason. Has she come across yet, Professor?"

Surling's face burned, and he knew it was red. Why should it be? He'd been acting a damn fool for almost twenty years now.

"I'll tell you, Professor, we hesitated getting you for this project. With all the time and energy you spend humping, at your age and all, we wondered if you still knew anything about chemistry. But you didn't disappoint us."

Applenu turned to Reedan. "Did you know he was a child prodigy? He was the youngest scientist on the Manhattan Project. Only seventeen, but he already had a year of graduate school when he went to work on the project in 1944. He's mentioned in all the books on the Manhattan Project. He's written a few of his own, in fact. There'd be more, if he applied himself. People figure he buggered it all away when his son killed himself."

"We're turning you loose," Applenu said, "but you know what you're going to have to do."

"I won't go to the police."

"If you do, your wife and daughters see those pictures and find out about your lunch hours and your Wednesday nights and Sunday mornings. You saw how Beecher and Maxwell operate. Need I say more? But to make it easier for you to keep quiet, we'll give you the two-hundred-fifty-thousand dollars we promised you."

"Don't worry. Nobody will ever hear anything from me."

- - - - -

After five days of checking for the big black car in the parking lot, Lori began to doubt what she had seen. Did they really get out of their car and go into the apartment building? Or did she lose them somewhere on the Turnpike and follow another car, assuming it was them? After all, it was dusk, and she was in pain. God, she didn't want to think of that day again.

She wondered if she was checking the right parking lot, so today she drove through parking lots for several identical buildings in the vicinity of where she thought she knew they had parked. She found no big black car with out-of-state plates in any of them.

She got home at six-thirty, exhausted, frustrated, and angry. While Beth went to watch TV, Lori read the newspaper account of the Chicago bombing. Why couldn't the FBI catch them?

Beth's scream erupted simultaneously with the doorbell. "Mommy!

It's them! It's those men again," she yelled as she ran up the steps and into the kitchen. "Let me stay with you, please."

Lori's breathing accelerated. She crouched down to hug Beth. "Everything will be okay. You can stay at the top of the steps and watch when I answer the door. Okay?"

Beth nodded, sending a shower of tears onto Lori's arm.

The doorbell rang again.

Lori inhaled deeply: Dad's advice to calm herself before she shot; it was her remedy to ready herself for a big exam. She grabbed her shoulder bag from the table and dug into it, fingering the cool handle of the pistol before coming out with a tissue to wipe Beth's face. After setting the shoulder bag on the bottom step, she checked the chain lock. If they made one move to come in, she would go for the gun.

A red-headed man stood on the porch. He held out a badge for her to inspect. "Mrs. Reedan, I'm Jerry Fortner from the FBI. I'd like to ask you some questions about your husband."

Chapter Thirty-One

Surling paced in front of the table where Reedan sat. He remembered telling someone several months after Al's death that he never realized life could get so fucked up so quickly. And here it was again, ratcheted up several more notches.

What could they do? At best, they'd have one more shot at an escape attempt. Nothing compared to the chance Reedan fucked up or the chance they'd have had with Drafton.

"We've got to make plans." Surling said. "They're coming for me in a few hours."

"Maybe Applenu will let you go. He sounded sincere."

Jesus, they feel up his wife, probably rape her, and show him videos and pictures of it, and he wants to trust them. "Sure, Applenu comes on like one of our friendly scientific colleagues. For non-scientific chores, he's got Beecher. He sends *him* to talk to your wife, and he sends *him* to pay us off and send us on our way."

"If they turned you loose, would you go to the police?"

"I don't know what I'd do, and they don't either."

Surling turned to pace some more. Tired, so tired. Maybe age had run him down at last. He trudged back to the table and sat down. "We can't let assholes like that gain control of these weapons. I was involved with two atomic bombs that blew thousands of people away. There was a reason then, but I sure don't want to be involved with another. When you were building bombs at Oak Ridge, didn't you ever worry that they'd be used to kill innocent people?"

"I never saw a bomb or bomb-grade uranium. I just developed computer programs."

"You just did your job, collected your check, and didn't even think about it. Those are some of the reasons Drafton gave for going to work for

Applenu. That's what we did on the Manhattan Project. Whatever happens, we helped make those bombs. When they go off, we'll be partly responsible...unless we do everything we can to stop them."

"But what if we fail? They'll..."

"It's the same either way."

- - - - -

Applenu answered the loud knock on the door to his apartment expecting to find Markum or Maxwell with his dinner. On most nights they brought dinner from a local restaurant.

Instead of Markum or Maxwell, a younger bloke with a shaved head and a full black beard stood there holding a large bag from Appleby's. "Your takeout meal is here, old chap."

"Steve? Uh...Derek?"

"The name's George Atkinson," he said, stepping into the room and sticking out his hand. He roared into a laugh as he slammed the door behind him and grabbed Applenu in a bear hug. "I've got a couple bottles of red in here along with steaks. Sorry I couldn't bring some broads to really make it like old times."

- - - - -

In the semi-darkness, Curt and Surling sat on chairs on either side of the door waiting, like early morning arrivals at the ticket counter for a major sporting event. A dim, green glow permeated the room, the light emitted from the open refrigerator, just enough light to distract whoever opened the door. Or so they hoped.

The refrigerator motor droned away.

Curt hefted his weapon, an empty green wine bottle. Could he live with it if he killed a man one on one? In Surling's argument to get him here, he reminded Curt of the pictures and video—as if he could forget. From the moment Applenu dropped the photos on the table and turned the laptop for him and Surling to see, his mind wouldn't release the image of Beecher's hand on Lori's breast and the agony on her face. What else did they do to her? When Beecher killed the video, his arrogant smirk hinted that the rest of the video held still more hideous scenes.

On the other side of the door frame, Surling twisted the cap off of a half-empty catsup bottle, studied it, and twisted it back on. "Deep down, I figured my philandering might kill me," he said, his voice stripped of its professorial tone, a quiet rumble to keep from being heard by their guard, who at night set up a cot in the hall just beyond the door. "I figured some guy would catch me in bed with his wife and shoot me." He forced a laugh. "Another way I visualized going out was a heart attack while on top of some young thing." His face clouded. "I forgot to tell you I turned eighty-five a couple weeks ago. I remembered yesterday."

"So why do you do it?" Curt asked, chasing the numbing thoughts of Beecher and Lori from his mind and tuning his ear for the key in the lock. Death, he thought, something he hadn't figured into his career calculations, except for the stray thought on the highway after a close call. If they guessed right, his own death was scheduled for the next few days. Should things go wrong tonight, they'd accelerate the schedule. Maybe doing something beat sitting around and thinking about Beecher and Lori, Drafton and AIDS.

Like a motor at idle, Surling's leg jiggled away, seemingly disconnected from his rigidly stiff upper body. "When Al...you know... when he did that, I flipped out. I wanted to strike out."

"At your wife?" Curt asked, wondering why they were talking like this.

"I don't know who. All I could think of was that I let him down. His life was fucked up, like so many kids. But kill himself? He tried drugs, but I figured all kids did that, a phase they go through these days. I talked to him about it, but we just argued, like we did whenever we talked...what little we talked. His first two years at Cal Tech were disasters...after being a Merit Scholar."

"Cal Tech's tough." Who cares, Curt thought. Beecher's coming for us.

"Anyway, when he was home that summer, I tried to listen to him, instead of doing all of the talking—preaching, you'd probably call it."

Curt nodded, wishing Surling would shut up and get ready.

"When I got to Los Alamos in 1944, everyone was older than me, most of them married with families, everyone with their PhD, sitting around talking about their science. At seventeen, I didn't fit in. Then one day Oppenheimer himself walked into my lab and asked me to hike with him in the Jemez Mountains. He talked to me like a father to a son, like my father never did. And he listened to me. It changed my life."

Curt nodded, listening for noise out in the hall. He wondered if he should know who Oppenheimer was.

Surling continued. "I remembered that experience with Oppie, so one day I suggested to Al that he and I go backpacking in the Sierras. I figured he'd say no, but he said yes. That's where I fucked up," he said, his voice rising slightly. He shook his head side-to-side. "I was finishing a textbook and had a deadline. When Al went back to school, I said we'd do it in the spring."

Curt remembered that the only place Dad ever took him was out on the driveway when he was about five. He handed him a basketball and told him to throw it through the hoop on the garage. Curt looked at Surling and saw tears rolling down his cheeks, just like they ran down Drafton's. "Bob, they'll be here soon."

"Less than a month after Al went back, we got the call..."

Curt swung his wine bottle at the air and thought about all those days on the driveway throwing the basketball through the hoop. Later, he sent Dad on trips. Dad never missed a game, and afterward he replayed it over and over. Was their relationship better than the one Surling had with his son?

Surling blew his nose. "Like I told you before, I wasn't connecting with my wife...or my other kids, for that matter. It started out with my wife's friend and went from there. It became a game. Like this beautiful Brigham Young graduate who'd do anything every Thursday afternoon while her graduate-student husband had a thermodynamics class. So I get enticed into bed by one more blonde and end it all in this god-forsaken place. Sometimes I think Al had the right idea. Not for himself, mind you, but for me. Just shut it down. Maybe...if I don't get out of here...it won't be all that bad."

Everybody changes one way or another, Curt thought. One farming accident and Dad changed. Why? It wasn't *his* accident. Curt never considered how he had been changed by the accident. He just changed his career plans—his plan for the rest of his life—and moved on.

"We're not going to die, Bob," Curt said. "That's why we're here." A few minutes earlier he hoped Beecher wouldn't come. Now he wished he would hurry up and get there.

"I told you about June, how I promised to make her my only woman. The one Applenu said I saw on Wednesdays and Sundays. I see her more often than that. Anyway, I've been thinking maybe I ought to rediscover my wife...my family...ask them to forgive me. She was good for me once."

Surling looked at Curt, as if trying to read something on his face. "Curt, you are right to want that kid, to want to be more involved with your wife and daughter. Just don't forget it down the road when some fucking robot project beckons at the same time your kid wants you to go to a ballgame."

"Hey, I'll make you the godfather, and you can keep an eye on me and the kid." Maybe if they have a boy, Dad could make him a basketball player. He'd ask his dad to help him put up a goal in the driveway.

Surling cleared his throat. "Your work's exciting, but your kids can bring something permanent to your life…if you're lucky. I was excited by work on the Manhattan Project, but then doubts set in about making atomic bombs. Oppie had doubts, and they fucked him over and drove him to an early grave. I got into research for nuclear reactors—atoms for peace, Eisenhower called it. That bogged me down in paperwork and bullshit, so I went to the university. Things were good there before the whores got control. I published four books and two-hundred-some research papers. But all the time my kids were growing up without me. I missed the whole thing."

As Curt strained to hear, he wondered if Dad had any regrets besides the accident. He thought he heard voices outside the door, meaning there was more than the usual one guard out there.

Surling didn't notice. "When Al died, I looked at all the *important* things I'd been doing and realized nothing's important."

Curt put his finger to his lips to quiet Surling.

Surling ignored him, his voice getting louder. "It's all a mindfuck. Eventually, everything turns out like the Manhattan Project. But your kids…you understand what I'm saying?"

"You convinced me what I did with Drafton was important," Curt whispered, "and now you say nothing's important."

Surling stared momentarily into the space above Curt's head. "Nothing matters when…"

A loud voice rumbled in the hall outside the door, and Curt waved a hand at Surling's face and pointed to the door.

Surling's head jerked sideways; his eyes widened.

In unison, they stood and moved their chairs to the side.

- - - - -

A key rattled in the lock.

Curt sucked in his breath and flattened his body against the wall. He rubbed two sweaty palms on his pants and grabbed the wine bottle from the floor.

On the other side of the door frame, Surling stood stiff as a corpse. He saw Curt looking and forced a smile, then flashed thumbs up. Curt returned the gesture.

The door opened. Bright light from the hall evacuated the green glow from half the room. Surling now stood behind the door and would have to work his way forward to make his attack.

"Why are the lights off?" Beecher growled. He flicked the switch. "Lights are burned out." He stepped into the room, standing barely three feet from Curt, and stared at the refrigerator.

Maxwell hung back in the doorway and watched; only his huge stomach protruded into the room.

Next to the light switch Curt pushed his back against the wall, wishing he could tunnel inside, hoping Beecher wouldn't look his way.

Beecher passed by him and called into the room, "You ready to go, Surling?"

Maxwell took a tentative step into the room, then another. Curt swung. Thunk: the bottle connected on Maxwell's forehead and bounced off like an axe from an oak log.

Maxwell's head snapped back. He grabbed at his face with both hands and staggered forward into the room, moaning as he crumpled to the floor at Curt's feet.

Beecher whirled to face Curt. He glanced down at Maxwell, and then his right hand dived into his jacket. "What the fuck's going on, Reedan?" He jerked his gun from his jacket.

Surling emerged from behind the door and slammed the catsup bottle against the back of Beecher's head.

Beecher staggered toward Curt, eyes glazed. Arm shaking, he struggled to raise the gun and point it at Curt. Slowly, he collapsed to his knees. "You sons of bitches." He toppled forward onto his hands, shaking his head and moaning.

Surling hurled the catsup bottle after the falling Beecher and stepped around him. Simultaneously, Surling and Curt tried to jam through the door. Curt stepped back.

Surling pointed to the floor, panic covering his face. "Watch out!"

Before Curt could react, he felt both of Maxwell's arms wrapped around his left leg, squeezing like a steel trap. Curt kicked at Maxwell with his right foot, but the trap tightened. He swung the wine bottle at Maxwell's head; it bounced off of his shoulder.

Surling stood rooted in the doorway, searching the floor for his catsup bottle.

Maxwell grabbed Curt's left arm, still holding the leg.

Curt strained to keep his body from being sucked to the floor like a roast into a meat grinder. He jerked back again and again, trying to break Maxwell's grip. It wouldn't give. Everything's over before it starts, he thought, just like the last time.

Surling stood and watched.

Beecher, still on all fours, shook his head and moaned.

"Get out of here, Bob." Curt yelled. He swung the wine bottle at Maxwell's head and missed. The bottle slid through his sweaty hand and shattered on the floor, glass swishing and clinking around the room. Maxwell held on, pulling and twisting Curt's bad leg. Pain shot up into his thigh.

Surling remained frozen in the doorway, searching the floor for his bottle, occasionally staring at Beecher, now on his knees.

With his right hand, Curt pried at Maxwell's hands; he kicked and connected with Maxwell's leg. Maxwell grunted, but held on, working to pull himself up while trying to pull Curt down.

"Get out of here, Bob! Run!"

Surling hesitated, saw Beecher struggling to stand, and turned and disappeared out the door.

Beecher heaved himself to his feet, his gun in one hand, his other hand pressed to the back of his head. "Hold that bastard," he yelled. He shoved Curt backward. "I'll get that other son of a bitch."

Beecher's push knocked Curt off balance. Curt's right knee connected with Maxwell's jaw.

Maxwell's head snapped back, and he lost his grip.

Curt landed on top of Maxwell and rolled off. He levered himself up, kicked at Maxwell's vast stomach, and then crunched through the glass shards after Beecher.

Out in the brightly lit hall, Surling was almost at the green EXIT door. Beecher trailed ten feet back, gun in one hand while his other hand fumbled inside his jacket pocket.

Curt followed on Beecher's heels.

Surling reached the green door and jerked at the handle.

Beecher stopped, screwed something on the gun, and aimed it at Surling.

Curt rushed toward Beecher; his only chance was to hit him and make him miss.

Thuck! Thuck!

As Curt approached Beecher, he caught sight of Surling.

Surling's head snapped back. He thrashed the air with both hands, like a drowning man about to go down. Slowly, he doubled up and pitched forward, his head crashing into the half-open green door.

Curt smashed into Beecher's back and bounced off, his momentum driving Beecher forward.

Beecher stopped, pivoted around, and faced Curt.

Curt lowered his shoulder and charged.

Like a bullfighter without a cape, Beecher sidestepped. "You son of a bitch, I'll get you for this." As Curt stumbled by him, Beecher kicked Curt's right thigh. "If Applenu didn't need you, I'd give you what Surling got!"

Beecher's kick sent Curt reeling, but he recovered his balance. When he turned to rush Beecher again, he stared into the muzzle of the gun.

Beecher waggled the silencer-lengthened pistol like a scolding finger waved at a naughty child. "Don't tempt me, asshole."

Breathing hard, Curt rubbed his aching thigh. He started to slump to the floor, then remembered Surling.

Surling lay on his right side, his left knee pulled toward his chest, still trying to run away. The back of his bald head glowed with reflected light. A rapidly enlarging reddish-brown circle on the lower back of his khaki shirt gleamed moist like spilled coffee. A smaller circle grew on the right shoulder.

Gently, Curt held his head and eased him onto his back. His light-blue eyes, wide open, stared at the ceiling, and blood oozed around the left eye and drained into the upturned socket to form a total eclipse. His glasses, the left lens shattered, hung from his right ear down the front of his face and glistened below his nose like snot blown out but not free. With his lips slightly parted, he appeared ready to speak.

Curt cleared his throat of the congestion that pressured his chest and pushed up into his throat. "Bob."

"Get your ass up, Reedan," Beecher growled from behind.

Curt searched Surling's limp wrist for life. "It's beating! There's a pulse." His pulse was weak, but present, constant, like the ticking of a watch. He twisted around to look up at Beecher. "He's alive. We've got to get him to a doctor."

Beecher kneed Curt in the right kidney.

Curt lurched forward onto his knees; he dropped the wrist and grabbed his back. "He's alive."

"Get your ass up."

Another knee from Beecher, and Curt crumbled forward and braced himself on the floor to keep from sprawling on top of Surling. He grabbed his back, and with great effort, he struggled to his feet, swallowing hard to choke back the vomit that stewed in the back of his throat.

Beecher grabbed Curt's shoulder, twisted him around, and shoved him toward his quarters. "No way is he alive."

Curt tried to go around Beecher to get back to Surling. "I felt a pulse. Bob!"

Beecher blocked his way, his gun shoved into Curt's stomach, his left hand probing gently at the back of his head. "That's it, Reedan. Now turn your ass around and get in that room."

Curt hesitated, and the gun penetrated further into his gut, stirring the nausea. He stepped back to relieve the pressure, his eyes never leaving Surling's face.

Beecher backed up until he stood over Surling. "He's done." He raised his gun.

"Hey!"

Thuck! Thuck!

Surling's body twitched slightly.

Before Curt could move, Beecher swung the gun around and pointed it at Curt's chest.

"You *killed* him."

Surling's expression hadn't changed. Two intersecting circular stains now raced across the front of his khaki shirt, heading for an intersection.

"Get back in there, Reedan. *Now.*"

He swallowed hard and slowly turned. Now what? Curt wondered. Maybe it was time to say the hell with it. Just take out after him and force him to use his gun one more time. Use it now, instead of two days from now. It'll all come out the same.

Beecher shoved him forward just as Maxwell stumbled into the hall, holding his stomach, blood coursing down his face from a gash above his left eye. A painted clown: one side of his face painted red with blood, the other side white. Blood polka dotted the left side of his short-sleeve white shirt. He shuffled across the hall into the change room.

"I said get your ass in there," Beecher said.

Curt cleared his throat and swallowed. He looked back at Surling one more time, as his last words hammered around inside his brain: *"Nothing matters."*

"It does, Bob," Curt mumbled. "It has to."

Beecher tapped the gun on Curt's shoulder and signaled for him to turn around and face him. He held the gun in his right hand while he probed the back of his head with a handkerchief in his left hand. He studied the blood-spotted handkerchief. "If anything like this happens again." He stopped to breathe, short quick rasps through his open mouth, like a winded dog. "If you even look like you're going to make a break for it, you're not only going to get it, but your wife's going to get another visit. And this time we won't just fuck the bitch." As if to summon more words, he waved the lengthened gun barrel like a baton. "Yeah, we fucked the cunt. We gave her what you haven't given her enough of."

Curt lunged forward, his fists ready. "Like hell you will."

Beecher stepped back, his face reddening, the gun still pointed forward. "Just don't tempt me."

Curt stopped and stepped back. No chance this time. There'd be a time to settle scores, soon enough. He turned and limped toward his quarters, his thigh aching from the kick, but his knee came out okay, despite the twisting Maxwell gave it.

Up ahead, Maxwell slouched in the entrance to the change room, watching, a white towel pressed to the left side of his head covering his eye. He shuffled toward Curt to block his way. They stared at each other, Maxwell's head cocked sideways to glare up at Curt with his good eye.

"I'd like nothing better than to get another shot at her," Maxwell yelled. "Next time I'll fuck her until her cunt's hamburger."

Curt started around him, but Maxwell scooted sideways to keep in front of Curt. He pulled the red-splotched towel from his face, leaving Curt to stare at blood oozing from a cut and rolling down his forehead. Without warning, Maxwell's fist smashed into the left side of Curt's jaw, spinning him around. Curt grabbed hold of the wall as it sailed by, a shower of blood from Maxwell's forehead sprinkling Curt's khaki pants and shoes. He choked back the vomit that seeped into his mouth.

Maxwell swung again, but Curt covered up, the blow bouncing off of his elbow.

Beecher grabbed Maxwell's shoulder. "We'll have time for that later."

- - - - -

Curt lay on his back and stared into the darkness, his body rigid with a tenseness that could not be drained. Across the room, the refrigerator hummed incessantly. His jaw and thigh ached. His brain ached with the memory of events of the past hour. Should they have tried it? If they intend to kill him when they're through with him, what would they do with Lori? She had seen some of them. What would they do with Beth?

He searched his mind for good memories to induce relaxation and ease himself into sleep. One memory—one he wanted to forget—crowded out all others: the night before Beth's birth. That night found him filled with tension produced by weeks of eighteen-hour days as he pushed to wrap up his PhD thesis.

On top of it all, Lori, two weeks overdue and climbing the walls of their one-bedroom apartment, ambushed him when he came home.

"Let's do something; I've got to get out of here," she said.

"I've got to go back to the lab. Once I finish the thesis, we'll have time for other things."

He capitulated: dinner at Legal Seafood in Cambridge and a movie with a metallurgical title, "The Tin Men," about two aluminum-siding salesmen. In the cool darkness of the theatre, his head spun with differential equations, a Bessel function solution he'd been wrestling with for days. Were the boundary conditions correct? Did they fit the problem?

Suddenly, he became aware of Lori holding his hand with both of hers, her swollen breasts pressing against his arm. He grew hard immediately. It dawned on him how long it had been. He caressed her swollen breasts, locked away in a tight bra beneath the sleeveless dress. His hand slid across her rock-hard stomach. Momentarily startled by the unexpected bumps and perturbations on the smooth surface of her abdomen, his computer-connected mind veered off in pursuit of the application of fractals to the mapping of the surface perturbations. Technical thoughts quickly vanished as his hand struggled to get between her legs. He wanted her. All those times he could have and didn't. Why now when he couldn't have her? He worked his hand up under her dress.

She pushed him away, but he grabbed her hand and coaxed it down between his legs. He glanced around the theater, unzipped, and his rock-hard penis jumped out as if spring loaded.

"Curt, don't."

"Do me. I need you."

"What?" She giggled, tentatively skimming her fingers across him, and then snapping her hand back. "*Curt.*" Giggling, she glanced around. "Watch the movie."

Later, standing in the shower, his soapy hands accomplished the hand job Lori wouldn't carry out in the theater, relieving some of his pressure. What were his thoughts? Thoughts of that hard bumpy stomach he hadn't really felt all those months as Beth grew within his reach? Thoughts of missed dinners? Missed conversations? No, just the thought of sex interspersed with calculations and finishing his goddamn thesis.

Three hours later, Lori woke him from a deep sleep and told him the pains had started. Throughout the day in the hospital and over the next few weeks as Lori recovered, his conscience nagged him for what he did in the shower. To some extent, it still nagged.

Was Lori afraid that night? Afraid of what she faced: labor pains, becoming a mother? *Now*, I think of that, five years after the fact.

Across the room, the refrigerator finally clicked off.

Curt flipped sideways on the cot, remembering Lori's hard stomach and swollen breasts. His left hand slipped between his legs. "Lori."

The future included all the things he'd been missing, always there within his reach. There would be a future for them. He'd see to that.

Chapter Thirty-Two

Applenu reached for his wine glass, hesitated, then jerked his hand back, aware of his wooziness and the effort needed to keep his mind focused. He again fixed his attention on Atkinson's voice, which seemed to flow from the far corner of the room, rather than from across the table. This was the closest he had ever come to being drunk, he thought, although maybe he was drunk, since he lacked a previous drunken experience for comparison. If only Sherbani could see him now—his good Muslim gone bad.

The evening began with a couple of scotch and sodas, followed by the steak and cabernet sauvignon Atkinson brought. They talked, catching up on where they had been and where they were going. Atkinson did most of the talking, describing what he had been doing since the reported death of Austin and the unreported death of Hearn. Although the shaved head, black beard, and brown-tinted contact lenses changed his appearance dramatically, his enthusiasm remained at full throttle.

He described his present work as strategist for the project. In that position, he claimed responsibility for the leaks to the press and the car bomb in Chicago. He expressed confidence that those actions had deflected the FBI's investigation far from where the two of them now sat. In addition, he supervised the machining in a Buffalo machine shop of bomb-mechanism parts that were on their way to Iran, and he was now busy planning the shipment of the machined nuclear materials.

"There will be more leaks," Atkinson said, smoothing his beard. He described how he placed trap door and Trojan horse programs in the DOE and FBI computers. In due time, those hacking devices were discovered and removed. However, Austin had set it up so that when they were discovered and/or removed, they activated new Trojan horse and trap door programs.

Atkinson sipped wine. "Once we find out they've got information on us that they want to keep quiet, we leak it. That shakes up their whole system, because it sends them off looking for internal leaks. We're also talking to Senator Hughson, which screws them up even more."

Applenu updated Atkinson on his progress in machining the nuclear material and how it would only be a week or two before the job was finished.

After dinner, Applenu's cell phone rang

"We completed your task," Beecher said.

Applenu knew he meant Surling. "It wasn't my task. It was yours and Lormes's. I told Lormes what I wanted to do."

"And he told you we didn't have a *bloody* choice. The reason I called was to tell you it was messier than we wanted it to be. Reedan saw the finish, and I called to warn you so you can be ready for whatever he might try tomorrow."

Applenu saw Atkinson watching from across the table. "You were supposed to take him out…"

"Things don't always work the way they are supposed to," Beecher said. "He ran, and there wasn't any other choice. Just be ready for Reedan tomorrow." He hung up.

"Is something wrong?" Atkinson asked.

Applenu eyed his wine glass but refrained from picking it up. "It was Lormes's man Beecher. They killed Surling tonight. He tried to escape, and they evidently shot him in front of Reedan."

"Those things happen," Atkinson said.

"Why couldn't we turn them loose? They don't know where we are."

"You know better than that. They can give the police descriptions of you and everyone else they saw. It will be okay," Atkinson said as he smiled and lifted his wine glass. "I want to propose a toast: To you, old chap, for a great job on the project. Sherbani and I are pleased with your work up to now."

Applenu smiled, picked up his glass, raised it, and sipped.

"There is one problem, however. Our boss is beginning to have doubts about your loyalty to your homeland."

"I'm doing the job he hired me to do."

Atkinson's smile drained from his face. "We don't trust you any more."

"You don't *trust* me? Why not?"

"For starters, it was that comment you made in New York about wanting to sabotage the project."

"You brought that up."

"I brought it up as a test. You flunked. And now there's the issue of your family. We want to know where you moved them."

"What are you talking about? My parents are in Amsterdam."

"Don't *bullshit* me. You moved them. It was a slick job, and we still haven't figured out how you did it. Was it the painters? You also moved your aunt and uncle out of Birmingham."

"What are you talking about?"

"I *said* don't *bullshit* me. Sherbani and I need to feel we can trust you to carry out this job."

"And to do that, you're telling me you need to hold me and my family hostage? I'm here to tell you my family is out of this game. I am still here, and I will finish the job as promised."

Atkinson reached for the wine bottle and drained it into his glass. "Sherbani wanted me to bring Mr. Lormes and some of his colleagues with me to talk to you. Maybe he was right."

"Does this mean I'm going to wind up like Surling and Reedan after I finish the job?"

Atkinson raised his glass toward Applenu, his California smile in place. "I sincerely hope it doesn't come to that, old chap. Cheers."

Chapter Thirty-Three

Saul's plane landed at Reagan National at two-thirty, and he was in his office at three-thirty. Two days in Chicago, another in Pittsburgh, and he had nothing to show for it. In Chicago, they turned McCormick Place upside down, but uncovered no leads on who booked the Lawless Room or who delivered the wooden box. Nobody at the Palmer House remembered anything about who delivered the note for Saul to the desk.

NEST searched over, around, and through Chicago for any indications of nuclear material, but they came up empty. Bureau bomb experts were still combing the remnants of the car-bomb explosion. Up until now, they had turned up tons of information, but none of it helpful in finding out who set the bomb.

While in Chicago, Saul received reports from the California agents who were trying to learn all they could about Austin, aka Hearn. Agents had been contacted by a classmate of Austin's at Berkeley, where they each obtained undergraduate degrees in electronics engineering. However, Steven Austin was not the name he used; it was Alfred Montgomery. This friend now worked in an electronics firm in San Jose, and he had helped Montgomery obtain the diodes, Zener diodes, capacitors, relays, MOSFETs, and other electronics components that showed up as parts for the bomb triggers in the design diagrams seen on the slides in McCormick Place.

His friend thought nothing about selling Montgomery the components, since he also helped him get electronics components when he was at MIT getting his PhD. The friend knew Montgomery as an extremely talented computer and electronics engineer, who built two high-tech computers while at MIT.

Following up the Montgomery lead, agents interviewed his mother, a Palo Alto lawyer, and his stepfather, a Stanford mathematics and computer science professor.

Montgomery had built a super-sophisticated computer while a freshman in high school—before he'd obtained his degree in electronics engineering at Berkeley at age 18. When he was thirteen, his stepfather found out he was illegally accessing one of Stanford's mainframe computers.

The video that showed the facilities for processing nuclear materials—the hot cells, atmosphere chambers, computerized machining equipment, and high-performance cluster computer—gave Saul an idea that produced another lead: companies that sell nuclear-handling equipment. Saul delegated eight agents to canvas all such companies with pictures of Hearn, Applenu, and Eric. They were to examine all big equipment orders to small companies during the last two years. Within a day, they turned up Eugene Slavin, a salesman for Reller Nuclear Equipment in Colorado Springs. Slavin thought he recognized the picture of Eric, who Slavin said called himself Eric Drafton. Slavin had sold him over three-hundred-thousand dollars worth of equipment to handle radioactive material. The equipment was delivered to Margine Nuclear Technology in Pittsburgh.

Saul flew from Chicago to Pittsburgh, where he was met by Spanner. They assembled ten local agents and headed for the warehouse on the north side of the city where the material had been delivered. The warehouse was now a furniture store. According to the building owner, the people who had rented it before were only there for three months. Apparently, they took delivery of the equipment and immediately shipped it out. Saul and Spanner flew back to Washington and left it to a task force of Pittsburgh agents to turn up information on the present whereabouts of the nuclear-handling equipment.

Back in Washington, there was little real progress. Scotland Yard had reported back on Brian Applenu. They had no information on him, and they were unable to turn up anything on him in the UK. An agent in New York City had spoken to a snitch in the Russian mafia, who said there was a rumor going around Brooklyn's Brighton Beach section that an Iranian diplomat was interested in bringing them in on a job for their government. There was also an indication from Austin's cell-phone records that he had contacted a bank in New York City that was known to have Iranian connections. They were now trying to determine what his connection was, but they needed a court order to get the bank to turn over any information they might have. Couple that information with Patricia Hunter's identification of Applenu and the indication that he could be Iranian based on facial ethnicity identification techniques, and it appeared to people like Saul and Spanner that the Iranian connection was verified.

Saul sorted through his messages. Field reports from Albuquerque and Boston indicated they had located the temporarily missing computer machining experts. Both provided satisfactory explanations on their whereabouts for the past few months. As to the missing expert in Oak Ridge, there was a message to call Jerry Fortner.

"There's something going on with that guy Reedan," Fortner said. "According to his wife, he's out of town. That's not unusual, I guess, because she says he travels almost every week. What's strange is that she claims she's not sure where he is or when he'll be back." He explained the conversation he had with her and her evasive tone. "All I can figure is they had an argument and he left. She had a bruise on her left cheek, like maybe he hit her. And when I rang the doorbell, I heard her daughter scream, like she was afraid of who was at the door. He probably beat her, too. At Y-12 they said he's a workaholic. Maybe that's the cause of their problems. You know how women can be."

How women can be, Saul thought, as he tried to make it all add up. Austin had made several trips to Oak Ridge when he was setting up the hijacking. Last month they had the Knoxville bureau check out the movements of Austin when he was there, but they drew a blank. They turned up no information except for the Double Tree Hotel in Oak Ridge that he stayed in on his trips to Y-12 ostensibly to confer on DOE computer business. Could he have known Reedan and recruited him for the job? Or was Reedan already in at that point?

"See if you can trace Reedan's travels the last few months," Saul said. "Find his bank and do a PPI. See if there were any large transactions lately."

"This is on the bomb thing, right?"

"Right. But that's not for release."

After hanging up, Saul called Philadelphia and Phoenix to check on the Surling case. Nothing. He was about to leave for the day when the phone rang.

"*Boychik*," Uncle Nathan said. "Glad I finally got you. I just wanted to let you know the Senator is grateful for your help."

"*My* help?"

"Enough already with the playing dumb."

"You mean my help with Saint Louis and Indianapolis? He had that all wrong."

"Like I know the *klutz* he can be sometimes, but we need him. Once

I make it to the governor's mansion, I won't need him as much. Maybe then, he'll need me. Until then, well...I know I make like a *nudnik* every once in awhile, but we're going to make it. By Hughson getting to Chicago right away, he scored in the media. And now this latest info you gave him ought to seal things for us with the Senator. I never heard him so happy."

"What are you talking about?"

"So play the *schlemiel*. Hughson said you found a new way to pass him info. That's what we need: creativity. Next year in Harrisburg."

- - - - -

Applenu sat on the couch and sipped whiskey, watching the TV. He glanced left at Atkinson, who sat on the recliner next to the couch. Over twenty minutes of CNN ten o'clock news had already been devoted to the missing bomb material and Chicago. Now they were reporting on the Energy Secretary's latest news conference.

"Do you think whoever stole the bomb material can make a workable bomb?"

The husky retired admiral with close-cropped gray hair glanced at the ceiling, as if thinking about the question, which he had answered several times from reporters the last few days. "No, it's not possible," he said. "I say that because..." and then he droned on about the difficulty of building a bomb, how it took over four years and over one-hundred-thousand people for the Manhattan Project to successfully build a bomb.

"What an asshole," Atkinson said. "It almost makes you want to explode one of ours, and maybe then they'll shut up."

Atkinson had spent the last three days with Applenu, sleeping in the other bedroom and going to the factory with him every day. He was leaving in the morning. At the factory, he spent most of his time in the office on his laptop, presumably communicating with Sherbani, although he did not tell Applenu what he was doing. It was obvious Atkinson was studying Applenu as he toured the facilities. He seemed impressed at what had been accomplished.

"He's like every bloody politician," Applenu said. "He's got to follow the script, cover his arse and his boss's arse because they let the material get stolen. I'm sure his technical people told him differently."

"You bet your ass—your arse—they did once they saw what we gave them in Chicago. Right about now they're pissing their pants." He laughed and turned to look at Applenu. "I thought you were trying to develop an

252

American accent. You need to drop words like *arse* and *bloody* from your vocabulary."

Applenu felt his face heat up. "I know."

Atkinson stared at him. "I've been in touch with Sherbani. He's not sure he can trust you, since you moved your family without telling him."

"Why should he know my family's whereabouts? My family has nothing to do with this job. You saw what I've accomplished at the factory. I've done everything that has been asked of me. I'll finish what we started."

"I told Sherbani you did a good job, and everything is in place to finish all the bombs. I think he bought it. Just don't get any ideas of disappearing like your family did."

On the TV, the Energy Secretary took another question: "Maybe they can't build a workable bomb, but what if they were to build a dud that spread a lot of radioactive material around when they tried to set it off?"

Pausing to reestablish his serious thinking-about-it look, the Energy Secretary said, "Obviously, that would be disastrous. Plutonium oxide is an extremely toxic material. If it were released in a populated area, even if it wasn't in a bomb, it could have horrendous consequences for the population living in that area. That's why I urge the people with this material to return it immediately. You've got to be highly skilled in the use of sophisticated equipment to safely handle plutonium. Should they be careless, they could very easily inhale a fatal dose."

Applenu drained his drink. The old sod had a point there, one that worried him every time he got near the plutonium-handling rooms. Images of Drafton's emaciated corpse flashed in his mind. He turned to Atkinson.

"Do they really need to do the same thing to Reedan that they did to Surling? They're just technical guys like you and me. I never signed up for anything like that."

"I just told you Sherbani and I think you're doing a good job. Your job is to machine the plutonium. You keep doing *your* job, and somebody else will take care of the other jobs. I might add that should you decide to suddenly do what your family did, we will hunt you and your family down. Without hesitation, they will give you what they gave Surling."

- - - - -

Lori turned off Vanderbilt Drive for one more try. She felt bad about waking Beth and making her walk to the car at eleven o'clock. Curt could have carried her.

With Beth asleep on the back seat, Lori headed for the dark parking lot she'd visited six or seven times during the last week, but only during daylight hours. If they left in the morning and came back at night, surely they'd be there now.

She turned left into a street that paralleled their building and ran between the curb on her right and the parking lot on her left with the first row of cars parked at an angle to the street. *Their* building loomed less than fifty feet to her right.

She stopped at the first out-of-state car: Alabama, wrong color car. She moved on to the next out-of-state: Indiana, not the right size car. At the end of the row, she made the U-turn into a double row of angle-parked cars.

Then she saw it. Parked to her left was a black Lincoln Town Car with New York plates.

She glared at the building they had gone into. "I'll be back," she said into the quiet.

Chapter Thirty-Four

With Beth again asleep in the back seat, Lori drove into the parking lot at five-thirty in the morning, two days after her previous late-night visit. Her breathing deepened to fight the tightness in her chest every time she saw the apartment building they went into, only more so today.

She parked across from the row of cars with the Lincoln, about ten cars down from theirs. After adjusting the outside and inside mirrors so she could watch the entrance to their building, she settled in with her thoughts to wait for Beecher and Maxwell to appear.

Daylight gradually brightened the sand-colored box behind her. Early risers brought movement in the form of two joggers and the driver of a car parked two spaces from hers. Drowsiness attacked, activating a string of yawns. She rolled down the window for an allotment of the chilly morning air. Although she got to bed after midnight, sleep eluded her, arriving only after endless hours of trying to scrub her mind of the awful visions that spewed from her brain.

Six-thirty. Two more cars drove from the lot. After another yawn, she looked up, and Beecher stood in the mirror, staring her way. She slid down in her seat, pulled her shoulder bag closer, and watched on the outside mirror, trying to blot out thoughts of what happened so she could reason clearly about what to do.

Another man joined Beecher, a dark-complected man with gray hair. She checked the inside mirror to see if Maxwell might be out of her field of vision. No fat slug in view.

Beecher paced the sidewalk, smoking and checking his watch, while the other man stood off to the side. Just as Beecher flipped his cigarette onto the street, a third man joined them. They headed for the Lincoln, and she turned to peer over the seat for a better look. The third man was not Maxwell.

She considered taking the forty-five from her handbag and confronting them, forcing them to free Curt. Before she could move, the Town Car backed out of the parking space. As they drove past, she flattened herself across the front seat, clutching the shoulder bag, her right hand inside and wrapped around the handle of the forty-five.

- - - - -

Applenu sprawled in the passenger seat next to Beecher with Simmons in the back, heading toward another day at the factory. He had just bid farewell to Atkinson, who had an early flight—he didn't say to where. It would be a better day with him no longer looking over his shoulder. Now, if only he could leave this place. Oh, to finish the job, he thought, and cut away from people like Beecher and Lormes. Although Atkinson didn't say it directly, he knew that Lormes and his men would be keeping an eye on him. So be it. His family was safely settled in Loughborough, England, a small town north of London where Malcolm Wilson, BahAmin's husband, had contacts at the university, and where Applenu's father might be able to resume his teaching career.

Applenu glanced at Beecher and remembered the phone call four days ago, telling him of the "trouble" they had in getting rid of Surling. Reedan saw them kill him, and somebody would have to calm him down the next morning and convince him that the same thing wasn't going to happen to him. That somebody was Applenu. A ghastly show. Did Reedan believe him when he told him that everything would have been okay if Surling had not run?

Applenu remembered Atkinson's reaction when he told him about it. He registered no surprise, no revulsion that Surling had been killed. He considered it part of the job, just as killing those people in the hijacked convoy was.

Applenu wondered if he was now technically a murderer, an accessory after the fact. No way did he want any part of it. At least don't tell me about it, he thought. Trouble is, he knew that they had no choice. Surling and Reedan could identify Lormes and his men. Applenu knew they could also identify him, but he could never agree to murder them. Applenu knew that besides Reedan, the only other people who could identify Lormes were Atkinson, Simmons, Sherbani, and himself. Not a comforting thought, that one.

The other reason he detested Beecher was the Lori Reedan incident. After Beecher showed Reedan the video of his wife and kid, he showed

Applenu the entire video. Applenu had never seen anything like it. The video Beecher showed Reedan was bad enough: It stopped after Beecher had ripped off her blouse and copped a feel of her tits.

That one bloody picture was all they needed to convince Reedan to give them the password. While Applenu watched the video, Beecher laughed as he narrated the part where he and that clot Maxwell were having a bash at her. Maxwell on top of her was like a bloody bull humping a collie dog. Beecher forced her to perform oral sex on them, the kid sometimes calling for her mother from some other room. At the end, they had that nice bit of crumpet flat on the floor, like she'd been run down by a lorry. He wondered: did that make him a rapist, too? Accessory after the fact, maybe?

While Beecher watched the video, he joked about taking Applenu along the next time they visited her. When Applenu brought up the police, Beecher said she wouldn't go to the police: "We fucked any thought of going to the authorities out of her," he said. At least that's how he saw it now. Would he see it the same way after they killed Reedan?

Beecher pulled into the parking lot of the Shoney's Restaurant, and he and Simmons got out for a newspaper and breakfast to go. Applenu rubbed both hands across his beard, good and black now with only a little skin showing through. Beard or not, he felt trapped, no longer able to go into the restaurant in case that blonde hostess would connect his face with the pictures in the paper and notify the police. She always made a thing about his British accent, because she'd been born in Britain.

Beecher handed Applenu a newspaper, a Styrofoam cup of coffee, and a bag containing his breakfast. "Looks like you made a good choice to re-grow your beard, Doc. Today they've got you in there with and without one."

Applenu grabbed the paper and found another story. It contained the now-familiar bearded sketch of him along with an artist's sketch of how he might look without a beard. It didn't look like him—at least he didn't think so.

Beecher roared into a laugh. "You better let Mr. Lormes get you a plastic surgeon to carve you out a new face."

Applenu concentrated on the Mosely story, everything in it attributed to an anonymous source. It began with the FBI now suspecting that Austin was still alive because of trap door and Trojan horse programs found on FBI and DOE computers. The FBI attributed the programs to Austin, and because they had been accessed recently, the assumption was that Austin was the only person that could access them.

"According to the paper, Senator Hughson says Iran is behind the hijackings," Beecher said as he pulled out of the parking lot. "It also says you are Ey-ranian. Are you an *Ey*-ranian, Doc?"

"Not really." He wondered if there was some way the FBI could identify all the Iranians in the country. His only hope was that his British passport would keep him from being singled out. If they got on to him, his only choice might be to play his *Ey*-ranianess for all it was worth and let Sherbani get him back to Iran. That, or rot in a bloody Yank jail.

"Does Mr. Lormes really know some discreet plastic surgeons?"

Beecher broke into a cackle. "Mr. Lormes can take care of anything you need for a price. But don't worry, those sketches of you are not very good."

- - - - -

When the Lincoln Town Car pulled into Shoney's, Lori drove on to the parking lot for the Days Inn Motel next door. Now back on the road and a safe distance behind the Town Car, she headed toward the rising sun. After two turns that took them away from residential areas, they turned into a wide, deserted street with three long, identical one-story buildings on each side. A sign at the entrance to the street announced that they were entering the new Melton Hill Industrial and Warehouse Park with space available for lease or purchase.

She continued past the entrance on a road that curved around the back of the buildings. After turning around and waiting to give them enough time to park their car, she turned into the park entrance and saw the Lincoln in front of the second building on the left. A small green car pulled away from the same building and headed toward her.

Was it one of them? She considered a quick U-turn and realized she couldn't make it. She whipped the wheel right and skidded into a parking space in front of the Morrison Tool and Die Company just as the other car shot by.

She shifted into neutral, her heart pounding wildly in her throat. It was Maxwell. He sat in the passenger seat with another man driving, and he wore something on his face, something white. A disguise? She wiped sweat from her forehead with a tissue and tried to calm down. Slowly, she turned and looked back. They were gone.

For several minutes, she stared through the windshield, wondering what she was doing there. Could they have Curt in that building?

"Mommy, where are we going?" Beth asked from the back seat.

"We're going home," Lori said.

258

- - - - -

Rick Saul dragged himself out of bed and into the kitchen, where he found Mary in her pink robe at the breakfast bar, concentrating on the front page of the *Post*. Although she'd been in the kitchen for ten minutes, no coffee brewed. Bad news for the Senator? Not Mosely again. Bad news for Rick Saul?

He glanced over her shoulder at the headline of the story she concentrated on:

MASTERMIND OF NUCLEAR BOMB MATERIAL HIJACKING ALIVE

He glanced quickly through the article. She had all the latest information they had dug up.

Mary glanced up, and he braced himself for her assault for not giving Hughson the information, but she went back to reading.

"What the hell is this," he asked. "How did Mosely get that about Applenu when we just got it the day-before yesterday?" He continued reading.

It was all there. "How did Hughson get onto this? She's inferring that *Hughson* gave her the story on Applenu and Iran. What do you know about this?"

"We've got our sources, too."

"Can't you see what this will do to me? They'll think I leaked it to him."

"If you'd have helped us earlier, we'd have made out even better. But this will translate into name recognition and get him up there in the polls with Mitchell and Morgan. By primary time in 2012…"

"It's as if somebody's setting me up."

"You're paranoid, Rick, paranoid and delusional. First, you think every guy that talks to me is trying to get into my pants, and you think I want him to. And now you think somebody is trying to set you up."

"How did you get this?"

"I can't say."

"I was one of the few people who were privy to this. Could this be what Uncle Nate was talking about last night?"

"Actually, I don't know anything about this. Senator Hughson set up the interview on his own. He just told me Mosely was coming in, and when she did, he talked to her in private."

"Find out what's going on, Mary, will you?"

Her blue eyes flashed. "The worm has turned, Rick. I'm supposed to help you, but all this time you wouldn't give me crap. I'll see what I can find out, but then I'll expect something in return."

- - - - -

Curt sat behind the monitor and typed: HIT.

The computer typed back: JACK OF HEARTS. BUST. I WIN.

Although he had been sent to the computer room to work on another machining program—the last one, according to Applenu—he'd spent most of the last two days teaching the computer to play blackjack. Anything to forget. He owed the computer twenty-two-thousand dollars.

Applenu gave him the job the day after they shot Surling. It came after he and Lormes spent an hour trying to convince him they had intended to turn Surling loose, and if Curt and Surling had not tried to escape, Surling would now be in Arizona, a quarter-of-a-million dollars richer. Curt wanted to believe, but knew better. Beecher just pointed the gun and fired into Surling's chest. At one point in the rambling discussion, Curt refused to do anything else for them.

Up until then, Lormes had let Applenu do the talking. When Lormes finally spoke, his voice was calm and quiet, but his gray eyes blazed. "You can reconsider now, Reedan, or I'll have Mr. Beecher and Mr. Maxwell visit your wife again."

Curt ached to ask about what Beecher and Maxwell did to Lori on their last visit, but he wasn't ready for the answer and remained silent. He knew the answer.

He typed: DEAL. With Applenu's new program finished, all he could do was wait and hope for one last chance.

Maxwell jerked open the door. "Simmons wants you in the machine room," he growled, barely looking at Curt with his open eye. A large white bandage covered the left side of his forehead, all the way back to his ear; his black-and-blue left eye was squeezed to a slit and toned down by his purple-tinted glasses.

At the sight of Maxwell, Curt waggled his jaw, and when he stood, he flexed his right leg to work the aching thigh where Beecher kicked him. Even Surling's gloom would have cheered the endless nights that large quantities of beer and wine wouldn't hurry. Loneliness and death haunted his every thought, dealt as arbitrarily as the computer dealt the jack of hearts.

In the machine room, Curt found Simmons at the grinder, gripping the frame of the machine and staring at the opposite wall. His shoulders and arms shook, like a man on the bed of a truck traveling a rough road. When he turned to Curt, he stared right past him, his eyes wide with fright.

"You look like you saw a ghost," Curt said.

"Maybe I did. Mine." Simmons stumbled over to the computer keyboard and monitor and collapsed onto the chair. "If we don't close this operation down soon, we'll all wind up like Drafton."

"And like Surling." Simmons never said much, but unlike Beecher and Maxwell, he did still talk to Curt.

Simmons ignored the comment about Surling and pointed a shaking finger toward the other end of the building. "That furnace room is as contaminated as a sewer rat. We're working in protective masks."

"Why don't you decontaminate again?"

"No time. We want to be out of here in two days."

"That soon?"

"Many things are happening, so we are moving fast." Simmons pointed to the monitor. "One holdup is the program you're working on."

"That's all?"

"I wish that *was* all. We have to machine two more pieces of plutonium. That means we will have to cast more plutonium ingots in that contaminated furnace room."

"That worries you, huh?"

Simmons jerked a handkerchief from his rear pocket. "Have you ever seen plutonium metal when it's exposed to warm air?"

"No. But I know it oxidizes rapidly."

Simmons looked for a clean part of the handkerchief. "It turns yellow with plutonium oxide almost instantly. If you're not careful and the oxide gets out of the atmosphere chamber, it gets all over the room. Soon, the air's full of the yellow shit, and you're breathing it." He roared into the handkerchief and then examined the effluent looking for yellow powder.

"And if you breathe it, you're finished. Like Drafton," Curt said.

"That's right." His voice quaked. "We worked too fast and got careless. I just hope those masks we're using work."

"Can't plutonium ignite and burn spontaneously when it's exposed to air?"

"You mean, is it pyrophoric? It is under certain conditions. According to Applenu, finely ground plutonium powder is pyrophoric, and certain plutonium alloys are. Actually, there were some pyrophoric alloys in one of the hijacked shipments. We don't intend to use them. They're those barrels in the chemical-processing room, boxed up and marked with all kinds of warnings." Simmons tapped the monitor. "Is the new machining program finished?"

"Just about."

"We've got to finish machining those pieces, so we can get out of here."

"I'll finish the program later today. Then you do me a favor. When my computer program is finished, turn your back, maybe distract my guard a minute, and let me slip out the back door."

Simmons stared up at Curt, his eyes filled with alarm. "I can't, man. Hey, I'm sorry about Surling. That wasn't in the plan."

"You don't believe that anymore than I do. What about you? You have seen all the people involved with this work. Maybe they won't trust you either when the work is done."

Chapter Thirty-Five

Saul knew better than plan anything for the morning. A meeting notice may as well have appeared in the *Post* next to Mosely's story. Dowel waited for them at the end of his conference table, and Saul again wound up sitting to Dowel's right and across from Spanner.

"So what the fuck's going on?" Dowel drawled, even before Saul sat. "First Mosely gets the information that we think Austin's alive, which we were keeping quiet, then we find out the Iranians might be involved, which has all kinds of ramifications, and Hughson gets that information at the same time. *You*, Mr. Saul, found out that Applenu could be an Iranian the day-before yesterday, and Hughson finds out about it the same day. And your wife just happens to work for Hughson."

"I didn't say a word to anyone."

"I'd like to think you aren't that fucking dumb, Mr. Saul, but it doesn't look good, does it?"

"If you don't believe me, give me a polygraph test."

"Give him a fucking *lie detector* test," Dowel mumbled as he turned to Spanner. "They want his ass off the case, George. Fact is some people are not too happy with you either. And no polygraph test is going to change that."

"I believe him," Spanner said. "Somebody's pulling our chain. Somebody was leaking information to Mosely, and now they are also leaking to Hughson. They're trying to rattle us and make us and the Administration look bad."

"If that's their objective, they are succeeding."

"What is the White House doing with the Iranian connection we turned up and essentially verified?" Spanner asked.

"According to the State Department, such '*vaporous rumors*' can not be used to conclude Iran is involved," Dowel huffed. "They spawned another fucking committee of White House and State Department types to *deliberate* on the *correct action* to take on the *vaporous rumors*. But that's not what we are here for," Dowel said and turned to Saul. "The Iranian leak was just the *latest* leak. Hughson also mysteriously showed up in Chicago the night of the bombing."

"The Hughson leak makes it look as if they're trying to make Rick look bad," Spanner said. "It's too blatant. That's why I believe him. In the media, we all look bad, but here, it's Rick who takes the heat. Besides that, it keeps us looking for the source in our midst, and while we are doing that, they are safe in their rat hole."

Spanner constantly amazed Saul on how he stood up to superiors with contrary opinions, and he usually prevailed, although it didn't look like he would this time.

Dowel leaned back in his chair and spoke to the ceiling. "You two convinced me the first leaks were the result of that trap door and Trojan horse. You concluded that meant Austin was still alive. But you closed that computer leak, so maybe Austin isn't alive after all and somebody else is doing it. So based on the timing of the leaks relative to when we learned the information, it all comes back to one or both of you being the source."

"Austin *is* alive, I know it," Saul said. "Slaughter and his people tracked an intruder in our computer system after they discovered the trap door. They just couldn't trace it."

"But they closed the trap door before the latest leaks," Dowel growled.

"I think I see it now," Saul said forcing himself to smile at Dowel. "Maybe he put more than one Trojan horse and trap door on the computer, and when we shut down one it activated another."

"Our people would have found them," Dowel said.

"Probably not," Saul said, "since they wouldn't be expecting that scenario."

"Get Slaughter to check it out," Spanner said turning to Saul.

"I'd like to believe you two," Dowel said, "but a lot of our so-called friends at the White House want Saul off the case. They want him off *now*. After Saul turned up evidence that Applenu was an Iranian, the State Department and the White House panicked and formed their committee. Like I told you last week, State's been doing the Neville Chamberlain waltz with the Iranians during the last few months. In those *private* talks, State concluded that the Iranians are taking a more reasonable stance concerning their nuclear ambitions. So the White House keeps waltzing with the bastards, trying to find any excuse they can to keep from having to come down on them. Besides that, it galls the shit out of me to have the White House and State accuse *us* of leaking, considering that information flows through those two places like shit through a tin horn.

"Then we have *your* friend Senator Hughson. No Neville Chamberlain waltz for him. He accuses the Iranians right off, and this morning Teheran Radio does one of their old 'U.S.-is-the-great-Satan routines'. It sounded like the *great* Ayatollah himself had risen from the grave. We are accused of being behind a Zionist plot to discredit Muslim people throughout the world. It's the same old Islamic-fascist bullshit we've been hearing since their revolution in 1979. Of course, that pisses off the White House and State, who probably adopted the go-slow dance strategy because they're incapable of thinking up a real one."

Saul knew he was off the case without appeal. His big chance, his career-enhancement case was gone. What career? He should have opted for computers after college, he thought, as a Dylan lyric flitted into his mind:

I was so much older then,
I'm younger than that now.

Spanner said, "I've been thinking about Mosely. We know her father and brothers were connected to the IRA. Her father was killed by a bomb, probably one he was trying to set, but the IRA blamed it on the Protestants. One brother spent three years in a British jail and he and two older brothers are still in Belfast. We also know that she was a radical in her youth."

"So?" Dowel said. "Besides, the IRA-British thing has been settled, and there has been little violence for years."

"That's right, but there are rumors of dissident IRA elements that still want to stir up trouble. What's to say that some IRA faction isn't mixed up in this, and they're using her to feed disinformation to us? Her information on Saint Louis and Indianapolis sidetracked us and the same with Chicago, where we learned a hell of a lot about McCormick Place, but not much else."

"Are you saying the IRA is in cahoots with Iran?" Dowel asked. "Don't let anybody at the White House or State hear you say that. They'll think you're crazier than Hughson."

"Stranger things have happened. There have always been rumors about the IRA getting weapons from Libya and other elements in the Middle East. If you read between the lines on this latest Hughson episode and the one in Chicago, you see that Mosely and Hughson are always acting in concert. She gets his wisdom for her column before he has his news conference. She could be feeding him information just to put pressure on Saul, figuring that would shake up our investigative team here at headquarters. Then again, if we assume Austin is leaking to Mosely, it could be him who is leaking to Hughson. While we're accusing each other, we're not finding those bombs."

"So bug her fucking phones," Dowel said. "Tail her."

"That's the other thing about her: she cooperates with us. She let us bug her phones, and an agent is following her. She forwards information she gets by e-mail. Trouble is, it comes from info4u@yahoo.com. When you trace it back, it is sent from a public computer at a library or some such place or routed through some computer in Romania or wherever."

"So what the fuck do we do besides taking Saul off the case?"

That's it, Saul thought. He'd have to go with Uncle Nate now, whether he wanted to or not. What if Nate doesn't win?

"What we do," Spanner said, "is take Rick out of his high-visibility role for the time being. Okay, Rick?"

Saul nodded. What else could he say? "I was thinking somebody should go to Tennessee to investigate the Reedan lead. He may be the computer expert they needed."

"Good idea." Spanner looked at Dowel for approval.

Dowel turned his chair toward Saul. "Okay, but if anything else goes wrong, you're finished. And you won't be saved by any would-be president of the United States."

- - - - -

Back in his office, Saul found a message to call Mary. On the phone, she sounded angry and just asked him to pick her up for lunch.

Mary's desk occupied a corner of a large room crowded with three other desks. She stood bent over some papers on her desk, head-to-head with Ross Lectner, Hughson's chief of staff. They began to laugh, and as Lectner straightened up, he rested his hand on her shoulder. He saw Saul approaching, and his hand bounced from her shoulder as if it were a rubber ball.

Saul followed her into the corridor of the Senate Office Building, trying to keep himself calm after seeing her short red skirt. Once they were isolated from others in the corridor, he let loose. "Is that all you have to do up here: play grab ass with the guys in the office?"

"Just can it, Rick, until we get out of here," she said quietly, not looking at him.

Once outside, she exploded, "You bastard!"

"*Me*, a bastard? You're the one with somebody's hands all over you."

"Is that all you think about: me and some guy? One of these days...if you keep this up, maybe then...What I'm talking about now is the story in the paper this morning. You asked me to find out how the Senator got it, remember?"

"I remember. And that's how you do it, by letting Lectner feel you up?"

She ignored the jab. "I expected this, since you obviously didn't want me to find out the truth. Or else you wanted me to find out, because you feel you're getting at me somehow."

He unlocked and opened the car door for her. "What's that supposed to mean?"

She made no move to get in. "I found out that you got Hughson that information on the Iranian connection. And on what was happening in Chicago, too. Jesus, Rick, why couldn't you give it to me first? I know you don't want me on this job, but as long as I'm here, you could at least help me."

"*I* gave it to him? Who told you that?"

"Ross. He said Senator Hughson got an e-mail with the information. Ross said the senator was vague on who the e-mail was from, but he thought you set it up with Mosely. You gave her the information with the understanding that she'd give it to Hughson, so she could be the first in the media with it, and he could be the first one in congress to run with it. You were doing just what Uncle Nate wanted you to, only this way you figured you wouldn't be directly involved."

"That's bullshit. I gave Mosely nothing."

"Ross said either you gave it to Mosely to e-mail the senator, or you e-mailed the Senator directly. Jesus, Rick, all I'm saying is you could have given me that information. It wouldn't have looked anymore like you gave the information to Hughson than it does now. In fact, I could have made it look better. But you'd do anything to get me away from this job."

"You're serious. I didn't give Mosely or Hughson or anybody else that information."

"You can't lie your way out of it this time. You said you had a funny call from Uncle Nate. I called him, and he verified it. Hughson told him what you'd set up."

Maybe Spanner had it figured right. "Somebody's doing me in. I'm off the Washington part of the case and on my way to Tennessee because of that story."

"Somebody's doing you in, just like somebody's always screwing me," she said. She turned and headed back toward the Senate Office Building. "It's all in your head, Rick."

He turned and followed her. "So how did Mosely or I get Hughson the information?"

"It came by e-mail from info4u@yahoo.com."

Chapter Thirty-Six

Standing tall in knee-high grass, her legs spread slightly for balance, Lori held the Taurus forty-five with both hands at arm's length and listened for Dad's words from ten years earlier: "Relax, concentrate on the target, take a deep breath, and squeeze it off. Steady. Squeeeeeze."

The gun barked. Her arms jerked back and thrust the gun toward her face. She flinched at the deafening explosion, but the foot-square side of the cardboard box on the ground twenty feet in front of her stood untouched. She couldn't even hit a box. Three more shots, and three more misses.

She sucked a breath of hot, humid air, suddenly aware of the hushed meadow surrounded by woods, the chirping birds silenced momentarily by the reverberations of the ear-splitting blasts. Sweating with gnats flitting about her face and diving for her eyes, she wiped her forehead with a sleeve of her plaid shirt and brushed her hand across her head to check her tied-back hair. "Concentrate. No flinching. Relax. Squeeze it off. Steady. Squeeeeeze."

The gun barked, and the box jumped.

Three shots followed, and each one found the target, sending the box into an erratic journey through the grass. She ejected the magazine and dropped it onto the ground next to the loaded one that she picked up and rammed into the handle of the pistol. She jerked back the slide to chamber a round.

Since she had followed Beecher to the industrial park two mornings ago, she made three more trips. Each time she eased the car into the street and fought the overwhelming urge to mash down on the accelerator and speed past their building. Instead, with every nerve in her body primed to explode, she slowed to look it over. Outwardly, it appeared no different from the five other long buildings on the street: two doors, a loading dock, and a sign that identified it as General Nuclear American Company.

It *was* different: Beecher and Maxwell went into the building. The other guy she saw the first morning could be the one in the sketch in the newspaper, the one the FBI wanted—Applenu.

During the day, she could only drive by and hold her breath, hoping no one would come out and recognize her. Once the black Town Car was there, twice the green car, a Toyota with Tennessee license plates, was there. Tonight she would determine what was in the building. Somehow, she'd find out if they had Curt in there.

Now, she glanced around the field surrounded by woods on the government reservation outside of Oak Ridge, well away from the road and houses. She picked up the other box she brought, about the same size as the first one. She took it to a large cedar tree and stuck it into the branches, about the height of Beecher's heart. This time she backed up twenty-five feet, concentrated on the box until she saw Beecher strutting toward her. She raised the gun and fired. Missed. "Clear your mind and concentrate on the target. Squeeeeze."

The box jerked. Another shot shoved the box deeper into the cedar tree. She paused, took a deep breath, and fired again, and again, and again.

- - - - -

Beth saw the car in the driveway first. "Mommy, they're back. Those bad men are back!"

Lori's heart jumped and jolted her thoughts back to the present. A black car? No, dark-blue, smaller. She sighed. It still meant trouble: Fortner and a curly-headed younger man stood by the car. "It's okay, Beth, it's not them."

- - - - -

Saul sat at a two-person table next to the darkened dance floor that was jammed with clutching bodies. On stage, a big round blonde sang about making it through the night. Your typical night in Babe's Lounge at the Knoxville, Tennessee, Howard Johnson, he thought. The only good thing about the hot day and night in Tennessee was that it wasn't a hot day in D.C., a day filled with telephones, meetings, and paper work, and nights arguing with Mary.

Before he left Washington, he debated on whether to call Uncle Nathan and tell him he'd be ready to join his campaign when it got going. Why not? His Bureau career was totaled. He wouldn't even get a chance to return to the statistics detail. Instead, he'd be dispatched to some backwater—like Knoxville, perhaps, Fortner's beat—that would make Spokane look metropolitan, back to the boondocks with an indelible mark on his record. Either get out or turn bitter, like a lot of the guys he knew that had been around too long, biding their time to qualify for their pension. Not him.

Although he shouldn't have, he called Mary before he left D.C. She told him to go to Tennessee and stay there, and by the way, he could go fuck himself.

Saul drained his Jack Daniels and water and ordered another. He turned and glanced at the wall behind the bar, where fifteen silent TV screens flashed a kaleidoscope of noiseless multi-color images into the noisy room. Half the sets showed a Chicago Cubs game, with all but one of the rest energized by a frenetic long-haired, big-mouthed singer seeming to be getting ready to eat a microphone. On the remaining set in the upper right corner, Larry King interviewed a fast-talking, long-haired man, his head shaking and eyes blinking in time with the turbulent animation of his mouth. Were they talking about atomic bombs, like every other talking head on TV seemed to be?

Someone somewhere was making atomic bombs that could blow away a city or two, and Doctor Curt Reedan of Oak Ridge was involved. Unfortunately, their visit with Lori didn't move them any closer to Reedan or the people making the bombs.

Saul reflected on his and Fortner's meeting with Lori Reedan. Tall and slim, she was a beautiful woman with long, coal-black hair. She was undoubtedly lovelier when she wasn't a nervous wreck, her hair wasn't drawn back, purple didn't ring her eyes like smudged mascara, and a purplish-yellow bruise didn't blotch her left cheek.

After she got her car into the garage, she led Saul and Fortner to the couch in her living room, a neat room with everything in its place. She wore blue jeans and a long-sleeved plaid shirt, as if she were a farmer just in from working the fields. Before she joined them in the living room, she took her daughter downstairs to watch TV. Her daughter fought desperately to stay, crying and hanging on to her mother.

Saul felt at ease in the room: a comfortable home, your wife taking care of the children instead of out trying to run the government. That wasn't the way your twenty-first century American man was supposed to feel, but sometimes it just seemed like the right way. Call him a chauvinist, but it worked for his mother, and it probably worked for Lori Reedan's mother and for Lori Reedan herself.

When she finally sat on the chair across the room from them, Saul let Fortner question her.

"We know your husband travels a lot and that he went to Miami on June tenth. He was scheduled to leave Miami for Cincinnati the next day. On the following week, he was scheduled to go to Raleigh. He had two more trips scheduled the week following that, and one the week after that. He was also completing a job for Y-12 right here in Oak Ridge."

She nodded, confused, looking to Saul, then to Fortner. "That's why he's accepting the professorship at the Colorado School of Mines," she said. "So he doesn't have to travel so much."

"We know he was scheduled to take all those trips, but he didn't take any of them. He didn't get in touch with Y-12 on their job either. As far as we can tell, he never left Miami."

"You're mistaken." Even with the long-sleeve shirt, she suddenly got cold and pulled her arms around herself. "He took those trips. Now he's in Pennsylvania. He's been away longer than usual. Like I told you the other day, he'll probably be back this weekend."

"Where is he in Pennsylvania?"

"I don't know exactly; somewhere outside of Pittsburgh. He'll call tonight or tomorrow. I'll let you know."

"Why did he go to Miami?"

"To give a talk at the A-S-M-E meeting."

"A-S-M-E?"

"The American Society of Mechanical Engineers."

"Why didn't he take the plane back from Miami? Why didn't he use those other reservations?"

"He used them. You'll see."

"Airline computers don't lie, Mrs. Reedan."

Her dark-haired daughter ran into the room and whispered into her mother's ear about something to eat, occasionally casting nervous glances at Saul and Fortner. Lori Reedan told her she could have cookies.

The kid would grow up to be as pretty as her mother, Saul thought. He wondered again why he couldn't talk Mary into a kid. It was time. His mother had his sister when she was twenty-one.

"Maybe Curt made alternate arrangements," Lori Reedan said, watching her daughter go into the kitchen.

"We checked all the airlines."

"Why do you want Curt? He hasn't done anything."

"We don't think he's done anything wrong," Saul said, as the daughter came out of the kitchen with cookies, hesitated at the top of the steps to look at her mother, and then went downstairs. "We want to question him about what he's been working on recently."

"I told you, when he calls, I'll let you know where he is."

Saul stood. "By the way, what happened to your cheek?"

Her hand jumped to her face and gently probed the bruise. She tried to laugh. "A stupid accident: I bumped into a door...in the dark."

Outside, he and Fortner agreed that she had run into somebody's hand—or maybe a fist. Was it Reedan's during a domestic quarrel like Fortner thought, or did it have something to do with the case? Perhaps they fought over him taking the bomb job.

After they left the Reedan house, Saul and Fortner split up and talked to neighbors, the few that were home. Most of them recognized the Reedan name, but little else, although one neighbor two houses down didn't even know their name. She said they moved into the neighborhood only a little over two years ago and hadn't gotten around to meeting the neighbors.

Only Sarah Eberhard next door seemed to know anything about them. She insisted that Lori always knew where Curt was, almost to the minute, because she took care of plane and hotel reservations and acted as his secretary. She believed the story about running into the door.

Reedan was their man all right.

Saul glanced around the lounge, filled mostly with people in their late thirties, forties and fifties, an intensity etched on their faces as they strained for fun and excitement. At the edge of the dance floor, a skinny guy in a white shirt and jeans with a dried-up face and a thin mat of gray hair sipped a long-necked Budweiser and studied the dance floor. Must be in his sixties, Saul thought. Not the crowd of people out having fun at night you saw on TV.

Saul sipped his drink and considered where they stood. They had someone checking whether Reedan gave his talk in Miami. Reedan was supposed to leave Miami the day before Surling got to Philadelphia. Maybe they were both in Pennsylvania. Were they there voluntarily?

Two tables away, Saul spotted a brunette about his age in a C-skimmer skirt sipping wine at a table filled with older women. Would she dance with him?

His mind wandered back to the atom bombs. Was participation by Reedan and Surling voluntary? Who knows these days? All kinds of military people were being caught selling secrets. Why not bomb makers for sale?

Some guy in a cowboy hat asked the brunette to dance. She refused and glanced Saul's way.

He remembered Harry Bryson saying that all you had to do to pick up women was say you were FBI. You didn't even have to show your badge. He decided to finish his drink and call Mary. Dancing with strange brunettes in HOJO lounges wasn't for him.

"You alone, man? Mind if I sit down?"

Saul surfaced from his thoughts to see a young black-bearded man looking around the room at the full tables. He wore an orange University of Tennessee T-shirt and a white baseball cap with an orange T. Saul motioned him to sit, thinking he looked vaguely familiar.

They exchanged pleasantries, discussed the hot-humid weather, and the upcoming first University of Tennessee football game. The stranger ordered a gin and tonic and bought Saul another Jack Daniels and water.

"I guess I'm not dressed for this place," the man said, pointing at Saul's tie. He removed his baseball cap to reveal a shaved head.

"I'm in town on business," Saul said. "What about you?"

"I'm a computer modeler over in Oak Ridge." He reached across the table to shake hands. "I'm George Atkinson."

Saul shook his hand. "Rick Saul. Do you know a Curt Reedan? He's a computer guy in Oak Ridge."

"Are you FBI?"

"FBI? Why do you ask that?"

"Because the FBI is looking for Reedan and a chemist named Surling."

"How do you know that?" They hadn't released that information and didn't intend to.

"It's on a new website, www.info4u.com. I got the website from a story on the AP website by that Sheena Mosely. The info4u.com website has everything that's happened in the stolen nuclear material case. So Rick, are you with the FBI?"

"Well, I..." He felt someone tap his shoulder and turned to find a smiling woman.

"Hey, love, are you stuck inside Knoxville with the Memphis Blues again?" she said, glancing quickly at Atkinson.

The play on the words of the Dylan song and the British accent: "Miz Mosely, is it?"

"Hey, good detecting. Recognized my voice, huh?"

Short dark hair and a pretty face, not bad for a fifty-something broad, at least in this light. Probably slightly overweight, because both times he'd seen her she wore a full dark skirt and ruffled white blouse—no C-skimmers for her. He remembered Atkinson and the website and turned back to find him gone.

"Where did that guy go? He said there was a new website spewing about the nuclear material case. He said he read about it in your story on the AP website."

"Right. I got an e-mail from info4u@yahoo.com about the website. It was signed: 'An Inquisitive Friend'. I forwarded it to you and to the other FBI address just like all the other messages I got." She explained the new information on the website—the same information Atkinson had. "Does this confirm your Austin is alive theory?"

Austin, he thought, which meant there was another trap door and Trojan horse. "What brings you down here?"

"You do. We've made some good trades on information up until now. Besides, you are one of the leaders of the investigation, so I figure you'll be where the action is."

"What trades? I never gave you anything. Anyway, you screwed up this time. I'm down here because of you letting Hughson in on your information. My superiors figured I gave it to him. So I'm no longer a *leader* of the investigation. Was that in the e-mail, too? Does the e-mail say I was kicked off the case and sent to Siberia?"

"It was there along with the information that you were coming to Oak Ridge, but I won't put that in tomorrow's story. That last e-mail said I'd be getting some really hot information later tonight that I can use for tomorrow's story. It wasn't there the last time I checked my e-mail. I'll let you know what it is as soon as I get it"

Saul twisted around to scan the entrance and bar area. He wondered who was tailing her, and what they would do when they saw her and him together. He knew damn good and well what they'd think. Dowel would say he knew it all the time.

"I hear you also forwarded information to Hughson."

"I did not. He got e-mails from the same Yahoo address that I did. I assume he hasn't forwarded them to you like I did."

"You know you've been used by Austin...or whoever sent the e-mails."

"What was I supposed to do: sit on the information? It would have gotten out. Besides, I turned all of it over to you and let your people bug my phones and e-mails. I haven't even complained about them following me."

Saul remembered Spanner's theory that she was working with the bomb makers. Could it be that when they heard he was in Knoxville they knew he was getting close, so they sent her to keep an eye on him?

"Are you working with the bomb makers?" he asked.

She sniffed a laugh. "Why would I do that? I guess you're referring to some of my anti-government writings years ago. That was another time, another me. On this story, I just took the information I got and went with it. You've got to look out for your career, right?"

"Everybody needs a career development plan," he said. He would like to pursue the Austin link, but he knew it would go nowhere. He drained his drink and realized the three Jack Daniels were having an effect.

She looked around for the waitress, and didn't see one. "Hey, if the action isn't in here, let's find our own. Like Dylan says: 'All I want to do, is baby be friends with you.' I've got two bottles of wine in my car, along with a couple of Zimmerman CDs. I'll check my e-mail to see if that hot information is there. I might also produce some controlled substance. That is, if you can forget who you are for awhile."

"I'll pass on the controlled substance. That was another time, another me, as someone said recently." He glanced back at the door, but the guy in coat and tie with the woman in the blue dress had been at their table for some time.

"Are you looking for my tail?" she asked. "They're not here. I'd say my tail is chasing his own tail up in Washington. Stupid bastards."

"Are you staying at this hotel?"

"I am now."

Chapter Thirty-Seven

Hunched behind the keyboard and monitor in the machine room, Curt waited for Simmons to chuck up the tapered steel cylinder in the lathe, getting ready for final machining of a non-radioactive bomb part. His shoulders ached from long work days that now extended into long nights.

"Why are we working so late, Perk?"

"We're finishing up," Simmons said, without looking up from the lathe. "You'll be home in a day or so."

Dead in a day or so, Curt thought. He figured they were finished when Maxwell and Markum showed up dressed in khaki work clothes, griping about having to load a truck. Besides that, Lormes, his whirlpool mouth quiet, appeared an hour ago and now roamed the building.

"Have you and Applenu finished machining the plutonium?" Curt asked. Applenu had taken over the computer for that job.

"Applenu's at the hot cell finishing the last piece right now. Once that's finished we're out of here. And that won't be a minute too soon for me."

Finished, Curt thought as he glanced at the twenty-four-inch crescent wrench on the work bench next to the teletype. One swing and Simmons's head would be a bloody mush. But he couldn't get by Beecher in the hall. Twenty-four inches of stainless steel was no match for a forty-five.

"You worried about being mixed up in murder?" Curt asked Simmons.

Simmons spun a wheel to align the cylinder in the lathe. "Nobody's going to get murdered."

"Not if you help me escape."

Simmons ignored Curt and tightened the wheel.

Curt stood, stretched, and walked to the machine-room door. Just up the hall to his right, Beecher watched as Markum and Maxwell passed with a loaded forklift truck.

What was in the crate? Machined plutonium? A few weeks earlier they had loaded another truck with the uranium they'd machined. According to Surling, that made Curt an accomplice. He'd soon be a dead accomplice, just like Surling.

Curt glanced left at the emergency exit. What was the probability he could make it through that door before Simmons or Beecher noticed?

Beecher turned and saw him in the window. He gently touched the back of his head, the spot that Surling hit with the catsup bottle. Then he tapped the left side of his light-blue sports jacket, the place he kept his gun, daring Curt to try it.

Back at the lathe, Simmons had the roughed-out blank in place. "This one's ready to finish."

Finish in sight, Curt thought, finish to a nightmare. He typed a command, and the lathe began to turn.

- - - - -

Shortly after ten o'clock, Lori drove into the wide deserted street between the two rows of long industrial buildings. The plan was to enter the General Nuclear American Company building to determine if Curt was there. She intended to enter at night when there should not be many people inside, maybe only someone guarding Curt.

She was surprised by the blackness of the street, with the only light being that beamed into small areas from widely spaced streetlights. The black Town Car rested in the shadow of their building with no indication of the green Toyota, which wasn't at the Garden Apartments either. Something new: a large yellow truck with Ryder on the side was backed up to the loading dock. Did they exchange a rental car for a rental truck? Why was it here tonight? Why was the Town Car here? Were they getting ready to leave? If so she would have to act before they took Curt away, assuming he was in there. Trouble was, if they were getting ready to leave and none of their vehicles were at the Garden Apartments, they would all be in there, not just the one or two she had counted on.

After a u-turn at the end of the street, she pulled in behind a pickup truck parked in front of the Environmental Disposal and Testing Company, EDAT, the building on the opposite side of the street. Grabbing her binoculars and shoulder bag, she stepped from the air-conditioned cool into a hot and muggy night.

Dressed in blue jeans and a long-sleeve dark-blue shirt and

concealed in the shadows of the EDAT truck, she scanned their building. By now, she knew every detail of that long structure, from the GENERAL NUCLEAR AMERICAN COMPANY sign next to the office door with a small porch and banister, at the far end of the building, to the boarded-up windows on the near end. In the middle, a large sliding door opened onto the dock.

Seeing the office windows dark, she decided everyone was in the back or in the room with the boarded-up windows. Did that make circumstances favorable for her plan hatched during target practice? If so, all she had to do was slip through one of those doors and catch them by surprise with her gun. She and Curt could then lock them up and escape.

Before she could move a sliver of light burst from the side of the building. Gradually, the loading-dock door eased open and illuminated the dock and the back of the truck.

Lori melted into the shadows. Maxwell. Her heart accelerated as he shuffled onto the dock and over to the truck, where he swung open the back doors. This time he wore khaki work clothes, not that awful red-and-white tee shirt.

With the binoculars trained on his face, she could almost smell his alcohol-and-tobacco breath and feel his sweaty hands on her body. He wore something white across his face, like the day she passed them in the green car. It looked like a bandage.

A forklift with a large box on the front emerged from the building, drove onto the dock, and eased into the truck. She recognized the driver as the one she saw driving the green car on her first visit out here.

Beecher ambled onto the dock and looked around, his swagger as cocky as his attitude *that* day. Curt *had* to be there.

Her body trembled as if racked by chills, and she jerked the binoculars away from her eyes and steadied herself against the truck. Her plan, which held such promise when every one of her forty-five slugs slammed into that defenseless cardboard box, no longer seemed like a sure thing. When she decided to come out here, she expected only one or two of them to be there guarding Curt. She thought about the FBI men. Mr. Saul came all the way from Washington. She recognized Saul's name from the newspaper articles; they were working on the bomb case and knew Curt was involved. Several times during their questioning, she ached to spill everything and was on the verge of telling them. Each time she hesitated, and then they were gone.

As soon as the three men were back inside the building and Maxwell closed the door, she made her decision. With sweaty hands, she rummaged through her shoulder bag and found Special Agent Saul's card with his cell-phone number.

- - - - -

Mosely was on top this time, working her body up and down on Saul. From his vantage point, he decided she had a hell of a nice body at fifty-one, although he didn't have too many samples to compare. How long since he'd done it twice in one night?

She guided his hand to her vagina to a spot she wanted massaged. She speeded up the rhythmic up-and-down, setting up an accompanying beat of the headboard banging the wall. Excitement etched her face, eyes now closed. She swooped down to kiss him, her tongue tangling with his, her hot face damp.

Her body quivered, the convulsions transferred to his. "Keep it up," she squealed, her voice too loud for the thin walls to contain.

Saul's body resisted for several beats before the tsunami hit, a chill coursing through his spine like an electrical shock pushing upward into his skull.

She collapsed onto him and lay there with him still inside her; his hand pinned between their bodies. She sighed and rolled off, breathing heavily. "That was good," she said.

He nodded, smiled, and wondered what he was doing. Was it the three drinks in the bar and then the wine? His knowledge of ubiquitous one-night stands came from movies and TV. Was it really like that? He lay there quiet, just wanting to sleep. "Why don't you check your e-mail again," he said.

His body jumped when his cell phone chirped inside his pants draped over the chair across the room. He listened to it, remembering that he was going to call Mary. Mentally, he kicked himself in his naked ass. What the hell was he thinking when he brought her to his room?

The phone stopped ringing, and he mentally played the leave-a-message voice now being listened to by the caller. Would Mary leave a message?

He debated whether to get up and listen to it. Maybe they tailed Mosely after all. They probably called Spanner for instructions, and now they were calling to ask him what he was up to. What could he say? He could say he was interrogating Mosely. That would bring a horse laugh. Maybe the hot information she was supposed to receive would save him.

Why didn't he call Spanner as soon as she showed up? He could have asked where her tail was and gotten them on the defensive. Now they had him. Even with the buzz from the alcohol, the evening didn't compare with the evenings of the Diane Fosbury summer. Nothing lived up to expectations anymore. Had it ever? He should have called Mary.

Words to a Dylan song tumbled around his mind:

Sweet Melinda, the goddess of gloom,
She invites you to her room,
Takes your voice, and leaves you howling at the moon.

The phone began another chirping session.

Mosely slipped out of bed, seemingly unaware of her nakedness. "Are you going to answer that or not?"

Saul watched her ass as she padded to his pants, rummaged in the pocket, sending her tits into a jiggle. She tossed him the chirping phone. Then she picked up her wine glass and padded toward the wine bottle on the table. Why did she wear the full skirts? She had a good body, might even say a great body.

He studied the phone, willing it to quit chirping. Finally, he snapped open the small phone and was relieved to hear Lori Reedan say "Hello" and identify herself.

"Did you hear from your husband, Mrs. Reedan?"

"No, but I know where they are."

He pictured the demure Mrs. Reedan at home with her daughter. Home and kids. Mary. "You say you know where your husband is? Where is he?"

"I know where the people are who are making the bombs."

She wasn't making sense. "What bombs?"

At the word bombs, Mosely hesitated pouring the white wine.

"I know where they're making the atomic bombs...at least I think I do. You know, the people in the paper and on TV...the ones that have Curt."

Saul pushed himself into a sitting position as Mosely headed toward him with the wine bottle, her ears tuned to the conversation. He pulled the sheet to his waist. "Are you sure, Mrs. Reedan?"

"Well...I'm pretty sure." Her voice sounded higher on the phone. Excited? Scared? "They made me promise I wouldn't go to the police. That's why I didn't say anything this afternoon. They came to our house... they threatened to hurt Curt and Beth. They did things to me...assaulted me...the bruise on my cheek you asked me about. *They* did that."

While Mosely poured the remainder of the wine into his glass on the night stand, her damp and matted pubic region hovered in front of his face like a black butterfly.

"Are you sure you know where these people are?" He glanced up at Mosely, who smiled, bent down and reached under the sheet and tugged gently at his semi-hard penis, her breasts swaying in front of his face.

"Yes, I'm sure. I followed them there. I think I saw the one the papers had a sketch of, the one with the beard."

"Applenu?"

Mosely watched him, listening. She bent down and kissed his cheek.

"Yes, him. He went there with the ones that…that raped me."

"*Raped* you?" She had to be making this up, probably fantasizing that Reedan was kidnapped, all because they had marital troubles. People everywhere had been turning in wild-ass tips ever since the government went public with the case.

"Yes…they said they had to teach Curt a lesson, teach him to cooperate."

Mosely ambled back to the table, and Saul's gaze locked on her ass. She tapped a key on her laptop, and the monitor lit up. Although a hard-on attempted to generate itself under the sheet, he knew he had to get out of this room and away from her.

"I'll be right there, Mrs. Reedan." It was worth looking into, if for no other reason than to get rid of Mosely. He'd call Mary on the way.

After he arranged the meeting place with Lori Reedan, he got out of bed and grabbed his shorts from the pile of clothes on the floor. "I've got to go out."

"I heard," she said, heading toward her clothes. "I'm going with you."

Her accent, which was sexy earlier, now grated. "No way can I take you along."

She glared at him. "You think I fucked you because I love you, because you're irresistible? Don't flatter yourself, love. We're together, you and me." She stepped into her black panties and pulled them up. "Unless you'd like me to call Mr. Spanner and fill him in on his fucking number one agent, I am going with you."

He got his briefcase and came out with the handcuffs he had never used. "You are not going along. You can stay peacefully, or I'll cuff you to that bed frame."

"How about a deal," she said. "I'll call you if I get that e-mail I was promised, and you call me if you get a break on the case."

"It's a deal."

As he left the room he saw her pull her cell phone from her purse.

- - - - -

Saul pulled into the Outback Steak House parking lot feeling cramped in the small Ford Focus. He found Lori Reedan's Honda, beeped his horn, and motioned her into his car.

"Where is Mr. Fortner and the other agents," she asked when she was seated next to him. "There are at least five people in that building."

"Just take it easy, Mrs. Reedan. We're not sure they're the people we want. From what you told me, they may be legitimate business people. So first, we'll check it out. If it's them, I'll call all the agents we'll need. How did you find out about these people?"

"You don't believe me, do you," she said. "They're there, and they're loading a truck, probably getting ready to leave. You need help to make sure they don't get away."

"Show them to me. If it's them, I'll get plenty of help."

- - - - -

Curt typed the command to begin the machining process one more time. While the machine did its job, his mind brewed the turmoil mixed by the past weeks. Images flashed into his mind like needle pricks on his skin: Lori, Drafton, Beecher, Maxwell, Drafton, Surling, Lori, Drafton, each image punching fresh wounds into his brain, pushing pain and nausea through his entire body.

A cryptic message appeared on the monitor screen. Curt typed another command, and the lathe spun to a halt. Simmons changed tools. Another typed command sent the lathe back into motion.

The smell of burning machine oil from the lathe activated a memory cell not connected to Drafton or Surling: the acrid smell of burning flux from a soldering iron and his blacksmith father at work in the Dref, Iowa of his youth. All he ever wanted was to escape from the corn-field walls that separated Dref from the outside world.

Like the reaction of someone hit by a terminal illness, he hoped for a miracle, but all the time his logical mind knew it was hopeless. It was so unfair. Lori, Beth, their future, the new child, all of his plans shot. His first five-year plan worked to perfection. Five more years, ten at most, he would have been a millionaire, and he would have proved himself to both their fathers. With everything within his grasp, Lormes and Applenu stepped in and grabbed him.

He'd done everything to survive. That thought nagged him, for regardless of how hard he tried to blame Surling, he knew he'd do the Drafton thing again. He now knew the stacked cards of death should be cheated at all costs.

As the high-pitched whine of the lathe spun away the final minutes, its sound pierced his brain and penetrated to the bone like a dentist's drill, numbing him to the inevitability of it all. Away from these ever-shining fluorescent lights, it was night. In Dref, Mom was at her night prayers. Pray for me, Mom.

He and Simmons both jumped when Maxwell burst into the room, his swollen black-and-blue left eye narrowed to a slit, his right eye wide open, as if fearing another blow. The white bandage across the left side of his forehead seemed to be the only thing that kept his lopsided head from deflating like a stuck balloon.

"Applenu wants you two," he said, his voice hoarse. "There's a fire in the room at the other end."

"The processing room," Simmons said. "Plutonium. We've got to get out of here."

Chapter Thirty-Eight

Maxwell herded Curt and Simmons toward the chaos at the other end of the hall, where Applenu and Markum waited outside the chemical-processing room. Half-way down the hall, they were joined by Beecher and Lormes, who emerged from the door marked OFFICE. As they approached Applenu, Lormes asked what happened.

Applenu, in a white lab coat, turned from Markum and said, "That's what we're trying to determine."

Markum, his face red like his hair, his freckles dissolved by the red sea, said, "Me and Maxwell were taking everything out to the truck like Applenu told us to."

"Right," Maxwell said in a strong accent, trying to one-eye everyone there, his wobbling head pivoting on his neck like a gyroscope. "We accidentally knocked a metal container off a workbench, and when it hit the floor, there was a whoosh. Like air coming out...or maybe going in... you know, like when you open a can of coffee. Anyway, this box had all these warnings about fire, about being highly flammable. It started to smoke, and we hauled our asses out of there."

"There wasn't a fire," Markum said. "Just some smoke. But we didn't wait around. We got our last load out of there as fast as we could. We don't want to end up like Drafton."

Curt watched, wondering if he could just walk away while their attention was diverted.

"That wasn't any bloody smoke," Applenu said to Lormes. "They probably saw dust from the top of the container. There's nothing dangerous in there, because we moved all the radioactive material into the furnace room." He turned to Simmons. "Isn't that right, Perk?"

Simmons, his hands stuffed into the pockets of his khaki pants, stared at the ceiling, as if trying to picture the inside of the room. He asked

Markum to describe the container.

"It was round like a barrel, a metal barrel. It had writing on the side, all kinds of warnings about not dropping the container or letting the contents get in contact with air. It said something about plutoni-something alloys..."

"The plutonium alloys," Simmons said. "That *was* smoke. We should have gotten rid of those."

"What alloys?" Applenu demanded.

"The pyrophoric alloy powders."

"That word was on the side of the barrel," Maxwell said. "Along with all those warnings about handling with care and not letting the contents get in contact with air."

"Pyro-what?" Lormes asked.

"Pyrophoric," Applenu said. "It means they can ignite spontaneously and burn when exposed to air. But if that's what it is, at worst, it's just smoldering. No bloody way could they have seen any smoke as soon as it hit the floor. From what I've read, those alloys only ignite and burn if they've got a good supply of oxygen, which they wouldn't have with just a pinhole knocked in the side of the container when it fell off the shelf. There might not even be a hole."

"It will probably depend on how it falls," Simmons said. "It could just as easily crack wide open if it fell right. It was piled fairly high."

"If it's radioactive, why didn't the alarms go off?" Lormes asked.

"They were disconnected after Drafton's accident," Simmons said.

Applenu pointed to the fire extinguisher in the corner by the door. "What we've got to do is to go in there and make sure no fire gets going. We can do that while any hole in the container is small. Hell, it could smolder for days before it really gets going. Or it could form a layer of oxide and stop all by itself without us doing anything."

Simmons nodded hesitantly. Everyone else stared at Applenu, who said, "Once we get the oxygen away from the alloy, we'll shut that room off and finish machining that last piece of plutonium in the hot cell. Then we'll load up and cut away."

Beecher pointed to Maxwell and Markum. "Grab that fire extinguisher and get in there. Smother it with foam, which should keep it from reigniting."

Maxwell's lopsided head bobbed up and down as it swiveled around on his neck, pausing first at Applenu, then Lormes. He turned back to Beecher. "Fuck you," he said. "I am not going to end up like Drafton. He breathed just a little of that shit and it killed him."

Curt glanced down the hall, his mind keyed on the office door halfway between where they stood and the corridor past his quarters. Was that door unlocked? Could he make it in there and lock the door before they grabbed him? Or shot him in the back like Surling?

"I'm not going in there either," Markum said.

"All you've got to do is put masks and protective clothing on," Applenu said, "like we did when we decontaminated the furnace room. That way you won't inhale any radioactive material."

Maxwell and Markum took a step back from Applenu.

Curt backed up, keeping his same distance from Maxwell, but getting himself a step closer to the office door.

Lormes pointed to the chemical-processing room. "What keeps those vapors from coming out and contaminating the whole building when they open that door to go inside?"

"There's an air lock with negative pressure between that door and the room the alloys are in," Applenu said. "After they stop any smoldering, they'll leave their clothes in the contaminated part of the air lock, just like Drafton did when he was contaminated."

"We'd better hurry," Simmons said. "The longer it smolders, the bigger that hole gets. Eventually, it'll get hot enough to blow the barrel apart, and the whole room will go up."

Lormes turned to Markum and Maxwell. "What are you two waiting for?"

The two sad faces stared at each other. Markum spoke. "I don't mean no disrespect, Mr. Lormes, but I saw what happened to Drafton. He breathed some of that stuff, and…"

"But he didn't have a mask on," Applenu said. "You'll have masks and protective clothing. There's nothing to worry about."

"Not me," Markum said and took another step back, still farther from the entrance to the chemical-processing room.

Curt shuffled another half step toward the office door. Was now the time to run?

"Let Simmons or Applenu do it," Maxwell said. "They're Applenu's bombs, let *him* do it. We're not getting paid to take those kinds of chances."

With his head cocked to the left, Maxwell scanned the knot of people standing there. His one-eyed stare landed on Curt, and a dark hatred burned through to Curt. He continued to stare at Curt, pushing at the bandage on his forehead as if trying to think. Then he smiled. "Let *him* do it. Let him earn *his* money."

All eyes turned to Curt.

- - - - -

Saul braked to a stop at the entrance of the wide deserted street, a typical deserted industrial area at twelve-fifteen on a Friday morning.

"It's the second building on the left," Lori Reedan said.

He drove into the street and stopped in front of the darkened building.

"You can't stop here," she said, her voice verging on a scream. "If they come out, they'll see us."

Saul drove to the end of the street, turned around, and pulled into the shadows of the building opposite the one she had pointed to. If they were threatened, he could take off fast. He turned off the engine and studied the dark building. "I can't make out that sign."

"It says General Nuclear American Company."

"There's nobody in there," he said, thinking Fortner's domestic quarrel theory was correct. She doesn't hear from him, goes to pieces, and starts manufacturing crazy scenarios.

He studied the building. His first reaction was that they would not set the manufacturing process up right here, less than five miles from where they stole the material? Then again, it made sense in a way. After they hijacked the load, they would not have to take it out on the road and risk getting stopped. It would not be expected. But why would they call it a nuclear company? Probably lots of nuclear companies in Oak Ridge, so it would not be out of place.

"There's a light in there," Lori said.

Saul rolled down his window. "It's probably some sort of night light, ma'am."

"What about the car and truck being there? When I was here earlier, they put something in the truck. I just noticed that car on the other side of the loading dock. It wasn't there when I was here before. You're going to need help."

"If we need more people, we'll get them," Saul said.

- - - - -

With his mind concentrated on the office door, the suggestion that Curt go into the chemical-processing room caught him off guard. He sensed hope in the gazes of the six men around him. After all, Surling charged into the contamination after Drafton's accident.

He remembered his panic when Surling nonchalantly helped Drafton get out. That was *before* they unleashed radioactivity in the room. His first impulse was to tell them to go in there themselves, but that would not get him through the office door. Instead, he decided to stall. "What's in it for me?" he asked.

Beecher grabbed the fire extinguisher and shoved it at him. "Just get your ass in there and put out the fire."

Curt ignored him and spoke to Applenu. "I said, what's in it for me?"

Applenu looked at Lormes and then back at Curt, but he seemed to look past him, as if trying to think it through. "What if we give you another hundred-thousand dollars?"

"Yeah," Lormes said, a tentative smile whirling to his lips. "You put out that fire, and we'll make it a nice round four-hundred thousand."

Applenu, his eyes still not on Curt, nodded.

Curt smiled and cast his gaze to the floor as if considering the proposition. He decided to assume the office door was unlocked.

Before Curt could reply, Applenu grabbed the fire extinguisher from Beecher and started giving orders, his voice filled with enthusiasm. "Get him some protective coveralls, gloves, and a mask from the change room. He can get dressed out here."

Beecher dispatched Markum after the requested items.

Applenu took several steps toward the chemical-processing room and motioned Curt to join him. He turned to Beecher. "He needs to take a second fire extinguisher with him. There's one in the machine room."

Beecher sent Maxwell after it and then stood across the corridor at the opposite wall, arms folded, staring at Curt. Simmons and Lormes joined Beecher.

Curt glanced once more at the office door, but with Beecher standing there staring at him, there was no way to make it through there, even if it was unlocked. He hesitated, but then advanced toward Applenu, who led him to the opposite wall from Beecher, set down the fire extinguisher and pulled a pencil from his shirt pocket.

Applenu sketched a diagram on the beige wall and quietly explained the arrangement of the processing room and the location of the pyrophoric alloys. "I saw you looking at the office door," he said in a quieter voice. "It's locked. I'll unlock it, and if you get a chance, go for it. There's no bloody way I would go in that room, and there's no bloody way I want you to wind up like Surling."

Applenu turned to Lormes. "I think there's a new mask in the office.

I'll get it."

- - - - -

What to do? Saul wondered. Was he sitting here with a crazy woman? Or was he in a position to solve one of the FBI's most important crimes of all time? Should he assume Lori Reedan was a spurned woman who had suffered a breakup of her marriage? Or should he call Fortner and tell him to alert his Knoxville colleagues and get over here so they can raid an illegal atomic bomb-making operation?

- - - - -

They waited. Simmons and Lormes discussed the situation as they backed further away from the chemical-processing room door. Applenu emerged from the office carrying a protective mask.

Now or never, Curt thought, before Markum and Maxwell got back. He hefted the fire extinguisher from the floor. It was too heavy and cumbersome for a club. He told Beecher to hurry up Markum and Maxwell.

Beecher turned, took a step down the hall and yelled.

Curt reached down and pulled the safety pin of the fire extinguisher. He jerked the canister off the floor, stepped into the middle of the hall and aimed the black megaphone nozzle at Beecher's head, just as he looked back from calling down the hall.

Beecher opened his mouth to yell, but before words emerged and before he could step toward Curt, white foam lathered his face.

Beecher screamed, took a step backward, and stumbled forward, groping for Curt like a grotesque mummy.

Curt pivoted around to Applenu, who tossed the mask aside and rushed toward him. Curt blasted away, aiming low to avoid Applenu's face, assuming he was making a show to avoid being accused of helping Curt escape. Applenu turned his head, and Curt lathered his lower body. Applenu stumbled backward and tumbled onto the floor.

Curt turned the megaphone on Simmons and sprayed. Simmons backed off, his hands across his face.

Lormes glanced around and then shuffled forward with both hands out in front of him as if ready to ward off an imminent attack.

Curt aimed for Lormes's eyes and scored a direct hit, as white foam splattered across the shoulders of his gray pin-stripe jacket, like the splash from a cream pie in the face.

Lormes yelled for Beecher to shoot.

With Beecher behind him to his left and the office door ahead of him on the right, Curt whirled to face Beecher.

Beecher rubbed at the foam in his eyes with his left hand, while he fumbled under his jacket with his right.

Curt blasted him in the face.

"You son of a bitch, Reedan. I'll get you."

Curt stepped back and sprayed the floor between himself and Beecher.

Beecher shuffled in the direction of the last blast, his outstretched hands grabbing wildly at the air in front of him. He reached the foam-covered floor, slipped, and went down hard.

Curt turned and found himself next to Applenu, who was trying to stand. "Sod you, Reedan."

Curt blasted the floor at Applenu's feet. Applenu started forward, slipped, and went down.

Curt turned back to Beecher, who crawled forward on hands and knees in the foam. He rose up onto his knees and fumbled in his jacket for his gun. Curt struck at Beecher with the black megaphone, trying to crush his head, remembering his big hands on Lori's breasts. He swung again, harder. The megaphone caved in.

Beecher, still on his knees, pulled back, both his hands covering his head.

To Curt's left, Simmons advanced tentatively. Curt blasted him with a flattened stream from the bent megaphone, completely blanketing his dark-brown face with a layer of the white foam.

Like an advancing ghost, Simmons kept coming. Arms extended, hands open, he groped forward one small step at a time.

Curt swung the canister and let it fly.

A strike: Simmons howled and crashed to the floor like a white-headed bowling pin.

Beecher regained his feet, rubbing his eyes with one hand and feeling forward with the other. Curt shoulder-blocked him back down, side stepped the foam, and ran for the door.

"Markum, Maxwell," Beecher yelled.

From the other end of the hall, Maxwell hurried toward Curt. Markum ran around the corner from the other corridor.

Curt knew that if Applenu had not unlocked the office door, he'd have to face them head on, without a fire extinguisher or a wine bottle. He would end up like Surling, banging into a green door.

"Shoot," Lormes yelled. "Kill the bastard."

Curt grabbed the doorknob and prayed.

Chapter Thirty-Nine

Like the waters of the Red Sea parted when Moses waved his staff, the office door opened when Curt twisted the cold brass knob. As he slammed the door, he heard Lormes yell, "Kill the son of a bitch." He locked it and plunged into the darkened room, lit only by the glow from the hall that seeped through the opaque glass window. Across the room, the window of another door glimmered from the street light, and he headed for it. Behind him, someone smashed the opaque window to get at the lock.

Curt unlocked the door to the outside.

Thuck! Thuck!

He heard the gun spit as he stepped through the door. The window of the door shattered and sprayed him with glass shards.

"Kill that son of a bitch," Lormes yelled.

- - - - -

Saul heard the noise and saw a second flash of light inside General Nuclear American just as Lori Reedan said, "Did you see that light? Did you hear that? It sounded like glass breaking."

Saul nodded, his gaze fixed on the door across the street, where a tall, gangly man charged onto the small porch to the accompaniment of the sound of more breaking glass as the window of the office door shattered behind him. He ran straight into the porch rail, looked both ways, turned to his right, and bounded down the steps.

"It's *Curt!*" Lori Reedan said.

Once off the porch, he turned and disappeared between the buildings.

"Curt! Curt!" Lori Reedan yelled and opened the door.

"Quiet," Saul said. "Close that door!"

"It's my husband."

293

Before Saul could move, a hefty man with a gun lumbered through the office door. He plodded down the steps and headed after Reedan.

"Maxwell," Lori Reedan said in a loud whisper. "He's one of the bastards that came to our house, one of those that…that raped me. I lost my child because of them."

"What do you mean raped you, lost your child?" Saul asked.

Lori Reedan ignored his question. "Mr. Saul, you've got to do something to help Curt. They've got guns."

Saul stared across the street, wondering what he could do. He fumbled his cell phone from his pocket, located the Knoxville office phone number in the directory and dialed. He got the duty agent in charge for the night and told him he needed a task detail to raid a factory that housed the stolen nuclear material. There followed a lengthy discussion about where the factory was located in Oak Ridge.

As Saul talked, he saw a stocky guy with a gun rush through the office door and follow Reedan and the fat man. Somebody yelled something indecipherable from around the side of the building.

Saul, his heart accelerating, turned off the phone and slipped it into his jacket pocket. Is this why he joined the Bureau? He'd never fired a gun at a man. Actually, he had only drawn his gun twice, both times in a relatively benign situation. What was standard procedure for an incident like this? He should have believed her and had a task force with him now. "How many more are in there?" he asked.

"Two or three," Lori Reedan said. "I saw Beecher, Applenu, and a dark-skinned man out here two days ago. I saw Beecher earlier this evening plus the two that just went after Curt, but that other car may mean more of them."

Saul knew he could not go running off after two men with guns and leave the others in the building to come after him. He started the engine. With a wide u-turn, he pulled up parallel to the Town Car, with the Town Car between them and the office door. Then he pulled forward so they could watch the entrance with the Ford Fusion headed into the street for a quick getaway.

Only one chance: catch those inside by surprise, while the two with guns chased Reedan. After that he would worry about the others.

He slipped his gun from the holster inside his jacket and jerked the keys from the ignition. He turned to Lori Reedan. "I'm going to try to get inside that dark room. I figure your husband can keep those two on the run for awhile." He handed her the keys. "Get over here in the driver's seat. Then give me ten minutes inside. If I'm not back, get the hell out of here.

If the other two come back, blow the horn, start the motor, and get ready to take off."

"Give me a gun, and I'll go with you," Lori Reedan said. "I can shoot a pistol. Or give me a shotgun."

He smiled. They might have torn this girl up, he thought, but she had *chutzpa*. "I'll be okay, Mrs. Reedan."

As he opened the car door, Lori Reedan reached out and grabbed his arm. "I can help," she said. "I want to help get those bastards for what they did to me and my family."

"We'll get them." He pulled away and headed toward the building.

- - - - -

Sweating and disoriented on a lifeless street on the other side of the building, Curt stopped to try and think. For the first time in what seemed like years, he could breathe fresh air and did not have fluorescent lights beating down on him. Here it was pitch dark, no way to see which way to go.

He shook his head and tried to concentrate on the situation. He was certain he heard his name called just as he left the building. Clear as a bell, he heard Lori's voice. It couldn't be. Now, he heard only the sound of footsteps. He began to run.

Maxwell yelled to Markum: "This way, around the corner."

Curt thought he heard the silenced gun spit, but he didn't hear the bullet hit. More importantly, he didn't feel it hit. He ran along the side of the road. A slight pain nucleated in his left side—dues for all that beer and no exercise.

Sweat rolled down his forehead and flooded his eyes, igniting a burn. Dampness in his arm pits grew to a puddle. After starting to unbutton the long-sleeved khaki shirt and strip it off, he decided against it; a white tee-shirt would make a better target.

He crossed the street and plunged into a thicket of bushes and scrub trees. Almost as soon as he hit the wall of bushes, he ran out of them and into an open field.

Maxwell yelled. "He went through there."

He ran through a mass of weeds and stubble where weeds had once grown; they slapped at his knees and thighs, while others brushed and scraped across his arms. Scattered around the field, black monsters of all sizes watched him stumble on. Only when he passed close to a tall one did he recognize the silent spectators as cedar trees planted at random by shitting birds.

Weeds: a tall one with leaves rough as a rasp raked across his hand, making him glad for the long-sleeve shirt. Dew-soaked grass and weeds cooled his ankles and soaked his socks and pants legs. If only he could collapse into their coolness and rest for a few seconds.

In his rush to move on, the only sounds to reach his ears were his frantic footsteps and his labored breathing.

Markum yelled: "There he is."

With each lung full of air, he sucked in equal amounts of fire that ignited in his throat and lungs. A knife sliced at his side, threatening to open it. He had to be in better shape than Maxwell, so he had to be moving away from him. A younger and leaner Markum posed a problem.

The uneven ground reminded Curt of running in a freshly plowed Iowa field. He stumbled more than he ran: one step on a mound, the next in a deep hole. He tripped, stumbled, and went down to one knee; he pulled himself up and ran on.

He thought he detected the sounds of two shots from the silenced gun, barely audible above his crashing feet and labored breathing. The shots triggered muscle contractions across his back and deep in his chest, while his brain transmitted memories of bullets ripping into Surling's body.

Up ahead, another row of tall bushes and trees loomed like those on the other side of the field. Another street? Houses? People?

Like the coxswain for a sculling crew, his brain called the cadence for the two pieces of lead that were his feet. Right. Left. Right. Leffttt... Instead of finding the earth in the same place as the previous step, his left foot kept going down. When it hit, his center of gravity leaned too far forward, and his momentum pitched him into a headfirst dive, like a belly slide into home plate.

He lay there, groaning, his sweat-drenched face cooled by the damp plants. His brain switched channels: from the cadence of escape to an urgent request for rest. His lungs sucked from deep within, rapid gasps that tore fire through his nostrils and throat down into his chest. Rest, got to rest, he thought. When he raised himself to his hands and knees, pain seemed to spurt from every region of his body.

"Where did he go?" Markum yelled.

"He fell down. Let's get him."

Curt levered himself up. Pain shot through his knee, twisted in the fall.

"There he is. Shoot."

Three hobbling steps and his left foot landed in a hole. His leg crumpled, sending him to his hands and knees. On all fours, he stumbled and crawled for the bushes. Once more he struggled to his feet.

Although he didn't hear the shot, he heard a bullet smash into a cedar tree to his right just as he crashed headfirst through the wall of bushes. He somersaulted down a steep bank, landing flat on his back on a rocky creek bottom, his left arm chilled in a water puddle.

His face burned, and he tasted blood from where a thorn-filled weed had clawed his face like an angry tiger. He lay on the damp rocks that cooled like a refrigerated bed. Rest, he needed rest, just a few minutes for the pain in his side to subside, and then he would be ready to get up and run some more.

He sucked more air, hoping it came with an escape plan. It came with an awful stench that singed his nostrils and threatened nausea. What to do? Run up the creek? If his throat hadn't burned so, he would have laughed at the thought. He struggled to his feet, hesitated, and ran up the creek.

- - - - -

Lori remained on the passenger side with the window rolled down to better see Saul sneak toward the building, his eyes fixed on the office door. He shouldn't go alone, she thought, too many people in there. She should have told him she had a gun and could use it, instead of expecting him to have a gun for her to use. How do you tell the FBI you're carrying a gun? Probably too macho to be burdened with a woman, knowing without a doubt she couldn't help. Should she take it out and just go along? What about Curt? Should she follow him and see if she can help? She knew she would never catch them, probably never find them. Curt had a head start, and even with his bad leg he would easily outrun that slug Maxwell.

She watched Saul work his way along the side of the building toward the door. Still no lights in the office, although light from an open door at the back of the room dappled the windows with shadows.

New shadows flashed across the office windows and then lights went on in the room. Saul froze in his tracks. The office door opened, and Beecher stepped onto the small porch, wiping at his face with a cloth while holding something in his other hand.

"FBI," Saul yelled, his gun held in two hands and pointed at Beecher. He moved out of the shadow of the building. "Drop the gun, or I'll shoot."

Startled, Beecher dropped the cloth. His head snapped around to locate the source of the voice.

"Drop it," Saul yelled, advancing toward Beecher.

297

Beecher hesitated and then slowly lowered the gun and laid it on top of the banister.

"Now raise your hands and step away from the gun. *Higher.*"

"Now, back down those steps," Saul said, his voice loud enough to be heard by Beecher, but hopefully not by those inside the building.

Lori watched Beecher hesitate, his gaze on the banister and the gun, his massive form looming at the top of the porch like a shadowy monster. Out of the side of her eye, she caught movement of a man running in the shadow of the building coming from the direction of the loading dock, maybe from the other car. He ran toward Saul, his arms extended. He had a gun.

- - - - -

Saul watched the big man on the porch stall. "I said back down those steps," he said, hoping no one inside heard him. Then he sensed movement behind him. Lori Reedan, he thought; she should be in the car.

"Drop your gun, Mr. Saul," a man's voice said from behind.

He turned his head, the gun still pointed at the big man on the porch, and glanced at a man twenty-feet away wearing a baseball cap with a gun pointed at him. "Atkinson? Austin, it's Austin," Saul said, recalling the NNSA picture and the face across the table at the hotel two hours ago.

"Enough with the introductions now drop your gun."

Saul glanced back at the porch, hesitated, his gun steady in front of him. Slowly, he lowered his hand as if to drop the gun. With one quick motion, he whirled to face the big man on the porch, whose gun pointed at Saul.

Before he could aim and pull the trigger, the big man fired. Two flashes at the end of his arm, two loud pops followed quickly by two louder pops, closer and without flashes. The impact of the bullets from behind propelled his body forward and sent him sprawling. The pain of the fall and the scraping of his face across the rough asphalt masked the location of the bullets in his body. Aware of the footsteps of the big man running toward him, he decided to stay down.

- - - - -

Horrified at seeing Saul gunned down, Lori grabbed her shoulder bag, opened the door, and started to get out.

"Stop her." the man in the baseball cap yelled. "Mosely said he was with Reedan's wife."

She realized that with Saul down, she would be no match for two men with guns. Footsteps pounded toward her as she slammed the door and scrambled across the front seat and slipped behind the wheel. As she fumbled to insert the keys into the ignition, she heard the passenger-side door open.

The motor turned over immediately, but as she reached for the gear-shift lever, Beecher's big paw grabbed her right wrist and twisted. Then he was inside the car, and he jerked her left hand from the steering wheel.

"Well, if it isn't the lovely Mrs. Reedan. You just can't stay away from me, can you, Lori?"

- - - - -

Applenu glared at Lormes, who dabbed at the lapel of his expensive gray pin stripe with a towel, trying to brush away the last bits of foam. "All you and your people had to do was keep one bloke in line, and you mucked it up," Applenu said. "Besides that, your people probably set this bloody place on fire."

Lormes glared back. "Those things *bloody well* happen. So what do we do now?"

Applenu toweled at his hair while he walked to the door that led to the chemical-processing room. He hoped Reedan made it and wished he was beside him running like bloody hell to get away from this place. He looked around and wondered what he needed to do to save his own skin. No more stalling, he thought. Time to find out where they stood with the fire, and he would have to be the one to find out.

Four closely spaced pops from outside broke the silence.

"That takes care of Reedan," Lormes said. "But they should have used silencers."

Applenu glanced back down the hall at Lormes. "Good. Now all we've got to worry about is whether we're looking at a bloody fire."

Applenu eased open the hall door into the airlock: nothing. He stepped into the airlock and went quickly to the door that led to the chemical-processing room. He placed his hands flat against the door. No heat. He put his ear against it: still nothing.

After slipping on a breathing mask, he slowly cracked open the door into the chemical-processing room. At the sound of a loud crack, he jumped back. Cautiously, he surveyed the room and located the source of the sound, the small barrel on the floor in front of the atmosphere chamber. No doubt about it, a fine plume of smoke curled upward from the barrel.

Another loud crack, as the barrel continued to heat up and expand. Much more smoke. They could have put it out easily if Maxwell and Markum had gone right in, he thought. Even if they let it go now, there was plenty of time before it would break out of the barrel. And still more time before it consumed the chemical-processing room and broke through a wall to a large source of fresh oxygen, plenty of time to make a fast and orderly exit.

How the bloody hell should he play this? All he wanted was to join Reedan on the run toward his former life. Although the amount of smoke curling from the barrel was increasing even as he watched, Simmons could dress out and go in and extinguish it. Then they could finish machining the last nuclear explosive. Trouble is, it would be hell getting Simmons in there—or anyone else.

Another loud crack and a small flame emerged from the side of the barrel. It was now just a matter of time—seconds...minutes...an hour?—before the barrel would fracture and spread the fire into the room. It would then be an hour, maybe several hours, before it broke through the thick walls of the chemical-processing room.

So be it, he thought. Time to put paid to the project and get serious about escape. While machining the final plutonium a few minutes before the fire broke out, he'd been assessing what they had accomplished: they essentially pulled off the whole thing just as planned. Although he knew Sherbani and Atkinson wouldn't admit it, they never expected to get close to fourteen bombs out of the fifteen for which they had nuclear material. They did it. He did it. Despite himself and the apprehension he felt about his future and about the future of the bombs they had created, he couldn't help feeling a pride of accomplishment. Maybe he shouldn't, but it was there. So unfortunately for the world, their success wasn't diminished by this little muck up.

A loud explosive whoosh and the smoke enveloped the barrel and the flame grew.

Applenu slammed the door to the chemical-processing room.

- - - - -

Bent forward at the waist, Curt hobbled along the creek bed, the thick bushes on the bank hiding him from Markum and Maxwell. Several yards up the creek he stumbled over a tangled mass of branches, jammed there by heavy rains during some part of the year. He climbed over them and ran on. The humid air reeked, further inhibiting his breathing, the stench getting stronger as he moved up the creek.

Now and then his foot splashed into a water puddle on the creek bottom. He kicked a metal can that clanged across the rocky creek bottom. His right foot plopped into a water hole; cold water soaked his foot to his ankle. God, what he would give for a cold drink. What was that stink? Smelled like something dead.

He stopped to listen: nothing but the roar from his nose and throat fighting for breath and not wanting to breathe. After a mental strangulation that pushed him to one knee, he concentrated to get the outside sounds past the thump-thump of his heart in his ears. Gradually, the screech and squeak of cicada and crickets seeped in. Then he heard them, forty-to-fifty feet down the creek where he went in, coming this way.

- - - - -

As Applenu stepped back into the hall from the airlock, the office door with the broken window opened, and a young woman walked into the hall, followed immediately by Atkinson and then Beecher, both men holding guns. Atkinson with a gun? He did it all, Applenu thought. He had come a long way from the Atkinson he met in Princeton.

"What the hell is this?" Lormes asked, pulling the towel away from his hair. "Hearn. I thought you went back to the base."

"The name's Atkinson, remember? I came back when I found out Saul, the dead FBI agent out there, was coming down here to nose around."

"Mrs. Reedan here brought the fucking FBI," Beecher said.

"The FBI. Where?"

"Don't worry, we took care of him. But if it wasn't for this guy, my ass would have been fried. All of us would have been fried."

Atkinson pointed to Lori. "Mosely said that bitch followed your guys out here and then called Saul." He turned to Applenu. "Is the job finished?"

"It's essentially done."

"We better get the hell out of here," Lormes said. "If there was one FBI man, there'll be more."

"I've got to go," Atkinson said, "and you better hurry. I'm sure Saul called for backup before he got out of the car to investigate. You've probably got an hour or so."

"We have to clear out anyway," Applenu said, "unless we can get someone to put out the fire." He explained the fire in the pyrophoric alloys to Atkinson.

"I should never have put that in the shipment we hijacked," Atkinson said. "Have someone get rid of Saul's car. I'll take an early morning flight back to our base, where I'll see you tomorrow night."

"Sounds good," Lormes said. "I'll be glad to wrap up this job."

Atkinson turned to face Lori Reedan, who stood next to Beecher, clutching her shoulder bag to her body. "You know she can identify all of us."

"Don't worry about her," Lormes said. "She won't be telling anybody anything."

- - - - -

Once he knew Atkinson, the big man, and Lori were inside the building, Saul assessed the damage. He hurt all over, especially his scraped and bleeding face from hitting the asphalt. One bullet smashed into his shoulder, and one burned into his thigh, the impact propelling him forward, and off balance, he slid onto the asphalt. Thank God, the once-dead Austin couldn't use a gun as well as he used a computer. It was Austin that shot him in the back when the big guy thankfully missed. His face hurt worse than the bullet wounds although he was aware of wetness around both.

Because the two men were busy making sure Lori did not escape, they momentarily forgot about him. After they caught her, they hurriedly checked him and from the blood concluded he was dead. In the chaos, he heard Mosely's name, another one of his fuck-ups. Ironic, he thought, playing dead was the only thing he did right in this sorry state of affairs. But because of him, they now had Lori Reedan.

The thigh wound throbbed when he flexed his leg. He probed his aching shoulder through the drenched shirt. What now? He wondered. How long would it be before the Knoxville office detail got here? How long before he bled to death?

He heaved himself into a sitting position, saw his gun two feet away, and stretched out for it. He patted his jacket pockets for his cell phone.

Lights flashed on and then off in the window above him, and then the door the three went into earlier opened. Saul flattened himself on the pavement, shoved the gun under his body, and reassumed the dead-man pose.

Approaching footsteps indicated one man. Foot steps stopped, a voice, which Saul recognized as Austin's said, "The computer game was fun, Mr. Saul. I win; you lose."

Austin began to walk, and Saul waited until he was past. He strained to sit up. "Stop right there, Austin, and raise your hands."

Caught in mid-stride, he halted, hesitated a second, and then turned and faced Saul.

In the dim light Saul could not read the expression on Austin's face. He levered himself to his feet with his left hand, keeping the gun in his right hand aimed at Austin. In his attempt at a quick movement to stand, a shimmering blackness momentarily blurred his vision. He steadied himself against a dizziness that clouded his vision and enveloped his entire body. He widened his stance for better balance, but felt himself sway slightly as if on a boat. "The game's not over," he said, taking a wobbling step toward Austin.

Austin stepped toward him, a smile now visible. "So you're still with us, Mr. Saul?"

Saul saw the gun at Austin's waist tucked behind his belt. "I want your gun," he said, taking another wavering step forward, now only a couple of feet separating them, his vision swimming in and out of focus.

Austin stepped back and reached for his gun.

Memorized FBI rules for firing his weapon flashed into his mind and vanished as Austin jerked the gun from his belt.

Saul fired, a loud blast of pain to his ears. He fired again, then once more. He saw Austin's body accelerate backward as a shroud of blackness enveloped him. As Saul's body slumped toward the ground, fading thoughts in his mind tried to assess the situation: Was Austin dead? Was the game now over? No...No...Bombs...Plutoni...

- - - - -

Curt eased himself onto his stomach and squirmed up under the overhanging bushes on the bank toward the direction he came from and the side Markum and Maxwell were on. In stretching out, his left leg was chilled by a puddle that extended from ankle to thigh. It balanced his soaked right shoe.

Water: just one drink, he thought, to quench the fire in his throat and douse his burning face. His cheek rested on his left sleeve, soggy from the water he fell into earlier. With his face turned toward the bank, a pungent stench of dead and decaying plants oozed into his nostrils, the odor of dank Iowa creeks from summers long ago, momentarily replacing the stink all around.

Behind him, bushes cracked as someone went into the creek. They crashed up the opposite bank.

"Nothing over here but more of the same goddamn weeds," Markum said.

303

"That means he's in the creek," Maxwell wheezed. "Be quiet a minute."

Curt squeezed back his breath; his chest quivered.

After several seconds of silence, Maxwell said, "He's laying low, hoping like hell we won't find him."

Bushes cracked. "It's dark as hell down here," Markum said. "And man, does it stink." More bushes cracked as he climbed back up the bank to join Maxwell.

Maxwell spoke, his words squeezed around forced breaths. "We know you're down there, Reedan. If you come out, I'm sure Lormes will make a deal with you. I don't blame you for not going in there to put out that fire." Maxwell paused to breath. "If you don't come out, we'll come down and find your ass. Then there won't be no deals."

Because of the mosquitoes that swarmed over his face like maggots on a dead rabbit's head, their whine sounding in Curt's ears like the sound of a high-pitched police siren, he barely heard Maxwell's voice. God, he wanted to slap and chase the mosquitoes, then scratch at the proliferating welts on his neck and splash something cool on the burning gash across his face.

"What the hell is that stink?" Markum asked. "It smells like something's dead down there."

Maxwell chuckled. "What do you think Beecher and I did with Surling? We had to do something with him quick."

Curt felt sick. He wondered how far he was from the body.

"I'd say we will have to go down and flush the bastard out," Maxwell said.

"No way will we find him without a light. It's darker down there than the inside of a black-cat's asshole."

Maxwell laughed. "Maybe a goddamned rattlesnake will crawl up *his* asshole."

Curt's sweat-drenched body froze. The fear of snakes crowded out thoughts of Surling and the stink. Goose flesh blanketed the mosquito bites.

"I'll wait here while you go back and get some flashlights and some more ammunition," Maxwell said. "If he moves while you're gone, I'll blast the shit out of him. We can lay him out right next to Surling."

Markum laughed. "No way am I going to get next to that stinking piece of shit."

Curt heard Markum run off, and then he heard something rattle on the bank a few feet above his head. The whining in his ears quieted.

Mosquito bites no longer burned and itched, and the air and water no longer stank. Snakes! He held his breath without trying. Snakes struck at heated objects. Though inwardly chilled, his body was one large heat source.

He raised his head from the rocks, ears cocked, his neck forced down into his shirt, waiting for a slimy rope to twist across his back, heading for his exposed neck.

- - - - -

After Atkinson left, the three men discussed what needed to be done before they left. Lori's arm ached where Beecher gripped it. She considered going for the gun, but she needed both hands free.

Three muffled pops sounded as if they came from outside.

"Maybe now they finally got Reedan," Lormes said. "But goddammit, they should use silencers."

Beecher jerked her arm and led her down the hall. He yanked open a door, shoved Lori into the room, and slammed the door.

Lori slumped onto the edge of a green vinyl couch, hugging her shoulder bag. She glanced around at the boarded-up windows, and then she recognized the suitcase on the floor next to the portable cot. She opened it: his suit, shirts, ties…Curt.

They had him here all the time. If only she had taken the chance and gotten the FBI sooner. If only Saul had brought help. But he had to see for himself. If he had just…Not Christmas today, she thought, remembering what Dad used to say: "If ifs and buts were candy and nuts, it'd be Christmas every day."

The cell phone, she thought, emerging from her gloomy thoughts. She dug into the handbag down below the pistol. It wasn't there. Where was it? She remembered using it in her car to call Saul. After the call, she placed it on the seat next to the handbag as she contemplated whether to call Sarah and see about Beth and tell her she would be late getting back.

"Shit." It's still in the car. "Shit! Shit! Shit!"

- - - - -

Minutes passed. How long would it be before Markum was back? Curt wondered. And then what?

The rustling on the bank stopped. Curt lowered his scratched and mosquito-bitten face onto the cool creek floor. Mosquitoes only quit whining long enough to land and sting.

Branches cracked and shook, and he sensed Maxwell on top of the bank, coming closer and stopping every few yards to part the bushes and try to look into the creek. Curt strained to hear, and he thought he recognized Maxwell's voice.

When almost directly above Curt, Maxwell parted the branches and spoke down into the darkness. "We're going to get you, Reedan. We'll let you down there in the ditch with Surling."

Could he rush Maxwell and bring him down before he could get off his first shot? Where exactly was Maxwell? His scientific mind dredged up Heisenberg's Uncertainty Principle: If the momentum of a particle is known exactly, it is impossible to know the exact position of that particle.

Mentally, he shook his head. No time for science. Time for action. If he misjudged Maxwell's position, he was through.

More bushes cracked. "I know you're down there, Reedan."

Thuck! Thuck!

The gun spit into the creek, the sound not as loud as a good fart. At close range, it reminded him of the sound that cut down Surling. How many bullets did Maxwell have left? Should he chance it?

"I'm going to enjoy killing you. I'll enjoy it just about as much as I enjoyed fucking your wife." He laughed. "She spread her legs just right. Even grabbed the old cock and stuck it in her cunt for us. And Beech taught her to suck. Suck and fuck. Not bad, not bad at all." He giggled. "We even got video of it. If Applenu had any balls, he would have let us show you those pictures."

Curt fought to control his anger, forcing himself to stay put. Got to wait for the right moment and then get them.

All was quiet except for the whining mosquitoes. How long had Markum been gone? He wondered. The rancid smell began to seep into his nostrils, evacuating the odor of rotten leaves and dank water pools. Had Maxwell moved? Or was he standing still waiting for Curt to move? If he decided to run, which way should he go to keep Maxwell from shooting him? How long before Markum would return?

More quiet and more passing time.

Maxwell spoke, his voice quiet. "Here comes Markum with the lights. When he gets here, I'm going to personally come down there in that stinking creek and blast the shit out of you."

Chapter Fourty

"What?" Maxwell yelled.

Markum shouted back, but Curt couldn't make out the words, which seemed drowned out by the horrible stench and the knowledge of its origin.

Neither could Maxwell. "Just get your ass down here," he growled.

In the silence, thoughts of doom scampered in and out of Curt's mind, thoughts of death twisted around thoughts of Lori and Maxwell, Lori and Beecher.

Concentrate.

He started to ease his legs under his body to assume a crouch, but the pain in his knee made him straighten it out. Somehow, just before the light hit, he would spring up and lunge for Maxwell or Markum. Get their gun and use it.

He wondered who would find his body, probably swollen by the hot sun and twisted grotesquely up against the bank. Was that how Surling's body looked? Where was Drafton's?

Concentrate.

No way did they do that to Lori. They'd be afraid she'd go to the police. How did she react? What about Beth?

He pictured his dead body lying in the sun next to Surling's and remembered a long-ago fishing trip and a dead hog at the edge of a corn field, ballooned, bloated, and stinking. Staying back where he could stand the stench, he heaved a rock and hit it. Immediately, the swollen carcass squirmed as if trying to stand up, and three slimy possums burrowed out into the sunlight and scampered off into the cornfield.

Pounding footsteps shattered his thoughts.

"You got the lights?"

Markum caught his breath before he answered. "God damn it stinks." He stopped to breath. "We got to get back. The place is on fire, and we got to get out of there."

"What about Reedan?"

"Let him go. He could be miles from here. Fuck him."

"He's down there. I can feel it as sure as I can smell Surling."

"We don't have time to look. We've got to get everything out of the factory."

"I want that bastard so bad I can taste it."

"Oh, we'll get him, and you won't have to wait too long."

- - - - -

Curt lay still in his soggy resting place to make sure Maxwell and Markum weren't faking him out. He willed himself ready to pounce should they move into the creek. All the while he could feel the stench of Surling's body attaching itself to his lungs. Finally, he could no longer keep his body motionless. He pulled himself upright, listened for any indication of Maxwell and Markum, and then he hobbled back down the creek and away from the origin of the odor. With an effort, he crashed through the bushes and weeds that lined the creek bank. Once out of the creek, he stumbled into another weed-filled field.

When he finally staggered out of the field, he found another warehouse and small industrial area, deserted except for an old Pontiac behind one of the buildings. How do you jump-wire a car, he wondered. He had a PhD, but no practical knowledge.

He tried the back door. It opened, and a high-pitched voice shrieked, like Beth's talking doll when the string was pulled. "What are you doing, mister? You can't come in here!"

Bodies scuffled in the back seat. A boy and a girl huddled side by side in the dim yellow light, both young and both naked.

"Get dressed. I need to get to the police station."

The boy tried to maneuver into his shorts with his knees held together, trying to hide his erection. "We don't have to take you anywhere."

Curt reached in, seized the kid's skinny arms and jerked him toward the door. He stumbled out, his shorts around his ankles. Curt grabbed his arms and shook him. "I said I need a ride."

"You got no right to do this, mister."

He shoved the kid against the car. "Get dressed and let's go." He turned away as the kid jerked up his shorts. The kid got behind the wheel, and Curt got into the back seat with the girl, now dressed and cowering in the far corner

Their first stop was a fire alarm on the side of the building. Curt ordered the boy to get out and pull it. Then, thinking the firemen might not see the flames across the field, since it would probably not be in flames, he asked if they had a cell phone. The girl had one, and he told her to call 911. He remembered his previous aborted escape attempt, and he told her to tell them it was in the General Nuclear American building. The girl knew the name of the industrial park and told the 911 operator. The girl started to say something else, and he grabbed the phone and shut it off.

Now, as the car accelerated, Curt leaned back in the passenger seat. Although nowhere near relaxed, for the first time in what seemed like hours, his breathing approached normal. The stench of Surling's body had almost cleared his nostrils. With an oily rag from his pocket, he dabbed at his cut face. No more blood, just the burning and the aching knee.

Time to think: he thought about using the cell phone to talk to the police but rejected the idea. He needed to talk to someone face to face, to inform them of what they were up against. He glanced at the girl huddled in the corner and staring out the window. Outside, a darkened city sped by, a city full of the same old eating places and gas stations: Phillips 66, Kentucky Fried Chicken, Burger King, Shell…Empty now, the buildings glowed with dim night lights, easily recognized by their emblems and distinctively shaped buildings and signs. Anywhere, USA. Wherever you traveled, only the sequence in which the familiar buildings lined the streets differed. Always home in America.

He realized he should have had the girl tell 911 that there was radioactive material in the building. Probably didn't matter, since they would not have believed her anyway. His best bet was the police.

Outside, more of America the beautiful: Crystal, Wendy's, Long John Silver, Chevron. The sequence of businesses and the buildings in between dawned on him. "What city is this?"

"Are you kidding, mister?" The girl squeaked. "Are you drunk or something?"

He wished he was drunk.

"You better go home, mister," the boy said. "The cops will throw you in jail for sure."

"What *town* is this?"

"Oak Ridge," the boy said. "Science City, USA. You ever been here before?"

The two kids began to giggle.

- - - - -

-

The door banged open, and Beecher ordered her into the hall, now filled with acrid fumes. Gasoline? Maxwell came from the loading dock carrying a five-gallon can. As he passed, he flashed his leering smile.

Beecher grabbed her arm and jerked her toward the door by the loading dock. Behind them in the other corridor, Maxwell, looking like a squat cardboard box in his khaki work clothes, splashed liquid onto the wall from a large metal can—the gasoline smell.

Outside, Beecher herded her toward the black Town Car and past Agent Saul's body. But his body had moved, and there was another body next to his. The guy that shot him.

Beecher saw it and pointed it out to Lormes who was following them. "The FBI guy must not have been dead. He got Atkinson before he went down for good."

"That will save us a job," Lormes said. "Sherbani was going to get rid of him anyway."

Beecher turned back to Lori and shoved her toward the car. He opened the door and grabbed at the shoulder bag. "You won't need that."

She clutched the bag to her body. "No...Kotex and stuff."

He laughed. "Don't say you got the rag on. But then we taught you some other tricks, didn't we?"

She saw the piece of rope entwined in his fingers. "Don't tie me up. I won't try anything."

"Okay, just get in there and don't move. I'll be right here." He slammed the door.

The short redhead trudged past the front of the car struggling with two of the large metal containers like Maxwell had inside, heading for the building next door. Maxwell came out of the building with two similar cans and headed to the building on the side opposite where the redhead was going.

She looked at Saul's sprawled body and then quickly looked away. Some other tricks, she thought, squeezing the shoulder bag. With no more worry about Curt's safety, it was just them and her. Earlier, in the hall while Atkinson had talked to Lormes and Applenu, she debated about going for the gun. There were just too many of them. Maybe there would always be too many, but they took her baby and they took Curt. When the time came for her, she intended to take at least some of them with her.

- - - - -

Just inside the police station, a well-built young cop blocked Curt's way. "Can I help you, mister?" Dressed in his navy-blue uniform trimmed with yellow insignia and a shiny silver badge, he swayed slightly, a tight grin on his thin lips as he looked Curt up and down. A white-on-black label above his right shirt pocket tagged him as T. Smith.

"I've got to see somebody about a fire and about the theft of some radioactive material."

Smith lifted his billed military cap and ran a hand through his sandy, close-cropped hair. "You've got to see somebody about a fire and theft, huh?" A smile splashed onto his lips and drained away.

"My name's Curt Reedan. I've been held prisoner..."

Smith laughed, a laugh that decomposed into a scowl. "You've got a kidnapping to report, too, huh?"

Curt's mind bucked. "Uh...I guess you'd call it that."

Smith sniffed at the air, like a coon dog searching for a spoor. He turned and led Curt from the foyer into a long corridor and past a closed door marked INVESTIGATION DIVISION. The wall on the right consisted of robin's-egg blue tiles with a large part of the wall filled by a glass, going from Curt's waist to the ceiling. A sign identified the dark-haired woman behind the glass as the dispatcher. She sat at a large desk filled with three telephones, a radio, two computer monitors, a computer keyboard, and a printer. For a second, Curt didn't recognize himself displayed on one of the two TV monitors on the back wall. Seeing the mess he looked, he realized why Smith was giving him a hard time.

Smith led Curt into the Shift Supervisor's Office across the hall from the dispatcher. There, a gray-haired man in uniform sat at one of the two desks, reading a newspaper.

Waiting until the red-faced man carefully folded the paper, Smith said, "Lieutenant Davis, this hippie here, who says his name's Reedan, claims he was kidnapped. He's also got a cock-and-bull story about some stolen radioactive material."

Curt dabbed at his hair and smoothed it down. It hadn't been cut in eight weeks or so. He must look awful. He rubbed a hand across his beard. They had not let him shave the last two days as they rushed to finish the last bombs. Besides that, his clothes were stained and stunk from the creek water and Surling. He probed gently around his face, wondering how deep the cuts were. No blood, just a burning as if he'd been in the sun for days.

Davis eased off his wire-rimmed reading glasses and glanced at the clock on the white wall: one-fifty. His pale blue eyes scanned Curt's face, ran down the front of his shirt, then came back to his face. "Kidnapped? Is that right, sir?"

"Let's give him a Breathalyzer test," Smith said. He turned to Curt. "I think we better have you blow into a balloon." He laughed. "Maybe you've been smoking dope—or something stronger."

Although Curt felt like he'd been chewed on by a school of piranha and was in no mood to be laughed at, he remained calm. Being just ten minutes from Lori and Beth, he contemplated walking out. Instead, he took a deep breath, ignored the young cop, and spoke to the older man. "I turned in the alarm for a fire in a factory out in an industrial area on the east edge of town." Since he found out he was in Oak Ridge, he figured out the approximate location of the factory. "It's in the General Nuclear American building."

Smith edged closer to get Curt to look at him. "Did you set it lighting one of those cigarettes?"

"There's a lot of radioactive material in that factory that will be spread by the fire. You've got to get some experts out there to analyze the situation. You'll probably have to evacuate people in the area."

"Is that right?" Smith said. He sniffed as he forced his thin lips apart to resemble a smile.

"There were people in that building making atomic bombs. They kidnapped another scientist and me and made us help them."

"Hey, man, that's a good one: making atomic bombs," Smith said. He turned to Davis. "Did you hear that? They'll probably be selling them over at Wal-Mart before long. You know, like computers. This guy is stoned, Lieutenant."

Davis's gaze swept slowly from Curt to Smith, then back to Curt. "Are you from Oak Ridge, sir? Are you a scientist?"

Curt nodded. "But they kidnapped me in Miami."

Smith giggled. "Atomic bombs, my ass."

Davis watched Curt's face as if trying to figure him out. "Where did these people get the radioactive material to make those bombs?"

"They stole it from the government."

Smith laughed louder. "He read in the paper about the stolen material, and now he's got the answer."

Davis turned to Smith. "Dammit, Tom, hush up a minute. Right now, we need some answers, not your smart-ass remarks."

They knew about it. Now if they could get rid of Smith, they could get down to business.

Davis stood and led Curt and Smith into the hall and to a room two-doors down from the one they left. He motioned Curt to one of the two worn wooden chairs in front of a scratched and faded wooden desk, its top clear. Davis pulled Smith aside, said something to him, and Smith left. He took a seat behind the desk across from Curt.

"You got any identification, Mr. Reedan?" he asked in a soft voice with a slight southern accent.

Curt shook his head. "It's back in that burning building."

"I see. There's been some nuclear material stolen, okay. It's been all over the newspapers and TV. But why should we believe you were involved? Why should we believe you on anything, if you can't even prove who you are? Who was the scientist with you, and what happened to him?"

"His name was Robert Surling, a professor from Arizona State. They killed him when we tried to escape. I know where his body is."

Davis nodded. "The FBI's looking for a professor from Arizona. You've got that right, but you could be making all this up, based on what you read in the newspaper or saw on TV. According to the newspaper, all kinds of people around the country have turned in false information on these bomb makers."

Even though the air conditioning blew cold air across Curt's shoulders, sweat beaded on his forehead and upper lip. As hopeless as running in the weed field, he thought.

"How come your wife didn't report you missing?"

"They told her they'd kill us if she did."

Smith, looking younger with his hat off, swaggered in and perched on the edge of the desk, squinting down at Curt like a vulture waiting for death.

Curt shifted in his chair, pointed to the clock that stood at two-fifteen, and spoke to Davis. "Look, we don't have time to play games. That fire is going to spread radioactive material all over the east side of town. Depending on the wind, it might be blowing it right down on top of us this very minute. You've got to do something."

"We've got to do something, alright," Smith called from his perch. "Let's throw him in jail until he sobers up."

Curt stood. "If you won't do anything, I'm going home. I haven't seen my wife in…"

Smith dropped from the desk and shoved his body up against Curt's, blocking his path, his right hand resting on the handle of the gun on his hip. "He's drunk. Look at his face. He's been in a fight. He ought to be arrested for public intoxication."

Davis glared at Smith. "Didn't I just tell you to cool it? When you were out, we got a report from the fire department about responding to a

313

fire on the east end. I dispatched two cars out there. Get in there and have Shirley find out if they got any more information on it."

Smith turned and bolted from the room. Davis followed him and returned with a wet towel he handed to Curt. "Smith may be a good cop some day, but first he needs to grow up."

Curt nodded. Although the towel cooled his burning face, it didn't relieve the discomfort inside that came with the knowledge that they had no time to spare. Across town radioactive particles filled the air like so much ragweed pollen, spreading a deadly hay fever. Human lungs would breathe that pollen; the firemen were already breathing it. Eric Drafton died from it.

Davis sat and leaned back in his chair, hands behind his head.

"Excuse me, sir, but you've got to get an expert out there to assess how much radioactive material is going into the atmosphere. Somebody's got to decide how much of that area needs to be evacuated."

Davis smiled. "You're still young, too. Just take it easy."

Smith returned, serious now, his pale face barely colored by his pink slit of a mouth. He ignored Curt and spoke to Davis. "It's in that new Melton Hill Industrial Park on the east end. It's bad: three buildings on fire. Lieutenant Majors figures arson."

"What's in the buildings?" Davis asked.

"I asked about radioactive material. Majors said the middle building where the fire started is General Nuclear American."

"They were written up in the paper awhile back," Davis said.

"Probably. Majors says they're new in town, and they were setting up to make something for nuclear reactors. He says…"

"That's what I told you," Curt said, remembering the sign he saw the night of his messed-up escape attempt about a million years ago. "It was a front. Don't you see they picked the perfect place to pull this job? Nuclear manufacturing facilities are always welcome in Oak Ridge. Here they could build nuclear-handling facilities, put out a good cover story, and no one would think anything of it."

Smith waited for Curt to finish and then turned back to Davis. "Majors says there's no radioactive material in the building. Or the other two either. A company has to notify the fire department whenever they introduce any hazardous materials into their buildings. It's the law, and according to the fire department's records, General Nuclear American didn't plan to bring in any nuclear material until after the first of next year."

"It was all a cover," Curt said, tossing the towel on the desk. "By the first of the year, they figured to have their bombs made and be long gone."

Smith ignored Curt. "Now for the interesting part, Lieutenant. Besides being arson, they found two bodies laying right next to the burning building. Majors thinks both were shot. One looked to be just about dead, and the other one looked to be completely dead. They got an ambulance to take them to the hospital."

Smith and Davis looked at Curt.

Curt didn't know who he hated most: He hoped it was Beecher and Maxwell. He hoped they were both dead. Or Lormes would be fine, too. He just hoped it wasn't Applenu. Maybe they found out that he let Curt escape.

He leaned forward with his hands on the desk and spoke to Davis. "Contact Lieutenant Majors. In this town, he's bound to have radiation-detection equipment with him. Tell him to use a G-M meter or an alpha-detector to check for radioactivity in the fire."

- - - - -

Lori stared into the bathroom mirror as she listened to Lormes in the hallway.

"Just be back within an hour so we can get out of here," Lormes said.

She pulled the comb through her hair, anything to get her mind off of what they were talking about.

"We'll be back in an hour," Beecher said.

"And we'll have that bastard Reedan with us," Maxwell said. "Either that, or he'll be dead."

She opened the medicine cabinet, looking for something—anything.

Lormes said, "Just bring him back, and we'll get rid of both of them later."

The apartment was like the dreary one they lived in their first year in Oak Ridge. She stared at the small window above the tub. It would be impossible to slip through it without making too much noise by banging the tub when she pulled herself up there.

"If he's not there," Lormes said, "leave a message."

A knock on the bathroom door, and Beecher said, "Ten seconds, Mrs. Reedan." The door burst open, and Beecher stood there, a rope in his hand. "Let's go."

She grabbed her shoulder bag from the lavatory with her right hand just as Beecher grabbed her left arm. He pulled her into the hallway. "You got your house keys in that bag?"

She hesitated.

He jerked her around to face him, his body up against hers. "Just give me the bag."

She shook her head and dug into the bag. Her hand rested momentarily on the handle of the pistol, but with Beecher in her face there was no chance. She pulled out the keys.

He snatched them, grabbed her arm, and propelled her into the bedroom, where Maxwell was stuffing clothes into a suitcase.

Maxwell grinned at her, his bandaged-and-swollen face like a Halloween mask. He stepped over to her, his grin never fading. "You look real good in blue jeans, too, cunt." Before she could step back, he grabbed her shoulders and shoved her onto the bed. He ran his hand up between her legs, probing. "Hell, she don't have no rag on."

- - - - -

While dabbing at the crusted blood on his face with the damp towel, Curt continued to insist they have the firemen check for radioactivity.

Davis stood and rubbed a hand over his thinning gray hair to assure maximum coverage.

Smith never faltered. "Let's lock him up. He's probably one of those anti-nuclear nuts, like the ones that showed up last week out at Y-12 for Hiroshima Day, or whatever they called it. You can see he's a hippie. The long hair. He needs a shave. He sets that nuclear company on fire and then comes in and says people are making bombs out there, something he's seen in the paper or on TV."

"It probably won't hurt to have the firemen check for radioactivity," Davis said, heading for the door. He returned ten minutes later with three cans of coke and sent Smith back to the dispatcher to wait for an answer to his radio query.

Half a coke later, Smith called for Davis.

Alone, Curt eased the coke down his abraded throat and looked at the clock. The waiting, the coke, and the thousand variations on the nightmare scenarios that inhabited his brain like ghosts—all of them too true—iced down the air-conditioned room. The ghosts, but not the cold, were momentarily chased when a worried-looking Davis hustled past the open door, never even glancing in at Curt. A few minutes later he rushed by the other way without stopping.

Curt stood and limped after Davis into the Shift Supervisor's Office, where Davis was behind his desk, talking on the phone. When he hung up,

Curt said, "What did you find out?"

Davis stared at him as if he had never seen him before. "Oh…you were right. Majors says the radioactivity's hotter than the fire." He stood and started past Curt headed for the door.

"I can give you descriptions of the people who were involved. They probably got most of the bomb material out…"

"What are you talking about?"

"The people that were making the bombs."

"That'll have to wait. We've got a fire to fight, and we've got to evacuate a hell of a lot of people." He started through the doorway and then turned back to Curt. "How many people you think we'll have to evacuate? You think the whole town will need to leave?"

"Depends on a lot of things, I guess. On how much radioactive material was in the building, on the strength and direction of the wind…"

"I guess it's not my job to worry about that."

"Can you get somebody to take me home?"

"No way. I'll need every man I've got."

Then he was gone, leaving Curt alone and suddenly very tired. Every muscle ached, like they used to after losing a basketball game. He decided that he had won this game even if he ached like a big loser. He had beaten Lormes and his goons, thanks to Applenu.

Although he hated to scare Lori at this time of night, he reached for the phone on the desk. After twenty-some rings, he hung up. The answering machine must be turned off, he thought. He decided she was afraid to answer, afraid it was Beecher. For a brief moment, he panicked. Maybe they had her. Not so. The pictures they showed him were taken in their living room. Maybe she was at the Motts or the Wilson's.

A taxi? Not in this town. They lucked out there anyway: better to have nuclear material spreading in a two-taxi town, none after ten o'clock, than in a large metropolitan area.

The silver keys glistened from hooks on the green wall, like ornaments on a Christmas tree, each set attached to a white tag. Why not, he thought. He had to get home to Lori, and he was too tired to walk the five miles. He picked one:

GREEN CHEV UNMARKED DCK 523

On the sign-out book below the key rack, he signed his name, listing his home address as the destination, letting them know he had no intention of stealing the car. He decided he'd get home, and then he and Lori could

317

bring the car right back before the police missed it.

Outside, even with dawn still hours away, the stars had faded into the dark-red glow that crawled up the eastern horizon spreading its ashes of doom.

He recalled reading some university professor's estimate that any plutonium spread around by a catastrophic nuclear accident would require the evacuation of several-hundred square miles for 250,000 years. Hyperbole, a scare statement and a gross exaggeration, but...

He shivered, remembering his last image of Drafton and remembering Surling's perilous panacea. Surling once spouted figures on Chernobyl: after the accident, over 100,000 people were evacuated from a 30 kilometer radius around the reactor. By the time they finished, they evacuated an area half the size of Iowa. A city of 45,000 had been turned into a ghost town. Oak Ridge contained only 30,000 people.

Chapter Fourty-One

Curt drove the unmarked car west and away from the plague-filled clouds churning in the eastern sky. A cool breeze from the open window blew across his face, soothing the burned skin. He fiddled in the dark with knobs and switches on the police radio and finally located the on-off switch.

Lieutenant Davis's soft voice rolled from the radio, talking to the fire chief, who was now at the scene of the fire. They discussed pulling all firemen back from the fire except for those with respirators. To add to their problems, the roof of a building across the street had caught fire.

The radio hissed and cracked, and the chief asked. "What about civil defense? Over."

"The head man's on his way. You think they've got an evacuation plan? Over."

"I don't know... Who would ever have thought we'd face something like this? You might have predicted it for one of the plants. They've probably got a plan for that with the reactor out there at the lab and all. I doubt they've got a plan for something like this. Over."

"I've got some squad cars on the way over there. You can tell them which houses should be evacuated first. Over."

"Right. There are houses fairly close on three sides. Maybe civil defense will have some health physicists from the lab who'll be able to assess the situation and put priorities on the evacuation. How the hell did all that radioactive material get into that building without us being notified? Over."

"We've got a guy here who claims the people the FBI is looking for were making atomic bombs in there. He's got a hell of a story, but there's no way it'll check out. Over."

"He's might be right," the chief said. "I didn't mention that a squad of FBI agents showed up about thirty minutes after we got here. They were going to raid the place based on a call they got from one of their colleagues confirming what you just said. Then they began looking for him, but they decided he must have left, probably following the guys that were in there making the bombs. They'll want to talk to the guy you've got. Over."

"I'll make sure we keep him here," Davis said. "Over."

"It makes you stop and think," the chief drawled. "My old man came here back in forty-and-three when he got a job on the project making the first atomic bomb. He used to tell the story about how they all cheered like hell when they dropped those bombs on the Japs. Now, it's like it's come full circle, and…"

A click of the off switch killed the chief's voice as Curt turned onto Wilden Lane. Home at last, he thought, and finally out of reach of muddled distant voices on radios, out of reach of the deadly rain, and out of reach of the fatal grasp of Lormes and company.

Scenes of the past weeks flashed through his brain like color slides from a vacation trip: Beecher and Maxwell boasting about Lori; Beecher's hand on Lori's breast; Drafton, naked, rambling on about love and their future, and Surling grabbing at the green door to freedom. It was all over at last. Mentally, he collected the slides and boxed them up, intending to leave them in the back seat of the car. Get out of the car and get on with life.

With his driveway up ahead, a heaviness lifted from his body as he contemplated his new future with Lori, Beth, and the baby. He anticipated Lori's pretty face peering cautiously through the space of the chain-locked door, then throwing it wide open so he could hold her, truly and completely hold her.

Spurred by thoughts of the future, his mind flashed to the MIT job offer, and he tried to recall the deadline date for accepting it. He decided to call first thing in the morning and ask for an extension. He smiled, seeing himself slipping into his old ways. He'd also call Colorado School of Mines and ask them for an extension. He and Lori would need some time to decide about their future.

Because of the large car with out-of-state plates parked directly across the street from his driveway, he cut the corner short and barely missed a shrub at the corner of the drive. As the headlights flashed across the front of his house, something on the porch moved. Was it a man?

He braked to a stop back from the house, leaned out the window, and called, "Who's there?"

Voices: two people talking. Two dark figures stepped off the porch

320

but stayed in the shadows. Once on the sidewalk, they moved faster. When the lead figure hit the driveway and began running toward the car in the headlights, Curt recognized him.

He shoved the shift lever into reverse and floored the accelerator. Tires yipping, he cut the corner too short, crushed a shrub and bounced across the curb, dragging the underside of the car. He screeched to a stop on the street, shifted, and sped forward, tires squealing.

In the rear-view mirror, Beecher bolted into the street, dragging a sluggish blimp in his wake: Maxwell.

Two explosions erupted in the back seat, as if someone had hit the trunk with a sledge hammer. Lights from the other car flashed in the mirror and died.

At the cul-de-sac, he slid into a u-turn. Floor boarding the accelerator, he raced out, only to find himself on a collision course with their car, now broadside in the street.

He shoved the brake pedal toward the floor and held on while the car screeched and growled as it squirmed to a halt sixty feet from the roadblock and forty-five degrees to the road. Smoke from burning rubber assaulted his nostrils before the squeals died.

A dog barked frantically.

Beecher and Maxwell hunkered behind the hood of their car. Their heads pushed forward, they stared at Curt, like hunters waiting for their prey to move.

A second dog joined in a chorus with the first. Windows lighted up around the neighborhood.

Curt backed up to straighten the car in the road; he gunned the engine. To get around them, he would have to jump the curb and dodge the shrubs that edged the street. If he stalled, they had him. Even if he didn't stall, they would get several good shots at close range.

He thought about the police radio, but rejected it. They would never make it in time. Besides, they were too busy evacuating the other end of town to bother with this little incident.

Beecher and Maxwell strolled around the long black car, which Curt now recognized as the Lincoln Town Car he'd been in the night of his escape attempt. Side by side, they marched toward him, their right arms lengthened by their silenced pistols. Only one escape route: get out and run, head for the woods behind the house. He knew he'd never make it this time, not with his aching knee.

Beecher and Maxwell stopped thirty feet in front of the car. They raised their pistols and aimed at Curt.

Curt tromped on the accelerator. Wheels screamed and sent more burning rubber into the air. His headlights splashed across the two startled men's faces as they scattered like scared rabbits, one to each side of the street. Ten feet from the Lincoln, he swung a hard right into Karl Eberhard's driveway.

Squealing tires re-energized the barking dogs.

He leaned on the horn and shoved the brake pedal to the floor, sliding to a fish-tailed stop five feet from Eberhard's garage door as upstairs lights flashed on inside the house.

Curt scrambled from the car and headed for the house yelling. "Karl! It's Curt Reedan, let me in."

Behind him, footsteps pounded into the driveway and climbed the hill.

"It's Curt Reedan, Karl. Let me in. Get your guns."

A foyer light flashed on.

Curt hobbled up the three porch steps just as the porch light blazed on, setting him up as a perfect target.

He shoved at the door. Locked. He hammered with both fists. "Karl, it's Curt Reedan."

Phutt.

A bullet clapped into the house above his head; a second one hit a few feet to his right. Another one, this one closer.

"Karl, open up." When he leaned his body against the door, it opened, and he tumbled inside, falling onto his stomach.

"Curt, what is it?"

Curt dragged his legs inside and kicked the door shut. "Turn out the lights." He pulled himself up the steps of the split foyer and ran into the living room to a window that looked out over the driveway.

Eberhard followed him. "What is it, Curt. Are you okay?"

Beecher and Maxwell stood half-way up the hill, talking. Beecher motioned at the house with his elongated gun.

Curt wiped sweat from his eyes. "Get your guns, Karl. Hurry, get a rifle." Thank God Karl was a hunter.

The room lights flashed on, and Sarah Eberhard appeared in the doorway. "Curt, what's going on?"

Curt jerked back from the window. "Turn out the lights."

"What is it, Curt? You look awful. What happened?"

"Turn out the lights, and call the police."

The lights went out.

"I've got a rifle," Eberhard said, out of breath from climbing steps.

"What the hell's going on?"

Curt eased open the window. "Shoot them."

"What? I can't shoot anybody."

Karl, the one always yelling about every man's right to bear arms and defend himself and his family, the one quoting the National Rifle Association's doctrine, *he* can't shoot anybody.

Beecher yelled at the house, "Just come out, Reedan, and no one else will get hurt."

"Who are those guys, Curt?"

Curt grabbed for the rifle. "Is it loaded?"

"It's loaded, but you can't shoot inside of town."

The slick wooden stock slipped from Curt's sweat-drenched grip, but he grabbed it with his other hand. He raised the window, rested the barrel on the window sill, and aimed at Beecher. He hesitated. If he missed, he'd hit the house across the street.

"I can't get the police," Sarah said from the doorway. "Nine-one-one's busy. What's going on, Curt?"

Curt raised the barrel to fire into the air. He pulled the trigger. Nothing. He turned to Eberhard.

"The safety's on," Eberhard said.

Curt wiped sweat from his eyes and fumbled around the trigger guard with his sweaty fingers.

Eberhard reached over and clicked a button on the rifle. "I see you haven't done much shooting."

Curt shoved the barrel out the window, and fired into the air, a loud crack that would get the neighbors dialing the police. Fat chance they'd have of getting through.

Beecher and Maxwell dropped onto their stomachs, leaving only their heads visible above the slope of the hill.

Curt fired into the air again, and they pulled their heads down until only the tops were visible. "We need a shotgun, so we can fire at them and not hit the house across the street."

"You can't just shoot people, Curt. Tell me what's…"

Curt yelled out the window. "It's two of us against two of you. We've got rifles."

Beecher raised his head and yelled back. "If you want your wife back, you'd better come with us."

Lori. They couldn't have her. They're bluffing. He fired two more shots into the air.

More lights blazed on around the neighborhood. Dogs barked

everywhere. Somebody hollered from across the street: "What's going on out there?"

"Okay, Reedan," Beecher yelled. "We're through with you for now. We're leaving. But before you go and do something stupid, you'd better read the note we left in your house. Otherwise you'll never see your wife again."

- - - - -

Curt sprinted from the Eberhard house across his yard, wondering how to get into his house without a key. He found the front door wide open. A note on one of Lori's yellow legal pads lay on the kitchen table on top of a brown envelope. Curt picked up the note and read:

Reedan,
If you want to see your wife again you better not go to the police. As far as the police are concerned just make yourself scarce. We will call tonight about six and tell you how you can get your wife back.

He ripped open the envelope and extracted a packet of eight-by-ten photos, the top one of Lori, naked and on her knees, tears streaming down her cheeks. Beecher was also in the picture.

Chapter Fourty-Two

Applenu listened to the one-sided cell phone conversation between Lormes and Reedan. Although Reedan was free, his wife, who sat between him and Lormes in the back seat of this automobile headed for wherever, faced the same fate Reedan escaped.

Lormes snapped shut the phone. "That son of a bitch is going to cause us trouble," he said. "It's your fucking fault, Applenu. You let the bastard escape."

"I did not let him escape."

"What do you mean, he let him escape?" Beecher asked, glancing into the rearview mirror to look at him directly.

"When we thought Reedan was going to put out the fire, I saw him whisper something to Reedan, and then he went into the office," Lormes said. "When he came out, Reedan took off spraying everybody with the fire extinguisher. Reedan heads for the office door, and it's open. From the beginning we said that door must always be locked."

"I didn't unlock it. Somebody else must have."

"The hell they did," Maxwell said from the front passenger seat. "I went in there just before you did, and I had to use my key."

"It looks like Hearn was right when he said he didn't know whether you could be trusted," Lormes said to Applenu. "He said even though you were an Iranian, Sherbani didn't trust you."

Applenu met Lori Reedan's sideways glance and detected the flicker of a questioning or grateful smile for helping Curt as she realized he was now in the same situation she was in.

- - - - -

"Curt, wake up."

Lori's voice? A dream? When he finally forced his eyes open, he was lost. He blinked, letting his mind catch up and unscramble itself from the nightmare jumble of dreams he had just escaped, dreams haunted by the demented characters that ruined his life these past months. He lay on his side, his cut face burning, and his aching legs folded into a space too small for his long frame.

"You awake, Curt?"

Not Lori's voice waking him. He twisted onto his back and gazed at the beige ceiling of the unmarked police car, the back seat shivering under him.

A thin voice called from far away: "Breaker-breaker, one-nine. Was somebody over there in the north-bound lane looking for one of them yellow Ryder rent-a-trucks? Over."

"That's right," the voice in the front seat answered. "We just heard it's up ahead."

"That's right, good buddy. I just passed it back at the eighty-nine-mile mark."

"I thank you, good buddy."

Curt sat up, his legs still stretched out on the seat.

Karl Eberhard laid the microphone on the front seat and glanced over his shoulder. "You think it's them, Curt?" Even with the front seat back as far as it would go, Eberhard filled the driver's seat up to the steering wheel. The large barrel of his upper torso dwarfed his head, which was further shrunk by his thirty-year-old crew cut. A smile usually decorated his baby-fat, smooth face with a never-changing youth. Today, without the smile and with the dark-blue, wrinkled circles under his faded-blue eyes, he looked as old and tired as Curt felt.

"You shouldn't have come along, Karl," Curt said.

"You're in no shape to do it alone."

Do what? Curt wondered as he recalled the waking nightmare that began when he found the note and pictures on his kitchen table. He collapsed into a chair, unsure about going on. Although totally spent emotionally and physically, it still wasn't over. How could he go on? Then he panicked: Beth. He bolted from the chair, his body moving while his brain remained in the chair, not catching up until he stood inside her bedroom and focused on her undisturbed bed.

Back downstairs, he ran into Karl and Sarah coming up the steps from the front door. Karl led him into the kitchen and calmed him down. Sarah told him that Lori had left Beth with them. "Lori said she'd be back by eleven. She didn't return, and she didn't call."

Sarah read the note on the legal pad and glanced at the pictures underneath. Horrified, she shoved them into the envelope and insisted he call Richard Saul, the FBI agent whose card she had gotten when he questioned her the previous afternoon. She ran home and returned with the card and her cell phone. She punched in the numbers and handed Curt the small phone.

He hesitated taking it. "Beecher's note says no police if I want to see Lori again."

Sarah persisted. "Just tell him what happened. He'll know what to do."

Curt took the phone and put it to his ear. After an eternity, the voice mail came on and Curt left a message for Saul to call him.

His first thoughts on Lormes and company centered on the small airstrip down by Oliver Springs. That's where they must have flown him in, based on the lack of air traffic when they landed and the time it took them to get him to their factory after they landed. He decided they would be leaving there once it got light, but there would be no chance to take them by surprise down there.

Then he remembered the Ryder rental truck parked by the loading dock when he ran out of the building, the one they'd been loading earlier in the evening. From what now seemed years ago, he recalled Drafton mentioning New York. They would head north with that truck full of nuclear material. Why wait for them to contact him? Follow the truck back to them. Lormes, Applenu, and some others who had Lori might fly north to meet the truck. He decided to follow it and catch them by surprise. A long shot, but what else did he have, besides waiting for them to call and tell him where they were going to pick him up and kill him?

It was then that he remembered the cell phone number, which he retrieved from a notepad in his office. He dialed the number. After four rings, Lormes answered.

"This is Curt Reedan. I want to talk to my wife."

"How did you get this number, Reedan?"

"You gave it to me when you *recruited* me for Margine Nuclear Technology." Curt could hear other voices and a hum indicating they were in an automobile.

Curt heard Beecher say, "Give me that." Beecher came on the phone. "Did you get my message, fuckhead?"

"Is Lori okay? Let me talk to her."

Lori came on the phone. "Curt, are you okay? I'm…"

"She's okay" Beecher said. "We will call you at six tonight. Just be there." He hung up.

Curt decided his only hope was to catch up to them and confront them. Karl argued against the plan, but when Curt insisted, Karl wouldn't let him go alone. It was Karl's idea to use the police car so they had access to a CB as well as a police radio.

- - - - -

Curt swung his feet off the back seat and arranged them around the two rifles, a shotgun, and two pistols—a forty-five and a thirty-eight—on the floor. He stared up ahead for the truck. A green highway sign approached. He blinked, read PULASKI, but didn't get the miles before it swung past. He stifled a yawn.

"How far have we come, Karl?"

"Over two-hundred miles. We're in Virginia. We made good time ever since we got through that mess in Oak Ridge."

When they hit the Oak Ridge Turnpike, it seemed everyone was trying to get out of the city, and they had to turn around and take the long way out of town. On the radio, the police were reporting that a big chemical spill was responsible for the evacuation.

In the front seat, the CB radio squawked about smokies up ahead. Eberhard lifted his foot from the accelerator, and the speedometer needle quickly dropped to the speed limit.

"There's the truck," Eberhard said.

Curt watched the big yellow box with black letters on the back and side strain up a hill half-a-mile ahead. It looked like the truck parked outside the factory, but this was the third such truck they had overtaken, the first two just outside of Knoxville. Maybe it wasn't such a good idea after all. Maybe he should have waited for their call and then made plans, depending on their instructions.

"You say they've got enough plutonium in that truck to blow away several cities?" Eberhard asked. "While you were sleeping, I was thinking about how I've spent thirty-two years working on nuclear reactors...over half of my life. And now, as if Three Mile Island and Chernobyl weren't enough, we've got this. Like always, there are some lines from Shakespeare that fit."

"Shakespeare?" Incongruities in Eberhard's personality constantly astounded Curt.

"Remember in Macbeth, where he says something like, 'That we but teach bloody instructions, which being taught, return to plague the

328

inventor.'? I don't know why those lines stuck with me."

"Bloody instructions" reminded Curt of Applenu. Was he also there against his will?

He saw the police car in the southbound lane as described on the CB and turned his attention to the yellow truck a quarter-of-a-mile ahead. Probably just another truck, somebody moving their family across country. No tension this time, not like for the other two. No tension, no disappointment. No stirring up the hate this time, he thought, leaving him with that constant ache of loneliness and apprehension that had settled into his bones like a crippling disease. What would they do to Lori this time?

After Eberhard saw the cops heading in the opposite direction, he speeded up. "When we catch up," he said, "duck down in the seat while I drive by and have a look."

"It's not them, Karl. They're probably somewhere in a motel asleep...or on another road."

"I don't think they're sleeping. They're probably trying to get to their home base as soon as possible. They intend to call you from there."

"We don't know where their home base is, so we don't even know if they're on this road. They might have taken I-75 north. Or they might have gone south."

"They might have, but I-81 is our best bet. It's the closest route to anywhere from Washington to Boston, from Pittsburgh to New York City. You said yourself they mentioned New York."

Curt laid his hot face against the cool, black-vinyl seat. Sun-scoured green hills slid across his gaze, inviting him back to sleep. He blinked himself alert. Although he needed more rest, chaos and terror awaited him in his sleep like twin assassins. He turned back to the approaching truck.

Eberhard glanced back at Curt. With his jaw set, his fat-man's smile from other days threatened, but did not surface. "You ready?"

They were in the right lane with two cars between them and the truck. Eberhard accelerated into the left lane and passed the first car, a yellow VW. "Okay, get down."

"That car," Curt yelled. "Drop back."

"What?" Eberhard let up on the accelerator.

"Get back in the right lane."

Eberhard drifted in behind the yellow VW. "What is it?"

"That black car behind the truck. A Lincoln, isn't it? White-and-black plates, right?"

"A big Town Car with New York plates, so what?"

"It's the car Beecher and Maxwell had out at our place last night."

"You sure?"

"We've got the right truck."

"*Holy Christ.* Now what?" Eberhard ran his left hand through his crew cut. *"Holy Christ."*

"Drive past and look them over. See if you can see Lori."

Curt stretched out on the seat as they approached the horror he had hoped to avoid.

"There's a big guy driving."

"Beecher."

"Looks like somebody else is in the front seat. And there's probably somebody in the back. They've got that dark glass, and it's tough to make out how many or anything else about them."

"Two in front and more in back?"

Lying on his back, Curt stared out the back window as they pulled up to the moving yellow box. Big black letters R-E-D-Y-R glided by the window as they moved toward the cab, which rode high above the road. Curt covered his face with his right arm so the driver would not recognize him if he looked down. When they rolled by the cab, Curt caught a glimpse of Markum—no mistaking his red head and freckled face.

"There's another guy in the cab besides the driver."

Eberhard accelerated away from the truck, and Curt raised his head to peer over the seat. He recognized the dark face of Simmons next to Markum.

In the front seat, the turn signal clicked a metronome beat, quick like Curt's pulse. Eberhard pulled off the interstate and up an exit ramp; at the top, they crossed a highway and pulled onto the entrance ramp. Eberhard accelerated, and they raced back into the northbound traffic, three cars separating them from the Town Car.

"They're all there," Curt said. "All five or six of them. They didn't take a plane out. Lori's got to be in there."

"Unless she's..."

"I don't want to hear it." His breath quickened as he thought of the ordeal she had been through. The pictures on the table and video flashed into his mind, probably never to be blocked out. And it still wasn't over.

"They probably had to fly the plane in to pick them up, and the fire changed their plans," Eberhard said rapidly.

No longer interested in why they were there, Curt's mind searched for a plan. Every time he was chased, he scampered around, running at random, never knowing what to do next, which way to move. Now the pursuer—or was he?—he still didn't have a plan.

"We can use the radio to call the police," Eberhard said.

"What good would that do? By the time we explain our problem, these guys will be out of the local jurisdiction. Besides, who'd believe somebody calling from a stolen police car?"

"Then call the FBI again," Eberhard said and pulled his cell phone from his breast pocket along with a calling card and handed them across the seat to Curt. "Call that guy Saul."

Curt dialed Saul's number and again got his voice mail. He left another message telling him where they were and to call Eberhard's cell phone.

Eberhard slowed. "They're signaling to pull off the road." He braked and quickly brought the car to a stop on the shoulder of the road about a hundred yards behind the Town Car.

Beecher got out of the driver's side, and Applenu got out of a rear door. They exchanged places and pulled back onto the road.

"If they're changing drivers, they're not going to get off this road for awhile," Eberhard said. "Get on that phone and get the FBI's number in Knoxville and see if they can find Saul. They can be here in no time with a helicopter."

- - - - -

In the middle of the back seat, Lori opened her eyes when the car pulled over and Applenu and Beecher changed seats. When she saw Maxwell stir in the front passenger seat and turn to look back, she again pretended to sleep. A torrent of questions, regrets, and fear whirled around her brain and kept her from sinking into the plush black-leather seats and falling asleep. Just remember you're a farm girl, she thought again. You're tough.

As soon as Beecher crawled into the back seat, he pushed his hot body right next to hers and ran his hand along the inside of her left thigh.

Faking grogginess, she opened her eyes and looked at his hand, now resting on her thigh. She shoved it away.

Beecher smiled at her and winked. "Good to have you with us, Lori." He squeezed her thigh.

Applenu hadn't bothered her when he was back there, and Lormes slept through most of the trip at her right, his head turned the other way.

She wondered about Applenu, who was now driving. If he had done what they said he did, maybe they could work together to escape.

She became aware of Beecher watching her, smiling. She eyed the door handle across Lormes's lap. She could grab it, shove the door open, and jump out. Push Lormes out first. She took a deep breath. No time to panic. With both hands, she picked up Beecher's hand and pushed it away.

"Did you see that car pull off the road back there the same time we did?" Maxwell asked from the front seat.

Beecher turned to look out the window.

"The second car back, the green one," Maxwell said. "They pulled back on as soon as we did."

"He's going to pass us," Beecher said.

Lori tried to see the passing car, but Beecher's body blocked her view.

"Just one guy in the car," Maxwell said. "A Chevrolet."

"If it's just one guy, it isn't the cops. They travel in groups, at least two," Lormes said.

"All the same, we'd better keep our eyes open," Maxwell said watching the green car accelerate away from them. He turned and one-eyed Lori. "We don't want to fuck this thing up, especially when we got some fun ahead of us."

Chapter Fourty-Three

Curt scrunched himself into the minuscule space of the back seat with the miniature cell phone pressed against his ear with his sweaty palm. "Now they're trying to find the guy in charge of the Knoxville office," Curt said to Eberhard as they sped past an exit to Newbern, Virginia.

Special Agent Saul had written the phone number for the Knoxville FBI Bureau Office on the back of his card. Curt had called the number, and this would be the third FBI agent he'd talked to. He glanced at the clock. Ten-twenty-five: he had been on the phone almost twenty minutes and had nothing to show for it.

"Jack Swain, special agent in charge of the Knoxville Bureau," the voice said. "How can I help you, sir?"

"Yesterday, an agent by the name of Richard Saul was out in my neighborhood asking about me. It had to be about the stolen bomb material, and…"

"I understand all that, sir. Agent Saul came down from Washington especially for the case. He was leading the investigation here, but he is not available at this time. Most of our agents are presently occupied trying to find out what happened to Agent Saul. There is also an emergency in Oak Ridge that we are involved with."

Curt struggled to keep from yelling. "Well get me somebody with authority in the case. They kidnapped me, and now they've got my wife. We know where they are, but we need help."

"Can you hang on a minute, sir? I have to call Washington."

Curt fought the urge to smash the phone onto the floor. Talking to these guys was like communicating with computer-automated answering systems. But with those systems, you eventually got through, even if it meant punching the operator key repeatedly until the system gave up with, "I'll connect you to a representative." These guys reminded him of another reason why he went into business for himself; they also reminded him of Surling's complaints. Seems everywhere you went in large organizations, the people you had to deal with always had the same evasive answers, only these guys pinned a "sir" on the end of it. Everyone was afraid to make a decision without the people above them approving, afraid it would inject a negative factor into their career trajectory.

"Listen, when you get the guy from Washington, have him call us. We are getting closer to Washington all the time, so they should be able to get to us with a helicopter fairly quickly."

"Sir, if you will just hold on while…"

Curt pressed the END button.

- - - - -

Exhausted, Lori had finally dropped into sleep, her first in over twenty-four hours. She achieved it despite the fact that every time she closed her eyes she saw Saul shot and falling onto his face. This sleep came without the dream of somebody holding her down, her unable to move and unable to scream. No dreams, even though she sat next to one of them.

Still exhausted, her neck and legs ached from being in the same cramped position for so long. She opened her eyes and glanced to her left at Beecher and decided not to stretch. She had been awakened by strange voices, suddenly loud after miles of silence. Maxwell, Beecher, and Lormes were discussing a green car that might be following them, the same car they had seen earlier.

"You're positive it's the same car?" Lormes asked Maxwell for the second time.

"I'd bet on it," Maxwell said, his one eye peering over the front seat to see out the rear window. "They are two cars back."

"Slow up and see what happens."

Applenu slowed, and three cars passed on the left.

"They're directly behind us now, trying to keep their distance."

"Pull over," Beecher said. "Let's see what they do."

Applenu eased the car onto the right shoulder.

Lori craned forward to see around Beecher, hoping the car contained someone she knew, perhaps the other FBI man, Fortner, although she knew that was impossible. They probably didn't even know Saul was dead.

"Here they come," Maxwell said. "It's the same green car with the same driver as before, but this time there's somebody else asleep in the passenger seat."

Lori saw the back of the light-brown head of the sleeping passenger pushed against the window. From what little she saw of the driver, he almost looked like Karl Eberhard. At least he had a square crew cut like Karl. But it wasn't his car.

"Tennessee plates," Beecher said.

"If it's cops," Lormes said, "there'll be more cars around. Those bastards never come alone. Anything suspicious behind us?"

"Nothing I can see," Maxwell said.

"Before we panic, let's see what these guys do. Just keep your eyes open to make sure they're alone."

- - - - -

Eberhard passed the truck and slowed down.

Curt straightened up and looked back. "Did you make out how many there were in the back?" he asked. They passed an exit for Lexington, followed by a sign that gave the distance to Washington as 198 miles.

"No. You don't think they know we're following them?"

"How could they?" Curt leaned over the back of the seat and grabbed the forty-five from the floor and shoved it under his seat.

Eberhard slowed, keeping the truck in his rear-view mirror. Once he was certain the Town Car had caught up with the truck, he took the next exit, slowing as they went down the grade. When they headed back up the other side onto Interstate 81, they were four cars behind the Town Car.

- - - - -

"They're back there again," Beecher said, looking out the back window.

Lori twisted around to look, but couldn't see the car. When she turned forward, she stared into Maxwell's swollen face, which set on the back of the front seat like a bandaged jack-o-lantern.

"The cunt's looking for somebody to rescue her," Maxwell said.

"You want to be rescued, cunt?" Beecher said and released a cackle. "You said she didn't have the rag on, right, Max?"

"No Kotex there; no bloody road to travel, as our friend Applenu would say," Maxwell said tapping Applenu on the shoulder and roaring a raucous laugh.

Applenu kept his eyes on the road and said nothing.

335

"Let me check it out," Beecher said.

Lori's heart jumped at the shock of his hand, his fingers squirming between her legs. She locked her legs and shoved at his hand with both of hers, her back thrust against the seat. His hand would not budge.

"Please don't. Please."

Beecher released his grip, and she collapsed back into the seat. Beecher's hand now danced lightly across her leg like a big spider, his long fingers crawling on her thigh. Spiders: the scream threatening in her throat was the same one that erupted years ago when her brother threw a large garden spider in her lap as she sat on the porch swing. The same chills coursed down her spine, but now there was no garden spider and no laughing little brother. No screaming this time, she told herself again; no panic allowed.

Maxwell continued to stare at her. "Maybe we ought to get out the pictures we took last time," he said. "Turn you on. Turn us all on."

Beecher grabbed her left hand and pulled it toward him. "Speaking of which."

She pulled back, crowding up against Lormes. Beecher bent her fingers backward, and she let her hand be led toward him, occasionally jerking back, only to feel a fiery ache engulf her arm up to the elbow.

"Just relax," he said, guiding her hand down between his legs and placing it there while he got a tight grip on her wrist.

She felt him beneath her hand. "Please don't. Please."

Beecher laughed. "Why don't you just unwrap what you've got in your hands, and then you can do that little trick with your mouth I taught you."

Maxwell laughed, his head high on the back of the seat.

Lori jerked back, but Beecher held on, squeezing her wrist. Searing pain filled her arm.

"Please don't."

"That's enough," Lormes growled.

"Yeah, we'll have time for that later," Maxwell said, laughing, "lots of time."

Beecher released his grip. She pulled back, shaken but momentarily relieved. She rubbed her hand and arm. That tingle of fear she felt with the spider blanketed her entire body and had her on the verge of screaming. With every incident, fear exploded anew from somewhere deep down inside, near where her baby had been. From there it roared into her chest, a spasm of chills and panic that surged down her legs into her toes, leaving her limp. She remembered Curt's laugh when she told him that some of her orgasms were toe tinglers. It wasn't anywhere near the same, but both left her exhausted. She longed for Curt; she longed to be held in his arms, to feel safe again.

"Those two blokes can't be cops," Applenu said. "How would they have found us?" He slowed. Three cars passed, but not the green one. "They're staying back there regardless of what I do."

"Maybe her old man tipped them off," Beecher said. "Maybe he won't be home when we call tonight. Maybe a cop will answer."

"Maybe he's trying to get rid of the cunt so he can find himself some sweet guy," Maxwell said. "Some guy like Drafton."

She wondered why Maxwell and Beecher kept making references to Curt's manhood.

Lormes spoke to Maxwell. "You're sure there aren't any other cars following us?"

"We've been watching for over an hour now, and I'd bet a million dollars there aren't."

"Okay," Lormes said. "Pass the truck and motion them to follow us. We're going to find out who those guys are once and for all."

- - - - -

Curt watched the Town Car lead the yellow truck off the interstate. Eberhard slowed to let two cars pass before he followed. At the top of the exit ramp for Raphine, the Town Car and the truck turned left; a quarter of a mile later they drove into a gas station on the right side of the road. Eberhard drove into a station on the opposite side of the road.

"You gas up and keep an eye on them," Curt said. "I'll call Knoxville again." He got Swain on the phone immediately.

"I was about to call you," Swain said. "We located Special Agent Saul. He's in the hospital in Oak Ridge, and we just got an agent out there. He had trouble getting there through the traffic. Seems they've had some sort of chemical spill, and they're evacuating half the city."

Curt got out of the car to stretch his legs. "I told you before, it's not a chemical spill. It's the bomb material you people are supposed to be looking for." The noon sun beat down, and the high humidity and his internal anxiety started to nucleate beads of sweat on his forehead. Nevertheless, it felt good being out in the open after being cooped up for the past several weeks.

"The official explanation is a chemical spill, sir."

"Did you call somebody in Washington who knows what's going on?

We're closer to Washington now than we are to Knoxville."

"We called Washington, sir, and they referred us to Saul. The people in Washington are all tied up with the Iran thing."

Unbelievable, Curt thought, politics and more politics. Was Surling right about everything? Couldn't anybody do anything anymore?

Swain went on. "It was in the paper this morning, sir, another story by that Sheena Mosely." He explained that the story indicated Iran sent a secret message to the U. S. Government that they had the stolen bomb material, and they had manufactured some bombs. "According to the story, they've threatened to blow one up in a U.S. city unless we meet certain conditions. And then that Senator Hughson just had a press conference."

For what seemed like forever, Curt had been energized by the fear eating away at his insides. He could no longer control his anger. "Dammit, we need help. *Now!*"

"Please hold on, sir, my agent in Oak Ridge is on another line."

Curt paced around the car twice before Swain came back on.

"Sir. Our agent talked with Saul, and he verifies your story. Based on what Agent Saul said, I'll take it on myself to contact our Richmond office and tell them to get a helicopter over to I-81. Then, the next time you call, we'll figure out how to get you all together with them. I'll also try Washington again."

"Have them call me immediately," he said and disconnected.

Back in the car, Eberhard handed him a cold can of coke without taking his eyes off the gas station across the road. "Best I could tell, four guys got out of the Town Car and two out of the truck. The Town Car is around the side now. They're probably going to the john."

"That means they're all there. The Oak Ridge cops said the firemen found two guys at the fire. It doesn't seem to be any of them. Did you see any sign of Lori?"

Eberhard shook his head slowly, never taking his eyes from the gas station across the road. "There they go, and the Town Car is in the lead this time. Hey, they're not heading back to the interstate."

- - - - -

When the car pulled away from the service station, Lori kept her shoulder bag on her lap. They let her use the restroom—the men's room. Beecher stood in front of the open door to the stall, spewing a constant stream of rude and crude remarks. She had no chance even to get the gun out of the handbag, nor was there a chance to yell or scream for help.

Beecher now drove, and Lormes sat beside him. Maxwell's humongous body sweated and smelled to her right; his hot leg pressed up against hers regardless of how she moved.

"They're following," Beecher said, looking in the mirror.

"Any other vehicles besides them?" Lormes asked.

"Doesn't look like it."

"Okay, we'll lead them through this burg and out into the country. Then we'll make our move."

- - - - -

Karl Eberhard's cell phone on the dash board chimed with what sounded like classical music. Probably Mozart or Beethoven, Curt thought as he grabbed the phone.

"This is George Spanner at FBI Headquarters in Washington," a deep voice said. "I was told you are Curt Reedan and you know where the people with the bombs are."

"We are following them in Virginia. They just got off Interstate 81 and are now on State Road 606. According to the sign we just saw, we are headed toward Raphine."

"I see that on the map. It's less than two-hundred miles. You keep them in sight, and we'll get on a helicopter and get down there. Richmond's closer, and they've got a helicopter about ready to take off. I'll be in touch."

- - - - -

As the car swerved around the bend and shoved his body against the door, Applenu felt Lori Reedan's body push up against his side. He wanted to reach out and protect her from Beecher and Maxwell. Was she frightened? She didn't show it. Considering their fates, she was holding up remarkably well. She reminded him of his sister, always strong.

On the other side of her, Maxwell crowded up to her, his pudgy hand now on her leg. She shoved it away, but it snapped back.

They sped up. Beecher swung the car into an opposite turn, wheels squealing. Applenu slid toward Lori Reedan and shoved her into Maxwell.

"Come on over here, cunt," Maxwell said, laughing, his right hand cupping his crotch. "Come to daddy."

"Why don't you let her go," Applenu said to Maxwell. He motioned with his head back to where the green car should be. "We need to concentrate on them."

"Don't worry about me, Doc. I'll take care of them when the time comes. Right now, I've got other things on my mind."

Beecher accelerated on a straight stretch. Applenu glanced back at the truck, which dropped back rapidly as Beecher speeded up. No green car back there now, although it lurked somewhere around the two curves they'd just taken.

"Speed it up some more," Lormes said.

"I'm going as fast as I can on this fucking road."

Back at the petrol station when they discussed the plan, Applenu had an almost irresistible urge to say "sod it" and get out and walk away. He would have, but he could not get to his backpack in the car boot that contained almost seventy-five thousand dollars—his emergency cash. With it, he could try to disappear, maybe take Mrs. Reedan along with him. She seemed full of the fight he felt waning in him ever since they left the factory in flames. He envied Reedan. She was the kind of woman that went well with his professor-at-Ohio-State dream.

Then he saw the headline on the paper in that petrol station: IRAN PLACES ATOM BOMB IN U.S. CITY. Mosely again. Fortunately, Lormes didn't see the headline. Lormes asked about the Iran rumor when it first hit the papers. He didn't seem too happy to be working for Iranians. That latest headline would cinch his unhappiness. In retrospect, he thought, maybe he should have shown him the headline.

Applenu's mind reverted to Sherbani's doubts about his loyalty. Could he stave off that inevitability with Sherbani by agreeing to go to Iran and work in their nuclear program? Perhaps that was the best he could hope for. After all, the FBI knew he had a British accent and was probably Iranian. Maybe walking away and becoming Ian Deby was not a possibility. What was Teheran University's Nuclear Engineering Department like? Was there a Mrs. Reedan type waiting for him in a lovely black chador? How do you chat up a bird in a long black robe and veil?

"Faster," Lormes said. "It's showdown time."

- - - - -

"Could they have a place out here in the boondocks?" Eberhard asked.

"Not likely," Curt said and reached under his seat and touched the pistol. His leg wouldn't stop its mad jiggle.

They were leaving the really small town of scattered houses called Raphine, which reminded Curt of some of the small farming hamlets in rural Iowa, such as his hometown of Dref.

Outside of Raphine, the road narrowed and the curves began. They were heading west past scattered farms and corn fields, like table-flat Iowa only set in a mountainous terrain. According to a sign they passed, Wades Creek was eight miles ahead.

The cell phone chimed. It was Agent Spanner reporting that they would be airborne in Washington in about thirty minutes. The helicopter from Richmond was on its way.

With no traffic in sight, Eberhard hung back to make sure they weren't seen. They glimpsed the other two vehicles in the distance only when they crested a hill or came around a long curve. After a couple of miles on the road, they crested a tall hill that looked over a long straight stretch.

"They're gone," Eberhard said. "They must have put the gas to it."

"Let's go." Was it a trick? Curt wondered. "Does that mean they know we are following them?"

"Maybe they turned off."

"No other roads. Just move it."

Eberhard floored it, barely got the speed to sixty before having to brake back to below forty for another sharp turn. "There's the truck. It's turning off the road. Where's the car?"

"They probably led the way."

Eberhard turned onto a much narrower road than State Road 606 and with more curves. Barreling around a blind curve, they suddenly found the truck crossway in the road. Eberhard hit the brakes, squealing the Chevy to a halt fifty feet from the truck.

Markum climbed down from the truck and ran toward them.

Curt braced himself on the dashboard and reached for the pistol. "Turn it around!"

Markum kept coming, one hand held behind his back.

Eberhard slammed the Chevy into reverse and tromped down on the accelerator, throwing Curt toward the dashboard. Wheels squealed, then squeaked to a stop, throwing Curt back against the seat. He turned and saw the Lincoln Town Car twenty feet from the rear bumper.

Beecher burst from the driver's side and ran toward them, his hand reaching inside his jacket. Maxwell pulled himself from the other side of the car and trudged toward them.

Curt hesitated, the gun held ready between his legs.

Markum jerked open Eberhard's door, and Beecher shoved his pistol through the door and waved it at Eberhard. "Okay, big man, keep your hands away from your body and get out of there."

Curt shoved the gun into his belt and pulled the tails of his light-blue shirt over it, just as Maxwell jerked open the door.

"Well look who we've got here," Maxwell said. "It's our old buddy, *Doctor* Reedan."

Curt turned, and through the back window he saw Lormes emerging from the Town Car.

Chapter Fourty-Four

Lori found herself alone in the middle of the back seat. As soon as Beecher slid the car to a halt, he and Maxwell drew pistols and rushed toward the green car; Lormes followed at a slower pace.

Applenu left the car, reached into the driver's side door and pressed a button to pop open the trunk. He disappeared behind the car. She heard the trunk lid close.

Seeing the corn fields on both sides of the road, Lori knew immediately what she had to do. Once she stepped between those rows of six-foot-high stalks, they'd never catch her. Her mind flashed on Iowa corn fields, remembering her young self dashing through the rows to elude her brothers, and in later years running and hiding from Curt and then letting him find and catch her. No game this time, but if they didn't see her slip out of the car, they wouldn't know which way she went.

Applenu, a backpack slung over his left shoulder, stuck his head into the back seat. "Mrs. Reedan, let's get out of here while we can."

"What...you're one of them."

"Not really. Come on let's go before they miss us."

Then, through the windshield, Curt appeared, stumbling around the side of the green car, being shoved by Maxwell. He looked terrible: a big red scratch across his face, oily, straggly hair, unshaven, and limping again. Karl Eberhard came from the other side prodded by Beecher.

"What in bloody hell is Reedan doing here?" Applenu asked, looking at her. "He's quite a good bloke, eh?"

She nodded and knew there was no running in corn fields, no escape. *Why now?* "I guess I'll need an alternate plan," she said.

Hands shaking, she dug into her handbag. She ignored the extra bullets floating around the bottom of the bag; there would be no time to reload. She should have brought an extra magazine. It would be eight shots and out, she thought, just like shooting bottles from the fence at home. Every shot would need to count.

Applenu saw the gun. "Where did you get that? You know how to use it?"

"We'll see," she said as she slipped onto the hot asphalt. She snapped off the safety and jerked back the slide to chamber a round. "Stay behind this door," she told Applenu as she slipped behind the open front door.

As she listened for their voices, she became aware of corn stalks rustling in the breeze—sounds of home.

Lormes was talking: "So it's just you two assholes. You thought you could take us, huh? The game is over, Reedan. Same for your fat friend there, whoever the hell he is."

"What do we do with them?" Beecher asked.

"Whatever it is," Maxwell said, looking at Curt and smiling. "I want Reedan."

Lormes looked around. "Why wait? Take them into that corn field, and get it over with. He nodded to Maxwell. "Go get Mrs. Reedan, and take her, too."

A cell phone began a musical interlude in the green car.

"Why don't we save the cunt till later?" Maxwell said. "Me and Beech have some romantic plans for her." He looked at Curt and began to laugh.

The cell phone music continued. It sounded to her like Mozart's *Eine Klinest Nacht Musak.*

"Take her, and take our former friend, Dr. Applenu. Hurry up before any cars come by here. And somebody shut off that fucking cell phone."

The cell phone stopped chiming as Maxwell started toward the Town Car.

Lori sucked for breath, her heart hammering in her ears. She stepped around the door and took a wide solid stance like Dad showed her. Arms extended, she steadied the gun in both hands. She aimed at Maxwell, who walked toward her, his eyes on the ground, his left hand pressing at the bandage on his head. Temporarily speechless while stupid phrases from police movies rattled around her head, she finally got it out: "Drop the gun, Maxwell. You too, Beecher."

Maxwell halted fifteen feet in front of her, his gun hanging in his hand at his side, his right eye wide open. Slowly, that evil grin from that evening spread across his puffed face. He cocked his head to take in all of her with his good eye. "How'd you get that gun," he asked. "You think you can use it?"

"Lori," Curt yelled. "Thank God."

She glanced at Curt, who started toward her.

Beecher stepped in front of him and shoved his gun into Curt's ribs. "Take the gun away from her," Beecher yelled.

Her eyes snapped back to Maxwell. Her arms began to ache with the heavy weight hanging out in front of her. Concentrate on the target, she told herself. Ignore everything else. "I said drop the gun, Maxwell."

She realized she'd have to keep track of the others. Beecher's gun was leveled at Curt. Who else had a gun?

Beecher kept his gun jammed into Curt's stomach and glanced at her over his shoulder. Although the redhead was partially blocked from her view by Beecher and Curt, she sensed his movement.

Maxwell just laughed and took a step toward her. "No way is a cunt like you going to use that forty-five."

"Well, this *cunt will* use this gun if she has to."

Maxwell took another step forward. His gun, held along his thigh and pointing downward, inched forward and upward.

Lori felt the weight of the gun tug at her locked arms, the pain building and setting off a wobble in her hands.

Concentrate, she told herself. Concentrate on what? Too many to keep track of: the redhead shuffled sideways, now behind Karl; Beecher looked over his shoulder, his gun still pointed at Curt; Lormes turned for a better look, and Maxwell's gun swept slowly forward like a pendulum, the motion at the direct angle meant to be hidden from her eyes.

Her heart beat quickened, a lightness spreading through her body. "I said *drop* the gun."

Maxwell stepped toward her, and with one quick motion he snapped the gun up to point the muzzle at her.

The explosion at the end of her arms snapped the gun toward her face, but she held it and did not flinch. As the sound echoed across the corn fields, she saw only his open eye, huge and gaping in startled terror.

His arms jerked outward, and his gun sailed off to his right. Like the cardboard box in the field, his unwieldy body leaped backwards and then collapsed onto the pavement, a red circle appearing on the dirty white shirt.

Lori stared straight ahead to where Maxwell had been, her thoughts careening to the rats her brothers shot behind the corn crib, their bodies jumping into the air, blood splattering the dust. She did not want to pull the trigger. He deserved it more than the rats did.

She swallowed back nausea that poked into her throat and threatened to gag her like morning sickness. She dropped her gaze to Maxwell's body

345

to see if there were any signs of life.

"Shoot the bitch," Lormes screamed.

Curt yelled. "Lori, watch out!"

She glanced up, just as Beecher turned from Curt and aimed at her. Curt threw his body at Beecher.

She stood rooted to the spot, arms outstretched. The roar of the shot swept over her as the bullet smashed into the windshield three-feet to her right.

When she saw the redhead aim, she dived behind the open door. His bullet shattered the window of the door and sprayed glass across her back. She heard Applenu's feet scrape the road as he ducked behind the back door. She peeked around the side.

Beecher recovered his balance and shouldered Curt against the green car. Curt bounced off the car and tumbled to the ground at Karl Eberhard's feet. Beecher turned and started toward the Town Car in long, swift strides, his gun out in front of him. The redhead fell into stride at Beecher's right.

Curt, now behind Beecher, dragged himself to his knees and pulled a gun from under his shirt. He pointed it at Beecher and yelled, "Drop the gun, Beecher."

Beecher and the redhead turned to look at Curt.

Lori jumped out from behind the door and pointed her gun at Beecher.

Curt pulled the trigger. Nothing happened. He tried again. Still nothing.

"For Christ sake," Karl Eberhard yelled, "chamber a round. Pull the slide back and get a round in the chamber."

Beecher laughed; he raised his gun and aimed at Curt.

Lori squeezed the trigger.

Beecher jerked forward, as if slapped on the back by a powerful hand. He grabbed at his back with his left hand and turned his head to look at her over his shoulder, his body bent forward. Slowly, he forced himself to turn and face her. He raised his gun to aim at her.

That look, that same superior look on his face that he had *that* day when he forced her to kneel before him.

She fired. Then she fired again.

The first shot straightened him up; the second one exploded his face into a violent red fountain as his body sprawled backward onto the pavement.

"Lori, get down," Eberhard yelled.

She glanced up to see the redhead aiming at her. Before she could duck behind the door, a shot rang out. Markum toppled to his knees, grabbing his shoulder.

Curt ran forward, his gun pointed at the redhead's face. He hesitated, and then tossed the gun at Curt's feet.

Curt turned to her, his relief shining through his scraped and tired face.

Lori's vision blurred and her mouth twitched uncontrollably until a surge of relief and joy coursed through her body and she was once again able to a smile.

- - - - -

Curt started toward Lori through the tang of cordite that floated over the hot pavement. He faltered; suddenly aware of the heat, his body quaked and his heart pounded. He wiped his scorched face on the tail of his drenched shirt. Everything happened so fast, with no time to think or be afraid until now.

In the darkest moment of an array of dark moments these past few months, he looked up and there she stood.

Lori smiled at him. At the sight of the tears glistening in her eyes, his eyes clouded. She started toward him, stopped suddenly and assumed that two-handed stance of hers, gun raised and aimed past Curt. He turned to see Lormes stooped over for Beecher's gun.

"Don't do it," she yelled, her voice husky and threatening to crack.

Lormes jumped back from the gun. He stumbled sideways and almost fell over Beecher's body.

Curt picked up the gun, shoved it into his belt, and then collected Maxwell's and Markum's guns.

Karl Eberhard emerged from the police car, the cell phone held to his ear. He shut off the phone and pocketed it. "The FBI should be here within an hour," he said.

Curt nodded, handed him the two guns, and turned back to Lori, who stood with her pistol pointed at Lormes.

Lormes suddenly spoke up. "You've got all the nuclear material, so what do you need me for? I can get you up to a million dollars if you turn me loose."

Curt shoved Lormes toward Markum. He turned and yelled for Simmons to come out of the truck with his hands up. The truck door eased open, and Simmons climbed down from the cab. Eberhard herded him over to the other two.

"You're making a big mistake, Reedan," Lormes said. "We've got powerful people behind us. You turn us in, and they'll get you and your family. You can mark my word on it."

Curt turned to Lori, who stared down at Maxwell and Beecher, splattered on the hot asphalt as if discarded by some giant hand. Maxwell lay sprawled on his back, arms and legs splayed, a shiny red stain growing on the front of his dirty white shirt, his mouth and one good eye wide open, permanently surprised by the scene. Beecher's body lay twisted, his upper body facing to his right, the left side of his face pulverized, his left leg crossed over the right. Four shiny green flies crisscrossed the red mush and the blood pool expanding on the steaming asphalt.

Curt touched her shoulder, and she melted into his arms. With his legs trembling, he closed his eyes to erase the scene and all the scenes of the past weeks. He pulled her head up, searching for her mouth.

When they parted, she gazed up at him and forced a laugh onto her bruised face. "The guns," she said, holding hers out and nodding toward it. "What a terrible way to have to get back together. What a terrible time this was." She stopped; her mouth quivered slightly. "I never thought anything like this could happen to us. Never."

"We made it, though."

She turned to look back at the Town Car as if remembering something. "I just thought about that other guy—the Iranian."

"Applenu? Was he with you?"

She nodded. "He was going to help me escape, but then I saw you. I think they were going to kill him, too." She laughed. "He must have vanished into the corn field."

"Good luck to him," Curt said and pulled Lori back to him. "Thanks to him, I escaped last night. Actually, I don't think he was with you after all."

She smiled up at him. "Come to think of it, I guess he wasn't."

They kissed, long and tender. They parted, and he looked into her brown eyes. "God, it's good to be with you," he said.

She nodded rapidly, smiled, and looked around. "In a way, it's like before we were married. We're surrounded by corn fields again."

He cleared his throat to get rid of his hoarseness. "I love corn fields. I love farms and farm girls. I love you."

"I love you."

They stared across the corn field to the side of a hill, where a tractor crawled silently through a hay field. A cool breeze stripped away some of the cordite haze, and for a moment, they smelled the freshly mown hay.

"There is a difference between here and Iowa," he said. "They've got hills here. I hear they've got hills in Colorado, and it's a nice place to raise kids."

Epilogue

Ian Deby clicked on the TV and settled on the couch with his mail.

Good Evening on this Friday, January 12, 2012. Today's top story comes from Washington, and it ties in with last week's unconfirmed report from Paris that Iran had exploded an atomic bomb. For the latest developments, we take you to Marvin Shorahm in Washington.

Two hours ago the Justice Department announced it was dropping charges against two Russians and an Iranian accused of stealing nuclear material, of murdering Professor Robert Surling of Arizona State University, and of attempting to murder FBI agent Richard Saul. They are Nakita Oleg Titov, a.k.a. William Lormes, Valentin Nikolai Fedorov, a.k.a. Richard Markum, and Farrokh Mohammad Bagheri, a.k.a. P. K. Simmons. Titov is reputed to be an ex-KGB agent and an important figure in Russian organized crime circles...

While the announcer described the charges against Lormes, Markum, and Simmons, Applenu opened a letter from Purdue University Nuclear Engineering Department, which indicated he was still under consideration for an assistant professorship. He looked up when the newsman said the three men were being deported immediately.

As he started to tear open the letter from North Carolina State, his attention was drawn to the TV screen where Curt and Lorain Reedan's pictures appeared as the shootout outside Raphine, Virginia, was described. When they began describing the disaster at Oak Ridge, Tennessee, five months ago, Deby returned to his mail, as this subject was in the news daily since September.

Over 25,000 people were evacuated—most of the city's population—with 90% of them now back in their homes. It should be noted that essentially none of the people evacuated from the immediate vicinity of the Chernobyl nuclear reactor that exploded in the Ukraine in the Soviet Union in 1986 ever returned to their homes. A special committee of federal and Tennessee state government officials has been formed to oversee cleanup, although no money has been appropriated for the cleanup. Congressman Roy Phillips of the Tennessee third congressional district introduced a bill in congress calling for the federal government to buy all affected property and declare the area permanently off limits to unauthorized personnel.

Meanwhile, a controversy has developed concerning the people exposed to the radioactive debris from the fire. Government medical personnel say it is too soon to estimate the medical effects, although several university scientists have made startlingly high estimates for cancers...

Deby unfolded the North Carolina State University Nuclear Engineering Department letter and read that they were offering him an associate professorship.

Senator Stanley Hughson, the front-running Republican presidential candidate has been in the forefront of revealing details of the disaster, as well as charging a cover-up by the Gordono Administration. Last week, Hughson stated that he has learned that since that bomb threat rumored for New York in August, State Department officials have been in constant negotiations with an Iranian delegation that includes Amir Akbar Maheri. Maheri posed as a diplomat in the Iranian UN delegation for the past three years under the name of Ahmad Sherbani. It was Sherbani who was contacted by Steve Austin, the mastermind behind the nuclear theft. The talks are reportedly deadlocked because U.S. authorities do not believe the hijackers could make an operating bomb. Last week's explosion in Iran's eastern desert region removed some of those doubts.

What bloody fools, Deby thought, that people like Hughson and the Administration think talking will solve their problems. Not when you've got blokes like Sherbani and his bosses. And how many more Austins were around?

Hughson said Iran had some of the stolen nuclear material secreted in this country for the bomb they were threatening to explode last August. By keeping it in this country, Iran hopes to insure that the U.S. government will not initiate military action against them.

When the White House was asked about the possibility of an Iranian bomb in this country, Press Secretary O'Connell said it is Administration policy not to comment on national security matters. He added, quote, The President wants to assure the American people that their safety is of utmost importance to his Administration, and they are not in any danger, unquote.

Deby clicked off the TV, still saddened by the havoc discussed by the newscast, havoc that he helped produce. He glanced at the letter. He now had offers from Texas A & M, North Carolina State, and New Mexico Universities. Maybe he could resume his place in the world, he thought, thanks to the foresight of a bloody computer genius. "Thank you, Steve Austin, Derek Hearn, George Atkinson…you bloody son of a bitch."

- - - - -

When Curt Reedan went to get a table for dinner, Lori Reedan saw the young blonde she met this morning on the whale-watching excursion arranged by the American Nuclear Society for accompanying persons. The two of them sat together on the bus to the pier with a bus load of mostly women who had accompanied their husbands and significant others to the ANS meeting. Because they enjoyed each other's company on the bus and neither of them knew anyone else at the meeting, they spent most of the boat trip together.

Juliet saw Lori, and they both laughed about the fact that they had spent the day together and then showed up at the same place for dinner. Juliet was waiting for her husband who was parking the car.

Curt walked up and touched Lori's shoulder. "No tables available for two hours," he said. "We'll have to find…"

"Please join us," Juliet said, turning to her husband, who had just walked up. "I'm sure Ian won't mind, and maybe Lori and I can plan

353

something for tomorrow."

At the sight of Ian, Lori's smile froze on her face. Momentarily speechless, she turned to Curt, who stared, his mouth open. She turned back to Ian, who appeared similarly paralyzed.

"We don't want to impose," Curt said.

"Nonsense," Juliet said and turned to introduce Lori and Curt to Ian Deby. After handshakes all around, they found themselves at a table for four.

Juliet turned to Ian. "This is Lori's first trip after her son was born. He's two months old, and their daughter is six." She turned to Lori. "I didn't tell you today, but I'm two-months pregnant with our first." She turned back to Ian, who smiled proudly.

After the waiter took their orders, the men finally got around to talking shop. "Where do you work?" Curt asked.

"I'm in the Nuclear Engineering Department at North Carolina State."

"I'm at the Colorado School of Mines," Curt said, "working on nano-materials in the Mechanical Engineering Department and on robotics in the Department of Electrical, Computer, and Environmental Engineering. I came to this meeting because I've been working on a robot for hot cells. I had some experience with hot cells about a year ago."

"Interesting," Ian said. "I've also got some ideas along that line, probably because of a similar experience. Perhaps we could collaborate." They exchanged smiles and business cards as their drinks arrived.

Lori raised her white wine. "Here's to future collaboration...and thanks for past collaboration."

"Hold the toast," Curt said looking around for the waiter. "For this toast, we need whiskey, corn whiskey."

The three of them laughed.

Juliet looked puzzled. "What are you talking about, past collaboration...corn whiskey? Do you guys...?"

"It has to do with running in cornfields in Iowa and elsewhere, especially elsewhere," Lori said laughing. She turned to look at Ian and then Curt. "It also has to do with open doors and running."

"You're quite right," Ian said. "There is much to toast. Make them double whiskies."

Ronald Klueh

Perilous Panacea

About the Author

A research scientist by training (PhD in Metallurgy and Materials Science, Carnegie Mellon University), Ronald Klueh brings a wealth of scientific knowledge and experience to contemporary techno-thriller fiction. He has worked as a research metallurgist at Oak Ridge National Laboratory and is presently a self-employed metallurgical consultant. As a freelance science writer of nonfiction, he has been published in the Washington Post, Houston Chronicle, and New Science. In his fiction, he strives to make the present and future interesting for adventure as well as romance readers.

Perilous Panacea

If you enjoyed *Perilous Panacea* consider
these other fine Books from
Savant Books and Publications:

A Whale's Tale by Daniel S. Janik
Tropic of California by R. Page Kaufman
Dare to Love in Oz by William Maltese
Today I am a Man by Larry Rodness
The Bahrain Conspiracy by Bentley Gates
Called Home by Gloria Schumann
Kanaka Blues by Mike Farris
Poor Rich by Jean Blasiar
The Jumper Chronicles by W. C. Peever
William Maltese's Flicker by William Maltese
My Unborn Child by Orest Stocco
Last Song of the Whales by Four Arrows

Scheduled for Release in 2010:
The Mythical Voyage by Robin Ymer
Ammon's Horn by Guerrino Amati
Charlie No Face by David B. Seaburn
Hello, Norma Jean by Sue Dolleris
Falling but Fulfilled by Zachary M. Oliver
In Dire Straits by Jim Currie
In the Himalayan Nights by Anoop Chandola
Still Life with Cat and Mouse by Sheila McGraw

http://www.savantbooksandpublications.com